BLOOD RED RIVER

Rohit Prasad is a professor at the Management Development Institute (MDI), Gurgaon. His academic research explores issues in the digital economy through the lens of game theory, politics and law.

He is the co-author of *The Dynamics of Spectrum Management* (Oxford University Press), and his research papers have been published in top international journals. He also writes regularly for financial dailies. His first popular book, *Start-up Sutra* (Hachette India), focused on the subject of entrepreneurship.

Rohit lives with his wife and two sons on the leafy campus of MDI, Gurgaon, and the whole family loves the opportunity to 'dog sit' every now and then.

ALSO BY THE SAME AUTHOR

Start-up Sutra

BLOOD RED RIVER

A Journey into the Heart of India's Development Conflict

ROHIT PRASAD

hachette INDIA

First published in 2016 by Hachette India
(Registered name: Hachette Book Publishing India Pvt. Ltd)
An Hachette UK company
www.hachetteindia.com

SRD

ISBN 978-93-5195-033-2

Hachette Book Publishing India Pvt. Ltd
4th/5th Floors, Corporate Centre,
Sector 44, Gurgaon 122003, India

Typeset in 11/14.5 Adobe Caslon Pro
by SÜRYA, New Delhi

Printed and bound in India by Manipal Technologies Limited, Manipal

MIX
Paper from responsible sources
FSC™ C043100

To my parents:
Suren Prasad,
who continues to open doors for me every step of the way,
and
Meera Prasad,
whose grit never ceases to amaze.

Contents

The State of Chhatisgarh

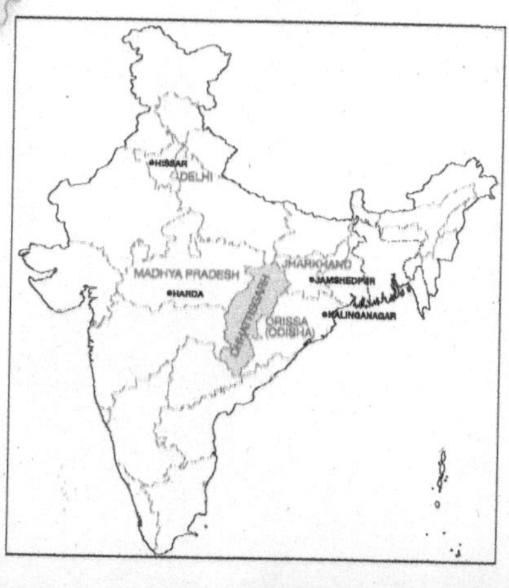

This map is a pictorial representation and not to scale. It is for general illustration only, and is not intended to be used for reference purposes or reproduction elsewhere.

Introduction

'Do I look like a Maoist?' asks a middle-aged man with burnished skin, bright eyes and a perfect salt-and-pepper mop of hair.

His voice is quiet. I am instantly uneasy.

We are at the Gandhi Smriti and Darshan Samiti in New Delhi, participating in a conference on Gondi, a Dravidian language spoken by tribals in southern and central India. My interlocutor, Professor Metry, is a professor of tribal studies at the Kannada University, Hampi. I have been introduced to him as someone interested in travelling to 'Left-wing extremist' areas, a euphemism for territories where Maoists wield influence.

I am obviously being sized up. Now people start pulling up chairs around us.

You need to stay calm, I tell myself.

'Do I look like a Maoist?' Prof. Metry repeats his question.

Seated next to him is a man with a friendly smile. 'Do we look like Maoists?' he asks, echoing the professor's words.

'No, no. Of course not, sir. But...'

Metry cuts me off. 'You people just talk about the Maoist problem for your own benefit. There are no Maoists in Chhattisgarh. No tribal is a Maoist.'

I contest his claim with facts and figures, but the professor stands his ground. I fall silent and recall Shubranshu Choudhary, a BBC journalist with years of experience in Maoist areas, telling me that the tribals bore no allegiance to either the Maoists or the government. They merely did what they needed to do, on a moment-to-moment basis, in order to stay alive.

For many months following that meeting, I would mull over Prof. Metry's comment, wondering what he might have meant. If, on the one hand, no tribal was a Maoist, I reflected, the Indian State was guilty of a grave injustice for targeting innocent citizens in its war against the Maoist insurgency. It might even be using the insurgency as a pretext to clear what it might perceive as human encumbrances on mineral-rich land. Further, if no top leader of the Maoists was a tribal, the indigenous population in the area might well be serving as cannon fodder in the ideological war being waged by the rebels against the Indian State.

As of today, 106 of India's 680 districts are said to be adversely affected by Left-wing extremism.[1] Of these, 35 are classified as 'seriously affected'. Most of the districts under Maoist influence are characterized by a potent cocktail of rich mineral resources, abject poverty, high rates of inequality, and the presence of a large adivasi population.

However, extreme poverty is not limited to Maoist-controlled districts alone. Uttar Pradesh (UP), for example, is largely free of Maoist influence. Yet, it is home to the largest number of India's poor, with 21 per cent of this segment of the population hailing from the state.[2] Even Bihar, where the grip of Maoism has eased somewhat after the separation of Jharkhand, performs poorly on human-development indicators, coming in at a lowly rank of 21 out of 23 states.[3]

---

[1]http://mha1.nic.in/par2013/par2013-pdfs/ls-050313/LSQ.1374.Eng.pdf

[2]http://www.in.undp.org/content/dam/india/docs/uttar_pradesh_factsheet.pdf

[3]http://www.in.undp.org/content/dam/india/docs/bihar_factsheet.pdf

Given the statistics, one might ask, how did the phenomenon of Maoism arise in some states and not in others, and to what extent is it linked to poverty? Does the birth of the insurgency in our country indicate flaws in our development model? Are mineral-rich areas suffering from a resource-curse, the phenomenon of abundant natural resources being accompanied by low rates of local Gross Domestic Product (GDP) growth and poverty alleviation? And why should you and I, individuals whose lives are seemingly untouched by the problem, care about these things?

About three years ago, I had started looking for stories of how common people in remote areas of India, and the government were championing the use of information and communication technology to transform society. My sunny sense of optimism was subjected to a reality check when I observed the prevailing conditions in these areas. I realized that while technology could play a facilitative role, the real drivers of the abysmal economic outcomes continued to lie in faultlines in the underlying model of development. I decided to realign my focus.

As a writer, I recognized that what I had stumbled upon was far more complex, and much more fundamental than what I had set out to find. I saw that I had an opportunity to illuminate an area of darkness situated in the heart of the country, where the darkness denoted both under-representation (and misrepresentation) in the media discourse, as well as the sordidness to which the ordinary citizen is subjected on a daily basis. In order to do justice to what I saw, I felt I needed to go beyond conventional tools of my discipline – economics – and delve into the nature of democracy prevailing in these areas. Even beyond, I was drawn to the tapestry of stories, legends, myths and rumours that formed the interwoven fabric of my subjects' lives, lives that seemed to follow an age-old dreamlike pattern, punctuated by birth, marriage, harvest and, increasingly, premature death. My eagerness to document the strife-torn land was quickened by my authentic encounters with adivasi culture that revealed that there was indeed something that we urgently need to salvage, to preserve and to nurture. I accepted the risk of venturing into this subject matter and this geography as part of the territory I had chosen to explore, although some of my friends characterized my new obsession as a somewhat unusual case of midlife crisis!

While empathizing with those affected by the juggernaut of development, I also felt that the perspectives of those attempting to kickstart industry demanded a fair hearing. As a result, I spent a considerable amount of time speaking to corporate executives, bureaucrats and politicians to understand the constraints under which they operated. At the same time, I delved into the ideology and methods employed by the Maoists – many of whom have brought an enormous amount of courage, sacrifice and erudition to their interventions – in order to assess whether their struggle offers any signs of hope for the local population.

The experiences of immersing myself in the world views of the various stakeholders enabled me to assess whether the insurgency, even though restricted to certain geographies in the country, reflects a wider social malaise in our nation.

Over the course of two years, I travelled through tiny hamlets, bustling village haats, sleepy highway towns, and cities bristling with ambition in Chhattisgarh and Jharkhand. I attended seminars and workshops in Delhi, the nerve centre of happenings in far-flung corners of the country. I hunted down clues in posh country clubs in Gurgaon, and quiet corners of public parks. I personally became embroiled in the proceedings of a criminal case, an experience that taught me more than any research carried out as a by-stander could. I invite you to join me on this journey – from the sterile invocations of information technology, entrepreneurship and good governance as the panacea for all evils into the heart of India's development conflict, a conflict whose contours we as members of a vibrant democracy must appreciate, and whose daily tragedies may reflect for some of us an urgent call to action. this led to the growing

Carved out of Madhya Pradesh, Chhattisgarh is one of India's most mineral-rich states, containing 19 per cent of the country's iron-ore deposits, 16.4 per cent of its coal deposits and 37.7 per cent of its tin-ore deposits.[4] It is, by all accounts, one of the success stories of post-liberalization India. Created in 2000, the state has been growing at an average of 7 per cent per annum. The mining industry contributes close to 10 per cent of the state's GDP.[5]

The state government's finances are also in excellent order. In 2012–13, its budget was ranked No.1 in terms of the percentage of social expenditure to total state GDP and the percentage of development expenditure to total state GDP. It was ranked second in the percentage of capital outlay to state GDP, debt to GDP ratio and gross fiscal deficit to GDP.[6]

Yet, Chhattisgarh is also the lowest ranked state in India in terms of the human-development index that assesses performance based on per capita income, adult literacy and life expectancy. It ranks 30 out of 35 states and Union Territories in the gender-development index that measures the gender gap in

[4]http://azimpremjifoundation.org/pdf/to%20know%20more%20about%20Chhattisgarh.pdf

[5]http://planningcommission.nic.in/data/datatable/0814/comp_databook.pdf

[6]http://dprcg.gov.in/news/budget-2014-15-press-note-english

human-development achievements in terms of health, education and command over economic resources. And that is not all.

Along with overflowing granaries that reflect one of the most successful public-distribution systems among Indian states, Chhattisgarh is also distinguished by the highest level of capacity utilization of jails in India (except for Dadra and Nagar Haveli which has a total inmate capacity of 60). The occupancy of jails across Chhattisgarh is more than two and a half times the capacity, while the national capacity utilization of prisons is just over 110 per cent. In 2012, the Dantewada district jail was filled to just over four times its capacity, while the Kanker district jail had an even higher occupancy rate of over four and a quarter times its capacity.[7]

Not entirely unrelated to the bursting-at-the-seams condition of its state prisons is the matter of Chhattisgarh's reputation as the breeding ground of one of the most serious internal security threats ever faced by the Indian State – the challenge of the Maoists, who have found a secure home in the forests of Dandakaranya that also straddle Maharashtra to its west and Andhra Pradesh to the south.

The ongoing saga of Chhattisgarh, with its lofty paens to industrialization, its bloody battles with insurgency, its constant grappling with the question of how the Indian State should address the rights of adivasis, and its virtual cornucopia of mineral wealth – which appears to be fast turning into a Pandora's box – places the conceptual questions of development in sharp relief.

And nothing highlights these critical questions as much as an examination of the ascension of the Maoists. To put it simply, how did a small group of ill-equipped revolutionaries come to be such a defining presence in Chhattisgarh?

---

[7]http://blog.mylaw.net/tag/jagdalpur-legal-aid-group/

It was 1975. *Sholay*, the iconic Bollywood movie set in the badlands of the Chambal valley, had just been released. The then prime minister, Indira Gandhi, was about to impose the Emergency. Meanwhile, the euphoria of Naxalism, the movement seeded in a small village in North Bengal, and inspired by Mao Tse-tung, who had established the one-party rule of the Communist Party in China using guerilla tactics and the support of peasants, had all but vanished. Following a brutal state-driven crackdown in West Bengal and Telangana, thousands of starry-eyed youth had either gone missing or fled the country. Faced with near decimation, Kondapalli Sitarammaiah, the head of the Communist Party of India (Marxist-Leninist) (CPI-ML), the political party floated by Charu Majumdar, Kanu Sanyal and other leaders of the Naxalite movement, decided that his group needed a 'rear area' to serve as a safe sanctuary. The forests of Dandakaranya in central India seemed to offer a promising option.

In June 1980, seven groups, each comprising seven members, were sent off to access the forests from different points.[8] Their initial supplies were meagre; each carried a spare dhoti, a couple of thousand rupees, a double-bore rifle, a pistol and a plastic sheet to set up shelter for the night. Hardly any one of them had studied beyond Class XII. Some had never been to school at all. They left for Dandakaranya with the instruction to visit the nearby villages during the day, explain their political ideology to the locals and, after gaining their confidence, home in on some of the problems they faced in their struggle for survival and launch a movement centred around them.

The grievances of the locals that allowed the Maoists to gain traction were not new. The inequitable practices involved

---

[8]http://www.outlookindia.com/magazine/story/walking-with-the-comrades/264738

in the tendu-leaf trade, for example, were at least a hundred years old. As far back as 1950, the first Indian district collector (DC) of Bastar, ICS officer (the Indian Civil Services as the Indian Administrative Services or IAS was then known) R.C.V.P. Noronha, had observed the prevalence of *begaar*, the coercive use of free tribal labour by the forest department to build roads.[9] The highly subsidized long-term contract for the purchase of 1.5 lakh tonnes of bamboo by the Ballarpur Paper Mill underscored the rapidly accelerating exploitation of forest resources for the paper industry since Independence, while the landlords within the tribal community had carried on their excesses, unchecked, for centuries.

Indeed, according to one narrative, the story of the Maoist movement can be said to have begun at the end of the eighteenth century, when Britain's ship-building, iron-smelting and construction industries began to feel the adverse impact of the dwindling reserves of English oak in Britain's forests.[10] An alternative source was sought and found in the Malabar teak forests in India that had come under the direct control of the British after the defeat and death in 1799 of Mysore's ruler, Tipu Sultan, the last bastion of resistance to India's colonial masters until the outbreak of the First War of Independence in 1857.

Given the vastness and density of India's forests, colonial administrators assumed that here, at least, there would be no problem of timber shortage. They blithely remarked on the 'seemingly immeasurable extent' of the country's natural resources.[11] Private contractors were, therefore, given a free run.

---

[9]R.C.V.P. Noronha, *A Tale Told by an Idiot*, Vikas Publishing House, New Delhi, 1976, 182.

[10]For the timeline of events leading up to the rise of the Maoists, see Appendix I.

[11]Elizabeth Whitcombe, *Agrarian Conditions in Northern India*, Volume I, Delhi, 1971, p ix.

The need of the revenue department to convert as much forest land as possible for agricultural use was similarly indulged. A status quo was maintained on the customary rights of forest tribes, although there were frequent skirmishes over the raising of the annual rent.[12]

Naturally, this approach led to rapacious exploitation of the forests. In the 1850s, with the forests of India as well as of Burma showing dangerous signs of depletion and the demand for timber soaring due to the proposed roll-out of the Indian Railways, the colonial administration decided that forests were to be state-managed. The Indian Forest Department was thus created in 1864 and the first Forest Act introduced a year later.

Nevertheless, in the course of the two World Wars, colonial exploitation of forests increased dramatically. The development of minor forest produce was also taken up in the twentieth century. As India was the Empire's only source for several of the more valuable products in demand – turpentine, for example, extensively used as a solvent for thinning oil-based paints – there was a rapid rise in the export of these products to other countries.

The bugle cry of state forestry ended the brief idyll of the adivasi, whose customary rights were now referred to as 'privileges' accorded by the Crown and held to be revocable. The Forest Act of 1878 tolled the death knell of the world as the tribal had known it. Large tracts of forest land were declared 'reserved forest', to the exclusion of all private or customary rights; a second category was classified as 'protected forest', where state control was exercised, with some recognition of customary use. Over a period of time, however, 'protected forests' would be reclassified as 'reserved forests'.

---

[12]The attempts to increase taxes, first by the Marathas and then by the British, the two forces that held sway over Bastar from the late 1700s, were met by the Halba (1774–79), Paralkot (1825) and the Tarapur (1842–54) rebellions.

Although the tribals would continue to enjoy their old privileges in a third category of forest known as 'village forests', they were baffled by the loss of their customary rights over the forests at large and insecure about their future where village forests were concerned. They felt they had been reduced to being trespassers on their own land and were uncertain about their right to access forests for their day-to-day requirements of food, fruit, fuel, wood, fodder and fibres. They had already taken on the British in the First Indian War of Independence in 1857 under the leadership of Dhruvarao, a Dorla tribal leader, and Vir Narayan Singh, a landowner. In 1859, the Koi tribals of southern Bastar refused to let government contractors undertake the cutting of sal trees, a precursor to the Chipko movement that would take place in Uttarakhand over 125 years later.

The most celebrated revolt led by the Bastar tribals was the Bhumkal rebellion of 1910, which took place two years after forest land in Bastar had been declared 'reserved'. Gundadhar, the rebel leader, set out with his army from a village called Nelnar, marched to Jagdalpur and was able to capture the Bastar Raj for two weeks, before the rebellion was crushed.

In all, there were close to 200 tribal revolts against British colonial rule. Each was ruthlessly quelled. However, on paper, at least, laws were enacted to protect the alienation of tribal land. These included the Scheduled Districts Act, 1874, and the Chota Nagpur Tenancy Act, 1908. Tribal communities were also given the power to administer justice in minor disputes.

The Maoists lay claim to this tradition of tribal rebellion. So, in fact, do a lot of others, including tribal-culture revivalists, campaigners for statehood, tribal politicians and, sometimes, even the tribals themselves.

The dawn of India's freedom did not bring with it any respite for the adivasis. There were two main approaches to the tribal question. Verrier Elwin, a Britisher, who would make tribal India his home after parting ways with Mahatma Gandhi, believed that there was much in tribal society that modern civilization could aspire to. He wrote: 'A gay freedom of heart is the most precious of possessions and simplicity of heart the greatest treasure a man or woman knows... The primitive world has a real message for our sophisticated modern world which is threatened with disintegration as a result of its passion for possessions and lack of love.[13]' He felt that tribals needed to be left alone till they had evolved to a point where they could interact with the outside world without being vulnerable to exploitation.

Elwin's position was disputed by G.S. Ghurye, who believed that the tribal belonged at the bottom of the caste-class-tribe continuum and needed to be brought into the mainstream as soon as possible – economically, as part of the Indian State machinery and, culturally, as a member of Hindu society.[14]

Jawaharlal Nehru, the first Indian prime minister, leaned towards Elwin's view. He said: 'People should develop along the lines of their own genius...tribal rights in land and forest should be respected...we should avoid introducing too many outsiders into tribal territory.' This view was reflected in a slew of laws giving tribals the power of self-determination over community resources.[15]

---

[13]Elwin, Verrier, *Leaves from the Jungle: Life in a Gond Village*, Oxford University Press, 1958.

[14]Hebbar, Ritambhara, 'Tribal Autonomy and Life Support Systems' in *Quality of Human Resources: Gender and Indigenous Peoples* – Volume 1, edited by E.B. Massini.

[15]At present, the Panchayati Raj Extension to Scheduled Areas Act (PESA), 1996, and the Recognition of Forest Rights Act, 2006,

However, there existed, alongside the sympathy for people who had been living for millennia in the midst of forests and streams, a firm determination to use India's natural resources for 'national development'. This goal was to be operationalized through the instrumentality of the state with the private sector playing a strictly supervised second fiddle. The use of natural resources for local development as well as the sustenance of traditional ways of life took a backseat. As a result, tribal-development programmes became, in the words of sociologist Ritambhara Hebbar, 'attempts at minimizing the effects of development processes without being critical of the latter'.

The 1952 Forest Policy document reiterated the essential principle of British doctrine: assertion of state-monopoly rights at the expense of forest communities. As late as 1978, the Inspector General of Forests in India celebrated Lord Dalhousie's policy that had 'laid down the ruling principle of management of a "state forest", namely, that timber standing on a state forest was state property to which individuals [or communities] had no rights or claims'.[16] The post-1947 scenario saw the rapid development of forest-based industries, necessitating a sharp rise in the production of industrial and fuel wood.

In the same spirit, the 1952 National Mining Policy

---

constitute two principal pillars of the rights of adivasis. PESA includes the right of the gram sabha to be consulted on land acquisition, to make recommendations on the grant of prospecting licences or mining leases for minor minerals and to safeguard and preserve the traditions and customs of the people. The Forest Rights Act, drafted by the Ministry of Tribal Affairs and enacted in 2008, grants legal recognition to the property rights of traditional forest-dwelling communities and gives communities and the public a voice in forest and wildlife conservation. For an account of the various laws enacted to protect tribal autonomy in the matter of properties and customs, see Appendix II.

[16]B.P. Srivastava, in R. Gupta, ed., 'Building Indian Institute of Forest Management', CMA Monograph No. 79, IIM, Ahmedabad, 1978, 14.

emphasized the urgency of mining for India's development, while putting in place a framework for responsible labour practices.

Yet, the Indian State's sights were trained on mining even before the prophetic midnight hour of 15 August 1947 had dawned. An account of its dealings with Raja Pravir Chandra Bhanj Deo of Bastar will make this amply clear.

In 1946, Pravir, a young man of twenty, leased the Bailadila hills, home to the richest reserves of iron ore in the world, to the Nizam of Hyderabad who had been chafing at the prospect of his state's assimilation into the new Indian State and evaluating his alternatives. This vastly increased the Raja's bargaining power with the Indian government. Days before Independence, the mining lease with Hyderabad was annulled, and Pravir was recognized as the ruler of Bastar. In 1957, he helped the Congress win the elections to the Legislative Assembly by a huge margin.

However, Pravir's days of contentment were numbered. Right from the early days of Independence, many princes had begun to resent the intrusion of the Indian State into the matter of their ancestral rights, and Pravir was no exception.

In 1958, the National Mineral Development Corporation (NMDC) was set up. By this time, Pravir had started objecting vociferously to the mineral exploitation of the Bastar area. He had found common ground with the adivasis who continued to feel dispossessed in the new dispensation, and adopted the stance that a period devoted to the development of basic services like health and education should precede the commencement of mining operations.

In 1960, he was arrested. In 1961, the police fired at a group of tribals protesting the arrest, killing 12. In 1962, Pravir formed a breakaway party, the Adivasi Sena Dal, which won 10 out of

12 seats in Bastar in the Assembly elections, even as mining operations in Bailadila commenced.

Validation from elections aside, the young raja had never entertained any illusions about his hold over the tribals. In 1965, he published an expansive autobiography entitled, *I Pravir: The Adivasi God*. While he seems to have actively abetted his own deification, he was generous enough to make room for other gods in the pantheon of his subjects, being a strong votary of traditional Hinduism.

The food crisis of 1965 and the Bastar forest scam triggered further protests by the tribals, led by their god king. In 1966, Pravir was killed at the entrance of his own palace, allegedly at the behest of the government. His brother was anointed king in his place and came to be known as the 'sarkari raja' on account of his conciliatory stance vis-à-vis the powers of the day.

Pravir, whose ancestors, the Kakatiyas, had migrated to Bastar from Warangal in the 1300s, has been described as a precursor of the Andhra-centric Maoists. But he seems to have been resurrected in a more direct fashion in the 1980s in the form of a proselytizer, Bihari Das,[17] who claimed to be his avatar and attempted to wean the tribals away from their heathen gods. The tribal pantheon, already swollen with the inclusion of the puffy-cheeked Pravir, was expanded once more to accommodate Baba Bihari as well.

The group of Hindu proselytizers would find an unlikely ally in the son of a tribal chieftain who had become a Member of Legislative Assembly (MLA) on the Communist Party of India (CPI) ticket in 1978, then left to join the Congress Party. His name was Mahendra Karma and over the course of thirty years he would play a definitive role in the state's approach to

[17] *Rise of the Plebeians? The Changing Face of the Indian Legislative Assemblies*, Jaffrelot, Christophe and Kumar, Sanjay, eds, Routledge India, 2009.

the Maoists and their consequent trajectory, even when not holding positions of power. The jury is still out on whether he was a curse or a blessing.

Short, squat and powerfully built, Karma resembled nothing so much as a Panzer tank. His political life began as a law student in 1975, when he became a member of the Leftist youth party, the Student Federation of India (SFI). When denied a ticket by the CPI in 1981, he joined the Congress. In 1996, he threw in his lot with Madhavrao Scindia's breakaway faction of the Congress and was elected as a Member of Parliament (MP).

In the beginning, the Maoists did not take on the elite of the tribal community. Consequently, the tribal landlords welcomed their interventions against the Forest Department. Understandably, Karma and the Maoists were on very good terms during this period.

They started falling out in the latter half of the 1980s, when the Maoists began targeting landlords who owned large tracts and redistributing their land. In 1987, a relative of Mahendra Karma, alleged to have captured vast tracts of land, was killed. At this point, Karma is believed to have sent an olive branch to the Maoists, but they did not respond to his overture.[18]

In the late 1980s, the Central Reserve Police Force (CRPF) started targeting the Maoists. It was during this period that the rebels underwent full-fledged military training under Suresh, a member of the Liberation Tigers of Tamil Eelam (LTTE) of Sri Lanka, whom the Indian Army had trained.[19] It was from

[18]Choudhary, Shubhranshu, *Let's Call Him Vasu: With the Maoists in Chhattisgarh*, Penguin Books India, 2012.

[19]Comrade Sonu, quoted in Choudhary, Shubhranshu, *Let's Call Him Vasu: With the Maoists in Chhattisgarh*, Penguin Books India, 2012.

him that the cadres learnt the techniques of setting up ambushes and installing landmines.

In 1991, the ruling Bharatiya Janata Party (BJP) government, the Congress and the CPI in the state came together under the banner of the Jan Jagran Abhiyan, led by Karma. During this campaign, villagers were forced to take oaths, swearing that they would not help the Maoists in any way. Those villages that did not join the movement faced police atrocities in the form of looting and rape.

Without a history of developmental intervention to strengthen its credibility, the Abhiyan made a serious tactical error, in forcing the villagers to align themselves against the Maoists. It merely strengthened the position of its adversaries – for the *dadas*,[20] as the locals called the insurgents, had several positive programmes to their credit. In fact, there was an exponential increase in the Maoists' recruitment of locals, which eventually led to a situation whereby, in the mid-nineties, they started setting up *jantana sarkars*, or people's governments, in villages under their control. It also reinforced the position of the BJP by projecting it as a strong pole for those who were being targeted by the Maoists and marked the demise of the CPI, whose traditional image as a supporter of tribal rights had been seriously undermined.

From 1992 to 1996, Karma collaborated with government officials, including a corrupt district collector, Narayan Singh, to pass off village-owned land as private land in 56 villages, acquire it at throwaway prices and sell the timber from trees growing on it at a huge profit. This came to be known as the Malik Makbuja scam.[21] In 1996, he launched another Jan Jagran Abhiyan to counter the growing influence of the Maoists, who

---

[20] Literally, 'older brothers', the term used by the adivasis for the Maoists.

[21] http://archive.tehelka.com/story_main11.asp?filename=ts031905The_Teak.asp

thwarted its progress by murdering a few of the movement's top leaders.

In the year 2000, the state of Chhattisgarh was formed. With 29 seats reserved for scheduled tribes (STs) in an Assembly of 90 members, it could claim to be a tribal state. However, the slew of corporate Memoranda of Understandings (MOUs) signed in the wake of state formation presented a different picture, given the history of forcible displacement that had characterized the trajectory of industrialization up to that point.

From 2000 to 2004, Karma was Industries Minister in the Ajit Jogi government. In 2005, the BJP came to power, with Dr Raman Singh at the helm. Karma continued to wield influence in the new government, and was referred to as Singh's 'sixteenth minister'. His bullishness on industrialization and devil-may-care attitude towards the Maoists were believed to be the source of his power. Two MOUs that would play a significant role in determining the events of the next ten years were signed in 2005. They involved the setting up by Tata Steel and Essar of two steel plants with a total capacity of 8.7 million tonnes[22] with backward linkages to iron-ore mines. These MOUs, along with actions taken to ensure their safe passage, would play an important part in consolidating the power of the Maoists and in Karma's eventual downfall.

Far away from Chhattisgarh, India is a country on an adrenaline high. So it would seem from the views of the CEOs invited to the Management Development Institute (MDI), Gurgaon, where I am a professor, on a sultry Sunday morning in September 2015 to

[22]http://www.business-standard.com/article/economy-policy/chhattisgarh-govt-renews-mou-with-tata-steel-112071902013_1.html

suggest changes to the curriculum of our executive management programme.

CEO after CEO waxed eloquent about the fast pace of change they were having to deal with and the exciting vistas of development and growth being revealed by new technology. Each one of them felt that old curricula were outdated.

'Why teach students about P&L [profit and loss] any more?' said one. 'Amazon did not make profits for its first fifteen years.'

Listening to them, I was carried away by their urgency, their feverish desire to grow. They were eager to get ahead, impatient with the need to exercise caution, unburdened by age-old prejudice, free of the stigma of exploitative practice. It was a simple crapshoot. May the best man win, I thought.

That night, I realized that the CEOs were all from the new economy – information technology (IT), knowledge process outsourcing (KPO) and legal process outsourcing (LPO) services. These industries are powered by a tiny enclave of elite Indians hooked into the global village and eager to take advantage of their shot at glory. They have reasonably fair labour practices, a relatively light footprint on the environment and could, justifiably, be proud of being at the vanguard of India's march into the world economy.

How, then, does one contextualize the conflicts of development starkly highlighted by the Maoists in Chhattisgarh? Are they an aberration? If not, how emblematic are the CEOs I have referred to of the Indian growth model?

India's realities include widespread deprivation, inequality and exploitation, not limited to pockets controlled by the Maoists. Ancient patterns of disadvantage based on caste, class and religion are primarily responsible for this lamentable state of affairs. But the one corporate process that lies at the heart of our paradigm of development and has a sizable effect on the impoverishment of people is land acquisition.

The conversion of agricultural or forest land for industrial use and the concomitant displacement of local inhabitants in India is often accompanied by tremendous distress in the lives of the displaced, with no concessions on offer in the form of employment or even compensation. Walter Fernandes[23] estimates in his essay, 'Singur and the Displacement Scenario', that during the period 1947–2000, the total number of Indians displaced or simply deprived of their livelihood, without physical relocation, because of development projects exceeds 60 million. Only about one-third of the people displaced by development projects have been resettled in a planned manner. This phenomenon is true of India in general, not just of Maoist-influenced territories. Of the displaced, 40 per cent are adivasis and another 40 per cent belong to backward castes, reflecting a disproportionate burden of displacement on the disadvantaged.

Before the liberalization of the economy in 1991, much of the acquired land remained in the control of the government or of public-sector corporations. However, after 1991, increasing amounts of land acquired for 'public purpose' have ended up in the control of private business interests, often in the name of public-private-partnership contracts.

Today, private parties can acquire land for a wide variety of purposes without carrying out a social impact assessment or obtaining the consent of the local population. The change in the purpose of land use is a critical component of industrialization and – let me be clear on this point – I am not arguing against industrialization. Every country that has developed has had to

[23]Fernandes, Walter, 'Singur and the Displacement Scenario', *Economic and Political Weekly*, 42, 203.6, 2007.

bite the bullet of land-use conversion. Most often, this has been achieved with very inequitable results. The enclosure movement in Britain that laid the ground for the country's Industrial Revolution was accompanied by tremendous bloodshed. Thousands of Native Americans were massacred by the country's founding fathers in the process of colonizing the West.

However, there are some important differences between our circumstances and those that had prevailed in the past.

First, the superfluous acquisition of vast tracts of land may have been acceptable in situations where it was available in plenty and environmental assets like clean air, water and forest were not scarce. In today's world, where food security assumes paramount importance and no country can afford to neglect its obligations to the environment (even if advanced economies agree to take responsibility for their history of environmental neglect), we need to minimize, along with our ecological footprint, the diversion of fertile land from agriculture.

Second, unlike in the past, the pattern of displacing people without rehabilitating them is the cause of much large-scale conflict. The direct impact is manifest in protest movements, both violent and non-violent. The indirect repercussions are evident in the rising lawlessness of our cities that are increasingly unable to handle the overwhelming influx of migrants, many of whom have been forcibly displaced from rural areas in the name of one project or the other.

The problems of environmental degradation, and of conflicts stemming from the immiserization of already poor people, are not disjointed from each other. Vast numbers of our poor depend on environmental goods – forests, underground aquifers and streams, for their sustenance. Thus, their displacement is a double whammy, simultaneously robbing them of their livelihood and their means of supplementary sustenance. The fact that in many cases they have customary and constitutional rights to the resources only adds insult to already grievous injury.

For reasons of environment, food security and law and order, we must remember, like British economist John Maynard Keynes, that a long-term view is all very well but only if our growth model does not come up against a logjam in the short run.

Fortunately, the trade-off between country and town is not the real one represented by corporate acquisition of natural resources in India today. Indeed, the same level of urban amenities can be developed at a less punishing cost in terms of distress caused to the rural poor if we address and fix the glaring inefficiencies and leakages that are features of our economy.

The leakages are not merely a reflection of simple wastage but also reflect the power relations prevailing in society today. The pervasive reality of excess capacity, including the widespread non-utilization of already acquired land, the chronic inefficiencies in the supply chain, the large-scale theft of minerals and the immunity of corporate promoters from the workings of bankruptcy proceedings, indicates that resources are being transferred from those who need them most urgently to those who may deserve them the least. The incidence of risk, on the contrary, appears to be moving in the opposite direction.[24]

---

[24]In his book, *Imagining India: Ideas for the New Century* (Penguin Books India, 2012), Nandan Nilekani persuasively argues that the much needed growth of our cities is hobbled, among other things, by escalating political tensions between the Centre and states, with state governments fearing that the empowerment of municipal corporations in areas like tax collection would result in an 'hourglass', with the state forming the tiny waist between an overweening centre at the top and an aggressive municipal administration at the bottom.

It is not as if the world we live in is not feeling the effects of all this bad karma. Indeed, the banking crisis in which the Indian economy is mired at present, imposing serious constraints on our ability to grow despite all rhetoric to the contrary, is a result of the specific nature of our crony capitalism. In any case, given the considerable slack in the system, the argument that an emerging economy like India cannot afford the luxury of caring too deeply either about damage to the environment or about the plight of the abjectly poor fails to stand up to scrutiny.

One might justifiably maintain that even if the leakages were contained within reasonable limits, there would still be a need to transfer resources to cities, for such is the magnitude of the need for urbanization. But in our eagerness to urbanize, we must not forget that cities need supplies of skilled labour and conditions ripe for businesses to thrive. We need to align our plans for urbanization to the existence of these complementary factors so that we do not end up creating ghost towns.

Further, in a situation where leakages are controlled, we would have the institutional capability to take care of the dispossessed and could, with greater responsibility, balance the needs of the different stakeholders concerned. The alternative approach – of turning a blind eye to the injustice that prevails in our system, simply because we believe that conditions are far from ripe for Maoism to take root and peaceful protest can be easily quashed, would not just be ethically indefensible but also strategically shortsighted.

In the face of our eagerness to race ahead, exemplified by the attitude of the CEOs who visited the MDI, our quickness to judge those left behind and our self-righteous rage at anyone who dares to disagree with us, this book attempts a radical immersion in a world far away from the drawing rooms and malls where hegemonic public opinion is fashioned and purveyed. It tries to establish that the conflation of GDP growth and development, accepted as a given in popular discourse, is conceptually erroneous; that growth has its costs, borne by some, as well as its benefits, enjoyed by others, and society must consider the trade-offs involved. It suggests that the commonly held views – that environmental considerations are an indulgence which only developed countries can afford and that climbing out of poverty justifies a less urgent concern for the fate of our natural resources – are misplaced, as it is the poor who bear the highest cost of environmental degradation and alienation from their traditional rights. It attempts to explain how the belief that our chosen development model is unrelated to the conflicts raging in the most backward regions of the country has led to a 'securitization of development', where suspension of civil rights is justified in the interest of GDP growth, exacerbating social conflict in the process.

In the first section, the book takes you into Kanker, a town in Chhattisgarh, to reveal the bewildering dynamics of democracy and development in a world where fact and fiction have coalesced in a vaporous cocktail. The second lays bare the tragedies of a village caught in the cross-fire as Maoists battle the government, even as it highlights the cultural transcendence that still flickers in a civilization under siege. Section Three attempts to understand the corporate viewpoint by probing the trajectory of the Tata Steel project in Chhattisgarh. It shows how the coterie of stakeholders muddying the waters extends far beyond the usual suspects – the government, mining companies, non-governmental organizations (NGOs) and the Maoists – to include corporates driven by internecine rivalries, an avaricious media – part extortionist, part sensationalist – and those members of the tribal community who have learnt that greed does pay.

The following section is a description of my own embroilment in the war over natural resources in the course of my research – an episode that provides a glimpse into the startling micro-dynamics of a conflict-ridden land, where no one can be trusted, not even the one whose cause you hold most dear. And the last section delves into popular myths and misconceptions about 'the real nature of the adivasi' and attempts a synthesis of the different voices given a hearing in various chapters of the book. It concludes that the question with which the book begins, 'Do I look like a Maoist?', has no answer, and therein lies the tragedy of a storm-tossed people.

The aim is to show you the world as it is. What you choose to do with the picture is your decision.

SECTION ONE

KIDNAPPING BY MANY NAMES

1

Rumours of a Kidnapping

Situated on National Highway 30 between two of Chhattisgarh's well-developed cities – Raipur and Jagdalpur – the brooding town of Kanker has yet to draw the attention of the sprawling Indian railway network. But for the Maoists, it would still be sitting squarely in the middle of the trash heap of completely banal towns that might as well have not existed, so little interest do they elicit from the rest of the country. The high point of such places is usually the bus stand, around which mushrooms a motley collection of dhabas, kirana stores and photography outlets. If one of these towns does especially well, a sign of its enhanced status might be a new bus stand in addition to the old one. There could be a government-run Circuit House nearby, built in the days of the British Raj. And there will be places of worship, family politics, petty political intrigue and a rich lore of sages and miracle workers – a healer, for instance, who acquired his powers from the goddess in a dream when he himself was afflicted with an incurable disease, or a man who can fight tigers with his bare hands. It is not clear if these legends thrive among the towns' residents because the freedom from the stressful lifestyle of modern cities allows the mind a greater focus on spiritual pursuits or because the deprivations of the here and now demand some compensatory make-believe.

Nevertheless, contrary to the usual run of play, rumours of

disappearing dervishes were not the main subject of discussion when I reached Kanker one evening in September 2014, after a bus ride spent dodging the spewing vomit of a passenger overcome by travel sickness. The town was agog with the rumour of a far more mundane vanishing trick. Squarely occupying pride of place in local gossip was a kidnapping – of six hopefuls in the by-election to the Antagarh reserved constituency vacated by a recent winner of the Lok Sabha polls. Antagarh is one of the seven tehsils or revenue-collection units of Kanker district, of which the eponymous town serves as the headquarters.

Apparently, the six worthies had been sequestered in a 'safe house', a controlled environment, where worldly temptations could not interfere with their inborn political convictions. The prime mover in the cloistering was supposed to be the Congress Party, which had suffered a body blow when its candidate, an acolyte of veteran leader Ajit Jogi, had suddenly stepped down from the contest, reportedly in response to material inducements having been accepted by his leader.[1] The party, recently dislodged from its seat in the union government, could not afford further reverses.

The identity of the agency that had stage-managed the forcible disappearance of the candidates from under the very nose of the Congress was a matter of some controversy, although the name of the ruling party, the Bharatiya Janata Party (BJP), was definitely high on the list of probables. It was even said that the state police force was directly involved – not as an

---

[1]The Congress immediately filed a complaint against the BJP with the State Election Commission, but it would take another year and a half before material evidence would emerge from a disgruntled candidate who had been asked to step down from an election he felt he was winning and not even given the compensation money he was promised for his sacrifice.

upholder of the law, but as the operative carrying out the act. The Superintendent of Police (SP) was himself said to be present on the scene of the crime.

Shortly before the elections the six 'kidnappees' had emerged in the broad light of day and withdrawn their nominations. Finally, there were only two names left on the ballot sheet: the first belonged to the BJP candidate, a long-haired gent who looked like a hippie from the '60s and was rumoured to have many 'wives'; the second to a hapless contender who had rushed to the nomination centre only to find that he had missed the deadline for withdrawal by a few minutes.

This was not the most bewildering rumour I would come across during the time I spent in Kanker. Although the space of a few months had weathered the sense of urgency in the minds of the people involved, the story of another kidnapping, that had happened during the 2014 general election, also reached me through a person who claimed to have been directly present at the scene of the crime. I verified the story later from an Additional Superintendent of Police (ASP) in Chhattisgarh.

An election was to be held in the remote village of Netram in the Orchha block of Narayanpur district. A party of thirty-five people was sent ahead to set up the polling booth. They were to carry out a variety of tasks, including creating the helipad for the election officers, setting up the booth and installing the electronic voting machine. The team was drawn from cadres of government schoolteachers, health workers and assorted government staff members.

The district administration offered to send a police escort with the team. To a man, the team refused. Each believed that in Maoist-infested territory, they were safer unescorted by the security forces. On the 35-km-long motorcycle ride to the site of the booth, things initially proceeded as foreseen, with the occasional felled tree placed strategically to block the road, or the hastily dug ditch to obstruct progress, being dealt with as necessary. The Maoists, who routinely put out a boycott call for elections, were expected to create such obstacles.[2]

All of a sudden, the splendid day in the middle of the forest took a turn for the worse. A man and a woman in green battle fatigues emerged from the forest on to the dirt track and waved the party to a halt with their AK-47s. Then a group of between 30 and 40 combatants emerged from the jungle and encircled the team. It was immediately clear to the team that these were Maoists, for the Indian counter-insurgency forces never included women in their ranks and this bunch consisted of an equal number of men and women.

After the purpose of the visit by the team had been ascertained, mobile phones were confiscated and the government party was escorted by a couple of Maoists through narrow pathways to a clearing about the size of a football field, where around eight tents had been set up. After providing the group with lunch and making arrangements for its members to rest, the Maoists returned to the clearing.

From the camp, the party would notice a few helicopters hovering above and then turning back on observing that the helipad had not been built. A few hours later, soon after they had finished lunch, the team heard the sound of sustained firing

[2]The Maoists have clarified various aspects of their standing call to boycott elections in an article in the *Economic and Political Weekly* (SPOKESPERSON, 'On the Election Boycott Tactic of the Maoists', *Economic and Political Weekly* (2009): 73-77). They regard security forces and candidates as legitimate targets. On the other hand, they state that the unfortunate attacks on poll officers that may have taken place on occasion were cases of mistaken identity and not a part of their policy.

from the clearing. It continued for a few hours and stopped just as suddenly as it had started. Half an hour later, the Maoist troops returned to the camp. They were in pitiable condition. Many were being carried on the shoulders of their comrades. Some had their innards visible through their open wounds, and blood flowed freely on to the dry earth below. Only a few of the guerillas were conscious enough to be aware of their pain and their incessant groans were clearly audible.

Apparently, the security forces had followed in the wake of the advance party to make provision for the helicopter that would be carrying the electronic voting machine. They were the targets of the Maoist-led ambush. Had things gone according to plan, the security forces would have got the worst of it. However, as it happened, it was the Maoists who were caught unawares when they broke cover for a sip of water from a nearby stream. As a result, they had suffered heavy casualties. After the encounter, the government forces, despite having the upper hand, failed to press home their advantage. They thought better of advancing and returned to the block headquarters.

Medical supplies from the captured government team were pressed into service to tend to the wounded. Finally, the Maoist camp was disbanded and the officials released. Their mobile phones were returned to them before they were let off.

When the party found its way back to the block headquarters, its members were confronted by an angry administration which wanted to put the blame for the entire fiasco squarely on them. They were threatened with suspension. The workers were nonplussed at their predicament, but found a way out when they learnt that despite no polling booth having been set up, the administration had managed to show that 98 per cent polling had taken place. In unison, the team members confronted their bosses and threatened to blow the lid off the scam if any action was taken against them. Faced with the prospect of a major embarrassment, the officials backed off.

Regardless of the truth of the matter, a few months later, it was announced that for the heroic achievement of holding exemplary elections in a remote Left-wing extremist area, the district administration – the Collector and the SP – had been singled out for praise by the Election Commission. Alarmelmangai D., district election officer of Kanker in Chhattisgarh, was recognized for 'micro-level planning at polling station level in Left-wing extremist-affected area to facilitate people to vote', while SP Rajendra Narayan Dash received an award for 'differential force deployment to counter Naxal threat during elections'.[3]

On a Friday morning, I am sitting in the Kanker Coffee House, the local version of the popular hangout place found in most Indian cities where members of the intelligentsia congregate to air their views on matters of consequence. Only, this place is even shabbier than the fashionably down-at-heel coffee houses of the metros. I had come here in search of a cybercafe to take some printouts, only to find that there are none in Kanker.

Which is how I find myself in a tea shop with a tin-shed roof, some long wooden benches, a steel water dispenser – a sign of unexpected affluence – installed for the purpose of washing hands and a bunch of people with time on their hands and the world's problems to solve. The walls are covered with hand-painted signs – 'Sai Kumbal Bhandar' (Sai Blanket Depot) being an example – and posters of candidates in the recent by-election.

Seated in a circle are four or five people, each nursing a tiny

[3]http://www.business-standard.com/article/pti-stories/national-awards-for-best-electoral-practices-given-away-114012500792_1.html

cup of tea in his hands. Among them is Mandawi, who, I am told, is a tribal leader in the Rashtriya Swayamsevak Sangh (RSS), the ideological parent of the BJP. When he is introduced as such, someone laughs.

'A tribal leader who is part of the RSS,' he quips, an oblique reference to the reputation of the RSS as a party with little empathy for the adivasis.

Mandawi smiles. There is about him the air of a person who has faced enough troubles in life to know that he cannot trust too many people and yet has learnt how to work the system to his advantage. Traces of the pain of a life lived on the peripheries of the mainstream still linger in his expression.

There is the bearded Rajen Gaur, a local Vishwa Hindu Parishad (VHP) leader. He works on bore wells in remote areas and must deal with the insurgents on a regular basis. He looks like a guy who knows how to work the system and is reasonably well-positioned in the little world he is a part of – high of caste, strong in body, clever in business and well-aligned in politics. Before joining the gathering, he spends some time sizing me up from his elevated perch inside a little unused stall just outside the coffee house, the kind used to dispense corn in city malls, except that this one is less fancy.

There is, of course, the sucker who pays for our cups of tea. A BJP honcho, he is wearing a nice pair of slip-ons in black leather. The reason those of us gathered here notice his footwear is because the guy who has fooled him into paying for us all points out his slippers as a sign of his prosperity. 'See, the nail in my slippers?' he says, to highlight the contrast. That seems to clinch the argument.

The tea we are drinking is indistinguishable from that served in any other roadside dhaba. What makes it different is the venue at which it is being consumed and the company I keep, the group of worthies who could tell me more about the recent kidnapping. Yes, that's right, the kidnapping of six by-election hopefuls, not the caper of the election officers in the remote forest location, which, in any case, they probably know nothing about.

'What they did was very bad,' one says. 'We heard this used to happen in Bihar, but never in Chhattisgarh.'

'The public is not going to tolerate this for long,' declares another.

The statements are vague enough to be interpreted in any manner one sees fit. I'm looking for greater clarity.

'Is what they are saying true?' I ask. 'That the BJP got six candidates kidnapped?'

I address my question to the patron of our morning tea, as he laughingly rises to go on his way. If a BJP member validated the word on the streets, I would need no further proof.

'I never disagree with them,' he says and leaves without confirming or refuting the story.

After my tea at the Kanker Coffee House, I hop across to the police station which is a stone's throw away. I am about to meet SP Rajendra Narayan Dash. My local contact had given me his mobile number.

'Come by in fifteen minutes,' the SP had said cheerily on the phone.

I walk into his cavernous office to see a mustachioed man who looks like Clement Rajkumar, the warden of one of the hostel blocks in my college who had suspended a couple of boys on my birthday for being drunk. Dash is tall and athletically built, with a forceful personality. His uniform lapel bears the name 'Rajendra', along with a circle and a plus sign. Behind him are two flags pasted to the wall – one of India, the other, a blue one with the emblem of the Chhattisgarh Police. High on the wall behind his chair hangs a large photo of Mahatma Gandhi as well as a plaque from the Election Commission acknowledging the SP's sterling performance in the 2014 election.

I am hesitant about plunging without preamble into my investigation of the stories of the various acts of forced bodily removal I have encountered since my arrival in Kanker. So I start off by discussing the vulnerability of the local population that has to satisfy two masters, one antagonistic to the other – the Maoists and the Indian government. The position of the local government representatives is especially delicate in districts like Kanker, where the two opposing forces are evenly matched. If the sarpanches align themselves with the Maoists, allowing them greater access to the development funds than deemed 'acceptable', they risk being called to account by the Indian government. If they lean the other way, they become cannon fodder for the Maoists. There is, of course, a third interest involved in this dynamic – the personal accumulation of wealth by the sarpanch himself, which happens either with or without the complicity of one or both sides in the conflict.

Given this complex tangle of motivations, it is not surprising that in the last two years, thirteen sarpanches have been killed by the Maoists, seven have resigned under pressure and fourteen accused of aligning themselves with the insurgents and imprisoned. With the power of the people thus hijacked by the power of the gun wielded by either the state or its enemies, there is a distinct possibility in the future of only stooges standing for election, regardless of which side they are affiliated to.

The calculus is somewhat different in areas where the Maoists clearly have the upper hand. In blocks like Orchha, one of the two blocks comprising Narayanpur district and the one more affected by the insurgency, the representatives of the people are hand-picked by the Maoists and expected to stay as far away from the action as possible. They do the bidding of the Maoists in the matter of diverting development resources to them; in return, they make a tidy sum of money with which they soon buy property and the four-wheel drives favoured in the roadless terrain. The semi-urban agglomerations to which they have been exiled are quite appropriate for their lifestyles.

Some squander their hard-earned money in less than profitable ways. The tehsildar of the Orchha block, for instance, chooses to spend most of his revenue on drink. Once, he was caught in his usual inebriated state on TV, declaring, 'I am the only tehsildar in the *world* who does not have a single subordinate staff member. Even if I have to get a *pauaa* (quart), I have no one in the office to get it for me.'

SP Dash's confident voice interrupts my thoughts. 'We are very sensitive about the vulnerability of villagers,' he says. 'They are caught in between. If they do small things for Maoists, we don't mind, but when they go out of their way then we have to take notice.'

'What do you mean by "going out of their way"?' I ask.

As I had gathered from my local contacts, half of almost every government service, including the public distribution system (PDS) rations and health services, was being appropriated by the Maoists as their inalienable right. Hence, I wondered where the boundary lines were being drawn.

'If a government schoolteacher is pressed into service for some small task like making posters, we understand. But not if they actively help with their operations.'

'I am sure the villagers are your eyes and ears when it comes to such things. Could local politics not have something to do with allegations levelled against certain people as Maoist sympathizers or government stooges?'

SP Dash smiles. 'We have ways of knowing what each one is up to,' he says. 'Many sarpanches steal money with the knowledge of the Maoists. When the villagers complain to us [about them], we ask them [the sarpanches] to resign. Only in rare cases do we imprison them. Our jail has a capacity of sixty-five[4] and it currently houses four hundred people. Where am I going to get the space to keep these people in jail? Of course, if the sarpanches steal money without telling [the] Maoists, they are killed by them.'

I probably look a bit concerned about the plight of the sarpanches, for SP Dash starts telling me about the police's latest scheme aimed at reducing Maoist influence in the area. The police, he says in a reassuring tone, have created ashrams away from the villages, where they house the children from Maoist-controlled villages. Dash claims that the tribals are happy to send their children away so they can grow up in a safe environment, insulated from the charismatic appeal of the Maoists. Once they come of age, many of those who have grown up in these ashrams are enrolled in the police force. There is, in fact, a long-standing guideline for the security forces to hire from the local district, especially at the junior level. Only recently have the police succeeded in implementing these norms, partly due to initiatives like the ashrams.

The prospect of many of these children carrying out operations against their elders and brethren, rightly or wrongly identified as Maoist sympathizers, does not lessen my sense of unease. The fact that the tribals have to send their children away, either to escape forced enlistment in the Maoist cadre or to avoid appearing sympathetic to the Government of India, appears to be

[4]The following site assessed in March 2016 lists the Kanker district jail capacity as 165, and the number of prisoners in the lockup as 425: http://jail.cg.gov.in/lockup.htm

just another form of abduction inflicted by a dysfunctional system on a hapless population. I am glad that I am not a sarpanch under these circumstances. Perhaps sensing my acute discomfort SP Dash continues his attempts to make me feel better.

'When I was in college at the Jawaharlal Nehru University I used to reproduce all these communist ideologies to get marks in my exams,' he assures me. 'We even believed in all that,' he goes on to add, 'but when I see the situation on the ground, it is different.'

He appears to be in an expansive mood. It is time to discuss the kidnappings.

'I have been hearing about the recent by-election,' I begin. 'People have been talking about irregularities. Apparently, there was a kidnapping of some of the contestants.' And then I let it slip: 'Did the police carry out the kidnapping?'

There is a moment of silence. I wonder if I have gone too far. After all, I have come to him with hardly any reference.

Dash smiles. 'You are not the only one who has said this to me,' he concedes. 'I know I will have to face this question for a long time [to come]. Others too ask me the same thing. But you can check my call records for that night.'

He stretches out his hand towards me, offering me a look at his mobile phone. I let the offer pass.

'You cannot imagine how difficult this election was for us,' Dash goes on. 'We are supposed to give one security personnel for each candidate. So many candidates refused the security cover. If someone does not want help, what can we do?' And then he puts forth his own allegation. 'I know who might have been involved. It was neither the ruling party nor us.'

I am unsurprised by his attempt to absolve the police of complicity in the matter, but shocked that he is making no effort to deny that the kidnapping had actually taken place.

'Do you mean the Congress?' I ask.

'I cannot say anything,' he replies.

He then points to the plaque on the wall. 'See that award? I got it for holding elections against all odds in Netram in 2014. And today I am being accused of such things.'

My ears prick up. SP Dash is voluntarily shifting the conversation to the other kidnapping.

'What was your particular achievement in that election?' I ask.

'I could not set up the polling booth in time,' he says. 'Due to opposition from the Maoists, the election officers had to return. Then I decided to hold an adjunct election and succeeded. That's what the plaque is for.'

'How did you succeed?' I ask. 'What did you do differently?'

As SP Dash grapples with the question, I muse: *Perhaps, you entered into a pact of silence with the party that was kidnapped by the Maoists?*

'We moved the polling booth,' he begins, by way of a reply.

'Then did the voters have to travel a long way to exercise their franchise?' I ask.

'No, not a long way,' he counters.

'Then what was different?' I persist.

There is some hemming and hawing. Finally, his eyes light up.

'I was able to deploy all my forces, who were now free from regular election duties, for the adjunct election. How proud I was when I took the Election Commissioner up in a helicopter and showed him the long line of people heading for the polling booth! Ninety-eight per cent of the people voted and we got the national award. So my humiliation at not succeeding the first time came with a sweet reward in the end.'

We go on to discuss several other issues, but I leave SP Dash's office with one thought uppermost in my mind – how does anyone separate truth from falsehood in this most surreal of lands? How do people living in the shadow of two competing threats retain their sanity and preserve their inner core, buried as it is under the layers of the camouflaging masks they must constantly don and peel off in order to survive?

I still cannot bring myself to believe that the candidates had actually been kidnapped. Many weeks later, I return to my contact with a barrage of questions. 'Did you actually meet the candidates who had been kidnapped?' I ask. 'Why did they not file a police report? Did they go to the press?'

I am told that many of the candidates are local traders and small-time crooks, susceptible to threats of court cases being filed against them for various transgressions or open to being won over by small favours. In fact, some may have stood for election precisely to be in a position to command such bribes. As a result, the matter has been discreetly buried, leaving no trace, and peace reigns once again in Kanker.

The real kidnapping, then, is the one being effected upon our democracy.

2

The Swami and the Sentry

Kamal Shukla is an irascible, unputdownable and incorruptible journalist from Kanker. For a life-long radical, unafraid of taking on the powers that be at some risk to life and limb, he is strangely observant of traditional customs: when I see him at the bus stop where he has come to receive me, I notice that he has had his head tonsured for *shraadh*, the month when Hindus customarily remember their male ancestors. Perhaps these concessions are his way of making up to his long-suffering family, I think. His flecked grey eyes appear the brighter for his bald pate, which seems to throw them into sharp relief.

The following story about him is a telling comment on the level of brazen insouciance he is capable off, even in the face of death.

On a day the Maoists had called a bandh, Kamal set out in his car to escort some journalists from Delhi. On the way, they found some trees and brush strewn across the road. Kamal got out of the car to clear the path and fell into a camouflaged hole. He realized it was a booby trap. If he attempted to get out, a bomb would go off. His best hope for survival was to stand absolutely still. His son, a budding journalist who was accompanying him, set about taking video footage of his immobile father. Others went back to seek help. Finally, when it became clear that no help would be forthcoming, Kamal extracted his leg from the trap slowly and carefully, praying that a detonator would not set off the explosive device. The moment passed, Kamal dusted himself off and the group resumed its journey.

Shukla is among those people who are more familiar than most with areas under Maoist control. In January 2014, he had led a padyatra of journalists through Abuj Maad, the unbreached citadel of the Maoists spread across the Narayanpur, Bijapur and Dantewada districts of Chhattisgarh, to protest against the killing of two journalists, Nemichand Jain and Sai Reddy.

According to the stated policy of the Maoists, they do not come in the way of freedom of expression. The padyatra undertaken by the journalists was thus intended to hold them to their declared policy in order to counter the wave of fear that had spread through the community following the murders.

Well-known journalists and litterateurs in Kanker, like Girish

Pankaj and Harish Singh Sidar, decided to join the padyatra. A group of 30 people set out from Orchha in January 2014. The police had tried to make them desist from their plan as they feared that those participating in the yatra could well become the target of Maoist violence, thus roiling the situation even further.

The journalists were adamant, however. Their only demand was that the police should refrain from providing them any kind of protective cover to avoid offering further provocation to the Maoists. After several hours of discussion and argument, the journalists were allowed to leave.

Over the next five days, they walked 110 km through Maoist-controlled territory. Every day, they would stop to address a public gathering in one village or the other. The meeting would start and end with the journalists shouting slogans of protest.

'*Patrakaron ki hatya…band karo, band karo!*' they would chant. 'The murder of journalists has to stop!'

'*Abhivyakti ki aazaadi…zindabad, zindabad!* Long live freedom of speech!'

At night, they would halt their yatra and set up camp either in the *ghotul* (community centre) of a village or in a decrepit ashram. Many of the villagers joined them in the march for short stretches. One of them was Sudhu Netam (name changed), who would eventually become a good friend of Kamal Shukla's and later serve as our guide in Abuj Maad.

As soon as the journalists had crossed the Orchha nullah, a stream that lay 5 km from Orchha town, they encountered members of the *jantana sarkar*, the parallel government set up by the rebels to administer areas under their control. Sometimes, as they crossed the boundaries of a panchayat, the journalists would be received and escorted by the Maoists. Everywhere, their audiences, packed with members of the jantana government, would listen to them in silence. It was obvious that the insurgents were embarrassed by their deviation from the stated Maoist principle proscribing attacks on journalists.

About five or six months after the padyatra, four of the journalists who had participated in it were invited by Ganesh Ukey, the commander of the South Bastar Division of the Maoists, for a meeting. The meeting was held in a forest clearing. Representing the rebel side was Ganesh, along with an escort of four – two men and a couple of women – in military fatigues. Kamal Shukla, Bappi Rai, Abdul Hamid Siddique and Jiten Chaudhry constituted the contingent of journalists representing the media.

Ganesh is a light-complexioned, parrot-nosed adivasi of medium build, known for his dedication to the Maoist cause. He has the habit of breaking into a booming, full-throated laugh – the kind favoured by larger-than-life Hindi film actors of the 1970s and '80s. He is also extremely sensitive to the matter of caste. When he first heard Kamal's name being mentioned during the opening round of introductions with the journalists, Ganesh's face had assumed a pained expression.

'Oh, a Brahmin!' he had remarked with evident distaste, before proceeding to ask each of the journalists his particular caste.

After introductions were over, Ganesh began the meeting by expressing regret over the role of the rebels in the death of Nemichand Jain, a newspaper distributor who had been killed in the process of mediating between a timber smuggler and the Maoists.

'Jain was innocent,' he admitted. 'We have expelled the party member responsible for his death.'

Kamal Shukla wondered silently if expulsion from the party was a punishment commensurate with the gravity of the crime committed.

'As for Sai Reddy,' Ganesh continued, 'he was responsible

for the death of many comrades. As far back as the Jan Jagran Abhiyan, he had caused us immense hardship.'

It is believed that Reddy was killed for unearthing scams in which both government officials and Maoists were complicit and extorting money from both parties.

On this matter, all that Ganesh was willing to concede was his party's failure to present matters before the people in their correct perspective. He promised that in future the Maoists would invite journalists to be part of investigations involving other members of the press.

Kamal Shukla asked, 'How will you decide which journalists should be involved, given their diversity and the difference voices in which they speak?'

Ganesh did not answer that question. Nor did the Maoists implement his promise of involving journalists in their investigations involving others from the same profession.

The question of which journalists to involve in a fair investigation is a pertinent one. The word 'journalist' itself has come to acquire a broad meaning, Kamal explains. Nemichand, for example, a distribution agent of newspapers, was deemed a journalist. So is Sudhir Jain, who runs a wholesale kirana store. And there are, of course, those journalists who have turned into petty contractors as the Chhattisgarh Police attempts to defang them with the promise of an assured income. Besides, many politicians run newspapers and TV channels. Often, members of the administration will access insurgency-affected areas sporting a press badge. So do the police forces, on occasion.

According to Kamal Shukla, the situation has come to such a pass that journalists who ply their trade with ulterior motives find themselves under pressure from both the government and the Maoists. Even those who attempt to abide by the truth as they see it usually fall foul of one party or the other. Sometimes the government brands them as Maoists and imprisons them under the Chhattisgarh Public Security Act, as happened to Santosh Yadav who was imprisoned in September 2015. The needle of suspicion fell on him for having reached the site of a Maoist ambush a short time after the incident took place. At such times, the media organizations that employ these journalists as 'stringers' often deny any connection with them. On other occasions, the Maoists accuse them of being police informers and keep them in custody or kill them. The exceptions are those journalists who have, over the years, acquired a reputation for probity and enough clout to command amnesty from both sides.

'They have a hard time making ends meet, though,' Kamal says ruefully.

Sudhu Netam, Kamal's friend from the padyatra, who joins us later that night, is an athletic tribal lad who sometimes has to trek 65 km from the nearest motorable road to get to his village. He is the first literate person in his family. As a small child, he was captivated by the monks of the Ramakrishna Mission when they came to his village in their bright robes and warm woollen caps, speaking broken Gondi as they handed out tasty toffees. He decided to take up their offer of education and studied till Class XII at their school in Narayanpur. Then, despite uncomprehending criticism from his family, he wanted to go on to college. Finally, realizing that his son was adamant, Sudhu's father gave him ₹200 and his blessings.

'If you feel hungry, eat something,' he told him.

Sudhu went on to complete a BA in Arts. Today he is a *shiksha karmi*, a government teacher in his village school. He is also a nationally accredited referee for kho kho, a traditional sport. His eyes reveal his wonder at having narrowly escaped the fate of his ancestors, even as his smile betrays the pain of not belonging anywhere.

I want to do two things, I tell Kamal: spend a night in a Maoist village, and see a working mine. These urges are driven by my belief that the quick transition from an insurgent-run zone to the operational site of a mine will allow me to test some of my hypotheses about Maoism and mining.

Later that night, we zero in on the plan. We will try to access Sonpur village in Abuj Maad,[5] where the weekly market is held on Tuesdays. This is one of the first large villages on this side of Maad, a 4,000 sq km 'liberated zone' where the Maoists are believed to run a parallel government. To access Maad, we have to drive south to Narayanpur town, the administrative headquarters of Narayanpur district, and then transfer to motorbikes to negotiate the difficult terrain. The plan is to spend the night in Sonpur. On the way back to Kanker, we will have a chance to stop at an iron-ore mine.

We have idlis for breakfast and head out in a car driven by Kamal's nephew Lokesh, also known as Bunty, who, on learning that I am a business-school professor, spends an inordinate amount of time picking my brains on how he could make lots of money.

Travelling through the countryside, one comes across a curious sight: clusters of people, gathered close to a tree, stretching their arms out and waving their cell phones about like arthropods intent upon sensing nourishment. All this activity, I soon discover, is aimed at catching a strong enough signal;

---

[5]The name Abuj Maad is usually translated as 'unknown forest'. However, while it is true that these forests have hardly ever divulged their secrets to the Indian state, the original meaning in Gondi, according to Gondi scholar Moti Ravan Kangale, is 'sal forest'.

the network strength is obviously better at higher elevations. In one particular location, we see how people have clambered on to the capacious branches of a hospitable banyan and settled themselves at three different levels. Each has a mobile device – one man is even carrying a WLL (Wireless in the Local Loop) landline phone – and all are intent on their own conversations, while others wait in the 'queue' below for their turn to get their places in the sun.

However, not all trees can be climbed. Nor do all those desiring communication have the time, inclination or agility to clamber up trunks and ensconce themselves on branches. In such instances, human ingenuity comes up with the appropriate technology to work around such problems. This technology is neither fancy nor state-of-the-art. It involves the old-fashioned pulley and the clunky mug once used in the washroom, but now rendered obsolete by shiny nozzles and sprinklers. A Bluetooth device, the only concession to modern technology, completes the circuit.

Here's how this works: a mobile phone is used to dial a number, then loaded in a mug which is hauled up to the top of a 20-metre-tall bamboo pole, using a pulley operated from the ground. Once the phone reaches a height at which the signal is clear, a Bluetooth device is used to redial the number continuously till the call goes through and the conversation can take place. Once the conversation is over, the mug containing the phone is hauled back down. Their purported backwardness notwithstanding, every child in a tribal village understands the value of a Bluetooth device.

According to the 2011 census, even in the major Maoist-affected states of Madhya Pradesh – Chhattisgarh, Jharkhand, Orissa and the North East – 40 to 45 per cent of the rural population possess a mobile phone, exceeding, by far, the number of people who have bank accounts in their name or toilets in their homes. However, it is the radio and the TV, rather than the mobile phone, that continue to be the main devices of access to information.

The mobile phone, however, is important, both for civilian use and from a strategic point of view; important enough for a force on the offensive – whether Maoist or national – to confiscate from targets so that no communication can be made during the operation. During one raid, the Maoists boarded a state transport bus and shot dead a passenger, a policeman in civilian clothes who was, perhaps, travelling on a personal errand. During the operation, all mobile phones were confiscated, never to be returned. Later, the Maoists issued a public apology. 'We forgot to return the phones,' they said. 'We are revolutionaries, not thieves.'[6]

When the Indian military forces attack a village, they too seize mobile phones to prevent strategic information from leaking out. The mobile is useful for yet another reason: when communication networks are based on mobile phones, the government forces enjoy an advantage over their adversaries. While they can eavesdrop on Maoist communications, their own conversations are inaccessible. This was not the case some years ago, when old-fashioned radio sets were the sole means of communication in these parts and messages exchanged between the combatants of one side or the other could be tapped equally by both.

In the early days of the mobile phone, the Maoists were indiscreet and arrests were made on the basis of exchanges

---

[6]Rahman, Shafi, 'Inside Maoistan', in Paul, Santosh, ed., *Maoist Movement in India: Perspectives and Counterperspectives*, Routledge, 2013.

overheard on tapped phones. In retaliation, the rebels blew up several mobile-phone towers.

The Ministry of Home Affairs lists 245 attacks on telephone exchanges and mobile towers between 2008 and 2013, of which 30 were carried out in Chhattisgarh alone. Twenty-five of the Chhattisgarh attacks took place in the years 2008 and 2009. After the first few years, the Maoists realized that their conversations were being tapped and started speaking in code. The number of attacks on mobile towers also dwindled. Nevertheless, the heavily fortified interiors of paramilitary camps still remain the preferred location for erecting mobile towers.

While the Maoists communicate in code to keep the military forces off their trail, even coded conversations are useful to their opponents, not because the code can be cracked but because their locations can be tracked using network records. So for important communications, the Maoists revert to the time-tested method of using a courier.

If a meeting is held in Aader, a remote village in the Orchha block, a courier carrying minutes of the meeting will set out for Kanker. Another courier will take over from there and head for Raipur. A third and even a fourth may be involved in the relay, before the message reaches the headquarters in some remote Andhra village. In hyper-local contexts, the Maoists use the age-old adivasi method of drumbeats and bird calls to learn about troop movements.

Indeed, in this war, the old-fashioned methods involving human couriers, audio relays and infiltration continue to constitute an important part of the arsenal on both sides involved in the conflict, but this is especially true of the Maoists.

The Ministry of Home Affairs plans to set up 2,200 mobile towers, run entirely on solar energy, in Left-wing-extremism-affected states.[7] The most obvious objective is to improve communications for the security forces. However, the impact of weaning the local youth away from Maoist propaganda by connecting them to mainstream communication lines should not be underestimated.

On our way to Narayanpur, Kamal promises to show me a cell-phone tower blown up by the Maoists. However, we forget to take the small detour involved and I miss a photo opportunity.

We reach Narayanpur a little past noon, eat a quick lunch and set out. Kamal is on one bike, Sudhu on the other. I am on Sudhu's bike, riding pillion.

We are moving towards Abuj Maad, fabled citadel of the Maoists, a rolling expanse of forest, stream and mountain twice the size of Mauritius, never surveyed[8] and breached by government forces only in 2012 as part of Operation Hakka. Expecting formidable encampments, bunkers and armaments, the invading army troops had only found forlorn villages and puzzled villagers. But the desolation did not signify the retreat of the Maoists as much as the inherent elusiveness of a force that carries all its worldly possessions on its back. It is into this fleeting fortress that I am now venturing – with racing heart and

[7]http://www.thehindu.com/sci-tech/energy-and-environment/2200-solarpowered-mobile-towers-to-be-set-up-in-naxalaffected-areas/article6346686.ece

[8]The revenue system in Maad was introduced by an English ICS officer, Grigson (his full name is not known), in 1929. The headman of the village, the Majhi, collects a tax for every male over sixteen years of age and pays it into the tehsil treasury. Census is taken every five years, again by the Majhi. (*A Tale Told by an Idiot*, R.P. Noronha, Vikas Publishing House, New Delhi, 1976, 182).

no small expectation of the thrill of coming face-to-face with a flesh-and-blood Maoist insurgent.

After fifteen minutes, we are on a dirt track. Forty-five minutes later, we pass the last village before Abuj Maad, cross a traditional tribal archway and enter.

Riding into Maad, I feel, curiously enough, as though I were entering an adventure park, perhaps even Disneyland. This may well be indicative of my naiveté, but the picture-perfect scenery does offer some justification for my state of mind. There are tree-covered hills gently undulating into the distance. Blades of the growing rice crop wave languidly in the breeze. Huts made of wooden logs dot the landscape and people appear with ready smiles on their faces. Enhancing it all is the delectable hint of danger, on the one hand, and the reassuring company of trusted guides, on the other – the precise cocktail of risk and security that makes a roller-coaster ride so exhilarating.

I have to get off the bike several times to cross difficult terrain. At places the water, running clear, rises to one's ankles. At one point, we meet three men. One of them has a mouth stained red, as though he were a habitual paan-eater. I learn that he is consuming *gudaku*, a combination of tobacco and *gud*, believed to be the biggest cause of oral cancer in Chhattisgarh. Its production is controlled by the family of the state health minister in the BJP government. The minister's family ensures that nothing happens to its thriving, though deadly, business by positioning one brother in each of the major parties and bagging key ministries like health.[9]

---

[9]In another case of piquant irony, the wife of Kedar Kashyap, the education minister of Chhattisgarh, was accused of using a proxy candidate to appear on her behalf in one of her MA English exams; http://indianexpress.com/article/india/india-others/impersonation-row-sister-took-exam-on-behalf-of-chhattisgarh-ministers-wife/

Finally, we are brought down to earth by a swollen nullah. Apparently, the government had planned to build a culvert bridge across this watercourse but the equipment of the contractor entrusted with the work was blown up by the local Maoist commander.

We get off our bikes and look this way and that. We notice a group of people bringing their bikes across, one at a time. I get ready to change into my shorts to take the plunge.

The people who have just crossed over tell us that there are more nullahs on the way to Sonpur. I glance at Sudhu. He looks doubtful. Even if we do manage to get there, the journey back is likely to be a challenge. If it rains, things will become still more difficult. Eight kilometres from our destination, we turn back. Later, I kick myself for failing to consider the option of heading for a branch of the Ramakrishna Mission Ashram, 3 km from the other side of the nullah, to spend the night before going on to Sonpur. Anyway, I would not have wanted to override the decision of my guides.

Tomorrow, we will try to access Aader, a remote village in the Orchha block. We will also have a chance to explore the Orchha market, held in Orchha town every Wednesday. Tonight will be spent in Narayanpur town.

En route to Narayanpur lies the vast Ramakrishna Mission property, a sprawling campus of school buildings, temples built in the traditional style with high, narrow, conical roofs and fields abundant with crops waving in the breeze. The mission, set up by Swami Vivekananda in 1897, is named after Ramakrishna Paramhansa, one of the most remarkable Indian mystics of the nineteenth century. Swami Vivekananda, his pre-eminent disciple, is known to have travelled through the length and breadth of the country, as well as to the West, spreading his master's message.

While travelling across India in the 1890s, Swamiji had been moved by the plight of the tribals and the ashram set up in Narayanpur in 1985 represents the mission's long-cherished dream of working towards their upliftment. Sudhu shows us around his alma mater with evident pride. There is an ashram, a school exclusively for tribal children, a remedial-education centre, a college and a large farm. The mission also has a presence in remote villages in the form of small ashrams and day-care centres.

I am in the drawing room of the Sadhu Niwas, the dormitory housing the monks, speaking to Swami Vyaptananda, the society's secretary. He is dressed in ochre robes and wears an ochre woollen cap. His face is calm, his tone measured, as he speaks in fluent, though slightly accented, Hindi. I guess he is Bengali.

Swamiji tells us that he has been in the area for close to fifteen years. The main change he has noticed over time is the increased interest in education. In the early days, the monks would have to visit the villages and literally lure the children into attending their school. The first step was to establish a rapport with them by enticing them with toffee and chocolates; the next was to focus on convincing the parents.

Today, the picture is very different; the mission has a total of 2,000 full-time students and several hundred in its remedial programmes. Yet it is unable to satisfy the huge demand for admission to its various educational institutions.

I ask Swamiji about the Maoist problem. There is a pause. Because of its reach in remote areas, the mission was used as a centre for the government's public distribution scheme. Accounts have described how the local *dada*s would come and take away half the ration from the mission, as they would from other PDS outlets in their areas. As a result, the mission's reputation came under a cloud and the PDS outlets were moved away from the villages to the block headquarters,[10] necessitating a 20 to 30 km walk for the villagers.

'We don't comment on political matters,' says the monk finally. 'But this problem does not have an easy solution. It is not likely to be resolved anytime soon. We have to be patient.'

The mission also instals tube wells in remote locations and has to negotiate with the Maoists to carry out its work. I ask if the insurgents have any objections to the setting up of tube wells.

Swamiji does not respond to the question. Instead, he says with a pensive expression, 'All I know is that the tribals are innocent. The tribals must not be blamed.' He repeats this statement a couple of times with deep feeling.

We chat for a while, enjoy a delicious tea served with biscuits and home-made gulab jamuns, and take our leave.

Later, we check into an abomination in the guise of a lodge, the bedspread in the room allotted to me a velvet horror, ripe for collecting dirt, with the motif of a rich red flower on it. The basin in the room is streaked with paan-stained spittle. The Circuit House in Narayanpur is no longer available to outsiders like us; a few months earlier, a Zee TV crew had consumed one too many drinks and created a ruckus.

Tomorrow, we will head to Orchha.

The problem faced by the mission in its humanitarian work is symptomatic of the challenge of bringing development inputs to an area controlled by a self-declared champion of the people and

[10]Mitta, Tusha, 'Life in the "Liberated Zone"', in Paul, Santosh, ed., *Maoist Movement in India: Perspectives and Counterperspectives*, Routledge, 2013.

enemy of the state. Inevitably, a large proportion of the inputs will be siphoned off by that enemy. This includes food and health services. Certain development inputs will be seen as a threat and not allowed into the area. These include any infrastructure that has the potential to aid security forces: hard-top roads, for example, along with bridges, concrete buildings with flat roofs that can serve as outposts and the occasional mobile-phone tower as well.

Every now and then, one hears of some person or agency being branded a Maoist sympathizer. These indictments have to be seen in the context of a situation where most of the resources enjoyed by the Maoists are generated from the Government of India itself, often with their complete knowledge.

In certain cases, the government's hands are tied and it has little choice but to allow this diversion of development inputs in the hope that at least some services will eventually reach the people. In other cases, government officials are actively involved in looting the public exchequer, appropriating resources along with the Maoists.

An example of a complex development input is a road. The construction of roads falls under the purview of a district *nirmaan* committee comprising the district collector, the SP and a few other district officials. The latter apportion the work of building new roads to contractors who are chosen on the basis of a bidding process. Often, however, there are no bidders due to the risks involved and the district nirmaan committee has to persuade contractors to take on the project by promising them adequate security.

All members of the district administration and the general public agree that a black-top road is anathema to the Maoists on account of the security threat it represents for them. But, according to the insurgents, roads, pucca school buildings and helipads in remote areas like Maad are unwelcome, because they are supposedly built as part of a 'long-term strategy to…loot the natural wealth that is lying unexplored and unexploited in the bosom of these regions…'[11]

Mainstream Leftist thinkers like Archana Prasad have other objections to the pattern of road construction. They claim that highways are built to 'facilitate the access of industrial traders to the main markets, but the condition of public transport and village and mohalla roads [is] ignored, thus denying access to markets for tribal forest-produce collectors.'[12]

In any case, the construction of a major road is regarded as a significant victory for the government. Indeed, SP Dash had proudly pointed out new roads – including a 55 km stretch from Durg Kondal to Bande and a 3 km road from Udhampur to Pratappur – to me on a wall-sized map in his office, frequently shining a pencil beam to track the paths.

However, the real gains from road construction are more nuanced and less unencumbered. Kamal Shukla claims that in all road projects, contractors have to pay off the Maoists. The amount of money due is worked out through face-to-face negotiations held against the backdrop of strategically timed acts of sabotage, kidnapping and arson perpetrated by the insurgents.

Further, Maoists are able to booby-trap the road with IEDs (Improvised Explosive Devices) before it is actually laid. I had to ask Kamal to repeat himself a couple of times before I could actually believe I had heard right. Yes, bombs are pre-laid under roads, he told me. I also checked this with the SP and the

[11]Maoist SPOKESPERSON, 'on the Election Boycott Tactic of the Maoists', *Economic and Political Weekly* (2009): 73-77.

[12]Prasad, Archana, 'The Political Economy of Maoist Violence in Chhattisgarh', *Social Scientist* (2010): 3-24.

Additional District Magistrate (ADM). Both, in different ways, confirmed that this was, indeed, true in many cases.

SP Dash conceded that this was the case with *some* roads, but added that daily checks by road-opening parties, apart from general security cover, were making such occurrences rare. The ADM went a step further, acknowledging that such situations were quite likely to crop up, and that if he belonged to the other camp he would also prefer to set up bombs before the road was laid instead of having to dig it up later for the same purpose and increase the possibility of detection by police sniffer dogs.

Even if true in only a minority of cases, the possibility alone contributes to the aura of fear surrounding the Maoists – exactly what the latter aim for. Like all guerilla forces, they thrive on a shadowy mix of bluff and genuine strength.

There are, of course, road projects which pose a threat to the Maoists and are laid against their will – although the two-fold gain of earning money and setting booby traps may accrue in such projects as well. An example is the road (and rail) construction from Dalli Rajhara to Rowghat, where iron-ore mining rights are to be given to the Bhilai Steel Plant. The Rowghat mine, much touted in the plans for Chhattisgarh drawn up by the National Democratic Alliance (NDA) government at the Centre, represents a serious threat to the Maoists, because it opens up an access point to Abuj Maad, their undisputed stronghold.

Such constructions are secured by the presence of a large number of CRPF personnel. Bastar has been described as 'the most-militarised zone in the entire country'.[13] The paramilitary forces from the CRPF, Border Security Force (BSF), Indo-Tibetan Border Police (ITBP) and Commando Battalion for

---

[13]http://articles.economictimes.indiatimes.com/2014-08-19/news/52983522_1_bastar-raman-singh-crpf

Resolute Action (CoBRA)[14] have been estimated at a lakh in number. In addition, there are estimatedly two lakh members of the State Armed Police Force spread across ten Left-wing-extremism-affected states. They are equipped with Kalashnikovs, INSAS rifles, satellite phones, unmanned aerial surveillance vehicles and Air Force helicopters. The participation of the Indian armed forces is believed to be restricted to training, although there are rumours of the feared Naga battalion having been pressed into service on a couple of occasions, an interesting phenomenon, if there is any truth to the reports, for it would imply that disaffected youth conscripted for military service from one insurgency are being deployed against discontented citizens involved in an insurrection in another part of the country. The Counter-Terrorism and Jungle Warfare College, situated just outside Kanker, is led by the colourful Brigadier B.K. Ponwar (retired) who claims that police officers 'arrive [at his academy] with pot bellies, chewing paan, and leave like tigers with a resolve to hunt and destroy the terrorist'.[15]

On my journey through the area, I see CRPF camps set up every few kilometres and frequently encounter troops of jogging jawans. In the remoter areas, the personnel are sequestered behind barbed-wire fences heavily barricaded with gunny bags. The standard roadblock is always unmanned. The driver of any vehicle wanting to pass through has to get out and remove it himself, while being watched from behind a barricade by a gun-wielding security personnel.

In contrast to the number of troops deployed in the area, the Maoists in Bastar are, reportedly, far fewer in number. Estimates

---

[14]https://en.wikipedia.org/wiki/Operation_Green_Hunt#cite_note-BS-113092700488-6

[15]http://archive.tehelka.com/story_main49.asp?filename=hub280511THELAWRENCE.asp

of their strength range from 10,000 to 20,000 only. And yet, even with the sheer strength of numbers in their favour, the Indian security forces are not having an easy time of it. To begin with, they suffer from all kinds of deprivations and challenges.

More of them die from malaria than from battling the Maoists. Posted in hostile territory, they have, on occasion, been set upon and killed by the rebels while in the middle of their morning ablutions in the forest. As a result, they started going out in heavily guarded groups for their personal chores, before solving the problem by building toilets inside their camps – entirely unbidden by the government's 'Clean India campaign', Swachch Bharat Abhiyaan!

The inside joke is that the CRPF should be called the 'Chalte Raho Pyaare Force' (roughly translated as the Neverending Footslog Brotherhood) on account of the inexorable demands it makes on its recruits. The pressures of living in the heart of a powerful insurgency include the perils of loneliness, sometimes verging on despair, that manifests itself in a desire for conversation with whoever crosses their path. This situation has resulted in our carrying on protracted and seemingly pointless conversations with security guards – a distance of about 10 to 15 feet separating us – with us on our best behaviour to avoid being held back and the guards taking full advantage of their power to wangle a banter in the middle of the boondocks.

'Who are you?' The beginning is gruff, almost menacing.

'I am a professor doing research on mobile towers.'

I do not want to mention my more exotic interest in the Maoists, as I fear that it might lead to immediate detention and interrogation.

'A professor, huh? A professor.'

Every statement is repeated once or twice.

'Where are you from?'

'Gurgaon.'

'So what are you going for? Oh, I see – research. I see. What are you carrying with you?'

'A laptop and some notebooks.'

'Okay. You know you have to be very careful in this area. Don't take unnecessary risks.'

Now they are paternal and concerned. The tough-love routine.

It is clear, given their refusal to budge from their checkpost, that they are following their own advice very carefully. By way of abundant caution, I have, before approaching the checkpost, removed the cap I usually wear, because it has faux military markings on it. I am not about to tell them that I plan to spend the night in a remote village.

'Who are these people with you?' they ask.

'They are locals.'

'Locals. I see.'

My interrogator has a companion who looks up from the newspaper he is reading.

'Which mobile phone do you carry?' he enquires.

'I have a Blackberry.'

'Oh, a Blackberry.' He nods. 'I see. Go carefully.'

'Okay, thank you.'

And we set off.

On our way to Orchha, we are unable to meet an officer from the Chhattisgarh Police force who had masterminded an infiltration campaign into the Maoist ranks a few years ago. Despite his urgent pleas for a transfer out of the area of operations, he is still posted within striking distance of his enemies. He spends his days in enforced confinement inside a CRPF camp. When we ask for him, we are told that he is fast asleep. It is about 12.30 p.m. His mobile phone is, apparently, always switched off.

Our most poignant encounter with a security personnel involves an interaction with a man who eschews all conversation and observes, seemingly to himself, like a person in a catatonic state brought on by severe concussion, 'Life is strange, very strange indeed. Life is strange.'

So we have a bunch of frightened contractors, propped up by gung-ho SPs, paying off a group of Maoists (and, probably, some government officials and politicians as well) who are busy setting up bombs and being chased down by jittery often lonely security forces paid for by the taxpayer's money – all in the name of development.

The Orchha weekly bazaar offers a colourful cornucopia of forest produce, agricultural implements, cycle tyres, water pots, perfectly motionless but promising-looking dried fish, and live fish wriggling about as their owner guarantees taste – all displayed for sale by a bunch of beautifully decked up women and more soberly attired men from neighbouring villages. A barber does brisk business, while a chicken coop promises to be rapidly emptied before the end of the day.

In the midst of this scene, seemingly set in antiquity, stands an electronics store of sorts, a makeshift set of stalls, as it were, mostly stocked with radio devices. There are only a few mobile handsets on offer, but lots of Coke-can-shaped, music-playing devices, with a USB port for a data card. It is obvious that no network is needed for listening to the latest chart toppers in the middle of the forest. I am told that the Maoists use such data cards to load their propaganda material – songs, lectures, educational talks – in the local Gondi language. So Bollywood hits alternate with Maoist jingles for the everyday listening pleasure of the local youth. Interestingly, some of these music devices have the words, 'Coming Soon – Modi Raj!' emblazoned on them. So mainstream politics, or at least the media-savvy brand practised by Modi, has caught on to the potential of these devices for low-tech advertising.

In the middle of this carnival of commerce and camaraderie, a group of five jawans skulks about, AK-47s slung across their shoulders, faces unsmiling, prospecting for a bar of soap here, a lucky bargain there. They are dressed in their civvies – a uniform of jeans, tees and keds. Nobody turns to look at them. It is as if they do not exist. Only a tot, no more than four, clings to his mother's hand as she leans unheedingly over a spread of greens, and looks back in wonder at the armed men in his bazaar. The soldiers, in turn, do not make eye contact with anybody. Not the merry widow on her haunches engaged in cheerful repartee with her prospective customers, not the proud fisherman with scarf draped across bare chest, not the schoolboy out for a jaunt. And certainly not the little child gazing at them so utterly intrigued.

3

Iron-Ore Fines and Tendu Leaves

At the Orchha bazaar, Sudhu has a conversation with a young man who is indistinguishable in appearance and bearing from the mass of shoppers milling around. He is the local *dada*s and he advises us against going to Aader. Preparations are under way for the tenth anniversary of the formation of the Communist Party of India (Maoist) the CPI(M) by the merger of the CPI-ML, the People's War Group (PWG) and the Maoist Communist Centre of India (MCC) and our visit would come in the way.

On our way back, Kamal asks if I would like to try and cross the nullah to Sonpur again. I think it over for a moment and decline his offer. Somehow, I feel that going there just to satisfy my curiosity or to proclaim to all and sundry that I had ventured where few dared to tread is not reason enough to take the risk. I am also less confident without the company of Sudhu, who bid goodbye to our party in Orchha to spend some time with his family.

Instead of another attempt at Sonpur, we visit the Ari-Dongri iron-ore mine in Kachche operated by Godawari Power and Ispat Ltd (GPIL). This mine has been at the centre of a fair amount of controversy on account of the manner in which it was privatized, accentuating the need for the Bhilai Steel Plant (BSP) to initiate mining activities in the Rowghat hills, an area critical for wildlife.

The government communiqués on Rowghat had emphasized that the iron-ore reserves in Dalli Rajhara, the BSP's main source of ore, would run out in 2015. Hence the urgent need to develop the mine in Rowghat as an alternative source of ore. However, critics pointed out, that if the development of the mine in Rowghat was, indeed, imperative, why had the BSP chosen to grant a mining lease in 2005 for the functioning Ari-Dongri iron-ore mine to Godawari Power and Ispat, a private company?

Senior executives in the BSP countered that the ore in Ari-Dongri was of inferior quality. If that was the case, it did not seem to be deterring Godawari Power and Ispat from seeking and obtaining a supplementary environmental clearance to mine an additional 33 hectares of land in the same area, doubling their capacity of iron ore with a mere 30 per cent increase in the area mined.

We reach the mine site to be greeted by several Shiv Sena posters painted on street walls. Apparently, they wield some influence on the workers in the mine. I recall the Shiv Sena's role in breaking the power of the trade unions in Bombay's textile mills in the 1980s and am struck by the irony.

At the mine, we are met by Mr Jha, a small-built engineer with a salt-and-pepper beard and a pleasing quietness of manner. We ask about the commercials of the mine, the number of workers, their welfare and that of their families. Mr Jha runs us through some numbers which indicate that after paying for labour, capital costs, processing fees and royalty, the mine makes a profit of 20 to 25 per cent on the iron ore. The mine occupies 139 hectares of land, formerly part of the Kachche Reserve Forest, and hires 1,100 workers whose main job is to separate the iron ore from the sand and other impurities at the last stage of the extraction process.

As I do not have the requisite permission from the zonal office in Raipur, I cannot access the actual mine site. From the reception, I am shown a distant hill from which iron is extracted by machines that cut step-like indentations into the hillside, enabling the ore to be accessed. This is truly iron-ore country, where the ore, located a mere three or four feet below the surface, would probably cause boot-shod steps to ring out on the hillside!

The rough ore is purified by a set of separating machines, after which manual labour is deployed for the final purification process. The work shift starts at 6 a.m. and ends by 10 a.m. Given that it is 11 a.m. now, no labourers are to be seen anywhere. We are told that most of the labour is hired from the surrounding villages and only 15 per cent comes from outside. The mine has hired a private security agency, but Mr Jha agrees that the lion's share of security for the mine comes from the various CRPF camps we have seen.

He mentions that the mine incurs significant health expenses of almost ₹10 lakhs a month on account of the workforce, their families and the inhabitants of the surrounding villages. I ask to see the medical facilities, expecting a sizeable establishment. What I am shown is a small room, about 10 feet by 10 feet in dimension, bearing the title of 'Chikitsalaya' (health centre), with no one manning it.

How many doctors, I ask.

'About two, no, three,' says Mr Jha.

Next to the dispensary is another small room bearing the legend 'Shala' or school. The 'Shala' too is deserted.

The Environmental Impact Assessment Report (EIAR), 2013, prepared for the public hearing to be held on the occasion of the expansion of the mining lease area from 106 hectares to 139 hectares,[16] states: 'GPIL is already actively involved in the CSR [corporate social responsibility] activities at its other project sites and will initiate either by providing or by improving the facilities in the area under like housing, education, health, medical services, occupation, water supply, sanitation, communication, transportation & road infrastructure for uplifting the living standards of local communities.'

In other words, it was a promise by Godawari Power and Ispat to improve the facilities mentioned for the welfare of the locals. However, the quality of services on the ground appears to be no better than the drafting skills of the person who has prepared the report.

I come away, unable to shake off my scepticism over the not inconsiderable medical expenses cited, along with the other claims – the number of workers employed, for example, as well as the proportion drawn from the surrounding villages.

---

[16] http://www.enviscecb.org/189/Execuitve%20Summary_English.pdf

Mining is an activity that is expected to expand the overall productive potential of an economic system. However, in reality, its direct benefits accrue to the wider economy, while its health-related and environmental repercussions are largely borne by local residents of villages displaced by mining.

With mechanization, the total number of jobs generated from a mining site is only a fraction of the total displaced employable population. Many of these jobs go to people from outside the mining villages due to the high levels of illiteracy and lack of skills prevailing there. The few jobs going to locals are in security or masonry, activities at the lower end of the value chain.

A study of Chhattisgarh's district-level data by Indicus Analytics[17] reveals that even in a leading industrial district like Korba, 40 per cent of the population live below the poverty line. Most of the district's poor are settled near mining areas; Korba has the largest open-cast coal mine in the world, where these people are subjected to 'unfair labour practices, meager wage rates, instability in working conditions, and long working hours.'

Greater benefits are available to the local economy if downstream industries, like power and steel plants, are located within close proximity of the mine. Although direct employment is limited, even in these industries, by the adoption of modern production methods, the demand for ancillary goods and services generates positive spillovers. But often, downstream industries are not located close to mining sites. In fact, the downstream industry may, sometimes, be located in another country altogether. For instance, from 2001 to 2011, close to half of India's iron ore was exported.[18]

---

[17]http://www.livemint.com/Opinion/TelfQDSiZ1IPufDbwZ526K/Spatial-poverty-in-Chhattisgarh.html

[18]Starting in 2011, increased export taxes and freight rates of iron ore, combined with a downturn in world demand, led to a reduction in

The royalties earned by the government from mining activities also tend to be low. On the other hand, the prices commanded by the mining companies are, for the most part, many degrees higher. In 2006, for instance, iron ore mined in Karnataka was being sold at ₹6,000 to ₹7,000 per tonne, while the royalties ranged from ₹16 to ₹27 per tonne.[19] In such a situation, under-the-table pecuniary benefits for sundry state-government politicians and officials become a necessary part of the deal, making corruption a systemic inevitability.

Mining companies too find it cheaper to make payments, not to the community at large, but to government officials and politicians, who then use the taxpayer's money to deploy the might of the state against the community when it suits their purpose. The community itself is divided by pampering a few members, who become champions, while leaving the concerns of the rest unaddressed. Select NGOs are bought off, the rest vilified. In this way, mining companies carry out the smart business practice of minimizing costs and maximizing profits. Democratic governance, environmental assets, social harmony and law and order are unfortunate casualties in the game of divide and rule.

As is often the case, value may be destroyed, not created, by a mining project if negative impacts on health, culture and environment are fairly factored in. However, the processes for measuring indirect impacts – a nascent science, at best – are further crippled by conflicts of interest (the EIAR, for instance, is prepared by a third party that is paid for by the mining companies), poorly staffed and equipped regulatory bodies

exports, finally resulting in India becoming a net importer in 2013-14 and 2014-15.

[19]http://timesofindia.indiatimes.com/india/-Ironic-Story-of-the-Great-Indian-Loot/articleshow/6012491.cms

and rampant corruption.[20] In 2011, the state government of Goa commissioned a two-year study of EIARs on the basis of which clearances had been given to every operational mine in the state. The preliminary results showed a blatant falsification of the facts relating to the extant forest cover, watercourses and tribal communities in the target area. In one case, the details of a bauxite mine were found to have been copied entirely from a document submitted for a mine in Russia![21]

Managing the chaos involved is often beyond the capabilities of companies which play by the book (not that this excuses errant mining practices). As the national mining policy states: 'The absence of a smooth and transparent process for granting these clearances has a twofold effect. First[ly], it keeps genuine miners, capable of best practice and willing to accept regulation and adhere to the Sustainable Development Framework, away from the industry; and, secondly, it leaves the field open to unregulated, often illegal, mining operations, with all the attendant risks of damage to conservation, environment, and governance.'[22]

I ask Kamal Shukla if my scepticism about GPIL's claims is justified. He merely nods and asks the driver to go back to Kanker via a small lake, located 2 km from the mine site. Although the EIAR states, 'There will be no outside discharge of liquid effluent from the mining project site; therefore no significant impact on surface water bodies is anticipated due to mining operations', the lake water is rust red in colour.

---

[20]In a letter to Human Rights Watch in 2011, then Mines Secretary Vijay Kumar wrote, 'There is no doubt that regulatory institutions of the [mining] sector are underfunded, understaffed and overstretched.'

[21]https://www.hrw.org/report/2012/06/14/out-control/mining-regulatory-failure-and-human-rights-india

[22]http://mines.nic.in/writereaddata/UploadFile/National_Mineral_Policy.pdf

In India today, over 80,000 mines operate illegally, as against 10,000 legitimate leases. A mere third of the legal mines actually report to the regulatory body, the Indian Bureau of Mines, while only one-tenth are inspected. Underground coal-mine operations result in one death for every 2.5 million tonnes of coal mined. Around 25 per cent of coal-mine workers suffer from pneumoconiosis, also known as the black lung disease.[23] Mining also has a significant impact on our water resources. For instance, the entire ecosystem dependent on the Mahanadi river is believed to be under threat on account of the large number of projects announced in its vicinity.

The penury of the tribals in the midst of abundant natural resources, not just under the ground, but also in their forests, has often been remarked upon. As of 2015, although 80 per cent of the minerals in India come from tribal areas, 50 per cent of the tribals live below the poverty line. Only 43.2 per cent have access to safe drinking water[24] and 28.9 per cent have no access whatsoever to doctors and health clinics. Among tribal children, only 42.2 per cent have been immunized.

Some commentators have suggested that tribals can gain from commercial exploitation of the minor produce of the forest, over which they have a customary and constitutional right. This is a pertinent idea, as 80 per cent of valuable minor forest produce reportedly goes waste every year.

Many tribals have, indeed, been involved in the commercial exploitation of minor produce, but not in the capacity of masters of the forests. On the contrary, they have been reduced to the level of petty thieves, wage labourers, scroungers and, ironically, exploiters at the bottom of the food chain.

---

[23]http://amrc.org.hk/content/mining-sector-and-its-future-india

[24]http://www.thehindu.com/opinion/lead/mihir-shah-writes-on-tribal-alienation-and-need-for-inclusive-growth/article7383721.ece

For years, tribals were cheated by traders because of their ignorance of the market values of their land's produce. Stories of how they would give up a kilo of *chironji*, almond-flavoured seeds much valued for their use as cooking spices, ingredients in sweetmeats and traditional medicine, for a kilo of salt are commonplace. The first stirrings of change in tribal fortunes occurred when the terms of trade of the tendu leaf were renegotiated.

The tiny, nondescript-looking leaf that grows in clumps on the tendu tree is one of the most valuable products of the forest. In its sere form, it serves as an ideal wrapper for the beedi, the pungent cocktail of nicotine, carbon monoxide and tar that gives the rickshaw-pullers, coolies and daily-wage labourers of India their rare moments of blissful oblivion, along with the risk of contracting a variety of cancers. The total trade of this leaf in India is estimated at ₹2,000 crores.[25]

The tendu leaf scores over other potential wrappers on account of its capacity to retain fire. In Chhattisgarh, the leaf has also shown its ability to set old commercial relations afire: the tendu-leaf trade served as one of the first points of access for the Maoists to infiltrate into the lives of the local people. By negotiating directly with the small set of contractors who controlled the trade in the 1980s, the insurgents were successful in bringing about a five-fold increase in the wages paid to collectors – peaking at ₹140 per 100 bundles – while also pocketing a tidy sum for their own operations.

Today, the successful implementation of the public distribution system for the provision of subsidized grain and kerosene and the rollout of National Rural Employment Guarantee Act (NREGA) have reduced the critical importance

---

[25] http://timesofindia.indiatimes.com/india/Tendu-leaves-little-hope-for-tribals/articleshow/8831314.cms

of the tendu-leaf trade in the day-to-day lives of the adivasis of central India, thereby striking at the very roots of the hold the Maoists have enjoyed over them so far. However, issues of community control over trade in minor forest produce remain integral to the long-term welfare of the adivasi.

4

A Pragmatic IAS Officer and a Troubled History

By now, I am beginning to feel like a person who has been plunged into a cesspool without warning. Moral dilemmas, political conundrums and economic paradoxes are swirling around in my head, making me feel not a little dizzy.

With little hope of gaining any fresh insights into the situation, I enter the office of Kartikeya Goel, ADM of Kanker. What follows is a pleasant surprise and an object lesson on the wisdom of not stereotyping government officers.

Kartikeya Goel is a fresh-faced young man who could well be heading the student placement committee at the institute where I teach, MDI, Gurgaon, instead of occupying a position of high responsibility in the Maoist-affected Kanker district. After an exchange of pleasantries and a brief account of my travels, we begin to discuss the situation in Kanker.

Within minutes I realize that Goel brings to his role as an 'agent of development' an enormous amount of commitment and competence. I also sense he is sceptical of the ability of an armchair theorist like me to understand the nitty-gritty of administrative challenges at the grassroots.

In the light of my discussion with SP Dash on the difficulties of providing roads in areas controlled by the Maoists, I am keen to find out what kind of development inputs are 'acceptable' to them. Goel confirms that anything that poses a security threat to them is unacceptable, but adds that many halfway solutions are fine. For example, while the proposal for a hard-top road would automatically be shot down, that for a second-grade road is open to negotiation. Similarly, the Maoists would certainly veto plans for a concrete bridge, but they could well agree to a compromise in the form of the construction of a culvert bridge.

'I did not want the villagers of Aader to travel thirty kilometres for their rations, especially in the monsoon,' Goel goes on. 'So I sent a tractor with the rations, but it got stuck in the mud. Finally, I managed to get all parties to agree to a second-grade road. The project is still stuck. Do you know why?'

It is obvious that he is testing me.

'The tractor can't travel on a second-grade road?' I venture.

'No, because the local Maoist leader will not let a temporary structure be built in the village to store the grain.'

'Is it because a security threat is perceived?'

'From a temporary structure?' Kartikeya gazes at me, the hint of a smile on his lips. 'No way! We were ready to build a structure that would satisfy the Maoists – sloping tin roof, with concrete wall ending below the roof to create an open structure. No, he wants a permanent structure to be sanctioned, so he can make more money than he would out of a temporary construction.'

Has corruption crept into the ranks of the Maoists, I ask. Kartikeya confirms that while the older generation of Maoists continues to, by and large, be free of the greed for money and material gain, some of the younger members have been unable to resist the lure of lucre.

'The Maoists are no longer a unicephalous organization,' says

Goel. 'They are multicephalous. In other words, there is no single, perfectly coordinated chain of command. The nullah at which you got stuck on your way to Sonpur was to be spanned by a culvert bridge. We know that the equipment of the contractor got blown up. But what is not clear is whether the local Maoist commander did this with the assent of the top brass or on his own volition.'

I have heard of certain fissures in the ranks of the Maoists that exist not only between different levels of the hierarchy, but even among the top leadership. Two major causes of dissension apparently relate to financial dealings and the demarcation line between 'necessary' and 'unnecessary' violence. The surrender of G.V.K. Prasad, a top Maoist leader, in January 2014 is said to be the outcome of his disagreement with his comrades over the degree of violence resorted to in the 2013 Jiram Ghati ambush, in which Mahendra Karma, the Congress leader who was the brain behind the 'vigilante movement' Salwa Judum, was killed.[26] Some Maoist commanders are known to have broken ranks after making off with protection money obtained from some corporation or the other.

'Sometimes, our own people use the Maoists as a pretext for their own acts of omission,' Kartikeya continues. 'For example, they may claim that [the construction of] a certain granary has been disallowed by the Maoists, when nothing of that sort has happened. They are merely covering up for their own lapses. So we are dealing with a complex situation with many shades of grey.

'It is also a very fluid situation that is constantly responding to societal dynamics. So far Maoists had no objections to [government] teachers, health workers or aanganwaadi workers [workers in the government's childcare centres] operating in

[26]The case of G.V.K. Prasad is discussed in Section 3, Chapter 4 of this book.

areas under their control. After all, apart from anything else, they do not want to be seen as inimical to the welfare of the tribals, as this would strike at their support base. But sometimes even education is seen as a threat.'

I remember Swami Vyaptananda's observation on the swelling demand for modern education. Kartikeya mentions that the days when the children of the village were easy recruits for the Maoist cause are passing. Young people are now able to get ahead in life by seeking an education in nearby towns like Narayanpur. They are not even averse to travelling in bore trucks to neighbouring states to work as construction workers under conditions similar to those that bonded labour endures, only so they can come back, once in a while, with a cap, keds and a shiny bag and avoid the life-threatening moral dilemmas of living in a contested zone. The appeal of the Maoist cause and the heady glamour of being part of a 'revolution' are being tested by the promise of working towards a better future, tenuous and chimerical though it may be.

During my trip, I have been able to spend some time with Sudhu. I learn that he has built a house in Narayanpur, celebrates Hindu festivals and has named his son Mayank, which is certainly not a tribal name. He avers that like his forefathers he too would like to be buried after he dies, but a question remains in my mind: While we, along with the Maoists, may want the Maadiyas, the inhabitants of Abuj Maad, to retain their old way of life and their ancient customs, do they themselves wish to do so?

It is difficult to coax Sudhu into sharing his views on the situation, so adept has he become at keeping his real feelings under cover. I see him heartily greet someone who, I am later told, is a local Maoist commander. Sudhu also agrees that no one, before the Maoists arrived, had ever tried to understand the tribals. But then I hear him say that the Maoists have changed local customs in small ways to conform to their ideology and their presence tends to be inhibiting, coming in the way of the spontaneous celebrations of yore.

'[The] Maoists are becoming feudatories who are loath to let go of their power,' Kartikeya declares, repeating his words a couple of times.

While this creeping corruption is 'the way of all flesh', with examples ranging from the Maoists of Nepal to the Shining Path, the guerilla-led insurgency in Peru, I feel he is being unfair to the many dedicated cadres in the Indian Naxalite movement who choose a life of extreme hardship and great risk, driven by the dream of a utopia they know they will not see in their lifetime. Many decorated police officers of the Indian government I have spoken to have commented on the extraordinary commitment and sacrifice their enemy is capable of. Earlier in my conversation with Kartikeya, he himself had acknowledged the idealism of the older generation of Maoists. The mixed signals I get from him regarding the nature of the beast probably mirror the fast-changing scenario on the ground.

Then he expresses a regret, bordering on reproach which, at that moment, I consider an insightful hypothesis made in the spirit of free trade-loving economists and worth testing empirically.

'Trade across the boundary of Maad has not increased in the last ten years,' he says. 'Maoists do not want [to encourage] an increase in exchange[s] between Maad and the outside world.'

I reflect that the tendu-leaf trade which represents the main export from Maoist territory is certainly tightly controlled. The development inputs from the government – the main imports to the region – are tightly regulated as well. The telephone network is still flimsy and the emigration of villagers to the rest of the country yet to become a flood. Given the circumstances, it would be difficult to predict how these interactions will be viewed if they acquire momentum. Goel seems to have struck a rich vein of thought.

Later, when I acquaint myself more thoroughly with tribal economics, I realize that there is a crucial point which Kartikeya has completely overlooked. The exchange relations of tribals in central India with the rest of the country, prior to the advent of the Maoists, involved the extraction of vast quantities of mineral resources and the displacement of large numbers of people, with next to nothing as compensation in terms of provision for jobs or development expenditure.

The Indian Social Institute, New Delhi, and the Global Internally Displaced People project place the total number of internally displaced people in India at 21.3 million. As mentioned in the introduction to this book, Walter Fernandes[27] places the number of displaced people and those rendered jobless (though not homeless) between 1947 and 2000 at 60 million. Tribals constitute 40 per cent of such displaced people, although they represent only 8 per cent of the total population. Thus they are five times as likely to be forced to sacrifice their homes to the claims of development, state management of forests or wildlife conservation[28] as an ordinary citizen.

The adivasis' traditional way of life came under threat the moment the attention of the British turned towards the timber available in the forests of India, starting with the appointment

---

[27]Fernandes, Walter, 'Singur and the Displacement Scenario', *Economic and Political Weekly*, 42, 203.6, 2007.

[28]Fernandes, Walter, 'Development-induced Displacement and Tribal Women', Govind Chandra Rath, Editor, *Tribal Development in India: The Contemporary Debate* (Sage Publications, New Delhi, 2006).

of a commission to enquire into the availability of teak in the Malabar forests in 1800.[29] The enactment of the Forest Act in 1865 led to the acquisition of forests by the state. The Forest Act of 1878 introduced the concept of the 'reserved forest' that was closed to local communities. The Forest Act of 1927 specifically denied local people any rights over forest produce 'simply because they were domiciled there'.[30]

After Independence, the Constitution affirmed the rights of adivasis over their traditional settlements, but they have continued to be vulnerable to forced displacement, be it for industrialization, forest conservation or wildlife protection.[31]

Some scholars have likened tribal areas to an 'internal colony exploited by the rest of the country'.[32] Although it might be deemed politically incorrect to acknowledge it, this unequal exchange has, to some extent, been curbed in areas under Maoist control. This is a point that the bureaucrat who dreams of the economic integration of tribal India with the rest of the country cannot overlook.

During my interaction with Goel, however, I have yet to research the subject further and do not have the benefit of this insight on

[29]Ravindranath, N.H., Chaturvedi, Rajiv Kumar and Murthy, Indu K. 'Forest Conservation, Afforestation and Reforestation in India: Implications for Forest Carbon Stocks', *Current Science* 95.2 (2008): 216-222.

[30]Arora, Dolly, 'From state regulation to people's participation: Case of forest management in India', *Economic and Political Weekly* (1994): 691-698.

[31]For a history of relevant policies, read Appendix II.

[32]Jones, Steve, 'Tribal underdevelopment in India', *Development and Change* 9.1 (1978): 41-70.

the exchange relations between tribal areas and the rest of the country. I am, therefore, not in a position to counter his argument about the Maoists discouraging such relations. I merely take careful notes as he develops the thesis that the Maoists cater, first and foremost, to their own interests.

'[The] Maoists promote community farming, because they want self-reliance in food,' he contends. 'Being dependent on the outside world for food is too risky. As Napoleon said, an army marches on its stomach. So they need to have assured food supplies in various places. In the same way, they need to explore the health benefits of local herbs for their own well-being. But development indicators have not improved much.'

By now, I have lapsed into silence, but Goel is not done testing me.

'Have you seen a child die of dysentery?' he asks. 'They should put up a video on YouTube to show how horrible it is.'

'When the children show symptoms [of the disease], they are put on a motorcycle and brought to hospital. On the way, they are given water [to drink] from streams which makes things worse. These clear streams are not as salubrious as they look. By the time they reach [the hospital], their eyes are bulging out of their sockets and it is too late – when only an ORS dose is needed. The level of maternal mortality is also very high. Lots of women absolutely need a hospital delivery. But that option is available to them only in an emergency. When the foetus is in a breach position, they are hauled on to tractors to be brought to the nearest hospital, which may be fifty kilometres away.'

If the Maoists had to choose between a higher standard of living for the tribals, based on government inputs, and a higher chance of their own survival, at what point would the calculations go against development? What is their long-term vision for the tribals? Do they wish to preserve them in a mummified state, bereft of interaction with the outside world, as the Indian government had tried to do for many years by imposing restrictions on access to the area? Do the insurgents wish to create a pastoral utopia of communism in Maad, buttressed by the tribals' innate freedom from concerns over property? And is this disarming absence of an acquisitive urge not changing in the face of modern currents? If so, can the Maoists realign their vision to accommodate the adivasi youth's new aspirations and opportunities? Does the freedom the rebels claim to protect on behalf of the tribals extend to the latter's freedom to become a part of the capitalist system?

It is not the Maoists alone, however, who have to answer difficult questions. The government too must do so. Is a policy of development at the point of a gun sustainable? Has the state tried to speak to the tribals in their own tongue and look at the world from their perspective? Does the development of mining and industry have to take place in a rush or can capitalism afford to progress at a more measured pace? Does the persistent dishonesty of politicians and bureaucrats not lend the Maoists a pretext to justify their methods? Who is the real Maoist sympathizer – the tribals or the corporate–government combine as it exists today?

That night in the Kanker Circuit House, as I toss and turn in bed, attempting to elude a persistent mosquito, I hear the sound of music in the distance. Having given up all hope of sleep, I grumpily leave my bed and head in the direction of the music.

It is midnight. In the portico of a nearby community hall, turbaned old men sit around a smoking fire. The moon is full. A huge banyan tree looms over the landscape like a friendly apparition. The men are smoking away and singing songs. Or rather, one song with new lyrics, which they make up as they go along. I catch a few words – '*gaari*', which, I assume, means abuse, and 'Ram', the name of the Hindu god. There is a smaller group sitting around another fire close by. It is quite dark and I am apprehensive about initiating communication. Have I stumbled upon a secret ritual? Would it not be discourteous of me to intrude upon their private moment and start an investigative conversation?

I greet a person standing on the fringes of the group with a 'namaste'. He nods. And that is as much attention as I get. I linger for about fifteen minutes more and then leave. Outside the structure, the pile of slippers and worn-out sandals, the tangled heap of rusty motorbikes and cycles, and the smoke rings from a dying fire, present a mundane contrast to the mellifluous melodies that emerge from the heart of an ancient tradition and soar into the night sky.

SECTION TWO

Legends of Markabeda

1

A Mobile Phone News Network

It is February 2014 and I am at Hackergram, a sprawling rundown campus on the outskirts of Bhopal. This is where the journey that led to this book begins, at the base camp of CGNet Swara, a mobile phone news network run by former BBC journalist Shubranshu Chaudhary. On my first visit, I venture into the neighbouring district of Harda.

My companion Mohan Yadav and I reach our destination four hours late on account of a delayed train and an unwise decision not to take the bus, instead. A trio of young men meets us on two motorcycles. Yadav, a tiny, disarmingly friendly man, who endears himself to me by opting to squeeze in as the second pillion rider on one motorcycle so that I can ride pillion in relative comfort on the other.

The road winds through Harda town and then veers into fields of corn and soya bean, its condition deteriorating as we move forward. Here and there, we see a water tank, built, we later learn, as part of the NREGA project. As we climb up a gentle incline, the fields become more barren and the road even patchier.

'This is a poor area,' my fellow rider tells me, his words carrying over the dust-laden wind.

Astonishingly, despite the delay, there are still some people waiting for us at the small village temple dedicated to Mahadeva. We sit in a circle in the temple's covered courtyard. After the formality of introductions is over, Mohan Yadav begins to speak.

'Sorry for being late and thank you for waiting. Who has a mobile phone here?'

Almost all present do.

'Okay,' says Yadav, 'why are we here? [Because] We all want to solve our problems. How do we solve our problems? First, we go to the panches, then to the secretary, then to the block, the district and, finally, to the state government. Is the sarpanch here?'

He's not.

'Any of the other panchayat members?'

There's one.

Anyway, now that he's broaching the issue of problems, people are interested, although nobody is particularly forthcoming. Yadav changes the topic.

'Do you get the newspaper [here]? Does news in the Jhiri language get published? Do you have a handpump?'

A man who has been leaning against a wall and listening to Yadav with a slightly disinterested look speaks up after the long pause that follows in the wake of his questions. 'We have a well, but it's full of fallen leaves and there's no handpump,' he says.

'The paper costs much more to produce than what you pay for it,' Yadav goes on. 'Who pays for the newspaper? Will they publish news that goes against the interests of the rich who pay for the cost of the paper?

'When there is wedding here, does the newspaper report it? We get to know when [film star] Shahrukh [Khan] has fathered a child, but not when you have a kid.'

There is laughter.

'When you don't have a voice, how will your problems get solved?' Yadav asks them. 'When each of us has an equal vote, why not equality in other spheres as well?'

Then he makes an abrupt switch to another topic.

'What do you use your mobile phone for?'

'To talk to people,' someone in the audience says.

'Do you talk to big officers on the mobile? The *patwari* (land revenue official)? The *nakedaar* (the security officer at a barrier point)?'

'No, just to each other.'

'I don't even have [enough] balance in my phone [to do so],' says one person.

'I don't have a sim card, but I use the phone to listen to music,' volunteers another.

Yadav raises his phone for all to see and says after a dramatic pause, 'The mobile can be used to communicate with the world. This is your friend, your leader, your teacher.

'You can use it to record your problems. These problems will be heard by the world. When your problems become news, they can be solved. Does anyone have a problem they'd like to share? Or a desi remedy they'd like to tell everyone about? Or a mela they want people to go to?'

Santosh Kumar, a young boy, mentions the absence of a hostel for girls in the nearest higher secondary school (meant for senior-school students) in Harda. His sister apparently had to discontinue her schooling for this very reason.

Mohan whips out his cell phone, dials a number and switches it off. Thirty seconds later, there is a call on his phone. He presses '1' and starts recording: 'This is Mohan Yadav speaking from the Ratamati village in Timarni block of Harda district. The people here would like to state that despite repeated requests no hostel for girls has come up at the government school in Harda. Santosh Kumar, a boy from the village, has more details.'

Santosh speaks hesitantly into the phone, 'We have reported the problem many times,' he begins. 'We even went to the

Collector's office. But nothing has been done. My sister, along with several of her friends, had to stop their schooling after Class VIII. We really need a hostel for girls so that the girls in our village can continue their schooling.'

Prompted by Mohan, Santosh signs off with his name and mobile number. A few days later, a recording of the message and a transcript are uploaded on the CGNet Swara site. Soon, the issue will be assigned to an 'urban activist', the name given to an informal network of concerned professionals who follow up the matter with the complainant and then with the concerned government officials to ensure that grievances are quickly addressed.

Mohan switches off the phone.

'Any singers here?' I ask.

I am sure there will be, given the vibrant cultural heritage still alive in tribal areas. One person among the audience volunteers, a quiet man with a wistful smile. His face is lined with the hardships he has endured in his life. He looks like someone who has suffered repeated tragedies to the point where they have robbed the spring from his step, but left him with eyes that speak more eloquently than words, eyes that well with immeasurable sadness and yet can laugh at the antics of a child, wonder at the beauties of nature and take pride in the ancient lore of his people.

We record two songs, one celebrating the Holi festival and the other, spring. The singer, suddenly animated as all performers are by the presence of an audience, wants us to play back his recording. We do so and he seems delighted.

Before we know it, the time has come for us to get back so that we can board the 6.30 p.m. train. I have not had a morsel since breakfast, but am chastened by the realization that the boys accompanying me on motorcycles (along, perhaps, with several among our audience) haven't eaten either – which, quite probably, is not an unusual occurrence in their lives.

The train leaves the station as a million people run, jostle, fight and demand their tickets to freedom. Heaving, lurching, puffing and sputtering, the train heads out – not to a physical location, but to the centre of a nation's collective aspiration, long denied. It is not 15 August 1947, with the ouster of a colonial power at hand. These are not dust-covered farmers, eager to reach Delhi and share in the magic of the midnight hour. These are digital pioneers, information-highway junkies, barefoot engineers, Indians like you and I; Indians we will remember decades later, not as sepia-tinted images, but as traces of aspiration frozen in cyberspace, their digital fingerprints telling the story of a nation riding on the wave of technology in search of a long-promised tryst with destiny.

The next morning I awake slightly sore from the exhausting visit to Harda. It is 7 a.m., but the cot next to mine is vacant, its occupant already up and about. My living conditions here are truly Spartan; all I have at my disposal are a metal-grid bed, a mosquito net, a toilet located 50 metres away and a tube light operated by connecting and disconnecting a plug outside my room.

I get ready and amble across an area overgrown with weeds and the occasional sprig of ayurvedic herb, passing by dilapidated buildings to reach the control room of CGNet Swara. From the outside, it looks like a massive medieval cathedral, but is actually a gigantic mushroom shed converted into office space. As expected of mushroom sheds, it has no ventilation. In the daytime, the iron shutter is rolled up and the side door left ajar to ensure air circulation.

In the centre of the hall stands a set of tables forming a large rectangle. The tables are actually mushroom beds, revamped to assume their present avatar. In fact, to say that such beds mushroom everywhere on this campus, serving as tables, beds, shelves, chairs and even clothes racks, would not, perhaps, be an overstatement.

At the head of the rectangular arrangement of tables sits Shubranshu Chaudhary, formerly a senior producer with the BBC. In 2014 he received the Digital Activist award, beating Edward Snowden, as part of the Index on Censorship's Freedom of Expression awards. With his glasses, thick beard and woollen beanie pulled low over his forehead, he looks like something between a Naxal revolutionary and a monk of the Ramakrishna order. A group comprising a dozen odd people is present, its members sitting around with the air of those who have been there all night.

'Good morning, Rohit-ji,' Shubranshu beams. 'I hope you slept well.'

'Like the dead,' I reply.

'How was the site visit?'

'Very useful,' I respond. 'It's amazing what you are trying to pull off.'

Shubranshu starts speaking slowly in measured tones, emphasizing each word and using well-rehearsed cadences. He has evidently done this before. He sounds like a priest intoning chants before a sacred fire.

'Rohit-ji, we need to create a democratic communication medium,' he says. 'Every democracy needs one. But the present structure of communication is skewed against the person on the ground. The result of this lack of communication is conflict. When a person is frustrated beyond the capacity to hope, he kills – either himself or others. So the Naxal problem is not a problem of violence; it is a problem of communication.'

I find the reference to Naxalism surprising. I had known CGnet Swara collected news from people in remote areas, but I had not realized that their users lived in districts affected by Left-wing insurgency.

Over the next few days I find myself listening to Shubranshu's views on the pattern of development, the structure of the news industry and his dream of setting up an 'air like' communication medium that would use verbal despatches in the mother tongue of the users and thus be accessible to all.

He tells me how CGnet had started as an email group on Yahoo, and succeeded in getting news dispatches from media-dark areas of Chhattisgarh during the time of the government-sponsored Salwa Judum pogrom. The dispatches alerted the international media and the resulting outcry played an important role in the termination of the organization. He spoke of how his dream was that adivasis in remote areas should become 'bolkars' or audio journalists on the CGnet platform.

Up to this point I had not really imagined that Naxalites would be part of the subject of the book. But I was intrigued by Shubranshu's references to them and by his diagnosis that the problem reflected, above all, a total failure of communication with the people affected by the insurgency.

In May 2015, I attend a workshop organized by CGnet Swara in Delhi that aims to standardize the Gondi spoken in the Gondwana region straddling eight Indian states – Jharkhand, Madhya Pradesh, Chhattisgarh, Maharashtra, Andhra Pradesh, Telangana, Karnataka and Orissa. The long association of native Gondi speakers with people from these states has resulted in different versions of Gondi being spoken in each state to the point that a Gondi speaker in one state cannot understand a

Gondi speaker in another state. The ultimate aim is to create a standard dictionary that can be consulted by all.

Native Gondi speakers from different states are present at this workshop. They are being facilitated by Professor Metry from Kannada University, Hampi. One by one, words are taken up for discussion. The version of the word as it is currently spoken in different states is noted and one of the versions selected as the standard to be used in the dictionary. The dance-and-music sessions, an essential part of the tribals' daily routine, are taken up during the breaks.

Every now and then, a tall, thin man in a dhoti, kurta and waistcoat, a turban on his head, makes charming interventions to explain the etymology of words and the genesis of the Gondi language itself. This is what I have understood from his interjections.

In times long past, Kupar Lingo, a redoubtable hero of the Gonds, had set out to unveil the mystery underlying the sorrows of his people. In the course of his travels, he fell into a river, was swept into a whirlpool and almost drowned. As the waters were about to swallow him, he was saved by Shambhu, the primal god of the Gonds, who was resting on a nearby bank with his consort Gaura.[1]

Kupar had lost consciousness by then. To revive him, Shambhu played his damroo, the drum that accompanies the tandava dance. Lingo emerged from his stupor with the percussion resounding in his ear, and uttered the vowels of Gondi-vani, the language of the Gonds. The birth of language coincided with the dawn of self-awareness, as the first sounds Lingo had uttered would signify the first person 'I' or ana. This was immediately followed

[1]It appears that the Hindu god Shiva and his consort Gauri are later versions of this tribal god.

by the consciousness of community, as the next sounds indicated the first person plural 'we' or *amat*. Subsequently, the words corresponding to the pronouns 'you', 'he', 'she', 'they' and so on were uttered. Thus, Kupar acquired the title of Lingo, the giver of *leing* or 'language' in Gondi culture. It is noteworthy that in the story of the origin of the Gondi language, the awareness of individual existence is immediately followed by the awareness of the collective 'we', consisting of one's kith and kin, a construct almost indistinguishable from the individual in tribal society.

Later, I have a chance to talk to the raconteur, who turns out to be Dharmacharya Sher Singh Anchala, a venerated elder of the Gonds.

Anchala highlights the close connection between the Gondi language and nature. At the passing of spring, the bird perched on the branch of the mango tree is heard singing, '*Markan kako*?' This bird call has been transposed into Gondi and means 'When will you ripen?' Similarly, just before the sowing season, the sparrow asks impatiently, '*Bas ke vitkit*?' This is now an expression in Gondi that means 'When will you sow?' The call of the thirsty bird, '*Pir, pir*!' means 'Water, water!' in Gondi. Thus, Gondi is a language born from the drum of the dancing god, flowering in the sounds of nature, giving its users a sense of self-awareness, but never distancing them from the importance of the collective *amat*.

In November 2014, it was reported that as many as twenty pictographs of Harappan origin had been discovered on rocks near Hampi, the UNESCO World Heritage Site located close to the Tungabhadra river in Karnataka. Experts in the Gondi script, including Dr Moti Ravan Kangale and Prakash Salame of Nagpur, argued that five of the twenty pictographs – *alin* (man), *sary* (road/way), *nel* (paddy), *sukkum* (star/dot) and *nooru* (headman) – seemed to be directly related to the Gondi dialect and were similar to drawings found in the interiors of ghotuls in the Bastar region.

When I take his leave, Anchala says with disarming sincerity, 'I try to spend my life in service to the Gond people and in being truthful. Not that I am always successful, but I keep trying.'

Language was the original information technology that enabled humans to communicate with each other. The revival of Gondi has strategic importance for it will connect several lakh people living in a contiguous belt in central India. This revolution in classical information technology, based on the standardization of a language that is believed to have originated in Harappan civilization, is far more empowering than the accretions of modern information and communications technology (ICT) can be at this stage. But ultimately, it is the combination of ICT – used as a news network or a data repository for traditional knowledge – and language that will be the game changer.

At the workshop, in addition to elders of the Gond community, I meet a number of people who live in areas inaccessible to the Indian government on account of the control of the Maoists. I hear stories of the lives of those people – some have to walk 60 km from the nearest road to get to their villages, others have to travel 35 km to the nearest town to access their weekly rations from the government PDS shop. I hear stories of the *dada*s, the Maoists who, for many of my interlocutors, are neither 'revolutionaries' nor 'criminals' but ordinary people who have become a part of their daily lives.

I recall that a mobile network equipment vendor, Vihaan Networks, whom I had dealt with as part of my core research into telecommunications policy, had participated in a tender to set up mobile towers in areas affected by the Left-wing insurgency. The dots seem to be getting connected. My vague search for a book based on solutions provided by information and communications technology in remote areas now seems to be getting focused in the form of a search for the realities of insurgency-prone areas and the possible impact of digital technologies in resolving the pressing problems of people living there.

It is at this workshop that I first tentatively ask Shubranshu if he could help me to travel to these areas with the help of a reliable guide. In response, Shubranshu introduces me to Kamal Shukla, who plans the trip I am to make to Kanker in September 2014.

And yet, as of December 2014, despite my visit to Hackergram and my foray into Abuj Maad, I am still not quite there. I have yet to reach a remote village, to get up-close and personal with people affected by the insurgency: bystanders, victims, sympathizers, thugs, revolutionaries – I want to meet them all.

Then, in December, Shubranshu reveals that CGNet is about to set out on a two-year yatra through remote Gondwana to persuade people to become bearers of good tidings and bad from their region. This is my chance, and I decide to grab it with both hands.

2

The Kolang Festival

The yatra starts on New Year's Day in 2015. Giving myself a day to usher in the year with the family, I join the yatra on the second day of January. I am met at the Raipur airport by Farid, an endearing fellow with a wonderful childlike quality and the habit of constantly chewing gutka.

We drive to Haat Kondal, a market where we meet the rest of the team that has gone ahead of us on a motorcycle and in two large Tata Sumos. They are an extraordinary group of young men and women from remote tribal villages and small towns, who have been selected on the basis of workshops and are fired by the zeal to serve society. Each one of this ragtag crew also has the charming gift of being able to hold a tune.

Their ability to sing is important, because every day, the team reaches a local market where they set up a stage to perform a street play. In addition to the cast of men and women actors, there are three beautifully crafted puppets that have to be carefully ferried in a steel trunk from one location to the other. Apart from some elementary sound equipment, there are sleeping bags for the team members to spread out and tuck themselves into, wherever night might fall. The team's energy is abundant and infectious.

The play delineates the travails of village folk who are being denied their dues for NREGA work. It presents 'Mobile Chacha', a charming puppet with a luxuriant moustache and a wobbly head, who can help by connecting them with the Swara network and, subsequently, the internet. It depicts the predicament of a district collector who is hounded by calls from urban activists the world over enquiring about an incomplete project.

The quality of singing is commendable, the performances more spontaneous with each show and the ability to improvise in the face of obstacles, like non-functioning amplifiers or inadequate lighting, something that could have done an experienced theatre group proud.

The leader of the group is Lalsu Soma Nogote, a Maadiya tribal. Lalsu's father had died young. His mother left him in the care of her deceased husband's family and remarried, choosing her spouse from a different village.

'In my uncle's home, I was an undernourished child,' he says. 'My life changed when I started going to the school in Hemalkasa run by Baba Amte's family.'

A much-admired social worker, Amte was known for his work with leprosy patients and his opposition to the Sardar Sarovar dam project.

'The principal's son befriended me,' Lalsu tells me. 'And the principal treated me like his own child.'

I can see how a simple and trusting young Lalsu would win his school principal's heart.

After graduating from Hemalkasa, Lalsu obtained his law degree from Ferguson College, Pune. He thus became not only the first person to have completed high school from his village, but also the first to obtain a professional degree. In the course of my journey with him, I would discover with relish that his many accomplishments include the ability to whip up a mean fish curry – just the thing for reviving the flagging spirits of his cast and crew.

Lalsu is assisted by Ankit Panwar, a burly, hirsute former music teacher who, it is evident, has been unable to resist the pull of his genes; both his parents are social workers. Ankit has left his wife tending a nine-month-old infant at home to come away on the yatra. His rich, zestful voice and supple grasp of Hindi and Chhattisgarhi are great assets to the troupe.

The first day, as expected, is the toughest for me, as I have to orient myself to a new way of being – devoid of frills, of the luxury of being waited on, hand and foot. All seating and sleeping arrangements are on the ground. Luckily, that night, there will be a welcome diversion in the form of the Kolang festival in Bogar village.

The Kolang festival is an annual gathering of Gonds from about 150 villages in Chhattisgarh.

It is being held on a sandy field, roughly the size of three football fields. There is an entrance fashioned like a straw roof, and a welcoming pathway lined by little flags of seven colours. At the end of the pathway is a temple, merely a little hut with walls made of grass stalks of the chhind tree. On the top of the roof of the temple is a large stick figure of a god alongside a white and red flag. Inside the hut, there is an altar made of many earthen pots decorated with leaves and an earthen lamp. At the end of the field there is a shamiana and a stage with carpets laid out along the sides of the stage where people can sit.

The origin of the Gond people is shrouded in mystery. According to a story from their mythology,[2] they are the descendants of a widow's children who were trapped in a cave by Sambu Madaav and his wife Gaura[3] and released through the intercession of the Gond hero Kupar Lingo and Hira Suka Patalir, a musician whose melodies evoked the *veera rasa*, the heroic impulse, in the children and enabled them to push away the rock that had held them fast in the cave. Lingo took the children under his wing and ensured their schooling in high culture, thus enabling them to become Gonds, standing apart from the rest of humankind, the Koyatur (born of the *koya* or womb). Hidimba, the wife of Bheem, one of the Pandava brothers in the Mahabharata, is believed to have been a member of the Gond community.

Any gathering of the Gonds is full of music and dance and the Kolang festival is no exception. The programme consists of a dance called the *madri*, performed for an entire night and a day in front of the adivasi god Burha Dev. Originally, only men were supposed to perform this dance. Now some of the troupes include women as well.

---

[2]http://www.downtoearth.org.in/news/legend-of-kachchargadh-46696

[3]The same as Shambhu and Gaura, mentioned earlier.

The dance can go on for over twelve hours, sometimes stretching to fifteen, with occasional breaks for meals. Once it is over, the performers return to their villages with their ceremonial sticks, which are now considered to be consecrated. They are not meant to sleep in their homes on the night they return, but have to turn in at the Sitala shrine in their village. Sitala is a folk deity who was later absorbed into mainstream Hindu religion to become a revered mother goddess. Many of her shrines in tribal villages simply consist of a muddy rectangular strip around a central plinth through which a luxuriously contoured termite hill emerges. The next morning, before returning home, the dancers immerse their sticks in the local stream in a ceremony called the *pandum*.

But at the venue where the Kolang festival is being celebrated, I notice that the dance performance is preceded by a concerted burst of speech-making, as one worthy of the Gond community after another extols the virtues of their culture and exhorts young members of the local audience to never forget their glorious roots. This marks the moment when I begin to wonder if I should have come at all. Far from being in a Maoist stronghold, I am sitting on a well-lit stage, sharing space with a former IAS officer, a local politician, a *dharmacharya* of the Gond religion and a bunch of stuffed-shirts who seem inordinately fond of their own voices. I have to endure this ordeal for almost an hour.

As the speeches are coming to an end, I hear a remark which makes me wish I had paid closer attention to what was being said. S.P. Shori, a retired IAS officer currently heading the All India Gondi Council, declares, 'When people in suits sitting on the stage fight along with people fighting in the forests, then the revolution will come.' I surmise he means that real change in the fortunes of disadvantaged communities will be effected only through a combination of a concerted push from within mainstream society led by those community members who have achieved a measure of success, and pressure exerted from the fringes by those who choose to combat entrenched vested interests through armed struggle.

When the speeches wind up, my attention is drawn to a set of dance performances starting in the large field in front of the shamiana under which the stage is set. These are group dances and many such groups perform simultaneously, the drum accompaniment of one merging with the plaintive chants of the other. The music reminds me of the aboriginal melodies of Australia and Africa.[4]

The dancers are dressed in a variety of colours. Many wear headbands with gorgeous flowers tucked into them. Some of the men wear ornate *lehenga*-like skirts, with large *ghungroo*s tied to their waist, a garment usually favoured only by women. All carry ceremonial sticks while they dance. Some of the performers are bare-chested.

Not only have I always abhorred long-winded speech-making, until now I have also had a lifelong aversion to most forms of ritualistic song and dance. I had regarded the singing of traditional songs at my wedding as a ceremonial dirge to be good-naturedly borne in view of the great happiness I had been gifted.

Quite unexpectedly, therefore, I find myself swept up by the tribal dances being performed now. As I go from one group to the next, clicking pictures, I sense a current of euphoria, of

---

[4]There is a consensus among geologists that Australia, India, South and Central Africa and South America belong to the same prehistoric land mass known as Gondwanaland. While the land mass separated before the advent of the first humans, there is genetic evidence that the

celebration, charging the atmosphere. I start feeling light, happy. The soles of my bare feet, smarting till now from contact with the pebbles and sharp stones underfoot, stop giving me trouble, and my mind is no longer preoccupied with the merits of the different means of cutting my trip short.

The tradition of Gondi song and dance is believed to have come into being when a group of Kupar Lingo's disciples who had set out for a bath became entranced by the *run-run-run* sound emerging from the humming of black bees and the heady fragrance of flowers blossoming on every tree. Hardly aware of what they were about, the disciples had held hands and started dancing around the trees, while mimicking the buzzing of the bees.

I am persuaded by a group of adivasis with friendly smiles to join their group dance. As I am led by my partners, I recognize a step I had learnt in my jazz dance class at an American university. Jazz dance draws heavily from ancient African traditions. The dance step I am performing is also akin to the four-step barn dance popular at summer fairs in the US. Perhaps this stepping forward, going across, shuffling back and returning to the starting point is an ancient ritual, handed down from generation to generation, spreading from land to land and used from time immemorial to symbolize the rites of passage of people who are increasingly disparate but never fail to return to elemental rhythms in their moments of joy.

---

aboriginal people of Australia are part of the same group of people who migrated from Africa 60,000 years ago, continuing along the coasts of Arabia and India and eventually heading south into present-day Australia, which was joined with the island of New Guinea at the time. Rock paintings, music and dance in these regions bear an imprint of their common roots. See http://www.biomedcentral.com/1471-2148/9/173/abstract. These regions are also believed to bear similar mineral resources in terms of quantity and grade.

After bidding goodbye to my newly acquired friends, I continue my walk through the groups of dancers. One group, in particular, blows my mind. There are about twenty men, many fairly advanced in years, standing close to each other in a straight line, holding sticks in their right hands that are slightly extended so that they are clearly visible beyond the line. These sticks are tapped in a gentle rhythm, as a repetitive, melancholy chant is sung over and over again.

At the head of the line is a quiet-looking man, obviously the leader, holding a stick with which he lightly strikes another that is held like a crossbar by two men who stand a little ahead of him on either side of the line. One of the duo holds an umbrella over the leader's head. In front of the entire group is a thin metal rod thrust into the ground, with a clump of straw crowning the top. It serves as the image of the god for whom this dance is being performed. At a certain point, the three men in front sit down on the ground. The music goes on and they continue tapping out their gentle rhythm.

It is difficult to describe the hypnotic spell this dance casts on me, a spell seeded and epitomized by the quiet man in front, who sways from side to side with eyes closed, seemingly oblivious of the world, lost in a trance as the music washes over and through him.

Like Wordsworth and his solitary reaper, I do not know how long I stand there, but I savour the slowly tapering rapture long after I have turned away for dinner, and even through the long and uncertain wait for the school master who will let us into his classroom to sleep the night. Even the shadows lengthening on the ground seemed to be suffused with colour, I think to myself as I turn in.

That night, I have a dream. The Kolang festival is over. The performance with the sacred sticks has ended, the intoxicating dance, streaming through the night like a sparkler of light, has finally run its course. The men and the boys return to their village, but not to their homes, where they can only go after the *pandum*, the ceremonial immersion of the sticks, is over. After a night spent in the Sitala shrine, the dancers leave for the river.

Day gives way to night. The trees change colour. The hills turn from green to brown. But still, the women wait for the return of their menfolk. The men and the boys of the village – soaked in celebration, bedewed with the spirit of their gods, plumed with flowers and tinkling with *ghungroo* bells – have been swept away in the currents of time. Their grimy shoes and the muddy termite hill are the only reminders that they once existed.

In the effortless shift of identity, possible only in a dream, I begin to think it is our team that has lost its way, not the tribal dancers; it is we who need to be led back to the path, not they – a not entirely farfetched scenario given the various existential crises facing our civilization.

Lost in my dream, I begin to panic. All of a sudden, the women of the village take up the drums left behind by their menfolk and set up an insistent beat.

I awake with a start. It is early morning. The vigorous drumming of another troupe, punctuated by virile war cries, pierces the air.

Don't they ever sleep, I wonder in mild irritation.

3
A Glimpse of Paradise

We reach Markabeda, a tribal village that lies 10 km off the road from Narayanpur, after a disappointing halt at the bustling Narayanpur haat, where our sound equipment fails us. It is dark by the time we reach our destination. We are to sleep in the *ghotul*, a thatch-roofed mud hut painted blue. The interior consists of a single hall, long, rather than wide. This is not the vibrant community centre of yore, but it does have a functioning power point that we can use to recharge our mobile phones.

Five of the girls in the troupe belong to this village. So we have no worries about being served a meal. While the troupe goes off for dinner to the nearby ashram school, I decide to open my can of baked beans, unpack my stock of crackers and make a meal of it so that I can turn in early.

The next morning, I wake up at 5 a.m. and have a bath at the handpump next to the *ghotul*. The girls have, as usual, risen before dawn and completed their morning ablutions. They must now be at home, being pampered by their families. Purushottam, a journalist who is travelling with the troupe, is still supine in his assigned place next to mine and Ankit is, as usual, sleeping like the dead. Shubranshu has authorized the team to empty a bucket of cold water over this prince of sleepers to wake him up.

While bathing, I find to my surprise that the well water is comfortably warm, even on a very chilly morning. When I am ready, I decide to go for a walk before breakfast.

The air is suffused with mist. There is only one narrow street with a concrete surface winding through the village. The houses flanking it on either side are large and painted in blues and greens;

often, more than one hut stands in a compound. Occasionally, a chicken scampers across the road. A woman is combing her hair. I greet her with a 'namaste'.

The sun is a golden disc in the milky sky, its heat devoid of enmity or bite. Every now and then, I come across a tree that makes me stop in wonder – a tall banyan, for example, or a willowy, luxuriant sal; a many-branched sulphi, with a matka, an earthen pot, tied at the top to gather the drops of sulphi juice that drip slowly from it at the break of day, giving the villagers an ambrosia they cannot get enough of. In the fields, I see the occasional turbaned man, squatting with a long staff between his hands, or women with pallus carelessly flung across uncovered breasts, pot-bellied, middle-aged matrons who stare at the stranger in their midst, even as I hastily look away.

Suddenly, I come upon a field of straw with a thatched granary in the middle. The mist hanging over the field cannot dim the incandescence of the granary's yellow roof that shines through like a golden orb, eclipsing the quiescent sun above. The caressing mist, the trees standing in a reprise of their ancient vigil over the landscape, the vast expanse of the field of straw and the flaming roof of the granary, shining like a surrealist's dream, transfix me.

With what enthusiasm we head for mountain resorts, I muse, for beach huts and places of pilgrimage! With what excitement, we set out on desert safaris! But what I am experiencing in a simple village in the heart of a jungle seems to transcend my most memorable vacation experiences. The greatest source of stress lies, perhaps, in the expectations we have of ourselves. In that village, in that moment, it seems as if those expectations don't matter.

Although that morning walk is steeped in a sense of ease, the next few days will vividly bring home to me the possible trajectory of an adivasi who joins the Maoists – the original state of grace, the loss of innocence, the consequent exile, the refuge in the band of rebels, the criminalization and death or, alternatively, surrender to the police and the donning of another uniform followed by the hunt for one's own kin on the other side of the fence.

As I walk back, I catch the strains of an old Bollywood favourite – 'Rooth na jaana' from the film *1942: A Love Story* – streaming through the window of a house. Its roof has a solar panel on it; obviously the creeper of modernity has reached even this remote place. I am not sure if I should be happy or sad about it. Are those cobwebs glistening with dew on the branches of banyans, as ancient as time, incompatible with the neat grids of solar panels? Obviously not, I tell myself, as I spy Shiv, a member of the troupe, looking for me.

4

The Loss of Innocence

We have been invited to Saroti's house. She performs the role of the worker in the play who faints in the middle of NREGA work. Seating is arranged on straw mats spread out on the floor. The food is served in steel plates, while drinking water is poured into steel tumblers. The girls in the group serve us. Here too it appears that women eat after the men have had their fill.

The menu is simple and delicious. There is *poha* – flattened rice – with a delicious tomato-chilli chutney and a serving of salad, fresh onions and radish. As is customary in our country, we eat with our fingers, scooping up the rice in tiny balls and biting off minuscule bits of the chilli to add just the necessary zing to our food. Every now and then, the girls come by with serving vessels laden with *poha* and chutney. We watch contentedly as they heap our plates with second helpings, then go back to eating.

If the principles of ayurveda are to be adhered to, we are not meant to drink water during meals. But with the piquancy of fresh chilli picked directly from the field setting our tongues on fire, the strictures imposed by ayurveda are the last thing on the minds of our team members. Shiv, who enacts the role of the Collector in the play, clears his throat with a vengeance. 'This chilli is good,' he remarks, gulping down a generous swig of water. Beads of sweat glisten on his face and on mine too, I soon realize. There is a crisp winter breeze blowing and the combination of hot and cold creates a very pleasant sensation.

Wherever we go, we are served simple food and offered the heartfelt hospitality of the village – the school or the *ghotul* to sleep in, the use of someone's pots and pans and wood-burning stove and the willing participation of village hands in the preparation of the meal.

All of this is very heartwarming, but nothing exceptional, for the hospitality of villagers, untouched by the very different ways of urban life, is well known. All the more telling that this old tradition of hospitality, the hallmark of a timeless way of being, has become the cause of immense trauma for the villagers.

At Saroti's house I met Arjun Yadav from the neighbouring village of Garam Bawali, Panchayat Moonj Metta. He is a farmer who works for six months of the year on odd jobs, when there is no water available for agriculture. Yadav is unlettered and unschooled, but adept in the ways of traditional farming. In 2008, he was delighted to get a job with Essar in Gujarat. The harvest had been bountiful and, with a job that brought him a monthly salary of ₹5,000, apart from giving him a bed in a dormitory, life looked good.

One day, however, he was summoned by the foreman to the manager's office, where he saw a couple of uniformed men waiting for him. They informed him that he was about to be arrested on suspicion of being a Maoist.

His face, usually expressionless in the presence of his supervisors, betrayed nothing more than mild chagrin.

'But I am not a Maoist,' he said finally. 'I never moved around with the *dada*s.'

Without addressing another word to him, the policemen had a talk with the manager. Soon, Arjun was walking out of the office, flanked by two police officers who bundled him into a jeep. Later, he was taken to Durg jail to await trial.

Days passed, but his hearing did not come up. Meanwhile, he heard rumours of the charges levelled against him, charges of being a ruthless killer and commander of the Abuj Maad division of the Dandakaranya Special Zonal Committee. He was alleged to have personally supervised many ambushes and killed a number of police officers.

The People's Liberation Guerilla Army (PLGA), the military wing of the CPI (Maoist), is organized into state-level committees and, further, into zonal committees which, in turn, comprise divisional committees. The Dandakaranya Special Zonal Committee is one of the Maoists' most powerful zonal committees, consisting of the divisional committees of South Bastar, North Bastar, West Bastar, Gadchiroli and Abuj Maad. The '*dalam*' or squad, constituted under the divisional committee, is the PLGA's lowest level of organization. In addition to the armed militia, the Maoists operate through a band of armed recruits who wear civilian clothes and maintain 'law and order' in the villages on a day-to-day basis.[5]

---

[5]https://wikileaks.org/gifiles/attach/9/9360_Naxalite%20brief.doc

Each story of his supposed exploits as 'zonal commander' increased the burden under which Yadav was reeling. He did not have the resources to seek the kind of help he required. His friends too did not have the means at their disposal to come to his aid or the necessary awareness that would have come in useful at this crucial time. Some of the jail officials were sympathetic, but none was able to tell him why he was there in the first place, when he had done no wrong, nor what lay in store for him.

The first court hearing, scheduled six months after his incarceration, led to an adjournment, as the prosecution lawyer was not present. The second hearing, scheduled another three months later, met the same fate as the cases of the presiding judge had spilled over, leaving no time for Arjun's case.

For three years, Arjun kept sitting in his ward, subsisting on jail food, which he says, tastes utterly bland, like water. He had brought ₹800 in cash with him to the jail and had deposited the sum with the jail superintendent. He was always tense that his money would eventually get stolen.

Meanwhile, he received news that the police had razed to the ground the two houses in which members of his extended family had been living. His wife and infant, his parents and young siblings, were left without a shelter. That would, perhaps, have been fitting punishment for the Maoist commander of Abuj Maad, but not for someone who claimed – truthfully, as the court was to discover later – that his only crime had been to offer a meal to the Maoists in his home when they passed by his village.

A villager extends this kind of hospitality to an itinerant professor, a visitor from a neighbouring panchayat and a Maoist alike, for in his mind, they are all guests; and turning away a guest is not part of the ancient ethos of the village, where a guest turning up without notice is akin to the arrival of a messenger from God. In the city the very notion of entering into a transaction with a fellow human being, without the exchange of currency, is fraught with so many negative undercurrents – grudging resentment over the effort demanded, fear of bodily harm and a complete sense of apathy.

Yet when the village is a site of conflict between the state and an insurgent group, the very act of hospitality involved in serving a meal becomes one fraught with grave peril, even the peril of landing in the lock-up some day. When that act is loaded with risk and liable to invite dangerous questions about loyalty and patriotism or the lack thereof, the abiding culture of a bygone age is forever sullied, irretrievably lost in the urban ethic of mistrust.

The very insurgency that has brought some benefit to the villagers, in terms of the protection of their community resources and of the more focussed attentions that a state – faced with the prospect of losing suzerainty over vast tracts of mineral-rich land – begins to lavish on them, has also robbed them of their innocence, an innocence epitomized by meals readily shared with a stranger.

After an ordeal stretching over seven years, Arjun was released.

The witnesses had testified in court that he was, indeed, no Maoist. While he has been redeemed in the eyes of the law, what of the years he has lost, the family homes that were burnt down, the trauma his near and dear ones went through and the death of his father, who could no longer bear the agony of witnessing it all?

Today, after his ordeal, he has a slight physique, a bony body, dark complexion and a crop of short, curly black hair. His large black eyes glisten like those of a frightened deer.

'I have no more blood left,' Arjun confides, perhaps indicating that he has become acutely anaemic as a consequence of his long incarceration in extremely inhospitable conditions.

'I did not get any medical attention in jail – neither in Durg, nor in Bastar, to which I was transferred, because the Durg jail could no longer accommodate additional prisoners. If I had had someone [influential] outside to help me, things would have moved faster. People with connections, with money, get good food in the jail. But the rest of us are given really inedible fare. [My years in prison have left me so malnourished that] it takes huge effort now for me to even move my limbs.'

Of the ₹800 he had entrusted to the jail superintendent, only ₹600 was returned to him.

'I am really afraid, sir,' Arjun says in conclusion. 'There are lots of people like me still in the lock-up. Simple, naive folk. Several women as well. We are all very frightened. What will I do if they [the Maoists] ask me for food again? What will we do if they ask us to attend a public meeting simply to make up the numbers? What will we do?'

Is he exaggerating his plight to arouse sympathy, I wonder. *Has he learnt the ways that enable people like me to survive in the city?*

Indeed, I will never be able to understand his predicament. Not till I am thrown into a lock-up and robbed of my youth. Not till I lose my ability to cry, because I have learnt after years of effort that no one cares. Not till my own children's futures are trampled underfoot, like so many fallen leaves, will I accept without an iota of scepticism that these stories are indeed true, that the trauma is real and that even as I eat my fill, drink to my heart's content and complain about the traffic, millions of lives are being wasted – far away, and perhaps right outside my car window, for who is to say I am more sensitive to the plight of the street beggar, the eunuch, the paraplegic than I am to the villager in a Maoist village.

Not knowing how to respond, I tell Arjun that his village is now free of Maoists.

'We are now afraid of going into the forest to gather wood or tendu leaves,' he replies. 'If the police are out on patrol, they thrash us.'

5

Damned and Dispossessed

The entry of Maoists into the life of the tribals was facilitated by the denial to the latter of customary forest rights by the Forest Department, along with unfair labour practices and the arrogation of vast tracts of land by the tribal landlords. Questions arise as to what extent the Maoists have sought to correct historical wrongs in their own fashion. To what extent are they guilty or innocent of similar transgressions?

Areas under Maoist control have been broadly identified as divided into two zones: the raiding zone (or the '*chhappamar*' zone) and the guerrilla zone. The latter is a fortified zone which has been described as a 'liberated area', where the Maoists run a parallel government called a *jantana sarkar*. The raiding zone, on the other hand, is a peripheral buffer zone from where surpluses are extracted to maintain the guerrilla zone.

In three of the villages I visit – Chahchaad, Mendo and Markabeda – I hear of Maoists confiscating the land of rich landlords. In Markabeda, a former sarpanch, Lachchman Wadde, eagerly shares his own tale of woe.

'The Maoists would say, "*Halka raho*, stay light. Why do you need so much land, so much grain?" They would work [in collusion] with the *patwari* to change land records and take away our land. They wanted everything *phiree* [free]. "Give us cows, give us buffalos," they would say. "Everything *phiree*".'

'If we took anything from the Forest Department, they would be angry. On one occasion, the Forest Department handed out shoes intended for the use of tendu-leaf collectors. I just happened to distribute them. As a consequence, I was summoned at night to the adjoining forest by a lady commander of the Maoists. She held me by the throat and abused me.

'"Why did you distribute the shoes?" she asked.

'"The government handed them to me [for distribution]," I replied, "and I gave them all to the villagers. I didn't keep any for myself." Then she kept quiet.

'Another time, when I had a second-grade road built [for easier access] to the village, they set my tractor and motorcycle on fire.'

Ram Kumre (name changed), a resident of the village who had spent six months with the Maoists and whose story appears in the following chapter, explains, 'The Maoists say, "The Forest Department will give you shoes. They will give you clothes. And they will take away your land. Don't cooperate with them."'

Like Lachchman Wadde in Markabeda, Santhuram in Chahchaad and Chhindi Lal Kumre in Mendo also complain of the confiscation of land.

On being pressed, Santhuram says, 'They did not take away land in our village, but in Mendo.'

In Mendo, on the other hand, Ram Kishore Sinna, a younger lad, distantly related to Chhindi Lal, laughs off the allegation. Lakhan Mandawi, a young volunteer in Markabeda, also pooh-poohs Lachchman Wadde's claims that his land was usurped.

Archana Prasad writes: 'Even at the height of the high intensity conflict with Salwa Judum, the committees confiscated approximately 1,526 acres of excess lands from landlords (most of whom were tribals) and distributed 743 acres to the landless, while also keeping the same amount for the "collective needs of the village"'[6].

---

[6]Prasad, Archana, 'The Political Economy of Maoist Violence in Chhattisgarh', *Social Scientist* (2010): 3-24.

While not intending to contest claims that the Maoists usurp land from rich farmers, I must mention that I was not able to verify the stories of such confiscation that I came across during my travels.

Apart from land, the Maoists also require villagers to contribute their labour. Large-scale irrigation works using traditional water-conservation techniques like stop dams are undertaken through *shramdaan* (voluntary labour service). This labour is meant to be entirely voluntary, but in many cases it is possible that fear and peer pressure play an important role in prompting the villagers to toil for such projects.

'Now that the Maoists have gone from Markabeda, are things better?' I ask Lachchman Wadde and his friend Phool Singh.

'Yes, at least we do not have [to go through] the daily tamashas,' they reply.

'How are your relations with the CRPF camp?' I ask.

'Good,' they respond. 'Every month, we take them a tonne of timber from four villages. In return, they give us a hearty meal.'

While talking to Lalsu (not to be confused with Lalsu Soma Nogoti, the leader of the CGNet Swara troupe) and Rajjawu Wadde after breakfast, I realize that nothing can divide a village quite as much as development. Lalsu is fifty-five years old. One of his daughters is a member of the CGNet Swara troupe. Ramvati performs the role of a harassed NREGA worker in the play and has a lovely, high voice, perfect for singing tribal ditties. She has studied till Class IV. Lalsu has two more children, one of whom has studied till Class IX. He himself is illiterate.

Lalsu has the air of a person whose very being has been numbed by the level of prevarication and betrayal he has witnessed in life. His eyes, gazing expressionlessly at the world, are hollow. Rajjawu, on the other hand, appears to be afflicted by the tribal predilection for alcohol. While he has a handsome face and a fine mop of long hair curling from under his headband, he is emaciated and his legs, visible under his short dhoti, are spindly. A faint aroma of *mahua*, the local brew, hangs around him at all times.

About twenty-five years ago, Lalsu, along with his friend Rajjawu and a few other residents of Markabeda, had decided to go across the small hillock surrounding their village and colonize some farmland in the uncultivated hillside. After a couple of years of strenuous labour, they managed to clear the area. Lalsu owns seven acres of land in Gutta Pal, as the settlement came to be known. Rajjawu owns five. Soon, a total of ten families started living there.

When it was clear that they had succeeded in their endeavour, a big feast was held to coincide with the *mitti puja*, the traditional worship of the soil performed by all villagers. Present at the feast was a government surveyor. Having such an august person attend the celebrations made Lalsu very happy.

Had he known about the kind of work the surveyor was engaged in, he would have tempered his joy. For the official had come to explore the possibility of building a small dam to bring irrigation to the adjoining villages, including Markabeda. Unbeknownst to Lalsu and his fellow settlers, Gutta Pal was going to be in the submergence zone of the proposed dam.

The surveyor did not, of course, mention this at the celebrations. He merely enjoyed the feast and left, continuing with the work for which he had been engaged.

It was not until the following year that news leaked out that a dam was to be built. The matter was discussed in the Aamgaon panchayat under which Gutta Pal falls. The gram sabha was favourably inclined towards the idea of a dam because of the irrigation benefits promised to the bulk of the villagers.

When Lalsu heard that his land would be taken away, he felt his world collapse. Lachchman Wadde, then sarpanch of Hallami Moonj Metta, which had jurisdiction over Markabeda, consoled the devastated farmer. 'The farmer's land is bound to go,' he said soothingly. 'We had better reconcile [ourselves] to it [the situation].' Lachchman, however, did not take matters quite so philosophically when the Maoists spoke of confiscating his plot of land.

Meanwhile, Lalsu remained inconsolable. He spoke to the sarpanch, the panchayat secretary and the Janpad CEO in Narayanpur.

'What will we get in return? Will we get land? Where will we go?'

With only ten families living in Gutta Pal and over fifty looking forward to the benefits of irrigation they had been promised once the dam was built, Lalsu did not have the power of numbers to strengthen his case. But when the Maoists arrived in Markabeda, he suddenly acquired the power of the gun. The one thing the *dada*s can be relied upon is to prevent the tribals from being divested of land, be it for mining operations or for the construction of dams, power plants, factories and roads.

Durusai, a boy from Markabeda who had joined the non-uniformed Maoist militia, was the henchman deputed to intimidate the engineer heading the project into withdrawing from it. A thrashing or two was enough to bring the work to a complete standstill. Peace returned to Lalsu's life and the pattern of one crop a year continued, till a CRPF camp was set up close to Markabeda. The Maoists retreated deeper into the jungle and work on the dam recommenced. A little greyer since the time his troubles had begun, Lalsu resumed his lamentations.

'Lalsu and Rajjawu are not opposed to the dam,' Lachchman now tells me.

Lalsu who had expressly voiced his distress earlier in the morning remains silent. Rajjawu shifts on his seat.

'He has no objection if he gets land in return,' Lachchman continues. '[And] he is going to get land in return.'

Lalsu continues to look impassive.

To understand the nature and depth of Lalsu and Rajjawu's distress, some familiarity with their current standard of living is imperative. Apart from the harvest from the land they own, both receive 18 kg of foodgrains a month from the government's PDS scheme, an amount that falls signficantly short of the 35 kg they are entitled to. Nevertheless, this ration, along with their own crop, provides them something to sell in the local market. At the price of ₹1,200 a quintal, they earn approximately between ₹10,000 and ₹12,000 a year on a single crop. Their sale of tendu leaves brings in an additional sum of nearly ₹4,000 a year. As things stand, they are doing reasonably well. It is interesting that today, their economy benefits more from the regular provision of PDS grain by the government than from the Maoist-led negotiation for higher rates for the sale of tendu leaves. Lalsu and his kind also have an opportunity to work on NREGA projects in the off-season, although payments to this region have not been forthcoming for an entire year. From the point of view of Lalsu and his fellow villagers, who could ask for more?

A couple of days later I speak to Mr Gawde, the Janpad CEO in Narayanpur town. Discussing the dam-related project, I am keen to know what kind of compensation the displaced farmers will receive. Mr Gawde tells me that they are to be compensated in cash. They will also receive money to build a house. But there is no mention of land. This is certainly not the impression Sarpanch Lachchman Wadde has been trying to convey to Lalsu.

'You will get land,' he had kept saying.

'What about alternatives to a dam, like surface wells?' I ask Gawde.

'The water table is too low,' he replies, relying on the findings of a survey undertaken twenty-five years ago. While it would be safe to assume that water tables could only have receded in this period, the mapping of watersheds (even if it had been carried out in the survey) would now certainly be out of date.

The Maoists protected Gutta Pal from submergence for about fifteen years. With their departure, plans to recommence work on the dam have regained momentum. Moreover, a new primary school has come up in the village and an ashram for residential students studying up to Class VIII has been built a few kilometres away. It appears that the attention of the Maoists to this area has provided a certain impetus to the government's educational initiatives, while not diverting their focus from the dam. Perhaps, the realization has dawned that if the authorities hope to acquire land they will have to provide some basic services in return.

6

Ram Becomes a Maoist

As I have mentioned earlier, the feeling most inimical to hospitality, most stifling to its open-hearted ways, is suspicion. In a village claimed by both the Maoists and the Indian military, every adivasi is always under suspicion – from both sides. The plight of Arjun Yadav, who was jailed for seven years on specious charges, indicates the perils the villagers face from the police.

The Maoists, on the other hand, will not tolerate *shikayat*, or complaints lodged against them with the authorities.

Present at the small gathering of people that I meet after breakfast, along with the former sarpanch of the village, Lachchman Wadde, is his friend, Phool Singh. It is 11 a.m. Already, both Wadde and Singh seem to be pleasantly tipsy.

A surge of feeling overwhelms me when Phool Singh narrates the following story.

A boy in Markabeda was suspected of having revealed the whereabouts of a passing Maoist patrol to the police by plucking a leaf off a tree in a prearranged manner – it was a signal that, allegedly, had been agreed upon in advance. The Maoists took him to the jungle nearby and, in the presence of a gathering of villagers, five of them set upon him, thrashing him brutally with logs of wood. As he screamed in pain, pleading for mercy with his palms clasped together, they struck him behind the knees and on his back.

'Don't take him to the hospital,' they warned the villagers, after they were done, 'or else we will shoot him.'

It was clear that the Maoists did not want word of the beating to get around. When the semi-conscious boy pleaded for water, they fetched it for him from the muddy stream flowing nearby. The villagers carried the boy back home and tended to his injuries as best they could.

Ram Kumre, an erstwhile Maoist who is also present, chips in with his own take on the matter. 'This is common,' he says. 'If the *dadas* suspect you are an informer, they will take action. They have no option but to do so.'

He seems to regard their behaviour as acceptable. But all I feel is a sense of outrage. Outrage at the thought of a bunch of barely literate villagers caught between two antagonists – expected, on the one hand, to turn down requests for information about the insurgents from the central forces and thereby be branded as Maoist sympathizers; required, on the other hand, to resist the demands of the rebels and, thereby, be singled out as lackeys of the police.

I acknowledge that the tribals are wise enough in the ways of the world; wise enough to know how to exploit their fellow tribesmen if they have the opportunity to do so; wise enough to recognize injustice when they experience it. But would they – or anyone for that matter – know how to react when caught in the crossfire between two implacable enemies, each with vested interests, but certain of the inexorable righteousness of its cause? Should those responsible for the tribals' predicament not hold themselves accountable for the situation and attempt to at least understand their plight?

I turn to Ram. He has joined an NGO after his engagement with the Maoists and after completing his graduation. He plans to devote his life to improving the lot of the tribals who, he says, have fallen on hard times.

'Did you join the *dada*s, because you liked the ideology, liked the people or were impressed by their uniforms?' I ask him.

'They used to come [to the village] and tell the elders that they would like [to recruit] one youth from every family,' he replies. 'There was no explicit coercion as such, but certainly a fair amount of pressure. The person who decided to join them would persuade others to accompany him. 'If I am going to die for the village, someone else should also join me,' says Ram, explaining the dynamic. 'But some people also go [and join the rebels] because they are idle in the village and [while living] with the Maoists they get food and training. They start enjoying that way of life.'

I remember asking another local contact from a neighbouring village if the Maoists ever used coercive tactics to get people to join their movement. According to him, the villagers enlist themselves voluntarily. The Maoists have wonderful dance troupes and inspiring music. They are pleasant to the locals, speaking to them in their own language. The children like to run small errands for the *dada*s and soon, they don't want to leave their company.

'What was your experience while you trained with them?' I ask Ram.

'Fear. Constant fear,' he replies. 'Fear of our instructor, who, like a sergeant major in the army, would hit us if we did not perform the training tasks [to his satisfaction]. Fear of coming across a police patrol and dying in an encounter.'

Finally, Ram could bear the pressure no longer. He pleaded ill health so that he could leave the training camp. He went for a six-month course to an Industrial Training Institute in Bhadrachalam and never returned. To this day, he has not told the Maoists that he has left for good; and to this day, they have not come after him.

'Aren't you afraid they might track you down one day?' I ask.

'Not really,' he says. 'I know others like me – people in the rank and file – who have been left alone after they decided to leave. But if the Indian police come to know, I could be in trouble, even though I have had nothing to do with the *dada*s for years now.'

'Maoists don't do anything wrong,' says Ram. 'They punish only those who are guilty of "mistakes" like complaining to the police or troubling people. Even then, they issue warnings and only take more serious action after repeated transgressions. [As Maoists] we would move from one village to another and get our food from the villagers,' he recalls. 'We never forced them to do anything for us. "If you have food and want to give us some, then you can," we would tell them.'

The assurance with which Ram Kumre claims that while training with the Maoists he had never coerced villagers into giving him food is belied by the candour with which he admits how nervous he would feel when the Maoists came around to his village, asking for a youth from every household to join their ranks. Is it simply that when Mohan left his life in the village to become a Maoist, his perception of the dilemma faced by the villagers was diminished? Or has his own ordeal of running with the hare and hunting with the hounds psychologically fragmented him?

During my own interactions with the adivasis, I come across the same shifting perspective, the same disconcerting dichotomy. If I ask them, for example, what kind of people the Maoists are, one villager after another will reply that the rebels can be both good human beings and bad. On the one hand, they protect the advisasis' lands, discourage them from quarrelling among themselves and caution them about the evils of drinking. Their music and theatre are entertaining. But, on the other, the Maoists are not averse to thrashing the locals for the smallest transgressions. They warn them against tipping off the police and force them to travel to faraway places to attend their public meetings and to fulfil their 'pledge' of providing voluntary labour. They also find out who is important in the village and set about clipping his wings.

Even as one villager or the other is holding forth, I notice how the prevailing trend of opinion is completely reversed if a new person joins the discussion and makes an observation that goes against the grain of what is being said. The villager who has been expressing his views will pause in mid-sentence and adopt the opposite stance before continuing.

This ability to shift gears and switch sides never failed to surprise me. I am inclined to believe that the pressures of living in contested territory have robbed the villagers of their natural candour. And I can hardly blame them; they are damned if they do and damned if they don't.

7

Durusai Dies in an Encounter

As is my wont, I ask Phool Singh about his experiences with the Maoists. In response, he tells me the story of two brothers in the village and the sad fate of one of the most promising adivasi leaders in the area. This story demonstrates how the Maoists may have a vested interest in preventing the rise of local leaders who wish to take advantage of government schemes to bring about development in areas under their jurisdiction. It also indicates how naive village youth are lured by false promises into being recruited, turned into criminals and killed when their existence becomes an inconvenience. It shows that those being killed as well as those carrying out the killings are usually adivasis, often joined by close ties of community and subsequently divided by the contemporary rite of blood-letting.

Noku Koram, was elected sarpanch of Chhota Dongar in 2009. A good man, he was driven by a burning desire to improve the lot of his tribal community. A few weeks into his tenure, he discovered discrepancies in the records of the various development works under way, works listed as having been completed without any actual work having been done, people mentioned as having received various payments whereas they had received none, and pensions falsely listed as having been distributed. He took up the matter at the next panchayat meeting.

The sachiv, the secretary of the panchayat who was also a government officer, nodded his assent when Noku proposed that the situation urgently demanded remedial measures. After the meeting was over, the sachiv took him aside.

'Noku, you are new,' he said. 'Please try to understand how things are done here. I will see you in front of the *ghotul* in the evening.'

That evening and the next, the sachiv sat with Noku on a charpai in front of the *ghotul* and talked of many things – the disunity among the tribals that had led to their exploitation, the problems caused by the local addiction to liquor, the new trend of boys and girls marrying outside the clan.

On the third evening, the sachiv said, 'Noku, how much do you earn? In today's world, we need money; money to send [our] children to private schools, money to meet medical expenses, money to pay for weddings and funerals. Now that you have become a sarpanch, take care of your family. This is an opportunity for you to put away a little something for your children.'

Noku got up and left.

That night, he confided in his wife. 'Sachiv *theek aadmi nahin hai*. He isn't a good man. He is encouraging me to do things that are wrong.'

At the panchayat's next meeting, Noku's response to the sachiv's suggestions was honest and unequivocal. Discrepancies were pointed out, junior officers roundly admonished and stern warnings issued. The sachiv could only watch the developments over the coming weeks and months as his empire, carefully built over years, began to be dismantled, bit by bit, by Noku's missionary zeal.

'That Gond is proving to be troublesome,' he told Ratan Dube, the *thekedaar*, or contractor, who was his accomplice in corruption.

The sachiv was a Halba. The Halbas consider themselves superior to the Gonds as they link their ancestry to former servitors of the Bhanjdeo royal family of Bastar. They do not break bread with the Gonds – a distinctly non-tribal custom – although they retain their tribal status and privileges.

The last straw was when Noku announced that he was going to stand for the assembly election. The prospect of this man acquiring political power in the state assembly threatened everything the sachiv had painstakingly put together, piece by piece.

The sachiv had been careful to maintain strong, mutually profitable ties with the local Maoist commanders whom he kept in good humour through timely payments from his cherry pickings. He once told Kamal Shukla, who had arrived in Chhote Donger to investigate allegations of corruption, that he was ready to pay the journalist as much money as he wished for in return for his silence on the issues in question. If Shukla refused to listen to reason, however, and continued spreading 'false rumours', he would not reach home alive. Shukla remained quiet and returned home that evening without being harmed. His story was not published anywhere and he received no further threats to his life. Of course, he never asked for a bribe either.

Coming back to Noku's story, the sachiv had reached the conclusion that he would have to 'take care' of the sarpanch. The Halba sachiv and Dube, the *thekedaar*, decided that Noku would have to be eliminated.

The brothers Durusai and Dalsai Wadde had been happy-go-lucky lads from Markabeda in the days before they became Maoists – Durusai a plain-clothes operative, and Dalsai a uniformed member of the rebel militia. When Durusai enlisted with the insurgents, he was not given a uniform to wear. Nor did he belong to a *dalam* or squad. But he was handed a rifle and had the run of seven or eight villages where his writ ran large. Quarrels among the tribals over livestock encroaching upon the fields of neighbours, unwelcome infringements by contractors, collection of weekly payments from government projects for non-interference in project work – he adjudicated on all manner of things. Despite being urged by his new comrades to do so, he had trouble giving up his addiction to *gutka* and *mahua*, and continued to indulge his habits on the sly.

There are many plainclothes operatives like Durusai in the Maoist camp. These young people are invariably used as cannon fodder by junior-level *dalam* commanders, sometimes in the interests of party work, often for their personal ends. As my local contact Lakhan Mandawi says, 'These operatives dance to the tune of the uniformed militia.'

The rank and file get their own kicks from the power they wield over former friends and relatives and the glamour of being associated with the *dada*s. I suspect, however, that in a few cases genuine allegiance to the Maoists' cause also has a role to play in their involvement with the movement.

Whatever be the reason, the hazards in store for men like Durusai cannot be overemphasized, as is borne out by his story.

One day, his boss, a uniformed local commander, summoned him to announce that Noku would have to be killed. The commander was confident his superiors would not object to this decision, as they knew how generously the *thekedaar* was contributing to their coffers – and the contractor's interests had to be protected. The local commander himself was a frequent beneficiary of the man's largesse.

Durusai was surprised, though only for a moment, by his commander's request, as he had high regard for Noku. Ever since he had been inducted into the Maoist movement, ostensibly as a reward for assiduously cleaning the local commander's rifle and running chores for him, the young man had become increasingly sullen, ever more anxious to please his superiors and progressively more unpleasant in his conduct towards former friends. Now the very same commander who had inducted him into the group of the *dada*s was ordering him to 'take care' of Noku.

The plan was carefully hatched. On 25 September 2011, Noku was to participate in an inquiry in the panchayat. In his convoy was an engineer, referred to as 'E-Sahab'. It was decided that the convoy would be ambushed.

While travelling in such convoys, Noku always brought up the rear. Durusai's comrades tracked the progress of the convoy through a pre-planned combination of traditional tribal signals and mobile phones – wherever the network was available. Meanwhile, Durusai and another man waited at a carefully chosen ambush point.

As the convoy approached, Durusai waved it to a halt, dragged Noku out of the car and knifed him. One, two, three thrusts, and the work was done. This was not the first time Durusai had killed a man, but this was the first victim he had held in some regard. He was now a certified mercenary.

The government swung into action. Suspicion fell upon members of the convoy. The E-Sahab, who was already embroiled in several other cases of corruption, became the prime suspect. As pressure began to mount, the E-Sahab was found dead from a fire that had broken out in his quarters in Narayanpur. Those in charge of the investigation had lost an important suspect and witness. Rumours of suicide and murder were equally rife.

The Maoists put out the story that Noku's assassin was also

dead, having been injured in the encounter. And so peace would have returned to the idyllic hamlet of Markabeda had Durusai not mentioned the details of the killing to one or two members of the community.

Word soon reached the Halba leader and Dube, the *thekedaar*. Both feared that the conspiracy behind Noku Koram's killing and their own role in it would be exposed. It was time to act, yet again.

'SP Sahib,' Dube whispered into the phone. His voice was tense, as if he were speaking under duress. 'I know who killed Noku.'

'Durusai, is it?' The SP clicked his tongue. 'That boy has become a hopeless case.'

The SP summoned Sukun Nureti, the Inspector at the Bhainsgaon police station nearby. Sukun himself was a former Maoist who had surrendered to the authorities and been subsequently hired as a Special Police Officer (SPO). Unlettered as this young man was, his value to the police lay in his ability to seek, find and destroy Maoists. In this function, Sukun was highly skilled and had earned several cash rewards for successfully carrying out his missions. He would now be informed that Durusai was wanted, dead or alive.

The problem with apprehending the quarry was that Durusai, for his own safety, kept himself constantly on the move, never sleeping in the same village for more than a night or even putting up for the night in the same house in a village. The breakthrough finally came from the boy who delivered Durusai's chicken for his *betia*, the Gondi term indicating the end-of-day sit-down dinner with friends.

'He is going to be dining in his own home tomorrow,' the delivery boy reported.

The next evening, as Durusai was enjoying his chicken dinner, surrounded by friends, waited upon by his anxious wife and romped upon by his little daughter, Sukun barged into his home accompanied by a burst of gunfire.

Durusai's face contorted with fear. 'Don't shoot,' he said, raising his hands in surrender. 'I will confess all. I surrender.' And then he started to run, still screaming, 'Don't shoot! Don't shoot!'

Sukun chased him down and smashed his knees with one blow of his rifle. Durusai continued to plead for his life, but Sukun's bloodlust was not yet quenched. Or, perhaps, it was his need for the extra ₹7,500 that a kill would fetch. In full view of Durusai's wailing wife and daughter, Sukun emptied ten bullets into him. The hatchet job that had begun with the killing of Noku ended with the elimination of his assassin, a Maoist who had been prepared to surrender when faced with death. Both murders were engineered by the same politician-businessman combine, with the local Maoist commander and the police acting as contract killers, each with a cut in the deal.

8

Dalsai Surrenders and Becomes an SPO

By the time Durusai was killed, his brother Dalsai had also joined the '*andar wale log*' – the people who lived deep in the forest. He was a member of a *dalam* and wore a uniform. After a period of gruelling training, Dalsai was posted in Maharashtra.

His posting merely followed the general rule by which the Maoists operate; they do not usually hire uniformed cadets from local areas in order to spare the latter's families the repercussions they would inevitably face from the authorities. It is the members of the non-uniformed militia, on the other hand, who usually belong to local areas.

The occasional overenthusiastic aspirant will, however, attempt to wangle his or her way into the militia. I come across one such recruit, who rose rapidly in the Maoist ranks, only to meet a sorry end. It is dusk in the Narayanpur bazaar. The surrendered cadet, Naveen, is standing with a group of police officers. He looks like a highly competent young man, with creased trousers and carefully combed hair. His face is impassive.

Naveen had joined the Maoists and, in a remarkably short time, managed to become the commander of the Narayanpur division.[7] Then the police started harassing his family. Beatings, incarcerations, cross-examinations accompanied by torture became common. Unable to bear their travails, Naveen and his wife surrendered to the authorities. They were given jobs as special police officers and became invaluable in identifying their former comrades.

A press release of the Maoists, dated 14 November 2014, denounces the surrender policy instituted in Maoist areas. They claim that it is being misused to siphon off crores of unaudited public funds by arresting innocent tribals and passing them off as Maoists. This release acknowledges, however, that some genuine cadres are also falling prey to the surrender policy. It goes on to condemn them in strong terms, stating that 'the revolutionary public has nothing but hatred' for such people. It claims that when surrendered Maoists join police forces in attacking villages, the villagers 'beat them up, abuse them to their face, and spit on them'. The communiqué singles out Naveen for special mention. It says that thousands of villagers demonstrated in front of the Dhanora police station, demanding that Naveen be either arrested or killed.

---

[7]http://timesofindia.indiatimes.com/india/Maoist-trained-to-evade-UAVs-choppers-Surrendered-rebel/articleshow/20389475.cms

The surrender-cum-rehabilitation scheme for Left-wing extremists in affected areas fixes a grant of ₹2.5 lakhs for cadres of higher rank and ₹1.5 lakhs for middle-level cadres.[8] A monthly salary of ₹4,000 is also paid, either for a period of three years or till a government job is secured, depending on which date arrives earlier. Most surrendered Maoists are given jobs as SPOs.

Whether the person giving himself up to the authorities is a genuine Maoist or not needs to be verified, as much as his stated rank in the hierarchy. For this purpose, there is a screening-cum-rehabilitation committee consisting of representatives of the state home department, the state police department and the CRPF. Given the level of graft generally observed in these areas, however, the screening procedure does not entirely eliminate the risk of people who are not Maoists claiming to be so and 'surrendering' to the police to reap the benefits, with the connivance of some of the concerned officials.

It comes as no surprise that the surrender of fake Maoists is commonly believed to be a rampant practice. The benefits are shared with select government officials, with the lion's share going to the officials. A villager I meet claims to know of cases where a number of youth have actually gone out and killed a couple of their fellow tribals, simply to establish their 'credentials' as insurgents. In the case of bona fide Maoists, there are stories of surrendering commanders coming away with stashes of money, part of which they share with the police.

It appears that the Maoists' questionable recruitment policy is mirrored by the fraudulent surrender policy of the police, a policy which ensures a steady supply of cannon fodder in the 'war against Left-wing extremism'.

---

[8]http://mha.nic.in/sites/upload_files/mha/files/NM-GuidSurReh_0.PDF

I recall SP Dash bringing up the subject of surrendered Maoists during my conversation with him. Many, he said, were less than thirty years old, but they bemoaned the fact that they had frittered away the best years of their youth in the quest of an elusive dream.

Naveen looks no more than 25. Despite his calm demeanour, I wonder what thoughts are passing through his head. I wonder how long he will be able to survive.

Durusai's death had hit his brother Dalsai hard. In accordance with tribal custom, he was obliged to wed his widowed sister-in-law. A conversation with her had decided his course of action.

'Will you take good care of me?' she had asked, tears brimming in her eyes, already swollen with crying.

'Yes,' he had replied, realizing in that moment that his life as a Maoist was coming to a close.

He surrendered to the authorities in the Narayanpur police station and was given a job in the police. He and his wife now live in a remote camp run by the government, where, hopefully, he is beyond the reach of his former comrades.

'Join the police, but don't do anything [that goes] against the *dadas*,' his friends had advised him.

Apart from the daughter Durusai had fathered, Dalsai and his wife have no children. The one pregnancy that had resulted from their marriage led to the birth of a stillborn child. When Dalsai meets friends, he never talks of the old days. For all practical purposes, those days have passed as if they had never been.

I ask Lakhan Mandawi, who had been a childhood friend of both the brothers, what became of Durusai and Dalsai's parents, Manku and Ratani Wadde.

'They were beaten badly, sir,' he says. 'As were other members of Naya Jungal, the small village they had moved to. The police held them responsible for their sons becoming Maoists. They [the parents] had tried to bring their children back [to the mainstream], but to no avail. Durusai would not even listen to Balsai, a tribe elder. Their mother ultimately died from the beatings and from grief. Their father has survived to see one son return to normal life.'

I gather most of the information about Noku Koram's case from two independent sources in Markabeda. I also contact Vishwaranjan, the then Director General of Police of Chhattisgarh, to verify the story. His response is brief and to the point.

'Dear Shri Prasad,' he writes, *'I tried to corroborate the information from some of the Police officers posted in Narayanpur. They confirmed the killing of Noku Koram, Sarpanch, Chhota Dongar, by the Maoists. Rest of the information could not be confirmed or corroborated by them as the incidents are very old.'*

SECTION THREE

In the Parlour of the Plutocrats

1

Clues from a Happy Childhood

I had played in this parlour, the parlour of the plutocrats, as a young child growing up in the august environs of the Tata Iron and Steel Company Limited (TISCO), perhaps one of the most highly regarded institutions of India in the 1970s and 80s.

While we did not seem to have the kind of money my friends from business families had access to, the absence of such a privilege was more than made up for by the perks that came with my father's position at the organization – the clubs, the parties, the entertainment allowance, not to mention the TISCO-dealers versus TISCO-officers cricket matches.

I grew up on a diet of legends surrounding the probity of the house of Tatas. Although the controversies of the 2G spectrum allocations should have alerted me that the world had changed and that even the Tatas had found ways to steer their boat in muddied waters, I am taken aback by the antipathy some of my contacts feel for them in Chhattisgarh, and by their sense that the Tatas were just like any other company. They are alleged by some to have transported fifty villagers to the Collector's office and obtained signatures in support of one of their projects in lieu of approval by the gram sabha. Others believe that the terms of the MOU they had signed with the Chhattisgarh government are replete with egregious clauses.

Given my understanding that no solution to the crisis in

Chhattisgarh can be arrived at without resolving the conflict between mining interests and the local population, I am eager to speak to Tata representatives. As a business house steeped in the philosophy of trusteeship, allocating 3 to 4 per cent of their profits to CSR activities, and as builders of some of the finest institutions in India in the field of basic research and social science, surely they would have a point of view, one that suggests a solution to the imbroglio?

My father puts me in touch with Mr B. Muthuraman, former Managing Director (MD) of TISCO, who had held the reins of Tata Steel during the initial years of the Chhattisgarh project. When I tell him about my proposed book project, taking care not to arouse any apprehensions about presumed radical leanings, his voice booms across the radio waves.

'Rohit,' he says, 'I have met many Maoists in my tenure at Tata Steel. I have sympathy for them. They are not at fault. But they get used by politicians and landowners. They don't have a job, so they join the Maoists. After a few years, they get disillusioned there as well. You must visit Jamshedpur and speak to Biren Bhuta, who handles our Rural Development Society.'

I decide to take his advice. But before starting out for Jamshedpur, for what I imagine might be a boring set of homilies about 'the Tata way', I intend to seek out those who will be able to offer me insights on the ground realities of Tata Steel's operations.

Through a former colleague of my father's, I manage to gain access to the first Chief Resident Executive of Tata Steel in Chhattisgarh. My desire to meet him intensifies when I learn that following his stint in Chhattisgarh he has resigned from the company. There can only be two reasons for his decision, I speculate. Either he had crossed the ethical boundaries acceptable to the Tatas and had paid for it or he had refused to cross those very boundaries and been made a scapegoat. Either way, I am interested.

I also secure an appointment with Dr J.J. Irani, former MD of Tata Steel.

In this way, I aim to acquire a certain understanding of the Tatas' foray into Chhattisgarh, before setting out on my journey to Jamshedpur.

2

The Agony of R.N. Singh

'I call the projects that corporates initiate with much fanfare nothing but a big drama,' declares Sudip Shrivastava, an activist-lawyer with extensive knowledge of the Tata Steel project in Chhattisgarh.

I am speaking to him on the phone.

'They sign a number of MOUs, far beyond their capacity to execute, only to capture natural resources, and prevent their competitors from gaining access,' he goes on. 'These resources will be used at some point in the future, when market conditions turn opportune. State governments, through a mixture of incompetence and lack of integrity, play into the designs of the corporates.'

Rajiv Narayan Singh, Chief Resident Executive of Tata Steel in Chhattisgarh, did not have Shrivastava's wisdom to comfort him when he emerged from Muthuraman's office in Jamshedpur in 2007. Muthu had sized RN up from his perch on a swivel chair behind a large oak table, as the younger man, mustachioed and thickset, walked the longish distance from the door to the seat opposite his MD's.

'Why are you getting cold feet?' Muthu had asked commandingly. Over the years, his voice had taken on some of the timbre of his former boss Russi Mody.

Then, taking advantage of the opportune visit of a local police officer, Muthu had signalled that the meeting was over. RN would leave dejectedly, without having had a chance to discuss the challenges of the Chhattisgarh project with his MD.

It was just over two years into Singh's tenure, two years since he had been sent off to the mineral-rich state nurturing great dreams.

'We are going to build a new Jamshedpur in Chhattisgarh,' he was told.

The entry was to be dramatic and grand. The company was not going to confine itself to mining and steel production.

'Find a nice piece of land in Raipur to put up a building that will become the Tata Centre of Raipur,' was the instruction. The Tata Centre, at 43 Chowringhee Road, is an iconic building on Kolkata's landscape, although somewhat eclipsed over the years by newfangled glass-and-chrome upstarts.

RN reached Raipur late one evening in May 2005, 'armed,' as he says now, 'with only a visiting card.' He took up residence in Hotel Babylon, the hotel of note in Raipur at the time.

'Had the Chhattisgarh project succeeded, I would have been happy to spend my whole life there,' RN confesses today. 'Not just I, many in Tata Steel were totally committed. Who would want to live in Gurgaon, when one could live in Chhattisgarh with such a visionary project to work on and with people as simple and lovable as the Chhattisgarhis?'

RN's father, T.N. Singh, had been a renowned freedom fighter and a successful politician of independent India. He had been chief minister of UP from 1970 to 1971 as part of the Congress (Organization) faction that was opposed to Indira Gandhi, and later became the governor of West Bengal. As Governor, he had chosen to eschew the palatial Raj Bhavan, official residence of the viceroys at a time when Calcutta was the seat of the British Empire, and live, instead, in the quarters allocated to the gardeners. His abstemiousness, inspired by Gandhi (the Mahatma not Indira), was sincere. He was a member of the aristocracy of simple living that had grown around the pleasure-renouncing Mahatma.

RN had had a middling stint at Tata Steel until he arrived in Chhattisgarh. As the son of a leading politician, he was part of a club comprising the sons of eminent people, like Ashok Shastri, son of India's former prime minister, Lal Bahadur Shastri, and Muzaffar Shah, scion of G.M. Shah, the one-time chief minister of Jammu & Kashmir and grandson of the redoubtable Sheikh Abdullah. RN's hail-fellow-well-met persona and his ability to launch forth into vociferous song held him in good stead in the company which, at that time, rather favoured the ability to hold a glass of whisky over a knowledge of the nuances of steel-making.

While RN was a happy man – others might even have described him as happy-go-lucky – he had a niggling feeling that his life was not playing out against the larger canvases that had given his father's trajectory its grandeur. For that reason, he saw his time in Chhattisgarh as a challenge and an opportunity to launch himself into his own rarefied atmosphere of courage and sacrifice. He was going to be an apostle bringing the 'good news' according to Jamshed Tata to the miserable and the destitute of the state.

RN was soon busy setting up office in his hotel room, scouting for land for a corporate centre and looking for a place that would serve as his home for the next few years. From his talks with government officials, he had concluded that there was so much goodwill for the Tatas that even if they had wanted to wind up and leave, they would not be able to. The district collector of Dantewada, Sanjay Srivastava, was most responsive and Raman Singh's right-hand man, Principal Secretary Shivraj Singh, was clearly committed to the project.

In the very first year of the project there was a brouhaha in the Chhattisgarh Assembly over the MOU signed by Tata Steel and the Chhattisgarh government. This was only to be expected, given the blunder the company's officials were alleged to have made, confusing hectares and acres and, thereby, more than doubling the acreage involved.

'You can verify the terms in my chamber,' was the chief minister's offer to his agitated legislators.

State government agreements with companies are usually kept confidential, although it is not obligatory that these be classified, except in matters of security and law enforcement. Most MOUs should be accessible through RTI (Right to Information) applications. But those were early years for RTI in India. Meanwhile, the public relied on the time-tested method of leaks.

These leaks indicated that a vast expanse of land – 5,000 acres – had been allotted, in principle, to Tata Steel to set up a 5.5 mega-tonne steel plant to be completed forty-eight months from the date of the final clearance. In addition, they were to be given a prospecting licence for an iron-ore mining block, Dantewada 1 in the Bailadila hills (so named because they resemble the hump of a bull), the richest iron reserve in the world. An assurance was given by the government for providing water supply of 25 million gallons a day. The coal requirement would be met from imports. A captive power plant would supply electricity. At the time of signing the MOU in late 2004, the company promised a total investment of over ₹12,000 crores.

The Tatas were granted a prospecting licence (PL) at the very outset, although this is the second stage of the three-stage licencing process for a mine that involves acquiring a reconnaissance permit to begin with and ends after a mining licence has been issued. The PL permits drilling activities necessary for ascertaining the quantity and quality of mineral reserves over a wide area. According to a report in a prominent national daily, soon after the MOU was signed, the government took away control of mines from the Chhattisgarh Mineral Development Corporation (CMDC) and assigned them to the Tatas.[1]

A colleague of Singh had also managed to submit an application for a PL for one of the blocks in Rowghat mine that contains the second-largest iron-ore deposits in Chhattisgarh after Bailadila. They were hopeful, even though other private companies like Nicco Jaiswal and Monet Ispat were in the running.

One fine day, however, Chanakya Chaudhary, Chief Resident Executive, Tata Steel, in New Delhi, told Singh dramatically, 'Rowghat *bhool jao.*' RN was to forget about Rowghat.

Obviously, something had not gone right in the confabulations with the central ministries involved.

Meanwhile, a piece of land in Sallepal Barupata only 100 km from the iron-ore mine had been rejected because of the presence of diamond tracts, and after three more sites had been rejected for their proximity to revenue forests, an area in Lohandiguda was identified. The land there was not level, as it had been in Sallepal Barupata, but the undulations would, at least, facilitate the building of water tanks. The problem was the significant forest cover and the need to displace 12,000 to 15,000 people to make way for the plant. Compounding the challenge was the absence of a water source in the vicinity to feed the easily created water tanks.

[1]http://www.thehindu.com/news/national/other-states/chhattisgarh-hc-issues-notice-to-tata-essar/article5012290.ece

The Tatas and the government had to convince the local people that building a steel plant there would be in their best interest. Varun Jha, RN's boss and the director appointed for the Chhattisgarh project, arranged for a well-rehearsed PowerPoint presentation to demonstrate how a steel plant would create a demand for transportation fleets, ancillary industries and supporting services. But the locals did not understand PowerPoint presentations.

A Public Interest Litigation (PIL) was filed in the Chhattisgarh high court by Sudip Shrivastava. Apart from the commitment guaranteeing water supply, the points raised included the pre-commitment in the MOU itself of specific mining tracts, the unconditional undertaking to supply costly minerals like limestone and dolomite and the acquisition of land in a scheduled area, without consulting the gram sabhas, as required by the Panchayati Raj Extension to Scheduled Areas Act.[2]

The petition filed by Sudip was rejected in the Chhattisgarh high court. The court observed that the petitioner's apprehensions were 'premature', compelling Shrivastava to move the Supreme Court. It was only in January 2013 that the PIL would be admitted in the high court, after the Supreme Court had asked Shrivastava to raise the issues again before the high court.

But despite a legal respite, the image of the Tatas suffered a blow in early 2006, when newspapers started flashing the news of a catastrophic episode at Tata Steel's proposed 6-million-tonne-per-annum steel plant in Kalinganagar, Orissa. On the very day that Tata Steel was taking possession of land allotted to them for setting up the plant, a group of locals, armed with bows and arrows and pickaxes, had turned up to register their

---

[2]http://www.thehindu.com/news/national/other-states/chhattisgarh-hc-issues-notice-to-tata-essar/article5012290.ece

protest and been fired upon by the police, resulting in the death of fourteen protesters and one policeman.

R.N. Singh decided to seek the help of the area's legislators. He recalls that all of them happened to go by the name of Kashyap, reflecting the success of Hindu proselytizers in the area. More to the point, all were from the BJP, the ruling party that was avowedly behind the project. However, none was willing to stick his neck out.

In RN's presence, they acknowledged the sound reputation of the Tatas, Kalinganagar notwithstanding, but regretted their inability to help. '*Aap toh theek hain*,' they said, 'we don't have a problem with you. Administration *ka kya karunga*? *Logon se kya kahoonga*? How do we handle this administration and explain ourselves to the locals? *Jungle-wale log aayenge toh unse kya kahoonga*? If the forest dwellers [the Maoists] turn up, what explanation do we offer them?'

Meanwhile, the Congress legislators were smiling smugly at the harried Singh. '*Yahaan se* clearance *mil bhi jaye, lekin* Centre *ki* permission *kaise layenge*?' they told him. 'Even if you manage permission from here, how do you propose to get it from the Centre?'

The central government was run by a different coalition and would, the regional leaders warned, oppose the state's ambitions.

After much cajoling, Lachchuram Kashyap, BJP MLA from Chitrakoot, offered to arrange for Singh to meet a group of villagers. Accompanied by Kashyap, RN and a few of his associates were driven to a village in the MLA's jeep. They reached a village *chaupal*, an all-purpose central square used for weekly markets and festivals alike, where a makeshift podium had been constructed. About 150 people, mainly women and children, had gathered there. It was 11 a.m. It was likely that at that hour, the menfolk were busy indulging their daily habit of consuming sulphi, the local brew.

Kashyap began to speak. 'The Tatas want to work in this area,' he announced. 'If you all consent to it, the work can begin. Mr Singh here is a senior executive of the company. If you have questions, he is ready to answer them.'

Before RN could speak up, he was assailed by a volley of wails, slogans and shrieks. Speaking in Halbi, their native tongue, the women screamed, 'Go on, slit our throats! Kill us! Slaughter our children, if you must, but we are not leaving our land!'

Singh attempted to pacify them. 'We will work for your benefit,' he assured them. 'You will be given new land [to compensate] for the land you give up. You will get jobs.'

But the raucous mob of agitated young mothers was implacable, refusing to be won over.

'I realized this was not the moment to speak of plant capacity and backward linkages,' RN says now. 'Besides, I did not want to linger long enough to make my defeat official. I sped away with the remains of my somewhat tattered dignity. Perhaps, I could have tried one of my songs. It might have worked better.'

While I am sure a soulful Bollywood ballad could work wonders even in Bastar, I know as much as RN does that this particular problem is not about to be resolved so easily.

While the legislators were busy acting coy, one person was totally bullish on the Tata project. RN had heard about him long before they met. He seemed to be that kind of a person – someone people knew of, even before he knew them. His name was Mahendra Karma.

Karma's name had been coming up frequently in RN's conversations with all kinds of people. He was said to have a considerable following among the tribal population. Although he was a member of the Congress, the opposition party in the state, and not even a legislator at that time, he seemed to be on very good terms with the government.

R.N. Singh was first introduced to him at the district collector's office in Jagdalpur, where a meeting of panchayat representatives had been convened to discuss the Tata project. Karma arrived in a government-owned helicopter, was greeted with lusty cheers and immediately launched into an impassioned advocacy of the project.

He was nothing if not determined to remove all obstacles that lay in the way. 'Tata *kaise nahin aayega*?' he declared confidently. 'What can stop the Tatas? If they are turned back, it will have to be over my dead body. Yes, I oppose this government, but not on this issue.'

'You cast a spell [on your audience],' RN told Karma.

'*Arre nahin*, Singh Saheb,' said Karma, 'These people insist that I come here and speak to them.'

Karma's was a voice that brooked no dissent. Even the insurgents, it seemed, would have to bow down before his indomitable will.

I ask R.N. Singh about his impressions of the man.

'He had a way with people,' Singh tells me. 'He would grab hold of them, abuse them and yet, it seemed, he was able to get across to them.

'I think he liked me. "Chaliye, Singh Saheb, *chai peetey hain*," he would say, grabbing me by the arm. "Let's go and have some tea."

'He was a volcanic personality; small, but powerfully built, with an unending repertoire of safari suits. He had a fleet of Mahindra Scorpio cars, direct access to the chief minister and a permanent entourage, consisting exclusively of the well-read, public-school types.

'We did not seem to be making any progress in getting across to the tribals. Neither the local MLA nor the district collector was of any help. Most of the journalists were only interested in free booze. The chief minister, Raman Singh, had been an acolyte of my father's, because he was from Pratapgarh, where our family has deep roots. But for some reason, Varun Jha dissuaded me from meeting him. The only ray of hope was Karma.'

According to RN, the Tatas had asked Karma if he would serve as their spokesperson and inform the tribals living in areas under Maoist control of their many proposed developmental schemes. Although he fobbed them off in the beginning, Karma eventually put forth a proposal.

'I can send my boys to the interiors to talk to the tribals, Jha Sahab,' he suggested to the director in charge of the Tatas' Chhattisgarh project, 'but they will need to be reimbursed for their travel expenses. They will need to go [to the villages] on scooters and you know the fuel costs these days.'

'How much would they need?' Jha asked guardedly.

'Not much, just petrol expenses for ten to fifteen vehicles,' Karma replied nonchalantly. 'About three to four lakh rupees a month.'

While repeating the conversation that had taken place, R.N. Singh falls silent, lost in memories.

'Did you accept the offer?' I ask breathlessly.

'No,' Singh replies, after a long pause. 'We told him that we only paid regular employees through lawful channels. That was the end of the matter, as far as I know. It is quite possible, though, that other companies were paying him.'

Three years of living and working out of a hotel room, without any visible signs of progress, were getting to RN. The government seemed unable to secure the land in Lohandiguda, the head office had made no progress in prospecting operations in Dantewada 1 and talk of building a Tata Centre in Chhattisgarh had fizzled out. Even Singh's house-hunting efforts were proving to be fruitless, as one good option after another was rejected by his management on some flimsy pretext or the other.

As he went knocking from door to door, everyone had a solution to offer. 'Why not start a cancer hospital in Raipur?' a principal secretary to the government suggested.

'Why should I start a cancer hospital in Raipur?' was Jha's curt response to Singh's suggestion.

He had evidently not bothered to explore the options that lay between building a gleaming cancer hospital and not building anything at all.

The CSR folks came and went, but it seemed as if the soul was missing from their endeavours. For all practical purposes, if they made any impact at all, it was only on the costs incurred by the company on travel allowance.

'Jamshed Tata's big plus point,' Singh now says wryly, 'was that he did not have a CSR team.'

The one group that Singh had no contact with was the Maoists. 'Naxalites, Maoists – I did not see them at all,' he says. 'Maybe, they would have come if we had progressed further on the project. In any case, I never felt any threat from them.'

The last nail in the coffin was the sudden parachuting of a contractor into the situation, one who, RN was told by his top management, would 'swing things for us'. The son of a prominent Indian businessman, this contractor did not intend to take things forward from the area of operations, but planned to press buttons from faraway Delhi through 'people who mattered'. Gram sabha clearances would soon be forthcoming through the network of the contractor, if assurances from Singh's bosses were to be given credence.

Despondent that external entities were being brought in without making more proactive attempts from within, and disappointed that distant levers were being preferred to grassroots advocacy, Singh called his MD. He and Muthuraman were not very far apart in age and RN had always enjoyed a halo over and above his role in the organization. In any case, as a person who was on a 'non-family posting' in a location fraught with risks, he felt he would be given special priority. He was confident he could unburden himself to Muthu and get the Tata charm offensive going to weed out the obstacles in the project.

'Why have you called during my golf game?' was the first question Singh had to field from the MD, whose golfing memories count as among the most precious from his stint in Jamshedpur.

That was the straw that broke RN's back. He could see nothing of any consequence taking place to propel the project forward. There was little support from the government, but he also felt that his own leadership was not doing enough to facilitate matters. Of course, no one was blaming Singh for the way things stood, but his superiors were also puzzled as to why he seemed unhappy and began implying that he did not quite understand the nature of his job.

I ask Singh if there was something that he, on his part, could have done better. He admits that due to lack of time, he had not been able to acquire the technical knowledge that allows a deeper understanding of mining activities. His daring and marketing skills had allowed him to traverse Maoist-controlled forest terrain to submit the PL application or talk a truculent clerk into giving him the prospecting maps of the area. But some geological knowledge of seams of coal reserves and 's'-shaped coils of hematite deposits might have given him an added advantage, he feels.

His next lapse, according to Singh, was that he did not kick up a shindy when things were not going well. His sense of loyalty prevented him from going over his boss's head, even when he had become convinced that Varun Jha was mainly interested in securing a smooth sinecure.

'I should have bypassed Muthuraman too, if necessary,' he now says ruefully.

Frustrated, he decided to resign from his job with the Tatas, a position most people regard as the acme of success and financial security.

'A man does not even consult his wife when he resigns,' he says. 'But I did. And Anshu said, "We cannot be happy if you are not happy. Please do not suffer any more for our sake."'

To make a point, Singh decided not to apply for the company's Voluntary Retirement Scheme (VRS), an option that was available to him.

'If I had taken VRS,' he explains, 'I would not be able to talk as openly as I am talking now. It is not that I have anything against the company. But when things are going wrong, the exemplars of society can either stem the rot or step away. The Tatas have got into the habit of stepping away. I fault them for a lack of courage.

'When so many people work so hard and have nothing to show for it, there is bound to be a sense of pain. Why did my MD not have the time and commitment vis-à-vis [urgent matters that] his Chief Resident Executive [had brought to his attention]? Why did he not make better use of me? Did he think that I could get everything done because I was from a political family? Then he has no idea at all of the kind of family I come from.'

And then Singh says something that brings to mind the grouse I had heard for Sudip Shrivastava, the activist: 'Was the steel project only a ruse to get mining rights for iron ore?'

3

The Lion in Winter

'Irani was a brilliant engineer,' my father had told me, 'but he was quite hard-headed. He did not hesitate to call a spade a spade and often rubbed people the wrong way.'

Cometh the hour, cometh the man. Dr J.J. Irani took over from Russi Mody as MD of Tata Steel in the early 1990s, a time described in an internal note[3] as a period marking the company's 'baptism by fire'. A thirty-year phase of controlled steel prices, high excise duties and quantitative restrictions on sales in domestic and international markets had contributed in transforming a thriving organization into one that had come to be known for its obsolete technology, high costs, a bloated workforce and lack of savvy in designing high-end products for new markets.

During Irani's ten-year tenure, Tata Steel became the lowest-cost producer in the world and cut its workforce from 78,000 to 40,000 by using a VRS scheme that seemed to keep heartburn at a manageable level, although someone did say that 'the golfers in the company found themselves at the short end of the stick'. In the 360-degree feedback process, MD Irani consistently scored abysmally low on inter-personal skills,[4] but explained that his wife Daisy more than made up for it. On average, therefore, he was doing fine, he concluded. In any case, by the time his tenure was over, Tata Steel was ready to capture market share following

[3]Mukherjee, Rudrangshu, *A Century of Trust: The Story of Tata Steel*, Penguin Books India, 2008.

[4]Lala, Russi Manekshaw, *The Romance of Tata Steel*, Viking India, 2007.

the rapid growth in world demand for steel in the first decade of the twenty-first century.

I meet Dr Irani at his son's house on New Delhi's Aurangzeb Road. Although he and my father were contemporaries in Tata Steel, I had never met him earlier, as he focussed on the works department in Jamshedpur, while my father was posted in the company's regional offices and in their marketing headquarters in Kolkata.

At close to eighty years, Dr Irani resembles nothing so much as an avuncular baronet from a P.G. Wodehouse story, one who would willingly rescue a favourite nephew from the ire of his fiancée's father. But it is evident that the man's punches have not lost their sting.

'We are not a soft target. We are not going to jump out of any activity, just because some Greenpeace or someone is targeting us,' he says, referring to the colourful NGO that had managed to temporarily hold up the Tatas' Dhamra Port project in Orissa's Bhadrak district on account of its potential impact on the nesting site for Olive Ridley turtles, apparently the largest in the world. 'But if we feel that we are breaking the law and the environment is suffering, we will pull out. We will not pull out when we know we are doing the right thing.'

I ask him about the willingness of corporates to abide by the rules, given the poorly funded, inadequately staffed and skill-deficient environment-compliance agencies. Irani is quite emphatic about the Tatas understanding their responsibility towards local communities and the environment, over and above contractual requirements. The obligation to carry out business in an ethical way is in no way undermined by the contractors that the companies employ, he declares, as they too have a responsibility to abide by the same ethical code. Nor would the Tatas be willing to ride on the government's unconscionable practices simply to flourish in business.

According to Irani, the Tatas have their own systems in place for judging whether they are fulfilling their commitments in a responsible manner, and they handsomely compensate the locals wherever the need arises.

'But even if we pave the streets in gold, there will be protests,' he remarks, drawing a distinction with China, where, 'on first June, the people [being displaced from their homes by a project] are told that on first July, they have to leave. They are given alternative accommodation and that is the end of the matter.'

I ask why, in the first decade of the new millennium, a time when Irani continued to hold a board seat in Tata Steel, there had been so many incidents where people expressed outrage against the Tatas – Singur, from where the Tatas had to exit after a mass movement led by the then future West Bengal Chief Minister Mamata Banerjee; Kalinganagar, where fourteen people and a policeman had died in a confrontation between the locals and the company; and Chhattisgarh, where there was widespread disapproval over the manner in which the MOU between the government and the Tatas had been signed. In addition to these episodes, the Tatas had also become embroiled in the '2G scam', in which spectrum was assigned to private-sector operators at highly subsidized prices, with many procedural irregularities in the assignment process.

Restricting himself to Tata Steel, Irani explains that the company had tried to expand too fast to take advantage of dynamic market conditions. The focus was on greater backward integration with raw materials, continued low-cost production and consistent expansion of the share of the high-end market. A number of acquisitions, including NatSteel in Singapore, Millennium Steel in Thailand and a coal mine in Australia, had left the company with a heavy debt, which became a millstone around its neck, especially as world markets collapsed after the financial crisis of 2008.

The big mistake, of course, was the acquisition of Corus.

In January 2007, after a four-month bidding war with Companhia Siderugica Nacional (CSN), a Brazilian steel major, Tata Steel had acquired the Anglo-Dutch firm for $11.3 billion, till date the biggest overseas acquisition by an Indian firm. The deal catapulted Tata Steel from the fifty-fifth to the sixth ranking in the list of the largest steel manufacturers in the world. The initial plan for financing the deal was that the group holding company, Tata Sons, would infuse $4.1 billion. The remaining amount, $7.2 billion, was to be acquired through a series of long-term loans which would be serviced through Corus's cash flows.[5]

The jury was divided on the wisdom of going in for such a large acquisition. However, Ratan Tata, chairman of Tata Steel, took a bullish view. 'I believe,' he said in an interview to a business weekly, 'that over the next few years, we will all come to think that this was a visionary move.'[6]

Cold logic aside, the deal also was imbued with a deep sense of poetic justice. When Jamshetji had started the Tata Iron and Steel Company and wanted to export steel rails to Britain, a Britisher called Sir Frederick Upcourt had said, 'Do you mean to say that Tatas propose to make steel rails to British specifications? I will undertake to eat every pound of rail that they make, if they do that.' Now, with Tata Steel acquiring Corus, formed as a result of a previous merger of Koninklijke Hoogovens N.V. with British Steel in 1999, the wheel would seem to have come a full circle.

The sense of sweet vindication operated at many levels. Nearly

---

[5]Freeman, Kimberly, Suresh Gopalan and Jessica Bailey, 'Achieving Global Growth through Acquisition: Tata's Takeover of Corus', *Journal of Case Research in Business and Economics* 1:1, 2009.

[6]http://www.bloomberg.com/bw/stories/2007-02-01/what-the-corus-deal-means-to-tatabusinessweek-business-news-stock-market-and-financial-advice

30 years before the acquisition of Corus, J.R.D. Tata, the then MD of Tata Steel, had lured away a young engineer from British Steel. That young Sheffield-educated engineer, knighted by the Queen of England in 1997, was Sir Jamshed J. Irani.

But today Irani is rueful. 'I can't escape responsibility for that [Corus],' he says. 'After all, I was still on the board.'

To appraise this expansionary streak in business and its impact on local populations, one needs to understand an important paradigm shift taking place in the steel industry in particular and in commodities, as a whole, in the first decade of the new millennium.

In response to the challenges thrown up by the bursting of the dot com bubble and the 9/11 attack on the World Trade Center, the Alan Greenspan-led Federal Reserve Bank brought down the benchmark Federal Funds rate from 6.5 per cent in August 2000 to 1 per cent in August 2004.[7] This is the rate of interest at which commercial banks in the US lend and borrow from each other on the overnight funds market to maintain their reserve requirements with the central bank.

The resulting flood of liquidity created a frenzy in the US housing market, unleashed a worldwide commodities boom and unlocked a wave of capital inflows into emerging economies. In India, the foreign direct investment and portfolio flows into the stock markets were focussed on the services and construction sectors (although the construction-sector investment must have included a disproportionate amount of domestic capital round-

[7]https://www.google.co.in/search?q=federal+bank+interest+rate&safe=active&espv=2&biw=1366&bih=667&source=lnms&tbm=isch&sa=X&ved=0ahUKEwji8eKGu4rKAhXDdCwKHewuBg0Q_AUICCgD#imgrc=fv7xEOzFCmxoRM%3A

tripping via Mauritius). The Indian infrastructure sector gained from being able to pick up debt capital on easy terms, albeit at floating rates, which made it vulnerable to the market risk of an increase in rates. The proportion of external commercial borrowings in overall corporate debt rose to 30 per cent in the 2000s, as opposed to 16 per cent in the 1990s. The external borrowings were supplemented by an avalanche of credit from public sector banks which were commandeered by the government to lend to infrastructure companies, even as private banks in India adopted a more cautious approch.

The first five years of the new millennium saw a rapid expansion in the demand for steel, a trend led by Asia. China continued to outstrip global growth rates and, between 2005 and 2006, accounted for 31 per cent of the world's consumption of steel. Some experts argued that the world economy had entered the early phases of a 'super-cycle' expansion, defined as 'decades-long', above-trend movements in a wide range of base material prices.[8]

The price of iron ore transported to China rose sharply from around $10 per metric tonne in 2003 to around $170 in April 2009. The price of steel (at steel plants in Japan) rose at a lower rate from around $300 per metric tonne in 2003 to $1,000 in late 2008.[9] This created a need for securing supplies of ore.

Between 2005 and 2006, Mittal Steel acquired Arcelor to become the largest steel producer in the world. They were also planning a steel plant in Orissa with a local iron-ore linkage. Tata Steel responded by acquiring Corus. It also signed MOUs both in Chhattisgarh and in Orissa.

---

[8]Rogers, J., *Hot Commodities: How Anyone Can Invest Profitably in the World's Best Market*, Random House, 2004.

[9]http://www.indexmundi.com/commodities/?commodity=iron-ore&months=180

Cyclical booms aside, long-term growth prospects for infrastructure in an emerging economy are, in any case, excellent. As stated by Chairman Ratan Tata in Tata Steel's 2005–2006 annual report:[10] 'The per capita consumption of steel in India continues to be extremely low at around 32 kilograms. If India were to have the same per capita consumption as China has today, then India could consume more than 260 million tonnes of steel annually.'

The combination of strong international demand, globalization of supply chains and robust long-term growth prospects saw a spurt of MOUs being signed in India, not just in iron and steel, but across the infrastructure sector.

Matters started unravelling after the subprime crisis in the US housing market spread across the world to become the 2008 global financial crisis. As Ratan Tata wrote in the annual report of Tata Steel in 2008–2009, 'After decades of global growth, the world watched in horror as financial institutions collapsed… It was a financial crisis of proportions approaching that at the time of the Great Depression of 1929.'

Iron-ore prices, controlled by three powerful international companies – BHP Billiton, Rio Tinto and CVRD – increased by 85 per cent, while steel prices remained depressed, causing immense stress on steel companies.

For three years, starting from 2005–2006, the Tata Steel annual reports refer to plans for steel plants in Chhattisgarh, Orissa and Jharkhand. In the 2008–2009 report, there is only a mention of a plan to expand steel-producing capacity in Jharkhand. In the report covering the period 2009–2010, when business conditions improved marginally, there is mention of

---

[10]http://www.tatasteel.com/investors/pdf/annual05-06.pdf

the Jamshedpur plant and the upcoming Kalinganagar plant in Orissa, but no mention at all of Chhattisgarh.[11]

During my conversation with Dr Irani, I observe that in Chhattisgarh the misdeeds of Mahendra Karma and the Salwa Judum seem to have rubbed off on the Tatas.

'That's why we pulled out,' he says. Later, he was to acknowledge that the debt overhang and weak world markets had also played a role in their decision.

I ask about his experience in dealing with insurgents.

'Yashwant Sinha [had] asked me the same question,' he tells me. 'He asked how we were able to operate normally in the Hazaribagh coal mine of West Bokaro, even when he himself did not have right of entry, though it was part of his own constituency. I replied that was because we are fair to people. Insurgents come from local people. Insurgents are not being imported from across the border or injected from outside. If they are happy with what's happening, there will be no insurgency. We move freely, because people want us. We carried on [our work in] the West Bokaro mine for years.

'Before we started mining in West Bokaro, we sent out teams to help with health and water facilities. Locals were suffering from malaria, hepatitis and a variety of other diseases. We built schools and roads. These expenditures are minor, compared to the cost of closing down a mine.'

I ask if the Tatas would ever consider paying insurgents, as Essar had been accused of doing in Chhattisgarh to safeguard their 267km-long slurry pipeline that transported iron-ore fines from the Bailadila iron-ore mines of the NMDC to Essar's pelletization plant in Visakhapatnam.

[11]http://www.tatasteel.com/investors/performance/annual-report.asp

'Absolutely not!' is Irani's emphatic reply. 'We would never pay anything. I became MD at around the same time that Laloo Prasad [Yadav] became chief minister of Bihar. I told him "The Tatas can't give you money. But if you want help for the people of the state, then we have ample money." And to this, Lalu said, "*Theek hai.*" We once built a children's hospital at his request. He never bothered us.'

If the Tatas had the understanding that the best strategy against insurgency was to provide welfare services, if the company had been founded on the premise that hospitals and schools should be set up at the same time that work started on the steel plant, why had they not built a cancer hospital in Chhattisgarh, I muse. Or a well-run hospital for general medical services? Or even a school, or a vocational training centre?

In October 1923, speaking to shareholders at a time of great struggle, R.D. Tata, director of the company and a first cousin of Jamshed Tata's, said, 'We are asked why it is necessary to spend so much on housing, sanitation, roads and on welfare... Gentlemen, people who are asking these questions are sadly lacking in imagination. We are not putting up a row of workmen's huts in Jamshedpur; we are building a city.' Later, urging shareholders to forego dividends, he would declare, 'We are like men building a wall against the sea. It would be the height of folly on our part to give away any part of the cement that is required to make the wall secure for all time.'[12]

From 2005–2007, before the onset of the global financial crisis, what had diverted the attention of a far more financially secure company than its 1923 forbear from its Chhatisgarh project? Was its preoccupation with the Corus acquisition or its chagrin over the Kalinganagar incident responsible? Was the

---

[12]Lala, Russi M., *The Creation of Wealth: The Tatas from the 19th to the 21st Century*, Penguin Books India, 2006.

company's failure in Chhattisgarh an outcome of internecine conflicts within the organization itself? Was its lack of focus on community development a result of the assumption that Mahendra Karma's Salwa Judum would pave the way for the Chhattisgarh project, making social spending unnecessary?

During our interaction, Irani says that he cannot explain what happened, since he was not involved with operations. The only point he does concede is that the Tatas had failed to understand that their reputation in Jamshedpur would need to be re-established in a greenfield project far away.

Despite Chhattisgarh seemingly falling off the Tata Steel radar, the MOU with the state government was periodically renewed. The fourth and last renewal took place in 2012. It prompted another PIL by the indefatigable Sudip Shrivastava, who objected to the fact that public resources were being locked up by a company which apparently had no intention of getting down to business and was using the Maoist threat, instead, as a lame excuse for its inaction.

I had not expected to get much 'dope' from Irani and, predictably, he does not, on the whole, deviate from the 'party line'. As our conversation is drawing to a close, however, he offers me an important lead. In response to my request for details about the Tata organization in Chhattisgarh, he reveals that the Tatas carried out their mining activities in the state through a contractor.

'He worked with us for a few years,' says Irani, 'and then left to start his own firm.'

Immediately, my ears prick up. Despite his earlier statements, I have not been able to quell my suspicions about the outsourcing by corporates of unsavoury work through the hiring of shrewdly chosen contractors, consultants, vendors and agents.

'Can I have his number, please?' I ask.

'Certainly,' he replies, seeing me off with a gracious request to convey his greetings to my father, a former colleague. 'I will sms it to you.'

But despite that promise and a subsequent reminder from me, that sms does not come.

4

The Death of Mahendra Karma

R.N. Singh's account is interesting for a number of reasons, not least for his run-in with Mahendra Karma, sometimes referred to as the 'Bastar Tiger'. His life and death are symptomatic of so much that transpires in Chhattisgarh that it would be remiss of me not to share the story of his meteoric rise and violent end.

He was the son of Bodda Manjhi and grandson of Maasa Manjhi, both tribal chieftains and landlords. His political career began when he was elected as an MLA on the CPI ticket in 1978. As a young legislator, he exhibited such a violent temper that he often had to be forcibly carried out in the middle of his speeches in the Assembly. In 1981, chafing at the restrictions imposed on him by his party bosses (even his MLA stipend had to be shared with the party) and stung by the denial of a ticket, he joined the Congress. Henceforth, he would not change parties. Instead, he would transcend party affiliations, uniting various stakeholders committed to the use of Chhattisgarh's mineral resources by corporate interests.

His relationship with the Maoists spanned the entire spectrum – from closeness in the early days to wariness when they turned against the landlords, from a subsequent attempt at reconciliation on his part to full-blown war. From his first attempt to rally the people against the Maoists in the Jan Jagran Abhiyan of 1991 till his death in a spectacular ambush in 2013, Karma was regarded by the Maoists as their prime enemy.

Their list of complaints was long. It comprised his repeated attempts to appropriate forest wealth by spurious means and – once he had discovered that the Maoists constituted a serious threat to his plundering ways – his unceasing efforts to turn the locals against them.

What deepened the Maoists' hatred for him were the two Jan Jagran Abhiyans of 1991 and 1996 and the Malik Makbuja scam in which Karma would make a financial killing by passing off the land to which fifty-six villages had natural rights as privately owned terrain, acquiring it on the cheap and selling off the timber from the trees growing on it. As industries and commerce minister in Ajit Jogi's government from 2000 to 2004, Karma is alleged to have assisted Romelt and National Mineral Development Corporation in forcibly acquiring land in Nagarnar by registering false cases against the villagers who had natural rights to it and using physical violence to subdue them when they protested against their displacement. To date, the Maoists allege that these villagers have received neither compensation nor employment in lieu of the land they were forced to surrender.

After the Maoists acquired power in Bastar in the years following the second Jan Jagran Abhiyaan, they would kill Karma's brother, Podiyaram, and some of his close relatives.

In the early years of the new millennium, in 2005, shortly after companies like the Tatas and Essar showed a keen interest in setting up projects in Chhattisgarh. Karma masterminded a vigilante movement against the Maoists, which he dubbed the 'Salwa Judum'. He claimed that the name meant 'peace march', but the more appropriate translation, according to his opponents, was 'purification hunt'.

As recounted by SP Dash of Kanker, the origins of the Salwa Judum lay in an incident dating back to 2005, when the police picked up three villagers from Kutru village in Bijapur district on suspicion of being Maoists. A group of fellow villagers subsequently turned up at the police station and informed the police that they had arrested the wrong people. Tired of living under the shadow of the Maoists, these locals promised to identify the real Maoists in the village and form a counter-insurgency group consisting of recruits from among themselves. It would be a citizens' force, as it were, challenging the rebels' reign of terror and coercion.

But as was later established from a Supreme Court judgement and a Citizens' Report, the Salwa Judum turned out to be a largely pseudo-vigilante movement funded by the government and orchestrated by Mahendra Karma. An alliance of citizens, the Danteshwari Samanvaya Samiti, had indeed been formed in 2003, allegedly with the blessings of the Shivanand Ashram in Raipur, to counter Maoist influence. It had spread to about 100 villages in Bastar. But the citizens' movement acquired scale and significance only when Karma convinced the state government to actively militarize the citizen groups, and hire members of the local population as SPOs, catering to their desire for government jobs. This force would form the front of the war against Left-wing extremism. In the period from 2005 to 2010, close to 5,000 SPOs were appointed.

Word goes that there was perfect concord between Karma and Chief Minister Raman Singh. The force's prime leaders – Karma's family members – had also cornered most of the important positions in the block and village administrations.

Karma was alleged to have received hefty commissions from his corporate clients.

From roughly June 2005 onwards, meetings began to be called in different villages to mobilize people against the Maoists. These so-called 'meetings' consisted of Salwa Judum activists and SPOs, in conjunction with the security forces, going from village to village, threatening to burn down people's houses if they did not join the movement and then acting upon this threat if the locals did not comply with their demands. The Maoists released a list of ninety-one villages where the Salwa Judum had made good their promise by burning down 1,857 houses. This estimate was later revised and it was stated that over 3,000 houses had been razed to the ground, affecting more than 500 villages. The people evicted from their villages were bundled into roadside camps. This tactic of 'clear [the land of people] and hold' was first used by the British in Malaysia and later by the US during the Korean and Vietnam wars (under the name of 'strategic hamleting'). Thus, in the war against its own people, the Indian government was following in the time-honoured footsteps of colonialists of various hues.

Villagers suspected of being pro-Maoist were killed outright. In the process, many innocents lost their lives. In retaliation, the Maoists carried out strikes against camps, initially targeting the Salwa Judum's prime movers and later resorting to large-scale 'counter-terror' strategies. Estimates of the death toll from such violence vary between 500 and 1,000.[13]

Extreme violence perpetrated by the Salwa Judum against women, including gang rapes, maiming and beatings, was reported. The Maoists released a list of thirty-one women who were allegedly victims of gang rape and other atrocities carried

[13]Guha, Ramachandra, et al, 'Salwa Judum: War in the Heart of India: Excerpts from the Report by the Independent Citizens' Initiative', *Social Scientist* (2006): 47-61.

out by the police, the security forces and the Salwa Judum and claimed that hundreds of other women had been brutalized in this manner. The government refused to acknowledge that such violence was actually being perpetrated against women. Five hundred ongoing cases of murder, 99 cases of rape and 103 cases of arson merely hint at the extent of the actual destruction that must have taken place on the ground.[14]

Approximately 46,000 villagers were moved to camps set up along the main road to hold internally displaced persons. The majority was either forcibly brought there or fled their native villages simply to pre-empt attacks by the Salwa Judum. Unable to bear the situation, some villagers emigrated to neighbouring states. The total number of displaced has been listed by the Maoists as 200,000. The possible motivation behind such mass displacement is captured in the following comment posted on a website: 'It appears as if the real aim of the movement is to clear villages of their inhabitants to remove any remaining shred of resistance to the mineral exploitation of the region.'

Mahendra Karma, for his part, seems to have harboured a fair amount of contempt for his tribal brethren. When the Citizens' Initiative asked him about fair compensation for the tribals, he is reported to have said, 'Since the tribals will consume any compensation they are given, they should be given work in ancillary industries. Instead of tractors, use them [the tribals] for land levelling.'[15]

---

[14]http://bannedthought.net/India/CPI-Maoist-Docs/Statements-2013/130526-DK-OnMahendraKarmaAnnihilation-Hin-corrected.pdf

[15]Independent Citizens' Initiative, 'War in the heart of India: An enquiry into the ground situation in Dantewara District, Chhattisgarh', 2006. Accessed at http://www.rightsandresources.org/wp-content/exported-pdf/warintheheartofindia.pdf

When I speak to SP Dash, he defends the decision to use ordinary citizens as de facto members of the police force. 'The Police Act of 1861 gives us this right,' he declares.

The Citizens' Report on the Salwa Judum took a different position, however: 'Under the Chhattisgarh Police Regulations, SPOs (appointed under sections 17, 18, 19 of the Police Act 1861) are meant to be recruited in special situations...they are not meant to counter a long-term problem like guerilla warfare. The SPOs are meant to be people of standing in the area who can ensure peace, not minors and certainly not lumpen elements with allegedly criminal pasts. On the ground, it is difficult to distinguish an SPO from an ordinary villager, leading to an absolutely seamless merging of illegal and legal authority.'

In a clear departure from SP Dash's stance, the Supreme Court, in its judgement of 5 July 2011[16] on a case against the state of Chhattisgarh brought by Delhi University professor and activist Nandini Sundar and others, rejected the state's claim that it had a 'constitutional sanction to perpetrate, indefinitely, a regime of gross violation of human rights...the power to arm, with guns, thousands of mostly illiterate or barely literate young men of the tribal tracts, who are appointed as temporary police officers, with little or no training...to fight the battles against alleged Maoist extremists.'

The court judgement pointed out that by handing over firearms to such poorly trained and barely educated youth, the state was opening a veritable Pandora's box, with the prospect of groups of armed men using weapons for their own sustenance and endangering society in the future.

When I ask SP Dash about the SPOs, he replies, 'The Supreme Court judgement was a blessing in disguise. The SPOs had done their work. They helped us identify [the] Maoists. Now

---

[16]http://indiankanoon.org/doc/920448/

we don't want untrained SPOs, but trained forces. Recruitment has gone up rapidly.'

The swelling ranks of SPOs were matched by a surge in the number of Maoist cadres, as hapless adivasis, unjustly accused of being Maoists and facing reprisal from the authorities in one form or the other, literally fled into the arms of the rebels. In response, the United Progressive Alliance (UPA) government at the Centre, led by the Congress, launched Operation Green Hunt in 2009. The central forces were believed to be assisted by special forces from the American army. Conservative reports say that close to 100,000 forces from the CRPF, BSF, ITBP and the CoBRA were deployed. According to an analysis of the news reports by the South Asia Terrorism Portal, 1238 Maoists, 1818 civilians, and 1076 armed forces' personnel have lost their lives in the battle since 2009.[17] Some top leaders of the Maoists, including Cherukuri Rajkumar, alias Azad, and Kishanji, have been killed, while others like Kobad Ghandy have been imprisoned.

In 2010, a CRPF battalion, out on a three-day combing mission in the Dantewada district, was ambushed near a village called Tadmetla. Seventy-six jawans were killed. Apparently, they had been lured into a spot that was perfect for an ambush, being vulnerable to attack from four directions. The complicity of local villagers was suspected.

The Peoples' Union for Civil Liberties reports that a year later, in what appears to have been a revenge attack, a 300-strong contingent of Koya commandos and CRPF personnel attacked Tadmetla and the adjoining villages of Morpalli, Timarpuram

---

[17]http://www.satp.org/satporgtp/countries/india/database/indiafatalities.htm

and Pulanpad, setting fire to 300 homes and granaries, killing two villagers, raping three women and beating and looting at random.[18] Several villagers went missing and were believed to be in police custody. Some who had tried fleeing into the neighbouring forest starved to death. Locals identified some of the boys from their own villages as part of the operation, for which they had been deployed in the role of SPOs.

The government tried to pass off the attack as a Maoist operation. The allegation, when I come to know of it, brings to my mind the story I had heard in the village of Chahchaad, where a village ruffian would get away with his heavy-handed bullying by pretending to be a Maoist. It appears that all kinds of people find it opportune to masquerade as the Red revolutionaries, their victims being, in most cases, innocent villagers.

The excesses of the village lout in Chahchaad had come to an end when the Maoists roundly thrashed him. The crimes of the Indian forces, on the other hand, abated when civil society took swift action and the Supreme Court ordered an inquiry based on the plea brought by Nandini Sundar and others.

In November 2015, four years after the inquiry had been ordered, members of a team from the Central Bureau of Investigation (CBI) deputed on the case informed the Supreme Court that they were walking a thin line between life and death in their investigation. They could not access the concerned villages without nearly 300 locals accompanying them, some out of idle curiosity, some to facilitate a genuine investigation, and some to keep the investigators honest. To avoid this situation, they began urging people to go to a central location to depose, but no one ever showed up.[19]

---

[18]http://www.pucl.org/bulletins/2011/PUCLJun11.pdf

[19]http://www.thehindu.com/news/national/naxal-threat-hampers-cbi-probe-into-dantewada-violence/article7924989.ece

In an affidavit filed before the Supreme Court in December 2015, the CBI alleged that the Chhattisgarh police was thwarting its probe into key cases in Maoist-hit areas. It cited instances when state police personnel had assaulted its team. The state's response was to refute the allegations.[20]

The Maoists never forgave Karma for organizing the Salwa Judum. Retribution was carefully planned.

It was 2013. A couple of years had passed since the Supreme Court verdict against the 'vigilante' force. In preparation for the Assembly polls, the ruling party of Chhattisgarh, the BJP and the opposition, the Congress Party, had launched yatras through the state. The Maoists warned that they would target both yatras.

In their press release claiming full responsibility, the Maoists identified, apart from Karma's misdeeds, the following incidents as having provoked the reprisals. According to the authorities, on May Day 2013, Maoists Phool Singh and Jai Singh from Madohanar village were killed in an encounter. The Maoists claim, however, that the two innocent tribals were picked up from the village, brought to the police station, dressed up in fatigues and shot dead. On 17 May 2013, eight tribals, including three children, were killed in Edsametta village of Bijapur district. Even before that, on the night of 28 June 2012, seventeen adivasis had been slaughtered in Sarkinguda village and thirteen of their women gang-raped.

On 7 May 2013, the insurgents targeted the BJP's Vikas Yatra without being able to inflict serious damage on its participants. Four or five days before 25 May, a date chosen by the Congress for their Parivartan Yatra in Chhattisgarh, the Maoist forces

---

[20] http://indianexpress.com/article/india/india-news-india/chhattisgarh-police-thwarting-probe-into-key-cases-cbi-tells-sc/

set up camp near two potential ambush points – Jiram Ghati in Sukma district, a valley located between the villages of Darbha and Tongpal, and a smaller valley before Nakulnar village. Their presence could not have been a secret to anyone. But two major events conspired to divert attention from their activities – a rally in Bijapur, held by the chief minister on 26 May, for which 2,500 security forces had been deployed, and a rally organized by the Maoists themselves on 25 and 26 May to protest against the operation carried out by security forces on 17 May during which eight tribals had been killed.

On 25 May, a Congress convoy that included, besides Karma, highly respected adivasi leader Kawasi Lakma, the veteran politician V.C. Shukla, and the state Congress chief Nand Kumar Patel was returning to Jagdalpur from a meeting in Sukma. When the convoy reached the deeply forested area of Jiram Ghati on the Jagdalpur–Sukma Highway, 50 km from its destination, it found the road blocked by trees that had been felled by the Maoists for this very purpose. The insurgents detonated an explosive near the fourth vehicle in the convoy, severely damaging it and leaving a five-metre-wide crater in the ground.

As the other vehicles in the convoy slowed down, around 250 Maoists, who had been hiding in the upper reaches of the adjoining Jiram hills, opened fire from the right. The convoy's security guards took up positions to the left of the damaged car and returned fire. The gun battle continued for nearly two hours. The rebels waited for the guards to run out of ammunition before ordering the Congress leaders to surrender.

Suddenly, a shout of exhilaration went up: 'Mahendra Karma *mil gaya*! Mahendra Karma *mil gaya*!' The insurgents had spotted Karma.

Now the Maoists trained their fire on his car. With Karma's security guards hard-pressed to respond on account of a lack of ammunition, he surrendered.

With his hands raised in the classic gesture of capitulation,[21] he climbed slowly to the top of the hill, where he knew certain death awaited him.

There was a sense of disbelief in the air. As evident from the press release issued by the Maoists after the ambush,[22] for years – they had dreamt of this moment. In their minds, they had built up an image of Karma as 'an inhuman killer, rapist, dacoit and a loyal broker of the big capitalists'. Their hatred for him must have been the fuel that carried them through days and nights of tortuous marches in leech-infested forest, through weeks and months of a life on the run. One day, they had promised themselves, they would finally get him. The masses eventually managed to exact revenge on their oppressors, they declared in the communiqué issued after his death.[23] 'In world history, Hitler and Mussolini were in the same pride that no one could beat them. In the contemporary history of our country, the fascists like Indira Gandhi and Rajiv Gandhi also were victims of similar misgivings. But the People are invincible. People only are the creators of the history. Ultimately, these handful exploiters and their pet dogs will only be thrown in the dustbin of the history.' While the declarations were emphatic, in tough times the rebels must have harboured their doubts. And yet on a clear May morning, when the promise of spring was giving

[21]The reconstruction of the ambush on Mahendra Karma and of his eventual demise is based on conversations with Kamal Shukla, reports on the events and the condition of Mahendra Karma's corpse in the local and national press, and on the press release issued by the Maoists after the ambush.

[22]http://bannedthought.net/India/CPI-Maoist-Docs/Statements-2013/130526-DK-OnMahendraKarmaAnnihilation-Eng-corrected.pdf

[23]http://bannedthought.net/India/CPI-Maoist-Docs/Statements-2013/130526-DK-OnMahendraKarmaAnnihilation-Eng-corrected.pdf

way to the burning hot sands of summer, that perfect moment had presented itself.

The leader of the Maoist squad sized up Karma.[24] Perhaps he thought of the 'attacks (led by Karma) on several villages in the name of conducting meetings and marches, the women (who) were raped by the goons with (his) direct instigation, incidents in which people were brutally cut into pieces before being dumped in rivers…'The names of destroyed villages listed like a roll call of hate in the Maoist communique may have played on his mind: 'Cherli, Kotrapal, Mankeli, Karremarka, Mosla, Munder, Padeda, Paralnar, Pumbad, Gaganpalli…'

One night imagine how his exhilaration gave way to hatred; the bile as it rose up within him, forming a hard knot that made his body taut, like the fingers on a trigger about to be pulled. In his mind, he may have seen the faces of his wife, his mother, his son, his brother… And then he noticed that Karma was no longer upright. While engaged in a re-run of his nightmares, he had bludgeoned Karma, striking him with his rifle butt – once, twice, thrice – on the head, the neck, the back, the knees. He noticed, as he came out of his daze, that his comrades had joined in the act; they were driving their knives deep into the prone Karma.

Their victim's screams died away after the first few blows. A gentle rain of spittle spattered his unconscious body, as the Maoists showered abuse on him. Suddenly, as the team was unveiling its blood lust, layer by layer, a guerilla, unable to hold back, pressed the trigger.

[24]The attack was believed to have been made by Maoist Platoon 26 of the Darbha Divisional Committee and led by Dandakaranya Special Zonal Committee member Paka Hanumanthu, http://www.uniindia.com/jiram-ghati-massacre-accused-held/states/news/292991.html, http://archives.deccanchronicle.com/130527/news-current-affairs/article/maoists-danced-over-mahendra-karmas-body-andhra-pradesh-group

The others realized almost with a sense of disappointment that the orgy of violence was coming to a close. Eager to make the most of their ebbing rage, they started emptying bullets into Karma. This they had planned many times. Their bullets would form a necklace around their dead tormentor, creating a halo of blood around his head. As they pressed their triggers, they hailed their movement with cries of 'Lal salaam! Lal salaam!'

The convoy at the foot of the hill watched the fate befalling their compatriot with a sense of dazed disbelief. Kawasi Lakma's eyes skimmed over the faces of the assailants to see if there were any he could recognize.

The sound of gunshots died away. Karma had been reduced to a mangled, bleeding mass of flesh. The Maoists wiped bits of his entrails off their uniforms. Then the party of rebels mounted his corpse and started jumping on it, shouting, 'Mahendra Karma, murdabad!' all the while.

Later, an autopsy would reveal seventy-eight stab wounds on his body and a string of bullet marks in a necklace formation. The Maoists had returned the Bastar Tiger in a state defying recognition: a battered shell of a human being, with knees shattered, ribs smashed in, guts wrenched out, eyeballs popping. The rebels would later claim that following the elimination of their class enemy non-pareil, a current of joy had passed through the oppressed villages of Bastar.

V.C. Shukla, who was waiting with other members of the convoy, had, by this time, sustained three bullet wounds.

The son of the former chief minister of Madhya Pradesh, Pandit Ravi Shankar Shukla, he was a strikingly good-looking man, known for his aristocratic ways and roving eye. During the twenty-one-month Emergency imposed on the country from June 1975 onwards by the then prime minister, Indira Gandhi, Shukla had served as the minister for information and broadcasting, exercising a cruel tyranny on both print and electronic media. The pattern of his later migrations to the Janata parivar and back to the Congress gives us cause to say his politics was characterized by an insatiable craving for power. A bystander may be accused of thinking that his family looked upon Madhya Pradesh as their personal fiefdom. While V.C. Shukla received the Centre in the division of the family assets, state politics had fallen into the kitty of the other members of the family. His older brother had been a three-time chief minister of the state. At eighty-four, Shukla had decided to throw his hat in the ring once again, not realizing that he was surrounded by enemies both from within his party and without.

His bête noir in the party, Ajit Jogi, symbolizes that breed of politicians who hail from very humble backgrounds and milk their modest origins to make disproportionate personal gains. Jogi had managed to gain a foothold in the IAS under the Other Backward Classes (OBC) quota, a step which would, subsequently, be challenged and proved questionable. He then resigned from the IAS and, in no time, became a very wealthy politician. Now Shukla, a pirate of the old school with a certain old-world courtesy to boot, had decided to take on Jogi, the new-age buccaneer. Had it not been for Shukla's advanced years, it could have been a stirring contest.

As V.C. Shukla lay grievously wounded in the Jiram Ghati ambush, perhaps unaware that he may have been caught in the cross-fire between the Maoists and his own security personnel, a couple of Maoist fighters went down to his car and carried out simple first-aid procedures on him. By this time, his bodyguard

Prafulla Shukla had shot himself with his last remaining bullet, after apologizing to the former Union minister for failing to provide him with the necessary protection. V.C. Shukla had to wait for seven hours before he was rescued and died of his wounds in a Gurgaon hospital in June 2013.

Nand Kumar Patel and his son Dinesh were singled out from a group abducted from the convoy by the Maoists earlier that day. A day later, their bodies would be found with axe injuries and knife and bullet wounds.

V.C. Shukla and Nandkumar Patel, and certainly Patel's son, were not direct targets of the Maoists, as they were not personally involved in Salwa Judum. The Maoists released a press statement specifically on V.C. Shukla's killing.[25] The statement, long-winded, somewhat lame, ended up saying that people like Shukla and Patel had blood on their hands because Karma's actions were carried out with the full backing of both the Congress and the BJP. So all members of these parties were, in this sense, culpable, although some members of the Congress contingent, including a prominent adivasi leader, Kawasi Lakma, were spared. The statement apologized for the unnecessary deaths resulting from the ambush, probably referring to the killing of the security detail of the leaders.

In all, 27 people died in that ambush. Thirty were injured. A large stash of arms and ammunition was looted.

It was not until 9 p.m., seven hours after the shooting had begun, that the Indian security forces reached the spot. Had they arrived earlier, a few casualties could have been averted. Even though ground forces would have been handicapped in the *ghati* (valley), the presence of a helicopter hovering overhead could

---

[25]http://bannedthought.net/India/CPI-Maoist-Docs/Statements-2013/130611-DK-OnVCShukla'sDeath-Hin.pdf

have scared away the ambush party, which seemed to have all the time in the world to carry out its operations.

On 22 January 2015, Mahendra Karma's younger son Chhavindra and family members of others killed in the Jiram Ghati attack met Chief Minister Raman Singh and demanded that the probe be handed over to the CBI, as the National Investigation Agency had neglected some basic angles in the case.[26]

In India, everything is invariably traced back to a conspiracy theory. In Chhattisgarh, in particular, where everything is, indeed, a conspiracy and not just in theory, all theories could turn out to be true, even those contradicting each other. However, certain questions beg answers: How did the police fail to notice the build-up of Maoist forces in Jiram Ghati that lay on the very route of the Congress's Parivartan Yatra? Did the decimation of the Chhattisgarh Congress and his own former industries minister yield any positive pay-off for Ajit Jogi? Could the BJP government have done more to safeguard their political opponents? These questions, like many others, disappear, unresolved, into the cavernous recesses of time only to resurface in new forms with new clues for old, once-forgotten issues now healed of the burning sting of emotion.

As testified by the activities of the Salwa Judum, the cult of violence openly espoused by the Maoists (even though they are at pains to distinguish between 'necessary' and 'unnecessary' acts of violence), is freely promoted by the government as well.

Respected public commentator and intellectual K. Balagopal has pointed out that while the state did much to fuel the Salwa

[26]http://www.thehindu.com/news/national/other-states/cbi-probe-demanded/article6809067.ece

Judum mess, missteps by the Maoists had also significantly contributed to it. In other words, the prevailing angst was not entirely state-manufactured. The brutal reprisals against alleged informers, the rejection of development schemes from the state, the failure to distinguish between power-drunk goons and politically aware revolutionaries and the indiscriminate violence against 'class enemies' had played a significant role.[27]

Long-time observers have mentioned the proclivity of the Maoist high command to back violent and regressive movements like those led by the Taliban, the Islamic fundamentalist group that has its base in Afghanistan, the ethno-nationalist ULFA in Assam and the Al-Qaeda. The rationale seems to be that they too are 'fighting state-sponsored oppression'.

The Maoists are also believed to have entered into an alliance with Chief Minister Mamata Banerjee's Trinamool Congress in West Bengal to counter the CPI (M) gangsters in Nandigram. Critics have identified this short-term opportunism and the focus on violence, to the exclusion of other modes of protest within the democratic framework, as a major reason for the erosion of ideological commitment in the Maoist cadres and their degeneration into roving gangs of 'paranoid, revengeful killers'.[28]

Criticism of the use of excessive violence comes from within the Maoist ranks as well.

Shortly after the Jiram Ghati ambush, the chief spokesperson

[27]Balagopal, K., 'Physiognomy of Violence', *Economic and Political Weekly*: 2183-2186, 2006.

[28]Banerjee, Sumanta, 'Critiquing the Programme of Action of the Maoists', *Economic and Political Weekly*, Vol. 44, No. 46, pp. 75-77, November 14-20, 2009.

of the Maoists, G.V.K. Prasad, who, in his role as the Maoists' chief spokesman, had issued an eloquent defence of the attack, surrendered to the police along with his live-in partner Santoshi Markam, also a Maoist. His legally wedded spouse Raje, from his second marriage, continues to be a part of the Maoist movement.

The text of Maoist despatches issued during Prasad's time reveals his fine grasp of Hindi, even though it was not his mother tongue, and his penchant for a cocky turn of phrase. He affirms, for instance, that the public will always annihilate their oppressors, despite the latter fancying themselves as '*tees mar khans*', an Urdu expression describing a person who moves with the swagger of one with thirty murders to his credit. While even Prasad was not above stooping to the usual brand of name-calling – referring to his enemies as 'pet dogs of capitalist forces' – he knew how to include key elements of Maoist doctrine into his missives. All in all, he was a class act, a man who could well have been an ace feature writer for a prominent national daily or a skilled, though polemical, poet, were he not committed to his role in the ranks of the Maoists.

During his twenty-year stint with the insurgents, his talents and natural inclinations had drawn him further and further away from actual combat. He was indispensable, both as an ideologue and as a teacher, introducing new recruits to the finer points of Marxist theory. His facility with languages was legendary.

His first wife, whom he had met at college, would die in action. A few years later, he married Raje who, like him, was educated and not a tribal. She was a member of a Maoist battalion. It was in the nature of things that they would live apart for long periods of time. Eventually, they drifted apart.

The story goes that Prasad first met Santoshi when he was training new recruits in the politics of world affairs. I could well imagine that for his sophisticated and often tortured mind, her earthiness and lack of guile offered a promise of tranquillity he could not escape.

But the exhilaration of his new-found love was short-lived. Operation Green Hunt, the government's military offensive against the insurgents, was, by then, in full cry and there were communiqués to draft. The police had occupied school buildings in the summer holidays, prompting the Maoists to blow them up. This deeply pained Prasad who venerated, above all else, the written word. The police had also stepped up its recruitment of informers, resulting in brutal reprisals by the Maoists against those they suspected to be guilty of such collaboration. The concern that innocent villagers might have been targeted in the process haunted Prasad, although in public he stoutly defended the need for punitive action against informers.

From the little I learnt about him, I can visualize this man camped out in remote terrain, his hidden world one of slow-moving streams and fields of grain, their stalks nodding in the breeze. I can imagine him lying under a star-studded sky on a night silvery with moonlight, sharing with his beloved a rare moment of privacy, precious and elusive, when one is part of a tight-knit community that is bound by joint initiatives rather than individual decisions, by a shared ideology and the ever-present threat of danger and death. And I can see him wondering if the beauty he sensed in that moment was a mere illusion. For crowding upon it would be the grim reality of his existence, the constant subterfuge and fear, the denunciation of enemies and perceived traitors, the cold-blooded killing of fellow human beings and the elaborate justification that would follow, the guilt engendered by innocent lives lost through error and misplaced suspicion…

Everyone did not have to be a Che Guevara, he could well have told himself. Prasad had venerated the legendary Cuban revolutionary since his college days. But now he may have been more inspired by the example of the Nobel Prize-winning Chilean Pablo Neruda – also a revolutionary, but one who attended state dinners and was fêted by the rich and powerful. Maybe there was another way for him too?

Besides, his own health and that of Santoshi had become a cause for concern. He was racked with chronic lower-back pain and Santoshi had discovered during a clandestine visit to the doctor that she had a hole in her heart. Above all, Prasad was tired of his life as a fugitive in the forest. He longed for a life that was closer to normal, less removed from the mainstream and less racked with the ethical dilemmas that beset him now.

When he surrendered, the Maoists promptly issued a detailed denunciation, condemning Prasad as a morally flawed person. They claimed that the reward of ₹20 lakhs, along with the prospect of a better life shared with his new love, was the real reason for his surrender.

Che once said, 'At the risk of sounding ridiculous, let me say that the true revolutionary is guided by feelings of love.' It would seem, at least if the Maoists are to be believed, that Prasad's love for Santoshi left no room in his heart to love the cause he had once so eloquently defended.

5

From Beijing to Bastar

I reach Jamshedpur as a hailstorm rages, at the fag end of an unseasonably pleasant April in 2015. The township is a bustling metropolis and home to 1.3 million people, only 26,000 of whom work in Tata Steel.[29] People from all over the country come here to seek employment. Adivasis constitute 28 per cent of the population, and a significantly smaller percentage of the Tata Steel workforce.

I am struck by the town's charm, especially the area that houses the Tata Steel buildings. Offices, either single or double-storeyed and made of old-fashioned cement, gleam a brilliant white in the moist sunlight of eastern India. Avenues are broad and lined with trees, of which one becomes a particular favourite of mine; it bears tiny yellow flowers which carpet the pavements below with its petals. The place abounds in parks, although some are not accessible for a snooze or a stroll.

I check into the comfortable Tata Steel guest house. The aura of noblesse oblige is everywhere – in the paintings of rickshaw pullers wearily lugging their burdens, the busts of tribal heroes, the displays of hard hats. Also manifest is the pride in industrialization – minimalist paintings of factories, where plumes of smoke float over tall chimneys arranged in geometrical precision, and the portrait of a beautiful woman, the wife of one of the founders, basking, it seems, in the aura of privilege her husband's stature as a captain of industry bestows on her. The waiters speak English. Their complacent smiles tell you they are a satisfied lot and their faintly supercilious air can make a guest conscious of his Ps and Qs.

JSR, as insiders refer to their city, was built over an area surrounding the village of Kalimati. That vast expanse of land once accommodated a hundred villages, all set in the midst of verdant forest. Today, the tribals from those villages, as well as the forests, are scarce.

[29] https://en.wikipedia.org/wiki/Economy_of_Jamshedpur

'People ask me what happened to the tribals who had occupied the 140 sq km over which Jamshedpur is spread,' says Biren Bhuta, head of the Tata Steel Rural Development Society, over a hearty breakfast in the guest house's dining hall. 'I really don't have an answer.'

An engineering graduate and an MBA, Bhuta left a job in banking to become a TV reporter for business news, but eventually moved from reportage to join the social sector. He chose 'Bastar over Beijing', he says, when he gave up a China posting with the *Indian Express* to work as a consultant for the Tatas in Bastar. In 2010, he joined the Tatas as a full-time employee.

Bhuta's experience in struggling with uncomfortable questions about the tribals would seem intriguing in light of the Tatas' welfare activities in the area. However, the hint of condescension in the company's earlier attitude to the adivasis may be only slightly exaggerated by the following extract from the famous book by R.M. Lala on the Tatas. Lala writes of the early years of Jamshedpur: 'Though the Maharaja of Mayurbhanj had given highly favourable terms to the Tatas, the local "kings" of the jungle were less hospitable. Tigers killed two tribal labourers.'[30] It is clear that in this case, the kings of the jungle were wild beasts, while the tribals, traditional forest dwellers now reduced to working as wage labourers, were their unfortunate victims. Whether intentionally ironic or unintentionally patronizing, the account seems to offer a foretaste of things that were to come for the adivasis.

In contrast, Verrier Elwin, who had lived among the tribals for over thirty years, regarded the adivasis as members of a regal martial race, adept in the ways of the forest and most suited to

[30]Lala, Russi M., *The Creation of Wealth: The Tatas from the 19th to the 21st Century*, Penguin Books India, 2006.

living in harmony with its myriad creatures. One of the many features of their society that he admired was the position of women. Of the Gond woman, he writes, 'Her free and open life fills her mind with poetry and sharpens her tongue with wit. As a companion, she is humorous and interesting.'[31] Elwin's views may well have been influenced, however, by his own marriage to a Gond woman.

On the one hand, the Tatas must have pitied the tribals for their precarious existence. On the other, they discounted the adivasis' distress over their forced displacement, because to an organization run by individuals with an urban perspective, their day-to-day lives seemed worth so little. This attitude, typical of a modernist mindset that is unable to appreciate modes of life different from its own, has been responsible for much of the misery suffered by tribal populations.

Today, however, the stated position of Tata Steel's CSR department appears to be closer to Verrier Elwin's than to that of its own founding fathers. The episode in Kalinganagar that Dr Irani refers to as a 'minor skirmish' in my meeting with him seems to have played an important role in changing attitudes.

Tata Steel's proposed steel plant at Kalinganagar had come up against strong opposition from the local population, which put forth a number of demands, including recognition of the customary rights of farmers settled on government land, higher compensation, provision of jobs in upcoming industries and involvement of a local organization, the Visthapan Virodhi Jan Manch, in deciding the provisions of resettlement.[32]

The situation reached a flashpoint on a particular occasion, when the company took the initiative of having the land allotted

---

[31]Elwin, Verrier, *The Aboriginals*, No. 14, H. Milford, Oxford University Press, 1943.

[32]http://www.pucl.org/Topics/Dalit-tribal/2006/kalinganagar.htm

to them for the project levelled. Arrangements had been made for significant police presence to deter anticipated opposition from the locals. A large contingent of armed adivasis also arrived at the site. Local resentment had been simmering for some time, for two previous attempts by Tata Steel to conduct a *bhoomi poojan* had been marred by vigorous protests. The latest incident that began with jostling and pushing escalated into a conflagration of violence in which the police opened fire on the locals, leading to the death of one policeman and fourteen tribals.

After the Kalinganagar incident, the Tatas reverted to some of the benevolent ways of their founders and commissioned the first phase of the plant in November 2015.

'Companies do not know how to talk to communities,' says Bhuta, 'and, more importantly, how to listen to them. They should talk directly, else middlemen come into picture.

'We have to recognize that land is a traumatic issue,' he declares emphatically. 'We should minimize land acquisition and [the] displacement [of locals] by better planning. We have to evolve a new definition of development. My definition of development is similar to that of the tribals – live off forests and natural resources, in harmony with nature. Tribals have a world view we can learn from.'

Bhuta had just come back from a conference of Tata executives in Mumbai, where he had addressed the CEOs of twenty-five Tata group companies and expressed such views. On his way back to Jamshedpur, he had thumbed a lift on the corporate jet of his MD, a fellow alumnus of IIM Kolkata.

'The Tata intent is genuine,' he insists, 'though our execution may falter.'

He tells me of being privy to a meeting of the CSR Advisory Committee to the board, headed by the Magsaysay Award-winner Deep Joshi, where a discussion on the tribals had been held for an hour and a quarter. In November 2014, Tata Steel organized a pan India tribal meet, where 1,500 people came from all over the country and abroad to discuss tribal medicine, their womens' issues, their livelihood and language. The organization is aiming to make it an annual feature.

'We need to listen more and bring people together,' says Bhuta.

'It is difficult for CSR to become a natural extension of the mining business, unlike in an FMCG company where, for instance, self-help groups can promote responsible saving as well as consumption behaviours. We recognize that we are in an extractive industry which has negative footprints,' he goes on. 'The negative footprint has to be converted into a positive handshake with the community, a social licence to operate, if you will.'

I learn that the Tatas have started a research project to study the geo-hydrological effects of mining in Joda in Odisha's Keonjhar district, where Tata Steel has a ferro alloys plant and a number of iron ore and manganese mines. In particular, they are keen on studying the difference in impact of iron ore and coal mining on the environment.

'We need to have a stable environment to grow, without [conditions of] widespread deprivation. Over and above that, we must be true to the Tata legacy of trusteeship. Politicians can speak against us for their own reasons, but we want the love of the people.'

A colleague of Bhuta's shares his CEO's dream with me: from a helicopter flying over Jamshedpur, one should be able to see scores of water bodies gleaming in the sunlight. Tata Steel is building ponds in and around the city – 300 in all. However, the case of the Dimna Lake shows that the Tatas will have to go beyond the mere creation of new water bodies to ensure their long-term sustainability. Located on the fringes of Jamshedpur between the Dalma range and the Sitarampur reservoir, Dimna was once a tourist attraction, but has now been reduced to a dumping ground for industrial waste and sewage.

Land for the lake was acquired by the Tatas in 1942 and the water body came into being three years later. Over the last few years, Tata Steel has been facing agitators demanding compensation for the land acquisition. The CSR wing managed to get hold of the land records which revealed that every bona fide claimant had already been paid compensation. They also discovered that the agitators were not the ones who had lost land. Choosing to ignore these persons, the company created a society of erstwhile land owners and entrusted them with the responsibility of cleaning the lake, paying each worker ₹120 per day for their labour.

While the agitators may have been mere opportunists trying to make a quick buck off someone else's trauma, one cannot deny the possibility of serious tension existing between the interests of those who have genuinely lost land and the members of the broader community adversely affected by a displacement episode through the loss of jobs or because of negative environmental impact.

In general, obtaining the consent of the locals before starting a project is often a process of playing off one group against another, co-opting leaders of different factions and severing the roots that keep common people attached to their milieu. For such reasons, a member of Bhuta's team admits, 'the fabric of communities is inevitably torn by the process of land acquisition'.

In any greenfield project, the Tata Steel Rural Development Society works with the broader community, while matters relating to the rehabilitation and resettlement (R&R) of those who have lost land are handled by the line manager in charge of setting up the operations of the steel plant and the mine.

While this official may succeed in persuading those who have lost land to accept the generous package on offer, it does not imply that the interests of all project-affected parties – sharecroppers, landless labourers and other landholders who stand to face deprivation in one form or another on account of environmental degradation, health hazards and loss of livelihood – will be fairly addressed. Perhaps, integrating the R&R and CSR functions could create the organizational structure necessary to consider the problems of the project-affected persons in a holistic way. If keeping the two departments segregated is necessary in view of the complex nature of the problem at hand, it is important that effective integration at a higher level is carried out to ensure an even-handed treatment of the community.[33]

Tata Steel makes a large number of contributions to the quality of life of people in and around Jamshedpur. The company is involved in family-planning interventions, AIDS prevention, making provisions for the supply of drinking water and improving maternal health care. On the issue of raising employability, they are partnering with Taj Hotels and the NGO Pratham to impart job skills for the hospitality sector. So integral are they to the life of the city that it is common knowledge that rentals shoot up in areas where utilities are provided by JUSCO, the municipal body controlled by the Tatas till a few years ago.

Commenting on Chhattisgarh, Bhuta says, 'Even though we have paid compensation for setting up the steel plant on land where

[33]Lawrence, Paul R., and Lorsch, Jay W., 'Differentiation and integration in complex organizations', *Administrative Science Quarterly* (1967): 1-47.

the locals had once grown crops, people continue to cultivate the land. We will take possession only when we are sure we are welcome and only after paying further compensation.

'Beyond a steel plant in Lohandiguda, an iron-ore mine in Dantewada and a two-acre plot for an office in Jagdalpur, we have no presence in Chhattisgarh. A hundred and five acres of revenue forest have been taken. Three sites before [we decided on] Lohandiguda were rejected, because they fell [within the] reserve forest.'

I observe that I have heard of the Tatas operating through a contractor in Chhattisgarh. Bhuta retorts that he has heard of no such thing.

I tell him that my investigations have yielded information of the Tatas' involvement in the mine at Rowghat.

'What is your source of information?' Bhuta's eyes have narrowed.

Unfortunately, the identity of my source has slipped my mind. I mumble something about the internet.

'There are a lot of rumours passing around,' says Biren, countering the allegation. 'We have no operations in Chhattisgarh as of now and, to the best of my knowledge, absolutely no involvement in Rowghat. The CSR team has started [its] activities in a small way.'

While the Tatas seem to be going slow today, they do have a history in Chhattisgarh. A despatch by Javed Iqbal in the *Indian Express*[34] describes a meeting called by the Collector, Fulsingh Netaam, in Lohandiguda in 2010 (before Bhuta joined the company), where the villagers vociferously opposed the project. It also alleges intimidation and the arrests of recalcitrant village leaders. Some villagers even claimed they were forced to sign

[34]http://www.newindianexpress.com/magazine/article206933.ece?service=print

blank sheets of paper. As per this version, the most effective tactic employed was the sowing of the seeds of distrust – turning family members against each other, one villager against another.

'Whoever took the Tatas' money should be thrown out of the villages,' an elder from Sirisguda, one of the affected villages, had said.

Yet many villagers surreptitiously withdrew the money that had been credited to their bank accounts, spent it and came back to join the movement.

'It's because of them that things are the way they are,' the elder would conclude.

One of Bhuta's most recent initiatives for adivasi youth in Dantewada, that aims to instil in them feelings of confidence and hope, has been to roll out in the form of three-day workshops the moral rearmament programme, a Gandhian movement based in Switzerland that inspires people to 'be the change they want to see in the world'.

Banking executive, born-again adivasi evangelist working in an extractive industry, Biren Bhuta hopes to fix the ills of mining from within. Such dreams serve as the foundations of an edifice meant to last an age or at least as a credo that lends meaning to an individual's life.

6

The Mysterious Contractor

While in Jamshedpur, I try to enquire about the company's elusive mining contractor in Chhattisgarh, referred to by both R.N. Singh and Jamshed Irani, but never named.

'Does Tata Steel operate through a mining contractor in Dantewada?' I ask Krishna Nandan who has taken over the Chhattisgarh project after R.N. Singh's departure.

Krishna Nandan, who has spent close to seven years in Jagdalpur, appears to search his mind for an answer. 'Yes, I think there is some company employed,' he finally concedes.

'What is the name of the company?' I ask.

'The name is eluding me,' he responds.

'Who is the promoter?'

'I don't know. Maybe some Agarwal.'

'Is it Mahesh Thakur,[35] by any chance?' I venture, having obtained his name from an independent source.

But Krishna Nandan expresses his inability to help me further.

In another meeting with a senior member of Tata Steel's marketing team, I broach the subject of the contractor.

'Mahesh Thakur!' the executive cuts me off heatedly. 'The less said about Mahesh Thakur, the better,' he continues. Then he checks himself and nips further reference to the topic in the bud. 'I have no comments. We don't get into politics.'

Given the general caginess about the contractor, it is obviously important for me to meet him. The only problem is that no one is willing to help me get through to him. After seven months of futile effort, through a chance encounter at a wedding in the family of someone who turns out to be a common acquaintance, I am able to get an introduction to Thakur.

'Dr Irani told me you would be looking for me,' he says when I call him up. The reader will remember that Dr Irani had informed me that the Tatas worked through a contractor in Chhattisgarh, a former employee of Tata Steel but had refrained from sharing his contact details with me.

---

[35]Name changed

And so I find myself sitting at the poolside of a plush Gurgaon club with Mahesh Thakur, a handsome man who resembles the actor Kabir Bedi, barring the full head of hair. Thakur is a consummate example of a man of the world, smooth and suave, but not one to suffer fools gladly. He has the air of a person at ease in the corridors of power, but also capable of the 'common touch'. A silk pocket square, along with a muffler that seems to have been carelessly thrown around his neck, suggests a man who takes pains with his appearance, even when it comes to his casual wear. Also with us is Ram Reddy, a tall, plain-speaking Telugu gentleman who is an associate of Thakur's.

Thakur's opening gambit is provocative. 'We can talk about the Tatas in Chhattisgarh, but first tell me: do you want to talk about it as a success or a failure?'

'A failure, of course,' I reply without hesitation. 'With no progress on the drilling in the mine site or [on] the development of the steel plant, what else could it be?'

Reddy refutes this vehemently.

'Our contract formally started in March 2009 and ran till February 2014. We were tasked with undertaking the survey of the mining area, road construction, drilling and obtaining approvals from the people for land acquisition for the steel plant. The official term used for the work I was asked to do was "Dissent Management"'.

'We got gram sabha approvals for five thousand acres of land in Lohandiguda, without a single person being slapped, abducted or killed. When another corporate tried to do the same, they suffered casualties. In our case, there was not a single shot fired. I am sure luck had some part to play. But whatever be the case, that was a success, not a failure.'

Thakur now intervenes. 'We built a twenty-seven kilometre road right up to the top of a hill on Bailadila, constructing nine bridges over nullahs, in an area where no government officer had set foot since 1961. That was a success, not a failure.

'We brought in our drilling machines thrice, put in sixty to seventy boreholes and, with great difficulty, under constant threat of getting killed, managed to drill down to a hundred metres. That was a success, not a failure.

'We managed to convince the local people that the Tatas were different from other corporates...they were the race horses in a field of donkeys. After much persuasion on our part, they developed the conviction that the Tatas were not there to take away their land, but to give them a better life. That was a measure of our success.'

I ask how they had managed to pull off their achievements. Thakur and Reddy explain that they had spoken to people at all levels – villagers, panchayat representatives, district officials, state-level leaders, national-level influencers and succeeded in getting everyone on board.

'I remember the first time I went to Bailadila,' says Reddy. 'I walked through five-foot-high grass, expecting a tiger to leap out at me any moment. For miles, there was no one in sight.'

'But we did not just restrict ourselves to the grassroots. We also held seminars at the India International Centre, the Institute for Studies in Industrial Development, and the Press Club of India, where all the top intellectuals participated,' Thakur adds. 'We had government officials, activists and Tata Steel people coming together on a single platform to thrash out a model of inclusive growth that would work for the adivasis.'

'Did you speak to the Maoists about this?' I ask him.

'No, but we spoke to highly regarded intellectuals, some of whom we thought might have the ear of the insurgents. We contacted everyone we thought might have influence – Swami Agnivesh, Professor Saibaba of Delhi University, the tribal-rights activist B.D. Sharma, Manish Kunjam – the CPI leader, Prashant Bhushan, Justice Rajendra Sachar, Professor Parashuraman of the Tata Institute of Social Studies. We even got a written statement from Kobad Ghandy, a member of the central committee of the CPI(M) who had been arrested and incarcerated in Tihar Jail. It was read out at one of our seminars. Based on all these inputs collected over a period of two years, a thirteen-point plan for rehabilitation and resettlement was formulated and given the go-ahead. After that, we had no problem in getting gram sabha approvals.'

I ask if they believe that movements like the Salwa Judum could help in kick-starting mining.

'They cannot, because the villagers seemed to be totally against such things,' Thakur replies. 'Our approval came from the people.'

Reddy tells me that he got a call from the SP of Bastar, when the latter was attacked and seriously injured by locals with a crowbar for being too high-handed. The SP stayed away from work, till Ram had mediated with the local people on his behalf.

'They trusted us,' he says.

Both Thakur and Reddy claim that people had voluntarily and gladly signed over their land to the Chhattisgarh Industrial Development Corporation, in return for the following promises that had been made to them: the setting up of an enterprise owned by adivasis over forty-five years of age to provide unorganized services to the Tata Steel plant; the creation of a technical training institute; bridge courses for the local youth at the secondary and matriculate levels; and the provision of a job to one adult member of every local family. Also on offer were a cash compensation of ₹5 lakhs per acre and a replacement deal of 'land for land'.

I ask why the project had not taken off after that.

'We were let down by a lot of factors – both governmental and non-governmental,' Thakur says angrily. 'We believe that we got caught in the crosshairs of corporate rivalry. Our drilling equipment, worth crores, was blown up thrice. Our inquiries led us to suspect that it was not only the Maoists who were culpable. On two occasions, the NMDC contractor himself might have been involved and the third time, it was alleged that the contractor of a rival corporate, aided by local politicians, was responsible.'

I recollect a senior executive of the Tatas telling me that the drills had been blown up by the Maoists and am surprised by the rather different picture of events that Thakur presents.

'So the Maoists were not the saboteurs?' I ask.

Thakur thinks over my question, before replying with a shrug, 'In that area, one does not know who is who and what is what and you cannot believe anybody. What we understood was that a number of lumpen elements, assisted by some factions of the Maoists, could have been the prime movers.

'We have to remember that the process of building roads and bridges took time. If the Maoists had wanted [to], they could have blown us up at any time.'

I am not sure I have understood the dynamics and probe further. 'Why do you blame the government?'

'It is common knowledge that [the] NMDC wanted to set up a steel plant in the area and had agreed to pay a much higher monetary compensation of ₹25 lakhs per acre,' Thakur replies. 'The talk doing the rounds was that legislators and ministers of the ruling party had bought land in the adjoining areas in the expectation of a huge windfall gain. So perhaps their priority shifted away from the Tatas. But it is also true that the people we were dealing with in the government continued to request us to regroup and try once more, as they had managed to identify a lot of local people and lumpen elements involved in the last attack.'

'And what about your corporate rivals?'

'Well, it is a known fact that some people had to make a hasty exit from the area. So they resented the fact that the Tatas were making headway. We had no problems with the village headmen or the villagers. Even though we never came face-to-face with any so-called Maoist, we have no doubt that the locals and some of the intellectuals were in touch at some level. We believe that our efforts had their approval, because they also realized that the adivasis need to develop. Today, all they do is drink sulphi and sleep for days at a stretch, only to begin again. Also, it is quite possible that the Maoists would have gained financially in terms of commissions from the various enterprises being set up as part of the project.'

Thakur declares that despite the setbacks, they had wanted to try again, as more and more villagers were coming out openly to help them.

'They supported us, because they all wanted development,' he says.

Based on local support, Thakur had wanted to try placing his drilling machines once more. He was sure that he would be able to succeed this time and take the last few steps needed to set the project well on its way. But the Tatas withheld their approval because of the possible threat to human life.

'When everything had been set with full public support, the Tatas, unfortunately, did not move.' His tone betrays a trace of disappointment. 'The equipment we had lost was worth crores, but the success of this project was of importance to the state's development. The mineral reserves of millions of tonnes could have fed the industrial growth of India, besides being an important strategic resource for the Tatas. They could, perhaps, have made one more attempt.'

'People talk about the Tatas' success in Kalinganagar,

but one of the biggest contributory factors [to it] was our work in Chhattisgarh,' Reddy adds. 'The master puppeteers of Kalinganagar are the same people who control things in Chhattisgarh. It was our negotiation with them and the thirteen-point plan we had evolved that facilitated the Kalinganagar success.'

I want to know why the Tatas had operated through a contractor in Chhattisgarh, rather than doing the work themselves.

'That is an internal decision of the Tatas,' says Thakur, a former Tata executive himself. 'I cannot comment on this.'

I recall R.N. Singh's dismay over the decision to hire a contractor. Perhaps he had paid the price for being the odd one out in a company keen to outsource the task of consensus-building in remote locations. I also remember Biren Bhuta's credo of talking directly to the locals and wonder if the Tatas will be able to pull it off.

According to Mahesh Thakur, what his company brought to the table was a specialized skill. Apart from drilling and surveying, they had the ability to talk across a wide variety of stakeholders and build consensus. He does not believe that the Tatas needed to build that competence within the company, but acknowledges that some executives might feel differently.

'The transfer of appropriate inducements in the form of money to the right people must have played its own part in your success,' I suggest.

Thakur disagrees. 'Everything was above board,' he claims. 'We approached the project with our hands clean and our heads held high, because we were certain about the cause we were fighting for – inclusive development.'

And then, perhaps to underline his integrity, Thakur explains his own motivations: 'I did not do the project for the money but with a sense of commitment – to the Tatas and to the country.

'Remember,' he says with evident pride, 'I have been trained by none other than Russi Mody. Otherwise who would take on so much danger only for the small sums of money on offer.'

I want to know why everyone working for the Tatas had seemed so reluctant to speak openly about his involvement in the Chhattisgarh project.

Thakur draws his chair closer to mine and looks me in the eye. '[Working] in the most perilous conditions, I put eighty to hundred workers on the ground and set up crores worth of equipment,' he tells me. 'There was constant threat of physical harm to our men and to our rigs. We had to move machines in the dead of night. Sometimes, we would even lie and say we were working for [the] ONGC and prospecting for oil. We were working in tandem with the government machinery, but the risk was on our heads. We were attacked thrice. In being secretive about us, the Tatas were merely ensuring we were not placed in greater danger than absolutely necessary.'

'But today, I cannot go to Bastar,' Reddy, who has been quietly listening to us, adds sadly. 'The tribals trusted us and signed over their land. I told them their children would become Tata officers and go to America. What face can I show them now? Of the thirteen points promised to them, they have only received the cash compensation. With no formal rights on their land, their dependence on the Maoists to protect their livelihood is greater now than it ever used to be.'

He goes on to say that the Tatas' MOU with the Chhattisgarh government formally lapsed in September 2014 and has, for all practical purposes, been given a quiet burial.

While I can understand that a company like Tata Steel would be cautious about business conditions that can only be described as chaotic, I cannot help wondering if the easing up of conditions for the Kalinganagar project also played a role in the Tatas' decision to not pursue the Chhattisgarh opportunity. With the market environment becoming difficult, and with the debt burden stemming from the acquisition of Corus proving increasingly unviable, would the Tatas have had the appetite to invest in both Chhattisgarh and Kalinganagar, even if the insurgency had not posed its own thorny challenges?

Ironically, the Maoists may have been the ones who rued the failure of the Tata Steel project in Chhattisgarh the most. Depending on one's view of them, they could have had two kinds of misgivings: they may have regretted that the promised development of the adivasis did not happen, or that their own sizeable pecuniary benefits from the project would never materialize.

7

The EMTA MOU

The evolution of a programme of rehabilitation and resettlement was one of the major achievements that the Tatas' contractor claimed for his client. But beyond the creation of an agreement lies the task of implementing its terms. In order to understand the ground realities, we move to the scene of a momentous MOU signed between a coal-mining company and the affected community, one that had promised much, when drafted.

In 2001, the Ministry of Coal had allocated the Pachwara central block, located near Amrapara town in the Pakur district of Jharkhand state, with reserves of 562 million tonnes, for captive mining to the Punjab State Power Corporation Limited (PSEB). The PSEB entered into a joint venture, named PANEM, with the

Eastern Mineral and Trading Agency (EMTA), in which it holds a 26 per cent stake. EMTA was appointed as mine developer and operator by the joint venture.[36] The Jharkhand State Pollution Control Board issued its clearances by March 2003. The Ministry of Environment and Forests' clearance came in 2005.

News of the mining project and the displacement of locals that it would bring about reached the villages sometime between 1998 and '99. Eight hundred and seven households, comprising 4,207 people, were to be displaced.

There were many voices of dissent which coalesced to form the Rajmahal Pahad Bachao Andolan (RPBA) in 2000. A Catholic nun who had settled in the area in 1998 was an important catalyst in the formation of the RPBA.

Sister Valsa Joan had joined a Belgian order of nuns called the Sisters of Charity of Jesus and Mary in 1983.[37] Her calm eyes and pronounced jawline suggested a woman capable of both strong feeling and great sacrifice. In the late 1990s, she was living and teaching in the convent in Amrapara. In her spare time, she would explore the neighbouring villages and strike up friendships with the local adivasis.

In 1998, Sister Valsa moved out of the Amrapara convent and into Pachwara for good and began living as a boarder in the house of Binej Hembrom, the *parganeith* (traditional head) of

---

[36]The information about this project is derived from 'Coal Lateral', a report of the independent peoples' tribunal on the project published by the Programme for Social Action; the jury included eminent lawyer-activist Prashant Bhushan, independent writer and academician Bela Bhatia and Venkitesh Ramakrishnan, Associate Editor of *Frontline* magazine. It also draws on conversations with Father Tom Kavalakatta, a social worker in the region, and on a report on the issue published in the *Wall Street Journal*.

[37]http://blogs.wsj.com/indiarealtime/2012/01/31/the-murder-of-sister-valsa-chapter-two/

thirty-two tribal villages, including Pachwara. The family had already forsaken the Santhal tribe's traditional religion to become Protestant Christians. Sister Valsa felt that by being less isolated from the people, she could best fulfil her order's mission to serve 'the poor and the abandoned'.

She was not in Pachwara to proselytize, villagers say. She lived as the villagers did and learned their tribal language, Santhali. She did, however, encourage them to change their ways as far as their addiction to alcohol was concerned.

'Follow your culture, but live well,' she would advise, urging them to lead a healthier life.

In 2000, Sister Valsa helped the villagers construct their own school, a thatched hut that sits out in an open field, and taught local children there for six years. Today, it has 170 students.

As news of the mining company's entry began to spread, Sister Valsa's thoughts turned to the state of destitution to which tribal people had been reduced by mining projects in other parts of the state. The RPBA, under her leadership, then launched and carried out a militant struggle against PANEM. Blockades prevented the entry of mining officials into the villages. Several leaders of mainstream political parties, like Shibu Soren and Babulal Marandi – both future chief ministers of Jharkhand – supported the movement.

It took six years for the mining company to succeed in undermining the people's movement. A select few in every village were offered jobs, cash, alcohol and the promise of contracts. This small group of privileged locals not only became ardent supporters of the project and began preaching its benefits, but also turned against the RPBA, even though this sudden shift in loyalties involved, in certain cases, breaking ties with immediate family members.

Those who continued to oppose the project were harassed

with false cases implicating them in acts of kidnapping, extortion and attempted murder. The threat of being picked up by the police loomed large over RPBA members. Between 2003 and 2006, it was common for families to either camp out in neighbouring villages or even take shelter in the adjacent forest areas for several weeks at a time.

A group of bodies aligned to the RPBA filed a PIL before the Ranchi high court in November 2003. They claimed that the acquired areas fell under the Santhal Pargana and were, therefore, governed by the Santhal Pargana Tenancy Act (STPA), prohibiting the transfer of land from an adivasi to a non-adivasi. PANEM countered the claim with the argument that the state's power of eminent domain, as per the Land Acquisition Act 1894, superseded the STPA. The High Court in its verdict of April 2005 ruled in favour of PANEM. The verdict was challenged in the Supreme Court.

By this time, the dual policy of favouring a few, while targeting others, had resulted in a breakdown of the traditional harmony that had prevailed in the villages all along. The High Court ruling was a further blow and resulted in the rescinding of the appeal in the Supreme Court and the signing of an MOU with the mining company.

The MOU was drafted by the RPBA leadership and, after negotiations, signed by PANEM. The *parganeith* signed the MOU on behalf of the RPBA. The three witnesses to the MOU were Stephen Marandi, the deputy chief minister of Jharkhand, PANEM's director, Bikas Mukharjee, and Shajimon Joseph, chief of bureau, the *Hindustan Times*, Ranchi. PANEM conceded in the MOU that violation of the terms therein would invite contempt-of-court proceedings.

The MOU was accommodative of the interests of the displaced. The provisions listed included monetary compensation, provision of a job in case over three acres of land had been taken, the creation of infrastructure, including schools and hospitals, and the return of 50 per cent of the land in cultivable condition after mining. Traditional places of worship were not to be disturbed by the mining activity.

An implementation committee comprising three representatives from the RPBA and PANEM, two from each village and three people nominated by the *parganeith* was formed to monitor the implementation of the MOU's provisions. Sister Valsa was to play a supervisory role.

The signing of an MOU with fair provisions and recourse to the judiciary in the event of non-compliance might indicate that the EMTA project was a success. However, the promises made in the MOU were, by and large, not kept. The process of reneging on stated promises without suffering the consequences was similar to the one by which community resistance had been overcome prior to the signing of the MOU – a few people were favoured, while most were ignored.

For instance, improper or unrecognized land records, technical errors and affiliation with the RPBA were some of the reasons cited for not paying due compensation to certain locals. The recognition of the land title was often not a mere technical issue, but dependent on one's proximity to company officials, as the gram pradhan was acting on PANEM'S orders.

The resettlement colony provided by the company consists of flats without toilets. Situated on low-lying land, the colony gets flooded every year during the rainy season and has not been provided the burial ground promised in the MOU.

A small percentage of project-affected people have been provided contract jobs and a minuscule number hired on a permanent basis. The jobs are related to either security or construction and not the more sought-after positions directly involving mining operations.

Due to the impact of mining activities on surface and ground water, cases of jaundice, malaria, typhoid and black fever have doubled in the area. Even though mining operations are complete in one village, there has been no move to take the promised remedial measures for restoring 50 per cent of the land used for mining to cultivable condition before returning it to the villagers. There is also a marked rise in alcoholism among people who have been left with neither land nor employment to sustain them.

Significantly, fatal road accidents have become commonplace in the area. Since 2005, more than 150 villagers have died after being run over by coal trucks. Most of the accidents involved dumper trucks used for the mining operations. There have been multiple instances of family members of RPBA leaders losing their lives in road accidents within short intervals of time. Many have come to believe that the accidents were pre-planned by the company and aimed at family members of those opposing them. Villagers allege that Joseph Soren, an RPBA activist who had spent a year and a half in jail on fabricated charges, was deliberately thrown off a bike by a contractor and run over by a tailing dumper.

Unjust though it was to many of the affected villagers, the rehabilitation and resettlement programme proved to be very lucrative for some members of the implementation committee who had to handle vast sums of cash in order to make disbursements. One of the committee members was Pycil Hembrom, the *parganeith*'s son, who had been treated like a younger brother by Sister Valsa during the time she boarded at his father's house.

At this moment, it is instructive to pause and compare the methods used by EMTA to bludgeon through its project with those resorted to by the Maoists to ensure the loyalty of the local population. There are differences in the details, but it seems to me that there are similarities too – in the use of fear as a pressure tactic, the instances of misleading naive villagers, the recourse to outright violence. There is not much to distinguish one modus operandi from the other and you are left wondering which group is the more exploitative of the two.

Sister Valsa observed the decline of the movement with dismay. She noted the broken promises and the large number of deaths of faithful associates. Then she started voicing her objections. Not diplomatically or quietly, for that was not her style. She objected to the committee's malpractices with the same grim determination with which she had taken on the company.

She knew that by doing so she was placing her life at risk. By this time, she had even moved away from the sanctuary of her religious order. Her visits to the convent in Amrapara had ceased in 2006.

'I am living the life our founder lived,' she would say to Sister Lilly, who heads the order's council that oversees the Jharkhand convents.

Sister Lilly told the *Wall Street Journal*, 'She felt she was living that life much more than the other sisters.'

Sister Valsa's views were not appreciated by her fellow nuns. Her objections on Pachwara were also making her unpopular. Certain individuals had already started objecting to what they perceived as her absolute domination of life in the village. But now, there was big money involved as well.

The committee on which Sister Valsa was training her disapprobation responded with strategies they had learnt from her. When she returned from her village in Kerala after tending to her critically ill brother, she faced a dharna, ostensibly targeted against PANEM, but actually aimed at getting the company to persuade her to leave.

Sister Valsa did not once think of giving in. But she did move from the Hembrom household to board at a house down the street. Now her adversaries allegedly resorted to a tactic they had not learnt from her, but one that the male of the species has used since time immemorial to subdue the female and establish absolute power over her – sexual assault. A twenty-two-year-old adivasi woman close to Sister Valsa was abducted and raped. The defence claims the act was consensual. When Sister Valsa took the woman to the police station to file a complaint, she was advised to go for mediation, instead.

With pressure being brought to bear on the deviant committee members and their accomplices, matters reached a breaking point. On 16 November 2011, Pycil Hembrom allegedly forced his way into Sister Valsa's room, accompanied by a group of villagers, and murdered her.

Interestingly, Maoist posters were found scattered around the scene of the murder. As the assassins left after accomplishing their objective, they apparently blew whistles, burst firecrackers and shouted, '*Inquilaab zindabad!* Long live the revolution!' The Maoists had previously attacked the Kathaldih mine, but denied involvement in the murder.

Sister Valsa was buried in an unmarked grave in a public Christian cemetery in the town of Dumka, about two hours' drive from Pachwara. Close to 700 villagers, nuns and priests attended the funeral, including thirty nuns from the religious order she had once belonged to.

In a prayer at the funeral service, the congregation said, 'We believe that Valsa has returned to the Heavenly Father after completing her mission here on earth.'

Can this saga, sordid and reprehensible as it is, be even partially justified by the compensatory provision of more efficient mining or cheaper power?

Not really, because Ujjal Upadhyay, MD of EMTA, and known to be close to Chandan Basu,[38] son of the late and legendary West Bengal chief minister, Jyoti Basu, had worked out a tidy scheme to siphon away all the surpluses.[39]

The joint venture, PANEM, was only a shell company, with actual mining operations being carried out by EMTA Coal, a wholly owned subsidiary of EMTA. As a result, almost the entire receipts of PANEM went to EMTA Coal, leaving little to be distributed, the terms of the joint venture notwithstanding.

In August 2014, the Supreme Court cancelled 204 of the 214 coal block allocations made since 1993 as being impermissible under the Coal Mines Nationalization Act 1973. Of the 204 cancelled blocks, only thirty-seven had been operational and fourteen of these were being operated by EMTA through joint ventures. As per this ruling by the Supreme Court, EMTA was liable to pay hefty fines.

PSEB, the Punjab state utility, did not fare much better. Even though it was re-allocated the mines through a bidding process carried out by the central government after the Supreme Court decision, the Jharkhand state government, citing a number of irregularities relating to non-payment of dues, excessive and unaccounted mining, infringement of forest land, illegal mining and lapses in the rehabilitation and resettlement of the displaced due to mining activities, refused to grant a fresh lease agreement.[40]

In October 2015, the court of the additional district and sessions judge of Pakur sentenced 16 people, including Pycil

---

[38]http://articles.economictimes.indiatimes.com/2012-09-06/news/33650222_1_coal-blocks-coal-secretary-emta

[39]'Coal lateral', a report of the independent peoples' tribunal on the project published by the Programme for Social Action.

[40]http://www.dailypioneer.com/state-editions/ranchi/no-fresh-coal-block-lease-to-punjab-power-utility.html

Hembrom, to life imprisonment for killing social activist Sister Valsa Joan. Valsa's sacrifice represents a victory of sorts – the victory of a simple, strong love of people and the earth that sustains them, over the machinations of those who have lost touch with themselves and the earth. But it is a victory that comes too rarely, and at too heavy a cost.

Whenever I find myself bewildered by the arguments presented by the various factions in the development debate, I think of Sister Valsa and others of her ilk, and know, despite the fakes and the pretenders, the hypocrites and the con artists who abound in every faction, on which side I must stand.

SECTION FOUR

Adventures in the Dirty Tricks Department

1

A Jindal Man

During my visit to Jamshedpur, I need a break from my back-to-back meetings with Tata executives and decide to head for XLRI (Xavier Labour Relations Institute or Xavier School of Management), the premier business school, where I intend speaking to academics conversant with land acquisition-related issues. I am told that the go-to person in this case is Professor Tata L. Raghu Ram. Evidently, it is difficult to escape the 'Tatas' in Jamshedpur!

Prof. Raghu Ram has a Master's degree in limnology and a Ph.D in biodiversity-impact assessment. He has keen, but kind eyes and an earnest way of speaking that immediately inspires trust. During our discussion, he refers to two of his co-authored papers, where he has identified the critical factors for successful land acquisition. These include a focus on fallow land, direct dealing with the community, non-alignment with political parties, maintaining a low profile (especially for high-flying promoters) and formalization of licences only after obtaining the free and informed consent of community members.

He believes that land acquisition should ideally be carried out through the market route. This would, however, require moving to the Torrens[1] system of land titles, where the title-holder cannot

[1]Torrens, named after Sir Robert Torrens, third premier of South Australia, is a system of land title in which a register of land holdings

be challenged by an improper chain of land transfers that have occurred in the past. Such challenges are more likely in the case of cultivated land.

Prof. Raghu Ram has studied twenty-four projects in India and classified them in terms of their potential for success.[2] For the purpose of this classification, he stops at the point where an MOU is peacefully signed between the company and the community and does not go further to examine whether the MOU is successfully implemented thereafter. As the case of the EMTA MOU indicates, this is a major lacuna in this particular research methodology as many land acquisitions begin with well-conceived MOUs but culminate in poor implementation. One of the projects the professor lists as a success is the Jindal Steel and Power Ltd coalfield in Raigarh. Prof. Tata speaks warmly about the best practices adopted in this project.

My ears prick up. A few weeks earlier, through a chance meeting with someone, I had the opportunity to learn a great deal more than I had expected about the Jindal coalfield. My experience had catapulted me from the position of an observer of the war being waged over natural resources in India, to that of an active participant, albeit in the role of a minor pawn. When I began to probe the reasons for the predicament I was in, I was led into over widening circles of causation, till I beheld the entire cast of characters involved-politicians, corporate leaders, lawyers, NGOs and adivasis.

The fact that Maoists are not a force in the theatre of action I became a part of, enabled me to observe the rich complexity of

---

maintained by the state guarantees an indefensible title to those included in the register.

[2]Raghu Ram, Tata L., Tigga, Nutan Shashi and Kakani, Ram Kumar, 'Insights into Land Acqusition Experiences of Private Businesses in India', 2008.

India's development conflicts, even without the presence of the insurgents. But before offering particulars of the Jindal projects in Raigarh, I must share the details of the strange encounter which had yielded such vital insights.

I am unlikely to forget Haripriya Patel, a plump, middle-aged lady, who had rolled into the room, swaddled like a baby in layers of clothing, her light eyes as clear as her complexion. A translucent white bindi shone like a pale moon on her forehead. Had the urban ways of the city not eroded my traditional upbringing, I would surely have touched her feet and addressed her as '*bua*', the term used to refer to one's paternal aunt.

'Namaste,' I said in greeting.

'Namaste,' she responded, adjusting the voluminous folds of cloth in which she was swathed, as she seated herself with a momentous air.

It was April 2015. I was meeting Mrs Patel in the office of Environics, an NGO run by R. Sreedhar that is dedicated to addressing mining-related issues in the country. Environics is also a prime mover in Mines, Minerals & PEOPLE, a network of NGOs, lawyers and activists working towards 'minimizing' mining. Sreedhar's name had come up repeatedly when I was looking for a respected name to educate me about mining practices in the country.

My request for an interview with Sreedhar had been promptly granted and I had gone to meet him at his ground-floor office in Neb Sarai in South Delhi, passing through the red gate that opened into the 'Freedom Fighters' Colony'.

I had entered and been hailed by Sreedhar from the only closed cubicle there, a conference room doubling as his office. Through the glass doors I had seen him clearly, a bearded man, slight of build, sitting inside an office that smelt of aromas I would recognize – cigarette smoke and Mysore pak, the much sought after sweetmeat from southern India.

We had started off with lengthy introductions. Sreedhar, a metallurgical engineer, told me about his evolution from a mining enthusiast to someone who saw the tremendous toll that mining was exacting on local communities. We spoke of the laws safeguarding the rights of adivasis and their relative dilution in various states and discussed the role of Maoists in mining areas. Sreedhar had mentioned the Maoists' tensions with NGOs working for tribal rights using non-violent means. The insurgents had, in fact, killed three activists from Samatha, the organization behind the landmark series of judgements that in 1995 proscribed the forced transfer of tribal lands to non-tribals, and later explained away the murders as an 'error in implementation'.

We went on to discuss the national obsession with starting new mining projects even though old projects were not working to capacity. Sreedhar had called it 'a fondness for ribbon-cutting'. I had quipped that it might have something to do with maximizing the personal wealth of the ribbon-cutters. I remember Sreedhar laughing as he lit a Malboro Light cigarette. Watching him, I had tried to look nonchalant though, if truth be told, I was concerned about the possible health consequences of inhaling 'second-hand' smoke. *Imagine you are a Ph.D student again in Pradeep's den*, I told myself, recalling the cigar smoke-laden atmosphere of my thesis supervisor's wood-panelled study.

'Do you have some racy stories about mining,' I had asked Sreedhar, 'like that of B.D. Sharma, the IAS officer and tribal-rights advocate, being paraded naked through Raipur for opposing a mining company?'

My penchant for the piquant and the controversial would not leave me alone. It was about an hour into our meeting.

'There is a lady from Chhattisgarh staying in our guest house,' Sreedhar told me. 'She is fighting a case against Jindal. They tried to seize her lands; she was threatened, beaten up, raped. Perhaps, you might like to speak with her.'

And that is how I was introduced to Haripriya Patel.

When she subsequently arrived at his office, Sreedhar spoke to her briefly about her case that was due to come up for hearing in the Supreme Court on 6 and 7 April 2015 and excused himself so that I could talk to her.

Haripriyaji and I were now alone in the office. I asked her about the effects of mining on the people in her village, about the pressures brought to bear on them so that they would agree to give up their land and how they were responding to such coercion. I told her that I had learnt from Sreedhar how her own land had been forcibly acquired and about the different pressure tactics used on her. I would like to learn more, I said.

She answered in Chhattisgarhi, a language that bears some resemblance to the dialects spoken in eastern Uttar Pradesh. Though I am from that region myself, quite a bit of what was being said went over my head. Since her voice was soft, I gave her the mobile-phone recorder which she held in her hand. People outside the room could see and hear what was transpiring.

'I hail from Tapranga village in the Raigarh district of Chhattisgarh,' Haripriya began. 'Jindal came in '96–'97 and seized my land. The company asked us all to sign over the land, especially Plot no. 62, to set up a godown for storing ammunition. Others agreed to it, but I did not. Starting from 1996–'97, the others received compensation ranging from ₹10,000 to ₹60,000 per acre. The sarpanch was from a different tribe and was happy to sign over the land for a few bottles of alcohol.

'I was opposed to the mine because of the impact I was witnessing [on those around me]. Many [in my village] were dying of jaundice, asthma and gastric ailments. I wanted to hold on to the land of my ancestors. But they forcibly took away six acres for a godown and, later, seventy-five acres for the mine.

'Besides taking the land, they also robbed me of my honour.'

The Chhattisgarhi expression she had used was '*bey-izzatti kiye*'.

As she spoke, her eyes welled up with tears. There was a pause. I looked at her tear-filled eyes, felt like a voyeur trespassing on her grief and looked away. The moment of silence lengthened. Then she began speaking again.

This welling up of tears and the ensuing pause, pregnant with feelings – compassion on my side and remembered humiliation on hers – occurred twice during the interview.

I asked her about her lawyer and she divulged a name: Sharma. As our meeting was coming to a close , I realized that I had failed to catch many of the nuances in her disclosures and statements. Perhaps, I had even misunderstood several things she had shared? I told her, therefore, that I would contact her lawyer for further details and thanked her for her time.

After the interview was over, I left the Environics office and returned home to the MDI, Gurgaon.

Next morning, as I was scrolling through a document sent by Sreedhar on an economic valuation of forests, I got a call from him.

'Rohit, I need your help,' he said, his voice urgent. 'The lady you met yesterday has filed a complaint with the police. She says you attempted, unsuccessfully, to inject her with poison, then forced her to consume it orally. After poisoning her, you took her thumbprints on some documents in which she has retracted her accusations against Jindal. She says you are a Jindal man, that you mesmerized her into issuing false statements and threatened to kill her if she did not sign.'

'Is this a joke, Sreedhar?' I asked.

It was 3 April, just two days after April Fools' Day.

'No,' he replied. 'I am at the Mehrauli police station. Haripriya Patel has been admitted to Safdarjung Hospital. And SI [Sub-Inspector] Mahipal Singh would like to speak to you.'

Jindal Steel and Power Limited (JSPL), a part of the US$18-billion-worth O.P. Jindal Group and the company I was allegedly representing, is led by Naveen Jindal, the youngest of four brothers. Naveen was a member of the 14th and 15th Lok Sabha from the Congress Party and also a member of the Indian Olympic shooting team. In the sphere of politics, he is best known for his initiative to change the Flag Code so that Indian citizens may fly the national flag in their private spaces, clearly a popular initiative, given the number of cars seen around the country with flags tethered to their dashboards. His contribution to the country's symbology was somewhat marred by his support for khap panchayats, a parallel form of civil law in rural India, infamous for condoning regressive practices like honour killings. In 2011, his alma mater, the University of Texas, Dallas, renamed its school of management the Naveen Jindal School of Management. His wife Shallu is a Kuchipudi dancer and, according to her website, 'an advocate of India's indigenous art and culture'.

JSPL's strategy is to set up vertically integrated steel-manufacturing operations, including coal and iron-ore mines, power plants and steel plants. It is also a merchant power producer, which means that it can sell power on the open market.

JSPL has a major presence in Chhattisgarh. The company's

1999–2000 annual report states: 'The operation of...coal mines in the Gare area of Mand in Raigarh has been further strengthened and production increased. Besides, the existing power-generation capacity of 95 MW is being increased to 150 MW by setting up an additional plant of 55 MW-capacity at Raigarh.'

JSPL first arrived in Haripriya's village Tapranga in 1996. Disputes between her and the company over the acquisition of land have been an ongoing affair since 1999.[3]

In 2008, Mrs Patel wrote a letter to JSPL, seeking fair compensation for the land purchased by them. She filed a civil suit in 2009 in the Gharghoda court on the acquisition of six acres of land for a workers' colony. She won it in 2013. The case is now on appeal.

In 2010, Mrs Patel wrote a letter to the SP, Chhattisgarh, about an unauthorized construction that JSPL had made on the land belonging to her and demanded suitable compensation from the company.

On 18 August 2010, she registered FIR no. 142/2010 under sections 147, 148, 149, 294, 506 and 323 IPC at the Raigarh police station. The afore-mentioned sections relate to rioting, voluntarily causing hurt, criminal intimidation and, curiously, running a lottery. On the same day, JSPL filed a counter-FIR at the same police station under Section 143 for unlawful assembly.

Haripriya's clash with JSPL took on a different complexion altogether with the appearance of a lawyer from Delhi – a certain M.L. Sharma.

A Supreme Court senior advocate, Sharma may not belong to the exclusive club of India's most revered lawyers. But he could easily make it to the cabal of those who grab the headlines most often. His latest claim to notoriety rests on his odious comments against women made in the BBC documentary

[3]http://indiankanoon.org/doc/115501094/

on the Nirbhaya rape case, in which a twenty-three-year-old physiotherapy intern in Delhi was brutally raped in a moving bus by five men. Sharma is the defence lawyer for the accused. In a previous defence of a Supreme Court judge accused of sexually harassing an intern, Sharma had argued that according to the ancient Hindu scriptures, a woman rarely speaks the truth for its own sake; hence, her words should not be relied on.

To the outside world, Sharma projects himself as a gladiator engaged in a righteous war. He is fond of filing PILs against the high and mighty. While such litigations have served in several countries to bring justice to the weak and downtrodden, Sharma appears to be more concerned with the public interest they tend to evoke.

His targets are invariably well-known politicians or businessmen, including Robert Vadra, the errant son-in-law of the Gandhis; Arvind Kejriwal, presumptive prince of India's new politics and currently New Delhi's chief minister; Akhilesh Yadav, heir of UP's Mulayam Singh Yadav; the head of the Ranbaxy pharmaceutical group; and last, but not the least, Naveen Jindal, the Chairman of Jindal Steel and Power Ltd. The only group exempt from Sharma's attacks appears to be members of the BJP, the party heading the NDA coalition currently in power in New Delhi.

Of the thirty-five PILs filed by Sharma in the Supreme Court, most have not been admitted. Whether or not he is redressing the wrongs that he claims give him sleepless nights, he is certainly racking up an impressive record in the matter of wasting the august court's precious time.[4]

---

[4]On 1 May 2015, the Supreme Court issued a show cause notice to Sharma for making 'irresponsible' and 'scandalous' allegations in his PIL challenging the National Judicial Appointment Commission (NJAC), saying, 'This is not a political platform.' A five-judge constitution bench, headed by Justice J.S. Khehar, directed Sharma to respond within a

On 6 September 2012, Sharma filed a PIL seeking the cancellation of all 194 coal blocks allegedly allocated arbitrarily during the period 2004 to 2011 in Jharkhand, Chhattisgarh, Maharashtra, West Bengal, Odisha and Madhya Pradesh. A day earlier, Prashant Bhushan, then leader of the Aam Aadmi Party and veteran PIL warrior, with triumphs such as the PIL on the 2G-spectrum allocations under his belt, had stated his intention to file an FIR on the issue 'in a few weeks'.

However, despite having apparently filed his PIL earlier, Sharma was defeated in the race. It was the PIL filed by the NGO Common Cause, along with high-profile personalities, including former cabinet secretary in the Government of India, T.S.R. Subramaniam, former Chief Election Commissioner N. Gopalaswami and Admiral (Retd.) R.H. Tahiliani, through their counsel Prashant Bhushan, that was admitted and credited with the cancellations of 212 of the 218 coal blocks allocated by different central governments since 1993.

But Sharma has nothing, if not staying power. Besides, this was not a war he needed to wage alone. He could ride on the coattails of an ally equal to his foes.

Subhash Chandra Goel is a larger-than-life entrepreneur, who started off in his family business of rice mills, but expanded to create a business conglomerate, spanning media, infrastructure, theme parks, education and precious metals. Even his failures – in setting up a satellite business and a 20–20 Cricket League – testify to the daring and chutzpah that saw him notch up a string

---

week as to why he should not be 'debarred' from canvassing any public interest litigation (PIL) (http://www.dnaindia.com/india/report-njac-issue-supreme-court-issues-notice-to-advocate-ml-sharma-for-irresponsible-pil-2082284).

of successes. In the satellite business, for example, he attempted to stitch up a deal with Sir Anerood Jugnauth, prime minister of Mauritius, to apply for a satellite from the International Telecommunication Union, since he had learnt that sovereign countries alone could apply for satellites.

Chandra has a flair for the dramatic, not limited to his band of white hair, reminiscent of the former Indian prime minister Indira Gandhi. In the 1980s, he had made an attempt to get the Kohinoor diamond back from Britain. When that failed, he would turn his efforts to buying the East India Company, the trading corporation that had served as the means by which Great Britain would gain power over the jewel in its crown – India. Chandra's initiative was ultimately foiled by the original 'Iron Lady', Margaret Thatcher, then prime minister of the United Kingdom.

His philanthropic ventures are as visionary as his business interests. He focusses on inter-faith harmony and education. He is also a much sought-after motivational speaker, who often cautions his audiences about the ill effects of greed. He publicly declared his support for the BJP during the Haryana Assembly election in September 2014.

Not every great man's life is defined by a great rivalry. Subhash Chandra, however, appears to belong to the coterie of those who thrive on a rivalry of their own choosing. His defining rivalry is the one he nurses against the Jindal family, also from Hissar. He is contemptuous of their entrepreneurial chops, disapproving of their ethical quotient and 'unable to digest the fact that with all his brilliance, he is not even the richest man in Hissar,' as a former employee puts it.

It was the scam in the allocation of coal mines and Naveen Jindal's involvement in it that would hand Chandra the opportunity he had been waiting for. In March 2012, a draft report on the allocation of coal blocks was leaked to the press by the Comptroller and Auditor General (CAG). It marked the beginning of what came to be known as the coalgate scam. The CAG estimated that the result of allocating coal blocks at subsidized prices determined by administrative fiat was a 'windfall gain' to the allocatees, amounting to ₹1.86 lakh crores. Over the summer of 2012, the BJP, the party then in the opposition, lodged a complaint, resulting in a CBI probe that sought to determine if corruption had made its way into the process of allocation.

The seeds of such corruption had been sown much earlier. While the coal industry had been nationalized by the central government in 1972, companies engaged in the production of iron and steel were allowed to retain their coal mines for captive use. In July 1992, the Ministry of Coal issued directives for the constitution of a Screening Committee that would evaluate proposals from private power-generation companies for captive mining. The Electricity Act of 2003 introduced competition in the power sector and opened the floodgates to a large number of private power plants (known as merchant power plants), whose developers were chosen by the states through non-transparent selection processes. The power companies were assured allocation of captive coal blocks and the freedom to sell power anywhere in the country at prices determined by market forces. Due to high spot prices in the power exchange during the period 2004 to 2010, a large number of power plants were set up. The total capacity of such merchant power projects – including those that had been cleared by the Ministry of Environment and Forests (MoEF) and those that were in the pipeline for clearance – exceeded by as much as 65,000 MW the total capacity projected by the Planning Commission up to 2017. This would create a huge artificial demand for captive coal. Between 2006 and 2010, approximately 40 billion metric tonnes of coal were allocated to public and private firms, in glaring contrast to the 9.6 billion metric tonnes that had been allocated between 1993 and 2005. The concerned companies paid highly subsidized prices determined by administrative fiat.[5]

It is interesting to note that the largest beneficiary of the new policy in the private sector was the Naveen Jindal-run JSPL. The coal blocks allocated to the company in 1998 during the NDA regime were followed by a slew of allocations under the UPA. This resulted in its reserves of 2,580 million metric tonnes of coal far outstripping the reserves of EMTA, the second-largest beneficiary in the private sector, which had 1,700 million metric tonnes.

JSPL's acquisition of coal at administered prices, combined with its right as a merchant power plant to sell power at market rates, resulted in operating profits of ₹6,399 crores for the company in 2010–11[6] on a revenue of ₹13,193 crores. According to the CAG report, JSPL was alleged to have made windfall gains of ₹21,226 crores as a result of the coal allocations. In an exclusive interview with *Headlines Today* editor Rahul Kanwal, Jindal explained that JSPL owed its profitability to its efficiency.

Not to be outdone by the CAG or the Parliament, the media was drumming up a frenzy on the coalgate issue. Zee, the media house owned by Subhash Chandra, seemed to have taken a special fancy to this case and came up with a series of exposés. In June 2012, it upped the ante when the CBI issued its twelfth FIR, naming

---

[5]http://cag.gov.in/sites/default/files/audit_report_files/Union_Performance_Commercial_Allocation_Coal_Blocks_and_Production_Ministry_Coal_7_2012.pdf

[6]http://www.jindalsteelpower.com/investors/annual-report.html

JSPL as an accused in the case of alleged cheating and criminal conspiracy in bagging the Amarkonda Murgadangal coal block in Birbhum, West Bengal, in 2008.

The media trial, being conducted simultaneously with the CBI investigation, was reaching its climax when, in a surprise move, JSPL played a hand that turned certain members of the fourth estate from the hunters into the hunted. At a press conference held on 25 October 2012, Chairman Naveen Jindal released video recordings which allegedly showed Zee editors trying to extort ₹100 crores as the price for not airing damaging stories on coal-block allocations involving his company. In a meeting captured on video, Jindal officials are seen protesting that ₹20 crores was the amount they were originally asked for to buy Zee's silence. The media house's editors take a swig of their coffee and reply that this was a 'communication error', a result of the earlier meeting having taken place in a noisy coffee bar with loud background music. Little did the editors know that JSPL was recording the entire proceedings.

Naveen Jindal, sharpshooter extraordinaire and poster-boy for the 'capitalism as a reward for merit' brigade, had struck again. His moment of victory at the press conference was only slightly marred by the presence of a man in a wheelchair with lucid eyes and a loud voice that he used liberally to shoot uncomfortable questions about JSPL's land-acquisition policies and raise lusty slogans against the hero of the hour. I was to connect with him later on a matter of pressing concern to me.

But this was only a tiny blip in a triumphal moment. Media houses tripped over each other to gather titbits of the story. Anchors breathlessly spilled details on national prime time. Viewers of the India's prime-time entertainment show sat back in their couches and roundly abused all concerned.

JSPL filed a criminal case against Zee, alleging extortion.

On 27 November, Sudhir Chaudhary, the head of Zee News, and Samir Ahluwalia, the head of Zee Business, were arrested by the Crime Branch of the Delhi Police. They were released on bail on 17 December 2012. A charge sheet was issued against the two journalists and Subhash Chandra, chairman of Zee, in July 2013. Simultaneously, Zee accused JSPL of defamation and registered its own slew of cases.

Despite the thicket of cases and counter-cases, Jindal seemed to have won the media battle. But not, perhaps, the war.

The cases of Mrs Haripriya Patel would soon take on a sleazier tone.

After having been upended by Prashant Bhushan in the coal scam PIL, and following Zee's humiliating reverse at the hands of Naveen Jindal, lawyer M.L. Sharma had started travelling to Chhattisgarh in 2013 to solicit cases from those affected by Jindal projects. He heard the story of Haripriya Patel through Jan Chetna, the NGO in Raigarh that supported her. It was the usual saga of forcible land acquisition. But Sharma was a Delhi lawyer. Land acquisition did not make for juicy sound bytes. He needed something more.

In 2014, Haripriya went to the local police station and claimed that in 2001 she had been threatened by D.K. Bhargava, a JSPL executive, to stop contesting the company's acquisition of her land. She went on to allege that she had been sexually assaulted by Naveen Jindal and Bhargava in her own home, after which her thumb impressions were forcibly taken by them on some documents. She also declared that in 2010, while she was standing on the road, she had been dragged inside the JSPL factory and raped.

The local police station turned Haripriya away. But Sharma

had not acquired his reputation for nothing. In December 2014, writ petition No.235/2014 was admitted before the Chhattisgarh high court. In January 2015, the writ petition was disposed of, holding that the concerned police station should immediately register an FIR in the rape case in accordance with the judgement of the Supreme Court in the case of Lalita Kumari vs Government of Uttar Pradesh & Ors. (2014).

This was all the pretext Zee needed. A series of news items on the allegations began running on the channel. Haripriya Patel, a loose polka-dotted headscarf pulled low over her face and her visible features pixelated to avoid identification, gave an emotional interview in Chhattisgarhi to a Zee journalist.

But despite the order of the Chhattisgarh high court and all the media hype, the FIR for the alleged rape has not yet been filed. The local police station claims that there was too long a time lapse between the date of the first incident and that on which the complaint was lodged. Some officers have also stated that had such an incident taken place they would have heard about it.

Later, D.K. Bhargava would file a counter-complaint against those who had allegedly grafted false charges against him and others, including Naveen Jindal. Based on Bhargava's complaint, the Tamnar police station registered a case against three persons, including Zee Group Chairman Subhash Chandra, Managing Director Punit Goenka and Haripriya Patel.[7] The news was widely circulated by a limited number of media channels. Most prominent among these was Focus News, a media house in which Jindal is believed to have interests through an ownership stake of Abhey Kumar Oswal, his father-in-law.

Meanwhile, having failed to have an FIR registered in Raigarh, Haripriya decided to petition the Supreme Court. Her

---

[7]http://newsworldindia.in/india/fir-registered-against-zee-group-chairman-subhash-chandra-and-his-son/60264/

case was to be heard on 6 and 7 April 2015. It was the reason why she was present in Delhi and available for an interview with me on 2 April. On 4 April, an FIR was registered against me at the Neb Sarai police station. On 6 April, Haripriya's case was 'dismissed as withdrawn' from the Supreme Court.

2

Negotiating Innocence

The FIR against me was registered under Section 328 of the Indian Penal Code 1860 Act. This section relates to 'causing hurt by means of poison, etc., with intent to commit an offence'.

The description of the 'crime' fills up one page in closely written Hindi script. Surprisingly, 70 per cent of the page's contents relate to a battery of rather egregious violations committed against Haripriya and others by Naveen Jindal and his associates, members of the police force and officials of the district administration. These range from multiple instances of rape and physical violence over a ten-year period from 2001 to 2010 to the forcible seizure of 81 acres of land, six of which were used to build a colony.

Almost as an afterthought, the FIR mentions the misdeeds of a 'Jindal man' from Haryana, introduced to Haripriya on 2 April, who unsuccessfully attempted to inject her with poison, then forced her to consume it, after which she was made to sign on some documents. For some reason, no name is mentioned, but the timing and location of the incident make it clear that it could only have been me. The mention of the Environics office as the venue of the interview also points the needle of suspicion at Sreedhar's organization.

My formal interrogation took place not in the Mehrauli police station to which I was initially summoned, but at the Neb Sarai police station. It was late in the evening. I was questioned by an impeccably dressed officer, recently promoted to the position of Additional Commissioner of Police (ACP). The questioning was thorough, polite and methodical. Between asking questions about my alleged links with Jindal, the good ACP thought it fit to inform me that he had also contemplated doing a Ph.D once. Given his obvious powers of systematic thinking, I was happy to aver that he would have made a dedicated scholar. After the information had been sought and given, I was offered a juicy slice from a Domino's pizza, which the officers on duty were sharing between them. I politely declined.

Later that night, as I waited for another round of questioning, I saw the ACP pacing the central quadrangle of the police station. He looked like a tiger prowling about his favourite jungle trail. '*Chal hat*!' he growled at some loiterers, who immediately obeyed his order to make themselves scarce and scurried away. I was glad I did not have to face him when he was in this mood.

In my travels through Chhattisgarh, I had heard of adivasis being thrown into jail on ridiculous charges levelled by mining companies or the government. My predicament seemed a bit similar. The only difference was that in my case, a member of the privileged set, I, was at the receiving end and the perpetrator of the atrocity was an adivasi woman.

In the light of what had transpired, everything she had told me so far seemed highly suspect – despite her amazing ability to cry in a convincing fashion. Everything the NGOs supporting her claimed was also open to question, although I did not want to write them off completely on the basis of how one of the people they stood by had sought to use me for her own ends.

I explored the possibility of applying for anticipatory bail, but was advised that it would be wiser to join the investigation, as the denial of anticipatory bail would weaken my position considerably. Apart from the fact that I was innocent, a few points worked in my favour. The meeting with Haripriya had taken place in an open-plan office and Sreedhar's colleagues vouched that there had been no untoward incident during the time I was there. My recording of the interview with Haripriya also established my innocence.

Regardless, a brush with the police is an unnerving experience and I was grateful for the help of friends who put me in touch with people in the right places, ensuring that the investigation was not more of a nuisance than it needed to be.

When I last spoke to the police, they told me there was little likelihood of the case going anywhere. To all intents and purposes, it was a '*maraa hua saanp*', as they put it in the vernacular – a dead snake. My phone, however, was seized as case evidence and is yet to be returned by the specialized investigating agency. Once it is back, I hope the case will be closed. The officer in charge of the investigation has told me that a minimum waiting period of six months is to be expected. The six months have now stretched to over a year.

The million-dollar question is: Who decided that I had to be framed and why? It is possible that Haripriya's lawyer had come to know – either in the time she took to reach Sreedhar's office to meet me or after she had returned to her guest house – that she was meeting someone. It may have been decided that framing me would enable an FIR to be registered, in which the litany of accusations against Zee would be repeated. This FIR could be useful in the case coming up before the Supreme Court and would allow the Zee media channels to start tom-tomming the charges against JSPL once again. Alternatively, it could be that Jindal had bought off the lawyer and/or Haripriya and was trying to weaken the tribal woman's previous cases against him and his employees by making her slap ludicrous charges on others that would eventually work against her.

Given the cooperation of Environics, I was sure that they were not involved in setting me up, although their helpfulness could have been motivated by self-preservation. The role of Jan Chetna, the NGO in Raigarh that supported Haripriya, was not clear. Were they an unscrupulous organization, like many NGOs today? Had their differences with the mining company made them forget their principles to the extent that they could drag an innocent bystander into the case merely to score a point? Or, perhaps, I surmised their campaign had been hijacked by an unscrupulous Delhi lawyer. It was also not clear whether Haripriya was being used without quite realizing it or was an active abettor in the set-up.

To get to the bottom of the matter, I had to talk to Ramesh Agrawal, prime mover behind Jan Chetna and winner of the Goldman Environmental Prize.

3

Jan Chetna's Lonely Fight

While the two heavyweights, JSPL and Zee, were squaring off against each other, a determined group of citizens was fighting its own battles against the mining giant JSPL.

Heading the group was Ramesh Agrawal, member of a community famous for both its business sense and its propensity for simple living. The unpretentious lifestyle of a Warren Buffet can be seen in varying degrees among many members of the Marwari community; G.D. Birla, a close associate of Mahatma Gandhi, and Jamnalal Bajaj, who, according to Gandhi, epitomized the ideal of wealth being held in trust for the public good, are two of the personalities who come to mind.

Agrawal, whose family runs a small oil mill, inherited the simple lifestyle preferred by several members of his community, but chose to focus his life on opposing business malpractice, rather than on expanding his own empire. His indifference to material possessions lends a certain aura to his bearing and a decisiveness to his thinking that can, sometimes, verge on obstinacy.

He started his career as an environmental activist with a stint in the Lok Shakti Samiti, an NGO seeded by Harsh Mander, an IAS officer who later resigned from service to become an advocate for social reform. In 2004, he formed Jan Chetna, a loose alliance of like-minded people, which Agrawal describes as an '*abhiyan*', a movement to sensitize the adivasis to their rights and to the transgressions of mining companies in the coal-rich Raigarh district. Other people involved in Jan Chetna include Rajesh Tripathi and Dr Harihar Patel.

The expenses for the movement are met from Agrawal's earnings from the internet café he runs and by dipping into his family finances.

Jan Chetna's major victories include the cancellation of an environmental clearance obtained by JSPL for the coal block called Gare 4/6, a four million tonnes-per-annum reserve, on the basis of the speciousness of the statutory public hearing that must be held as part of the Environmental Impact Assessment of a project. In its judgement of April 2012, the National Green Tribunal bench, comprising Hon'ble Justice C.V. Ramulu and Prof. R. Nagendran (an expert member), described the public hearing as a 'farce', in which 'all the norms required in conducting a smooth and fair procedure were given a go-by.'[8]

The second significant breakthrough was the suspension of a JSPL project to add 2400 MW of capacity to its 1000 MW capacity power plant. Agrawal discovered that the land on which this expansion was taking place belonged to the government. He sent Jairam Ramesh, the then Union Cabinet Minister for Environment and Forest, an email about the matter and dispatched a hard copy of the complaint to him.

Ramesh replied immediately. 'Let me see what I can do,' he wrote.

A team was sent from the MoEF. They found that the transgressions in question were more serious by far than the complaints Agrawal had listed in his email.

'This company has no land to put up new capacity,' they agreed.

'Perhaps, they intended to put up a second storey on the existing power plant,' Agrawal joked.

The ministry suspended the project and directed the state government to initiate action against the company. The ₹10,000 crores public issue for the thermal power plant had to be postponed and has not taken off till date.

As reward for his troubles, Agrawal has spent 72 days in jail on charges of defamation and of inciting a mob at a public hearing organized to grant clearance for the 2,400 MW thermal power plant.

Shortly after his release from prison, on 7 July 2012, Agrawal was sitting in his cybercafe when unidentified assailants fired at

[8]http://www.elaw.org/system/files/3-2011t_20apr2012_final_order.pdf

him, wounding him in the thigh. According to him, they had intended to kill him, but failed because he managed to distract them by throwing his cell phone at them.

Seven people were accused of the crime. The shooter, a security guard in the firm providing security services to JSPL, is in jail. Jan Chetna alleged the involvement of JSPL and demanded a CBI probe. The demand was denied by a judge, alleged by Agrawal to be a former lawyer of the Jindal group. JSPL strongly condemned the incident and denied any involvement.

In Delhi, I chanced upon a Jindal lawyer at a social gathering and broached the case with him. He was familiar with the details and said that the shooting had been engineered by a criminal Agrawal had met in jail and fallen foul of.

I check this allegation with Agrawal when I call him in June 2015. He laughs it off. 'In jail, all the inmates thought I had beaten up or killed a man,' he says. 'So they held me in very high regard indeed. They would seek me out for advice on how to free themselves from their own assorted murder and rape charges. '*Hum bhi* murder *karke aaye hain*,' they would confide in me. '*Humein chhudaaney ki koi tarkeeb bataiye.*' They too were there on murder charges, they told him, and sought his advice on a way out. 'I had no problems with anyone in jail,' Agrawal says, by way of conclusion.

Despite being in a wheelchair – the result of the injury he had sustained from the attempt on his life – Agrawal made it a point to be present at the press conference called by Naveen Jindal to share details of his reverse sting on Zee. It was an opportunity for Agrawal to register his loud, if limited, protest.

In 2014, Agrawal was awarded the Asia Goldman Prize for organizing villagers into demanding their right to information about industrial development projects and succeeding in shutting down one of the largest proposed coal mines in Chhattisgarh. I ask Agrawal if he has considered the possibility that Western countries are unfairly trying to close down coal plants in India through the funding of NGOs, while refusing to take responsibility for their own long history of carbon emissions.

Agrawal explains that the resistance to mining does not stem from foreign-funded NGOs alone. There are many domestically funded movements as well, including Jan Chetna. The struggle to protect the environment is ultimately one taken up by project-affected people to retain their livelihood and traditional ways of life, not a grudge match between the North and the South about how the costs of global warming should be distributed.

Mathew Cherian, a Keralite with a penchant for breaking into accented Hindi and head of Voluntary Action Network India, a network of NGOs working on issues of '*jal, jangal, zameen*' (water, forest and land), had offered some pertinent details earlier on how NGOs working on development issues were funded.

'The annual funding under the Foreign Contribution Regulation Act is ₹10,000 crores,' he had said. 'Of that, ₹6,000 crores goes to religious organizations of all denominations. Of the remaining ₹4,000 crores, a lion's share goes to campaigns on vision or tobacco or children. The funds channelized for development activism amount to as little as ₹1,000 crores. Most of the resources [for this] are generated from the contribution of local people or [from] fellowships obtained by activists from domestic sources.'

I ask Agrawal if the Maoists have attempted to spread their influence to Gare.

He replies that they are present in the town of Ambikapur and are slowly advancing upon Pathar Gaon and Dharamjaigarh. 'If mining continues in the way it has and non-violent agitations are clamped down on, the people will have no alternative.'

I now broach the matter of Haripriya Patel and her various charges against Jindal. How many of them does Agrawal think are valid and on how many cases is he supporting her?

'The only case I am helping her on and the only case I know to be true is the forcible acquisition of six acres of her land to build a workers' colony. She received no compensation for this land. The company was not willing to give the compensation demanded. The case was registered in Gharghoda. The court has ordered that the colony be cleared and the matter is now in appeal in the district court.'

I ask if there is any truth to the rape cases filed. Agrawal replies that he has never heard of any such incidents and doubts their veracity.

I ask him about the lawyer M.L. Sharma and his link with Jan Chetna. Agrawal says that Sharma has been coming to Gare since early 2014. He had apparently asked for a meeting, but Agrawal was not that keen and the meeting did not take place.

'In general, people were quite in awe that a Supreme Court lawyer was in their midst and was willing to take up their cases. They did not know [about] his reputation. He took lots of files back to Delhi. After hearing about your case, they will understand the kind of things he is up to.'

I ask if he has been in touch with Haripriya Patel from the time she brought charges against me. Agrawal says he has not.

After speaking to him and delving into the history of the Jindal–Zee feud my best guess is that M.L. Sharma has used the false case against me to strengthen his hand ahead of the Supreme Court hearing of Haripriya's complaints against Jindal.

As for Agrawal's claims against Jindal, the judicial records attest to their veracity. I am inclined to believe, however, that Agrawal may be underplaying his knowledge of and involvement with the cases that M.L. Sharma is fighting on Haripriya's behalf.

Haripriya Patel is a member of the Jan Chetna community; she appears in a video film made on Agrawal on the occasion of the Goldman Prize award ceremony. On her trip to Delhi, the purpose of which was to be present when Sharma appeared before the Supreme Court to get a case registered against Jindal, she was accompanied by Rajesh Tripathi, an associate of Agrawal's. It is beyond credulity that Tripathi was entirely unaware of the details of the cases being pursued and only slightly less difficult to accept that Agrawal was in the dark.

Perhaps they went along with Sharma because, like the local people of Gare, they too were impressed by him and hopeful that he would be able to make a dent in Jindal's armour. It is possible that they did not fully comprehend the mischief the lawyer was capable of.

When reviewing the draft of this chapter I realize that as an economist I have come a long way, not just in terms of kilometres clocked during my field research but also in my understanding of how the dearly held credos of my breed – the benign role of global financial flows for an economy, the invigorating effect of competition in economic development and the ability of democratic institutions like the media to withstand the relentless power of money – play out in the harsh light of human greed. No doubt my insights have come at a price – the bother of a legal case. Yet, this experience is perhaps the most valuable that I have had during my research.

SECTION FIVE

The Search for a Synthesis

1

The Many Colours of Displacement

Having experienced the lawlessness characterizing the political process in Kanker, the deceptive charm of Markabeda, a village in an erstwhile Maoist-controlled territory, the Tatas' new thinking on CSR and its denouement in their foray into Chhattisgarh, the brutal consequences of mining on tribals and the dirty tricks played by parties involved in the high-stakes game of capturing natural resources, I returned to the point where we first began to ask: what is the adivasi's real nature, and does he look like a Maoist, as my interlocutor at the Gondi language workshop had so evocatively asked me? I also subjected the Maoist himself to scrutiny and asked if he has any hope to offer to the tribal whose cause he claims to hold close to his heart. What are the new developments that loom on the adivasis' horizon, and what is his level of preparedness to deal with them? Who are the heroes and heroines emerging from within tribal communities to lead their people to the promised land? And what does the predicament of indigenous people say about us in a world facing existential crises along several dimensions?

Addressing these questions and issues, I discovered, required me to make one last field trip – right in my backyard, Delhi, where so many answers for happenings in remote corners seem to lie. Being away from the field also gave me the distance I needed to make sense of what I have seen and heard.

The tribal condition is unique because no other community has been promised so much and received so little. Not only do the adivasis lead lives of extreme deprivation, they do so despite a raft of constitutional safeguards designed to give them their due and their moral right as original inhabitants of the land.

Policies relating to the tribals have traditionally been characterized by the contradiction between two themes: self-determination in the matter of their community resources and restrictions on freedom in certain respects, including the sale of tribal land to non-tribals. This tension reflects the assumption that while the adivasi has a right to the forest, he or she is unschooled in the ways of the world and must be protected from inimical interests.

Unlike the agricultural class as a whole or even Dalits in particular, the tribals owe the privileged position accorded to them in the Indian Constitution not to their political power but to the spirit of socialism and largesse that imbued ruling elites in the early years of the Indian republic.[1]

In the 1940s, the Jharkhand Party was formed under the leadership of Jaipal Singh, a tribal leader who was a member of the Constituent Assembly. He was also a stalwart hockey player for India. For sixty years, the party fought for a separate state, but its effectiveness was undermined by a series of schisms. When the state of Jharkhand was created in 1998, it consisted only of the tribal districts of Bihar, rather than being, as Jaipal had hoped, a much larger province covering, in addition to Bihar,

[1]Guha, Ramachandra, 'Adivasis, Naxalites and Indian democracy', *Economic and Political Weekly* (2007): 3305–3312.

the contiguous tribal districts of West Bengal, Orissa, Madhya Pradesh and Andhra Pradesh. In the form in which it finally came into being, Jharkhand is home to an overwhelming majority of non-tribals, as is Chhattisgarh. Consequently, the adivasis of central India have a fragmented presence across ten states[2] – Chhattisgarh, Gujarat, Jharkhand, Rajasthan, Maharashtra, Madhya Pradesh, Andhra Pradesh, Odisha, Bihar and West Bengal.

Apart from Jharkhand, where parties headed by tribals have held power, albeit with a high turnover of governments, the importance of adivasis is restricted to a few legislative and parliamentary constituencies, where they call the shots. In the remaining constituencies, they are virtually voiceless. Thus, despite constituting 8 per cent of the population, tribals have very poor representation in positions of executive power in the judiciary and in the bureaucracy. In contrast, Dalits and Muslims have achieved significant success not only in the executive, the legislature and the judiciary, but in the armed forces as well.

Inevitably, privileges accorded to the tribals have ended up as mere lip service and the story of a close-knit community like a tribe has come to be defined, ironically, by its relations with a variety of outsiders, including petty traders, large mining companies, environmental crusaders, the Maoists and, of course, the nation state. This is typical of a collective that lacks the ability to articulate its own needs and desires and, therefore, ends up either as a reflection of someone else's fantasy or the victim of another's greed.

The absence of leaders among the tribals is also a direct result of the conflict raging between the Indian state and the Maoists. Both may consider an independent, non-violent voice as a threat

[2]These now constitute ten states after the formation of Jharkhand and Chhattisgarh.

to their turf. The travails of Noku Koram are being echoed in the challenges that Soni Sori, an emerging tribal leader, is facing in Bastar. When she takes up cases of 'encounter' killings of innocent tribals falsely accused of being Maoists, her efforts are confounded by the actions of the Maoists themselves, who carry out their own revenge killings even as Sori is protesting peacefully. In the toxic stand-off between the government and the insurgents, the space for a citizen hoping to get by simply on the promises upheld by our Constitution shrinks significantly. Such a person becomes an inconvenience for law enforcers and rebels alike. The lure of the enormous amount of money available to tribal leaders, even mere greenhorns, on account of mining interests, could well be another impediment to the emergence of authentic leadership.

One may argue that the many issues tribals face, like displacement, are not unique to their situation; Dalits and other backward castes are just as vulnerable to these challenges. If tribals constitute 40 per cent of the displaced, Dalits and other poor rural communities comprise an equal share. Even though 80 per cent of mining areas fall in scheduled areas, where adivasis represent the majority of the population, a significant number of Dalits and other backward castes live in these areas as well. In fact, the landless Dalit is usually not even entitled to compensation, unlike the adivasi who may have formal rights over land (30 per cent of the members of scheduled tribes and 45 per cent of the Dalits have been listed as landless, according to the Socio-Economic and Caste Census 2011) and can, thereby, salvage something by way of compensation. Therefore, the problem to be tackled is forced displacement in its totality, not just the injustice suffered by the dispossessed adivasi.

And yet there is something uniquely tragic about the adivasi ousted from his own home and land.

With his long strands of hair knotted in ringlets, his luxuriant white beard and his emaciated frame, K.B. Saxena is the epitome of a forest-dwelling ascetic, except that he is ensconced behind a desk in the middle of Lutyens Delhi – at the Council for Social Development, a think tank, to be precise. The think tank is located at the edge of Lodi Garden, a sprawling city park in the heart of the national capital, dotted with architectural works from the fifteenth century.

Saxena has been a career bureaucrat and is now a professor at the Council. He has a habit of fixing a piercing gaze on those with whom he is engaged in conversation, albeit with his left eye half shut, a tendency that would be disconcerting, were it not for his rare and sudden smile, which transforms his face into that of a delighted child's.

'For millennia, the adivasi was cut off from mainstream Aryan civilization,' he tells me. 'After the initial displacement from the Gangetic plain, waves of conquerors came and went, kingdoms arose and disappeared into sand, but the adivasi continued in an age-old pattern of life in the heart of the jungle. This led to a communitarian, egalitarian life, with very little market exposure. The idyll was interrupted by colonialism, with the creation of the Forest Department and the onset of [a system that introduced] state-managed forests.

'However, even today, the entire life of the adivasis is woven around the land they are born into, live on and are buried in. Land is a symbol of their identity, a mark of their dignity, as close to their sense of self as their own physical bodies.'

I protest that not just adivasis, but all Indians are inordinately attached to land. As a member of a 'zamindar'[3] family that

---

[3]India's British colonial masters had appointed zamindars to collect revenue from areas under their control. Zamindari, regarded as an exploitative system by the leaders of India's freedom movement, was abolished in 1952, five years after Independence.

had experienced its own richly deserved dispossession and having witnessed, at just one remove from a lost generation, the psychological trauma it had caused, I am indignant, even resentful, that the adivasi's love of land is being treated as a matter of such special concern.

'The displacement of the adivasi leads to the breakdown of the community, the living heartbeat of adivasi life,' Saxena explains. 'The ethnography of displaced tribals is very different from the ethnography of other displaced people. For the adivasi, all economic indicators apart, it is a fall from grace.

'The connection of the adivasi to the land is natural and inborn. Land, to others, is merely an economic resource, a sign of power and prestige in the world.[4] For the Dalits, displacement is less traumatic for two reasons. They move from one landless state to another. Further, they have been integrated with mainstream society, albeit at the lowermost level, for as long as the adivasi has been cut off from it. Hence, they [the Dalits] are habituated to their abject condition. That is why adivasis always ask for alternative land, where the community can be rehabilitated together.'

If Saxena is right, the tragedy of the adivasi is far more devastating than the misfortune of the displaced Dalit. I find myself lacking the data or experience to assess the validity of this conclusion. All I can assert is that the phenomenon of development through displacement and displacement without rehabilitation, aided and abetted by the state's military might, is a deeply disturbing feature of the national model of economic growth since the British Raj, a feature whose consequences have assumed an alarming magnitude in the new millennium.

[4]Indeed, the Permanent Settlement of Cornwallis that had given birth to the zamindari system marked the beginning of the commercialization of land in India.

Jo Woodman is a petite Britisher who works for Survival International, an organization that pledges, in connection with indigenous people, to 'defend their lives, protect their lands and determine their own futures.' She is an anthropologist and geographer who did her Ph.D from Cambridge University, training the focus of her research on the condition of tribals displaced by the twin Pench tiger reserves in the central Indian state of Madhya Pradesh.

I did not have the pleasure of meeting Jo (she is prohibited from entering India for reasons I will elaborate upon later), but managed to speak to her for a few hours on a slightly dodgy Skype connection. She was voluble and articulate. She obviously feels deeply about the pattern of development that sees fit to ride roughshod over the rights of indigenous people.

'We should be deeply, deeply horrified by the violation of tribal rights, which is a serious international problem,' says Jo. 'These are people who have learnt to adapt to their local conditions over countless generations. They have an incredibly light ecological footprint and a humbling knowledge and understanding of the world they live in. They have been self-sufficient for a large part of their history. Now our paradigm of development appears to be intent on destroying that self-sufficiency and knowledge, and taking away their self-respect.'

Jo argues that those who claim to be sympathetic to tribals imagine a future in which they could live the high life in Delhi and shop at malls. But the reality is that tribals are not actually in a position to make a choice between retaining their way of life and opting for a more comfortable urban lifestyle. They are, in fact, given no options at all, but forced to surrender their current means of livelihood, their lands, their knowledge and their self-sufficiency. All they are left with is dependency on their labour and on the whims of the state, and a life on the margins of the 'mainstream'. This, Jo says, is true not just in India, but across much of the world.

As she sees it, it is not the tribal peoples who pose a threat to conservation, but the logging and mining companies and the insatiable desire of urban societies for resources. Her first involvement with tribal rights in India in the year 2000 as part of Survival International was in the Niyamgiri case, where Vedanta, a mining company, was trying to mine on land vital and sacred to the Dongria Kondh tribals. Vedanta's keenness is not difficult to understand: there is, reportedly, two billion US dollars-worth of bauxite lying under the surface of the Niyamgiri hills.

Survival International had come to know about the case through the anthropologist Dr Felix Padel. Jo and her colleagues spent time with the Dongria and Kondh adivasis, learning about their lives in the hills and their fierce determination to defend Niyamgiri. They lobbied hard at state, national and international levels and, as Vedanta is a British company, they lobbied the British government and the company's major shareholders, including the Church of England.

After a visit to Niyamgiri, Jo was placed on a 'visa list' by the UPA government, denying her access to the country. But the concerted efforts of the Dongria and the Kondh and their many local, national and international supporters paid off: the Supreme Court of India upheld the right of the gram sabhas to give or withhold their consent. And the sabhas' response to the mine was a loud and resounding 'no'. It was, in Jo's eyes, a 'historic moment' in the movement for tribal rights.

Jo is still persona non grata in India. However, the internet and mobile phone have enabled her to remain engaged. CGNet Swara is one of her primary sources of news from the field. It was on CGNet swara, in fact, that she found a post filed by Mohan Yadav, my companion during the excursion into Harda, regarding evictions of members of the Baiga community from the Kanha Tiger Reserve – an issue she had remained concerned about from the time she was pursuing doctoral studies in Pench in the early years of the new century.

'When I spoke to Mohanji, using the number listed on the CGNet site, it was immediately clear he cared and would do whatever was possible to help the community. It seemed obvious that he had no axe to grind.'

Jo found that extremely refreshing and decided to get involved.

Since her preference is to personally speak to the affected parties herself, Mohan went to visit the Baiga villagers, carrying his mobile phone. Jo has only a smattering of Hindi, but she was assisted by an interpreter who called in from London while she herself was in South West England (for security reasons, Jo's exact coordinates, as well as the name and coordinates of the interpreter, cannot be shared). Mohan Yadav and the affected villagers were standing by a radio mast so that they could get a decent signal.

'They told me what they were going through', says Jo, 'and expressed what they wanted. Under no circumstances did they want to be evicted. After speaking to them, I spoke extensively to Mohan about forest rights and urged him to do the same with the communities.'

The community wanted Survival International to write to the authorities. Jo suggested that their message would carry more weight if they were to write it themselves. Mohan helped them to put down their thoughts.

'We are continuing to talk with the community, with Mohan and others at CGNet and to lobby for their right to stay in their homes. Mohan has helped the Baiga tribals travel to Bhopal to the Human Rights Commission to seek redress for some evictions that have already taken place. The threat of eviction still hangs over these communities and we'll continue to do what we can to help them.'

As I listen to her, I feel that in this transaction-oriented world in which we live, mainstream attitudes towards tribals is influenced by what they 'bring to the table'. Blinded by the man-made wonders of our civilization and too impatient to search for the treasures found in a different way of life, we regard the tribals as incapable of contributing anything of worth. Our best instincts urge us, therefore, to try and mould them in our own image. Our worst drive us to dehumanize and exploit them. What kind of environmental or humanitarian disaster will it take to open our eyes?

In 2005, the tiger-conservation movement in India woke up to the alarming news that tigers had disappeared from Sariska, one of the first few tiger conservation parks in the country. This led to a re-evaluation of the conservation paradigm which had previously focussed on denying locals access to protected zones through improved surveillance and control. It was recognized that the interests of indigenous communities and the survival of the tiger were aligned, though not congruent. The 2006 amendment to the Wildlife Protection Act explicitly included the protection of the rights of local communities in its framework of tiger protection.[5]

Tiger reserves were to be divided into core areas and buffer zones. The former were to be treated as inviolate sanctuaries, while the latter would be considered areas of co-existence, inhabited by both humans and tigers. This was in addition to

[5]http://www.vakilno1.com/bareacts/wildlifeamdtact2006/wild-life-protection-amendment-act-2006.html

the already existing provision for wildlife corridors – also regions of co-existence – that allowed the king of beasts to roam freely from one reserve to another.

But old attitudes die hard, even in those aware of the paradigm change after 2005.

'Talking about the co-existence of man and tiger is easy for those who do not have to face the day-to-day problems of living with a carnivore. Humans breed buffalos and tigers hunt buffalos,' says S.P. Yadav, Deputy Director General of the Global Tiger Forum, an association of tiger range countries usually chaired by a minister for environment and forests of one of the member countries. 'In Cambodia, the tribal appetite for meat has led to the extinction of the tiger.' Yadav is on secondment from the Indian Forest Service. He is a strongly built man with a professorial air and a pleasant smile. Under the glass table top of his wooden table is displayed a photo of a yogi sitting on a tiger-skin mat. 'If you fly over the Dang forest in Gujarat, you will see a rich green cover,' Yadav goes on. 'But it is a dead forest – not even a squirrel stirs there. Everything has been eaten up by the tribals. The tribals' love for meat is such that they have been known to fell a tree just to hunt the squirrels nesting on its branches. The presence of important temples in the core area can attract lakhs of pilgrims on special days, again destabilizing the eco-system.

'Co-existence is possible in African reserves, stretching over thousands of square kilometres, not on our reserves, which are barely a few hundred square kilometres [in area].'

In India today, the core areas measure 45,000 sq km out of the total area of 68,000 sq km reserved for tiger sanctuaries. The high percentage of core areas shows that Yadav's pessimism about the co-existence of tigers and tribals continues to be the standard operating assumption in tiger conservation.

According to him, 44,000 families continue to live in the core areas of 49 tiger reserves. These families cannot be evicted because they are protected by the Forest Rights Act (FRA). Unlike in mining, he says, where coercion is often used as a strategy for displacing recalcitrant locals, muscle power has a smaller role to play in conservation because there may be no major commercial interests involved.

The alleged encroachment of villagers on core areas is accompanied by infringements by the urban tourism lobby which is eager for access to such areas to set up 'VIP resorts', special sighting privileges and exclusive pilgrimages to places of religious importance. This particular lobby is not merely restricted to India, but has international backing. In May 2015, when the tiger referred to as 'T-24', also known as Ustad, was placed in captivity after his fourth human kill in five years in the Ranthambore Tiger Reserve, there was an outpouring of indignation on social media, with hashtags like '#JeSuisUstad' and '#BringUstadBack' being used to drum up support and candlelight vigils and protests being held in cities like Jaipur, Agra, Hyderabad, Mumbai, Nagpur and Bengaluru.

A documentary film, highlighting the need for Ustad to be placed in captivity, provoked hundreds of personal accusations and enraged comments against its makers on online forums. The filmmakers would later remark that there had never been a similar level of outrage against the biggest threat to India's wild tigers — the destruction of their habitat. Regarding Ustad's fate, however, the local villagers and wildlife conservationists were united, for once: both groups demanded the tiger's immediate eviction from the reserve and its confinement in a restricted environment, where it could do no further harm to humans.[6]

---

[6]http://news.mongabay.com/2015/06/social-media-firestorm-defends-popular-man-eating-tiger-in-india-raising-conservation-questions/

In waters already roiled by mining interests, conservationists and upholders of adivasi rights, the presence of the lobby of urban tourists adds yet another layer of complexity.

Having been presented two diametrically opposing views on the tribals, I seek out an academic to play the role of referee. Prakash Kashwan is an Assistant Professor at the University of Connecticut's Political Science department. He has a Ph.D from Indiana University, where he was one of the last students of Elinor Ostrom, Nobel Prize winner in Economics for her work on common property resources. I meet Prakash at a conference in IIM Bangalore, where we find ourselves positioned next to each other at the welcome photo shoot.

He is measured, as academics ought to be.

'Tribals have found ways of interacting with the institutional status quo to get by,' he tells me. 'They have bought into the status quo because of compulsions. But still, it is only the elite in [among] the adivasis who join the exploiters and broker access between the locals and the government. The vast majority would still be simple in the ways of the world and skilled in the ways of the forest.

'But the romanticization of tribals is also wrong,' he goes on. 'They used to practise shifting cultivation and protect sacred groves and watersheds for specific reasons. Since respect for the sacred has gone down in youth everywhere, including tribal youth, we need to give them new reasons to protect the forest.

'People's aspirations have changed and there is nothing wrong with that. There is no need for tribals to be damned to subsistence-level aspirations. But these aspirations should be met from forests. Allow them to harvest timber and hold their hands to build capacities.'

But if Kashwan is measured in his assessment of tribals, he is nothing if not scathing in his evaluation of the Forest Department. He describes an occasion on which he was visiting central India as part of an international NGO team. Over drinks, a forest official had apparently stretched his hands out, as if to encompass the world – here, Prakash mimics the gesture – and proclaimed, 'This whole fucking town belongs to me!'

Kashwan feels that while Forest Department officials have bragging rights, they have no accountability.

'If you add up all the plantation-covered areas for which the Forest Department takes credit and divide the figure by five or six, you will get a number representing twice the area of forest land than actually exists in the country! And if you bear in mind that only one-fifth of the country's forest land has fertile soil where plantations can come up, the Forest Department's claim suggests more than a fifty-fold wastage of effort on their part – assuming, of course, that all flourishing forests in India owe their existence to the department.'

'Despite this record, also scathingly remarked upon by the Comptroller and Auditor General of India, the Forest Department continues to claim money for reforestation. No one asks: what have you done with the money you already got?'

Kashwan feels that while the FRA is a major blow to the Forest Department's hegemony over the country's forests, it retains its formidable power at the grassroots level by shrewdly manipulating micro-level politics.

'Activists need to focus on grassroots mobilization, [a sphere of necessary activity] which many are getting out of,' says Prof. Kashwan. 'Rights have to be asserted,' he concludes, raising his hands and bringing them down repeatedly for emphasis. '*Haq lena padta hai.*' But given the current system of patronage and privilege, the ability of grassroots activists to achieve anything significant is open to question.

'What do you see as the future of the adivasi, sir?' I had asked K.B. Saxena.

'They are doomed,' was his immediate response. 'Without the support of the mainstream, they are on their way to becoming the untouchables of the future social order of the world.'

2

Soni Sori Rises from the Ashes

History has established that Lakshmibai, the Rani of Jhansi, revered by many as an icon of India's initial resistance to colonial rule, had no intention at the outset of taking up arms against the British. All she had wanted, really, was that her adopted son be recognized as heir to the throne left vacant by her deceased husband. If things had gone in her favour, she might well have spent the rest of her days ensuring that the boy was groomed into a fine king and basking in the warmth of his lifelong devotion. Her maternal wisdom might even have prompted her to advise him to choose pragmatism over emotion and tolerate minor slights from the country's foreign rulers as part and parcel of statesmanship.

But life had other plans for her.

The British refused to recognize the four-year-old Damodar Rao as the rightful heir to the throne and invoked the Doctrine of Lapse that held that any princely state or territory under the direct influence of the British East India Company would automatically be annexed if the ruler was either 'manifestly incompetent or died without a male heir'. Lakshmibai rejected the pension offered in compensation and rode into battle against the greatest colonial power of the nineteenth century, wielding double swords as she took on the enemy.

It is rare to find a modern-day personality who can match the Rani's desperate courage in a more contemporary context, but certain parallels do come to mind when considering the life and predicament of Soni Sori, who might emerge as something of an icon, not merely for adivasis, but for disempowered people as a whole.

'I was happy as a schoolteacher in Jabeli,' Soni muses, sitting across from me in the cafeteria of the Press Club of India in New Delhi, where she has just concluded a press conference.

It is August 2015 and the evening is warm. The who's who of the breed recognized as India's 'liberal intellectuals' had been present at the press conference where Sori was the cynosure of all eyes.

'Unlike my father, my husband did not own land,' she now continues. 'But he had a hotel.'

I realize that she is referring, in the lingo used by many Indians, to a restaurant.

'He came from a trader's family,' she says, continuing to speak of her husband, Anil Futane, 'We had a car. Our children were growing up. I was happy.'

I contemplate this simple, slightly built woman, with her sisterly air, and note with what unaffected humility she carries her celebrity status. Who is this woman who has earned the unstinting attention of the most battle-hardened Delhi cynics? What is her life story? And why does she represent one of the last flickering embers of hope in Bastar today?

The story begins, as much in Bastar does, with the Salwa Judum pogrom. As the campaign to forcibly evict adivasis from mineral-bearing land was gathering momentum, the police started identifying educated young adivasi men who could be a potential obstacle to the evictions and concentrated their efforts on enlisting them as special police officers. They also sought information about the Maoists, information that everyone living in a 'liberated' village would possess.

One of the people thus identified was Sori's nephew Lingaram Kodopi, known as Linga who hailed from a prominent land-owning family in Bastar. His grandfather Mandru, who had been a sarpanch, owned close to 200 acres of land. His two grand-uncles had been CPI MLAs.[7]

For several months, the police had been attempting to lure Linga into joining the force as an SPO. When they failed, he was picked up from his house in August 2009 and locked up in a police station toilet for 40 days on suspicion of being a Maoist courier.

After Linga's elder brother Masaram, and Himanshu Kumar, a Gandhian peace activist who had been running an ashram in the area since the 1990s, filed a habeas corpus application in the Chhattisgarh high court, Linga was released on 10 October 2009.

The harassment continued, however, and not merely from the police. Keen to have Linga join their movement, Maoist leaders too spared no effort to try and win him over. This would go on until Himanshu, concerned that one or the other of the war

---

[7]The Soris have large landholdings and Soni's father Mundra Ram was Congress sarpanch of Bade Bedma for over a decade. Sori's estranged brother Sukhdev and his wife too have held positions in the panchayat, representing the Congress. Two of her uncles were MLAs and Sori's cousin Amrita is DSP in Jagdalpur (Bastar). (http://archive.indianexpress.com/news/soni-s-story/983928/0).

fronts would end up destroying Linga, persuaded him to leave Dantewada and go to Delhi, where he enrolled in a journalism course.

In December 2009, Himanshu Kumar's ashram was razed to the ground by police bulldozers. His efforts to bring justice to the scores of people affected by the Salwa Judum had made him the administration's bête noire, a far cry from the early days when he would be inducted into every government committee on account of his easy familiarity with tribal communities and his knowledge of Gondi.

The next year would be the bloodiest in the history of the Maoist movement, ending in 1,180 deaths.[8] (It was also the year in which the maximum amount of forestland – about 14,500 hectares – was diverted for mining in any single year.) In April 2010, an ambush by the insurgents would lead to the death of 76 CRPF jawans. In July 2010, the Maoists attacked Awdhesh Gautam, Congress leader, who was a prominent contractor in the area. Close to 100 Naxals and 150 villagers, led by the Maoist commander Ganesh Ukey, circled his house. Gautam escaped, but his sister and an employee died. Several members of his family were injured. Almost simultaneously, a 150-strong group of uniformed Naxal cadres attacked Kuakonda Police Station and the CRPF camp with rifles and mortar fire. On 5 August 2010, a bomb blast completely demolished the new tehsil office in Kuakonda. In September 2010, Naxalites stopped some trucks in Nerli and set them on fire.

The police, now led by S.R.P. Kalluri, Senior Superintendant of Police (SSP) in Dantewada, listed Soni Sori as an accused in all the FIRs and declared her to be absconding, even though she was reporting for duty at her school every day. Her husband

---

[8]http://www.satp.org/satporgtp/countries/india/database/indiafatalities.htm

was listed as a co-accused in the Gautam case and put behind bars in August 2010.

Why, one wonders, would the police declare an easily accessible person, that too one accused of heinous crimes, as 'absconding'? Were the charges against Sori fabricated and levelled at her with the intention of deterring any possible action she might consider in future, either directly in support of the insurgents or against the police in the event of human-rights abuses against the tribals? Or were the charges intended to bring pressure to bear on Soni and blackmail her into becoming an informer in the war against the Maoists?

In August 2010, Maoist Politburo member Cherukuri Azad was killed while in the process of initiating peace talks with the Indian government, an event I elaborate on subsequently in the book. This would mark an important turning point in the fate of Essar's slurry pipeline, which passed through densely forested areas controlled by the rebels. Azad had opposed the project on environmental grounds. After his death, his colleagues would support the project, but not without levying the requisite 'tax'.[9]

In March 2011, a 300-strong contingent of Koya commandos and CRPF soldiers are alleged to have attacked Tadmetla and later attempted to pass off the operation as a Maoist-led one. Ignoring repeated warnings by Himanshu Kumar to stay away, Lingaram Kodopi returned to Chhattisgarh to cover the atrocities perpetrated on the locals during the attack. He was now a trained reporter and more dangerous than ever to the police.

Meanwhile, in the chronology of events in Bastar, things were about to change for Soni Sori.

In March 2011, Ankit Garg took over from Kalluri as SSP

---

[9]http://archive.tehelka.com/story_main50.asp?filename=Ne151011 coverstory.asp

of Dantewada when Kalluri was promoted to the position of Inspector General of Police (IGP) in Bastar.

In June 2011, Soni Sori's father was attacked and shot in the leg by the Maoists. Just as the police suspected Soni of being a Maoist, the Maoists had been watching her frequent visits to the police station in connection with her cases and concluded that she and her father were informers. They had been summoned twice and charged in the people's court set up by the insurgents. Soni challenged her accusers to prove her complicity with the police.

Given the new stance adopted by the rebel powers following Cherukuri Azad's death, the Essar pipeline project had made significant progress by now.

While the 'cut' of the Maoists is commonplace in such projects, for some reason,[10] the police asked Soni in September 2011 to help them catch R.K. Lala, the Essar contractor, in the act of handing over money to the rebels. Mankar, a constable from the Kirandul Police Station, wanted Lingaram Kodopi to pose as a Maoist, accept money from Lala, then hand it over to the police. If Soni could persuade Linga to do the needful, Mankar promised that all the police cases against her would be withdrawn. Soni refused, but alleged that Mankar himself had made a call to Lala from her phone, impersonating a local Maoist.

On 9 September, Lala and Kodopi were both arrested. According to the police, they were caught red-handed while exchanging money in a market place. They also alleged that Soni, who was present at the spot, had managed to escape. The accused men maintain, however, that each was picked up separately from

---

[10]One hypothesis is that the police were not getting their desired share of the pie.

his home. Later, D.V.C.S. Verma, an Essar manager, would also be arrested. Both Lala and Verma were immediately released on bail, while Linga was left to languish behind bars.

Expecting to be rounded up next, Soni, disguised as an ailing woman, fled through the jungles of Chhattisgarh and made her way to Delhi. On 4 October 2011, she was arrested in the capital and booked under various sections, including extortion, criminal conspiracy and unlawful activities. On 7 October, despite her statement to the Saket court that she feared for her life, she was transferred to the custody of the Chhattisgarh state police and sent back to Chhattisgarh.

Soni Sori alleges that on 8 and 9 October, she was tortured in custody – stripped naked, administered electric shocks, sexually assaulted and violated in other ways, with stones being inserted in her vagina.[11]

By now, through the Human Rights Law Network which had taken up her case, Sori had become a cause célèbre for leading activists and intellectuals all over the world. The National Human Rights Commission took suo moto cognizance of the case, and questions were simultaneously raised about it in the Indian Parliament. Human Rights Watch wrote to the then prime minister Manmohan Singh, seeking an independent probe into the matter, while Amnesty International declared Soni Sori a prisoner of conscience.

In late October 2011, the Supreme Court issued a directive ordering a medical examination of Sori. According to the report of the NRS Medical College and Hospital in Kolkata, 'two foreign bodies recovered of sizes 2.5 cm x 1.5 cm x 1.0 cm each from the vagina and one foreign body of size 2 cm x 1.5 cm x 1.5 cm was removed from the rectum'. Some news reports

[11]http://www.tehelka.com/2011/10/the-inconvenient-truth-of-soni-sori/

disputed the veracity of the medical report, because the latter apparently contradicted the findings of a previous X-ray and CT scan carried out on Sori in Chhattisgarh.[12] It is not clear how the Supreme Court came to choose the NRS Medical College and Hospital in Kolkata as the test centre.

On 26 January 2012, Ankit Garg, the SP of Dantewada, whom Soni had accused of masterminding her torture, was given a Presidential gallantry award for killing six Maoists in the Mahasumund encounter in October 2010. Again, there was an outcry from human rights activists, protesting against the honour bestowed on an officer who had been accused of violating a woman in custody. In response, the Director Generalof Police, Vishwaranjan, issued a clarification that Garg had not been given an award for meritorious lifetime service, but for gallantry displayed in a specific encounter.[13]

In May 2012, the Supreme Court directed the Chhattisgarh state to bring Sori to the All India Institute of Medical Sciences (AIIMS) in Delhi for full medical treatment. In January 2013, at Soni's request, she was transferred to Jagdalpur Central Jail from the Raipur Central Jail. In May 2013, her husband Anil Futane was acquitted of all charges against him and released. While in jail, he had become paralysed from the waist down, allegedly due to torture. According to some reports, he blamed his wife for his predicament, complaining that she had been free for over a year while he languished behind bars.[14]

When he died in August 2013, Sori approached the Dantewada district court for a limited-period bail to perform

---

[12]http://archive.indianexpress.com/news/soni-s-story/983928/0

[13]http://www.thehindu.com/news/national/activists-shocked-at-gallantry-award-for-chhattisgarh-cop/article2834675.ece

[14]http://www.thehindu.com/news/national/other-states/soni-soris-husband-dies/article4985885.ece

her deceased husband's last rites. But her request was denied by the same Sessions judge who had acquitted Futane.

In November 2013, Soni Sori and Linga Kodopi were granted bail, but barred from entering Chhattisgarh. In February 2014, they were given 'permanent bail'. Though they could now travel freely, they would have to report to the police station every week. In December 2015, the conditions of bail were relaxed further.

In May 2014, Sori fought the Parliamentary elections on the ticket of the Aam Aadmi Party from the Bastar constituency, New Delhi's giant-killing political party that is yet to build a strong presence elsewhere in the country. She lost to Dinesh Kashyap of the BJP. She says her decision to join a national political party was driven by her need to 'stay alive and fight'.

There are three possible interpretations of what happened to Sori: first, that she was completely naïve and got embroiled in a quagmire not of her own making; second, that she made the mistake of acting as a conduit between the powers running the area – the Maoists, the contractors and the government; third, that she was a 'double agent'.

For someone to work as a double agent, it is necessary for the two sides involved to be locked in an adversarial relationship. If on the other hand, the parties concerned are playing a 'mixed strategy' of conflict and cooperation, the double agent is as much a conduit as a mole and becomes all the more vulnerable to the shifting contours of the relationship.

Even if Sori was a double agent, the ruling elite must ponder why some people would be driven to take up this option in a Left-wing extremist area.

Did the police gain anything from Sori's intermediation, thus giving her impunity for the time that Kalluri was the SSP? Had she slipped through the cracks during the handover of authority from Kalluri to Garg? Are Sori and Kodopi as vigilant about

Maoist misdemeanours as they are about the transgressions of the Indian state? Is it fair to expect them to be? Why do armchair theorists expect local leaders to have spotless histories? Why do activists object to attempts to probe into an individual's tangled past?

What really happened to Soni Sori is a matter of endless debate and of sensing the imperceptible inner shifts through which irreproachability may or may not give way to silent complicity. But it is her transformation in the wake of her incarceration that is remarkable. To understand the kind of work she is currently engaged in, we must return to the scene of her press conference in Delhi.

There is a definite buzz in the air. We are in a wood-panelled room with a projector and screen. The legend 'Press Club of India' is emblazoned on the opposite wall. It is obvious that this is not any old press conference. Prashant Bhushan is here; author and activist Arundhati Roy walks in; the well-known human-rights lawyer Vrinda Grover greets her; Annie Raja of the CPI makes her entrance...

Suddenly, Roy spots someone behind her and greets her warmly. The woman in question is dressed in a salwar kameez with a floral pattern in purple and yellow; I recognize Soni Sori. I also spot Himanshu Kumar, Sori's guruji, a powerfully built man, who speaks passionately in Hindi and carries a head of scanty but carefully dyed hair. Later, Linga Kodopi, a lithe young man with a charismatic, devil-may-care air about him, takes his place at the table facing the audience. We are ready to begin.

We start with a film based on Linga Kodopi's footage on different human-rights abuses in Chhattisgarh. Three incidents are highlighted: in one, we see a long line of people, about 500 to 600 in number and dressed in dhotis and saris, walking on both sides of a highway and heading for a police station. Next comes a scene where a large gathering is being addressed by Sori at the police station. They are protesting against the abduction of a woman called Sukdi. As a result, three days later, Sukdi will be returned.

The second scene shows Linga pointing out bullet marks on a small embankment. These were apparently the places where bullets fired by the police had landed, when they shot at a villager who was on his daily visit to the river. The police blamed the Maoists for the man's death. Again, the villagers call Soni and Linga, who organize a rally. The matter has not yet been resolved. At the end of this footage, Linga introduces Hidme, a ten-year-old girl in a bright frock, who is the daughter of the dead villager.

The third story is the most heart-wrenching of all, because the person concerned is present at the conference and presents a pathetic picture of a young woman with the bloom of youth all but gone. In 2008, on her way to a fair in Sukma, the seventeen-year-old Hidme was picked up by the police in a case involving the killing of 23 policemen by a team of 350 Maoists. She was charged under sections 302, 147, 148 and 149 of the Indian Penal Code and different sections of the Arms Act. Upon her arrest, she was taken to the local police station, from where she was transferred to the Dantewada thana and, the next day, to the Bhansi police station. There, she alleges, she was kept bound and blindfolded and her sari and gold ornaments were taken away. She was raped by the policemen and relentlessly beaten for six days.

'It was only when they feared I might die that they gave me some water,' she says in a later conversation.

She describes how her body had swollen up so much after she was tortured with electric shocks that she could barely walk. Also, her clothes were taken away, leaving her only in the petticoat she had been wearing, without a sheet to cover herself with or lie down on. Only when she was being sent back to Sukma were her clothes returned to her.

'The policemen there helped me to get [medical] treatment, but warned that if I wanted to go home safely, I was not to tell the magistrate that I had been beaten,' she states.

She says that numerous other women are being systematically abused in jails.

For years, Hidme was transferred between the Raipur and Jagdalpur jails. Her health deteriorated rapidly; multiple operations were necessary to treat her condition. Getting each surgery performed was a task in itself, she says, as jail authorities would often claim they didn't have enough guards on duty to escort her to the hospital.

In the course of her imprisonment, she met Soni Sori. According to the latter, her condition after undergoing police torture was far worse than Hidme's. The young girl would apparently massage Sori's brutalized body and comfort her during those difficult times.

Sori, in turn, turned up at the Dantewada jail to receive Hidme on her acquittal. However, she was initially prevented from doing so by a stranger who insisted that he had been sent by Hidme's family to pick her up. By the time Sori managed to stall him and fetch Hidme from inside, the man had disappeared. Neither Hidme nor anyone in her family has a clue to his identity. Her lawyer informed her that Bastar's IGP S.R.P. Kalluri had ordered his men to look for any case in any police station that might have the name Hidme, a fairly common adivasi moniker, on the list of accuseds. Allegedly, the name was all he needed to send her back to prison on the very day she had been released from the Dantewada jail.

By the time Hidme was acquitted, Sori had gone a long way from being a village schoolteacher in Jabeli. She was, by now, a leader with stature and authority and used her network to draw attention to Hidme's case. As a result, on 1 October 2015, taking suo moto cognizance of the atrocities committed by the police against adivasi women, the National Commission for Scheduled Tribes issued a notice to the Director General of Police, Chhattisgarh, instructing him to lodge a formal complaint against the accused police officials under the SC/ST (Prevention of Atrocities Act), 1989.[15]

'Things have become worse in Bastar in the last year,' says Soni, as I sit with her and a few of her associates in the Press Club's open-air cafeteria, soon after her interactions with the media. 'I could have stayed in Delhi, but I went back to fight. The good thing is that now the villagers are fighting too.

'Kalluri had said to me, "Don't do rallies. You will not want for money." He summoned Linga and spoke to him, with a revolver placed on his desk. "We will give you ₹25,000 a month," he said.

'When we refused his offer, he accused us of being Naxal agents and started a campaign – a *nikaalne ka andolan* – to isolate and exile us.

'He got some people to stone my home. Leaflets, with "Leave Bastar" written on them, are thrown into the homes of colleagues. My in-laws don't speak to me any more. My colleagues in the Aam Aadmi Party are under pressure from their families to distance themselves from me. I urge them not to take the risk of associating with me.

'But the people are with me. They have learnt to fight,' Soni

[15]http://www.thehindu.com/news/national/st-panel-issues-notice-to-chhattisgarh-dgp/article7743876.ece

goes on, adding quietly, 'my children encourage me. Muskaan is sixteen, Deependra, fourteen, and Amrita, eleven. They feel I am doing the right thing.'

By now, a gentle drizzle has started and we move to a table under a tree which affords some shelter. Hidme shivers and draws her sari pallu close around her.

Soni looks at her affectionately. 'I am trying to infuse Hidme with my own strength. I want her to fight,' she says. 'Perhaps we can do something for all the women who are being unjustly kept in jail. Maybe, Hidme will emerge as the strongest of us all.'

I tell Soni about my interactions with the Tata Steel executives and list the plans they were making for the welfare of local communities. I ask her if she would be willing to speak to the company.

She gives me a patient hearing. Then she says, "The Tatas cannot succeed in Dantewada, because people have the bad example of sixty years of NMDC before them,' she says, alluding to the National Mineral Development Corporation. 'No adivasi can hope to get free treatment in their hospital. Jobs go to outsiders, even when we are qualified [for them]. People will not forget all this easily.'

I venture to ask a question, a question that, I realize, really has no answer in the present. 'We have seen so many people come up from penury, from exploitative conditions, to become mass leaders, Soniji,' I say. 'But they all get co-opted into the mainstream after a while. How do we know you will remain true to your cause?'

Soni thinks for a moment, before replying. 'I never wanted this,' she says. 'I was happy as a schoolteacher. Now I have lost my old life, and all that I held dear. But I have found the affection of the people. They are my family, my treasure.

'I am not afraid of dying or going to jail. Even a thousand Kalluris can't stop me.'

Unfolding events in Bastar would soon present Soni an opportunity to make good on her bold declaration of intent, as described later in the book.

3

The JagLAG Girls Take the Plunge

Soni Sori is not alone in her fight. She has the support of a vast network of activists, the backing of the Aam Aadmi Party and the constant guidance of her 'guruji' Himanshu Kumar. One of her most important sources of strength is a group of lawyers – all women – armed with degrees from prestigious universities, who help her navigate the legal minefields that the adivasis face on a daily basis. Here is their story.

During the years she spent in the USA, Shalini Gera, a Ph.D in neuroscience, with a successful career as a consultant in the pharmaceutical industry, had been involved with a number of social causes and realized that they gave her greater fulfilment than her professional work. In 2010, she decided to return to India to work in the NGO sector. She began by working with the Chhattisgarh Mukti Morcha, a group set up by the legendary trade-union organizer Shankar Guha Niyogi. Keen on being useful to them in some way, Shalini decided to study law, expecting to spend her time mainly on trade-union issues.

She enrolled in the law programme offered by Delhi University and interned with the Human Rights Law Network (HRLN) headed by Colin Gonzalves. This is where she learnt about Sori's case.

'The Soni Sori case was a watershed,' Gera, a confident

woman in her mid-forties, recalls in a Skype interview in October 2015. 'Before that, very few cases from Bastar reached Delhi. Her case gave us a ringside view of what was happening. The charges were so specious that no one in Delhi believed they would be admitted, but they were.'

At HRLN, Gera met twenty-four-year-old Isha Khandelwal, who had switched over from her studies in computer programming to the study of human-rights law in Delhi. Members of the Human Resources Law Network began to believe that they needed some lawyers on the ground in Chhattisgarh to address the many travesties of justice similar to those Sori was facing. But whom should they send? They needed someone experienced, someone with the stomach for the battles they would have to wage, someone who cared deeply about what was going on in Bastar.

In this situation, with the need for 'boots on the ground' becoming paramount, three people raised their hands. All three were women; they had a combined total of zero days of experience between them as full-fledged lawyers and none had worked in Bastar before. Shalini Gera and Isha Khandelwal were joined by the twenty-five-year-old Parijata Bharadwaj, a graduate from the Tata Institute of Social Sciences and a recent law graduate.

'It was certainly not ideal,' says Gera. 'All we had was a strong sense that justice was not being delivered to local communities. What drove us here and what keeps us here is an abiding interest in what is happening to the adivasis.'

Gera was in her second career and did not have too many family commitments to hold her back. Bharadwaj was an army kid; so her family had some understanding of life in conflict zones. But Khandelwal's banker father was distraught. The Jiram Ghati ambush in which Mahendra Karma had been killed had just taken place in May 2013 and that news did not help to ease his anxiety.

Finally, when the three women did leave for Chhattisgarh, they were joined by Rupesh Kumar, a paralegal who, however, had to leave after a couple of months due to pressing family commitments. Twenty-five-year-old Guneet Kaur, who had a Master's in law, with a focus on transitional justice, from the University of California at Berkeley, completed the all-girl group. Guneet worked as a Research Fellow and did not appear in court.

Supported by fellowships that a few Supreme Court lawyers, like Colin Gonsalves, and Rajeev Dhavan, a commissioner of the International Commission of Jurists, the international human rights NGO, had put them on, the women would not need to charge their clients who, in any case, did not have the wherewithal to pay for their legal services.

Through a series of RTI applications, the group, which had started referring to itself as the Jagdalpur Legal Aid Group, or JagLAG, began discovering that the ground realities were every bit as alarming as they had suspected.[16]

Adivasis between the ages of 18 and 35 were being rounded up in groups on heinous charges, crammed into overcrowded prisons and kept incarcerated for extended periods of time. They were often completely innocent and just happened to be at the wrong place at the wrong time. Sometimes, their only crime was a relatively minor one, like offering a meal to a Maoist, although they would invariably be booked on grave, non-bailable sections of the law. A rare minority was, however, guilty of the charges levelled at them.

Close to half of the cases had more than five accused named

[16]Data provided on Chhattisgarh prisons is taken from information gathered by JagLAG from government departments through RTI applications.

in the FIR. Five per cent of the chargesheets had between 21 and 100 names listed. In one case, the testimony of the witness failed to mention two people who were in jail, but no one discovered the oversight. The two spent six to seven years in jail waiting for the prosecution witness, before JagLAG discovered the lapse.

In the Jagdalpur and Dantewada district jails, the percentage of cases in which bails were granted amounted to half the national average. And even on the occasions bail was granted, often, the undertrials were unable to furnish the required surety.

Trials would tend to drag on for an inordinately long time. For instance, in 2013, the average duration of imprisonment of undertrials in the Jagdalpur and Dantewada district jails was 70 per cent higher than for Chhattisgarh as a whole. Trials would not come to a swift end, because prosecution witnesses – often soldiers in the CRPF or Naga battalion or other kinds of government officials, including doctors – just would not show up. In one case, the witness belonged to the Naga battalion, which had left the place long since. The court waited for over six years for the battalion to return, before finally closing the case. Precedents set by the Supreme Court in the matter of imposing a cap on the number of days taken by the prosecution to present its witnesses – between sixty-six and seventy days – were regularly breached by several orders of magnitude.

On certain occasions, hearings were postponed, because no armed guards were available to escort the prisoners to court. Sometimes, the judge did not show up; at others, one of the lawyers would fail to appear. And so, date after date would be strung together, with no reprieve for undertrials, their hope slowly ebbing away, till months stretched into years and lives unraveled entirely.

As a result, Chhattisgarh, today, has the dubious distinction of harbouring one of the country's highest percentages of jailed citizens. Jail-occupancy rates in the state are 253 per cent of capacity, with the number going up to 600 per cent in areas affected by Left-wing extremism. Inmates sleep in shifts at night and live in filthy, unhygienic conditions. Despite this state of affairs, the system does not appear to have either the will or the ability to achieve a speedy resolution of pending cases, with the time spent by undertrials in custody rising to twice or even thrice the national average.

The high proclivity of the police to keep adivasis in these areas in prison becomes clear when looking at statistics related to the final element of the legal process – the sentencing. The complete acquittal rate during the period from 2005 to 2013 was between 91 and 99 per cent, where 'complete acquittal' means that if ten people are charged with five sections each, all ten are acquitted of all charges.[17]

According to a member of the Bastar Bar Association, the unwillingness of people to testify against Maoists is also a contributing factor for the high acquittal rate, a feature of trials across India, but one that is even more glaring in the insurgency-affected areas.

The spate of imprisonments is accompanied by a spree of 'encounters' – some genuine, but many largely fake – in which adivasis are killed by other adivasis who have signed up as SPO to escape the fate of their tribal brethren. These SPOs are often the ones tasked with the most brutal missions.

The Maoists have responded to the SPO-ization of the populace by killing these special police recruits, not in armed battle, but by catching them unawares when they are going about their daily business – en route to their wife's village for a visit, for example, or out shopping at the market[18] – and least

[17]http://blog.mylaw.net/tag/jagdalpur-legal-aid-group/

[18]http://www.thehindu.com/news/national/other-states/maoists-targeting-local-tribal-cops-in-chhattigarhs-bastar/article7739269.ece

prepared to defend themselves. It is no surprise that a number of villagers are choosing to leave the forces to avoid the menu of traumas offered to them.

It does appear that ordinary people are being stung by the kiss of death on a daily basis – killed in fake encounters, imprisoned for extended periods on specious grounds, 'SPO'd – that is, recruited as Special Police Officers to turn on their own kith and kin – and scared into running away to neighbouring states. Meanwhile, attempts to kick-start mining and make Chhattisgarh the 'Number One Indian state' continue apace.

JagLAG decided to work towards fulfilling two main objectives – documentation of the situation and legal intervention. Till October 2015, they had dealt with close to fifty cases, involving sixty to seventy people. They have managed to secure forty bail orders. But they have also made qualitative contributions by being the only ones to challenge illegal detention and raise the issue of custodial torture.

'Checking police impunity with respect to the adivasis is a start,' says Khandelwal. 'But we have a long way to go. We would like to involve local lawyers more. They have a number of advantages, like greater acceptability in the courts. But so far, we have not been able to get any meaningful participation.'

JagLAG also works closely with Soni Sori.

'Soni has emerged as the go-to person for adivasis in these parts,' says Gera. 'Other adivasi politicians feel hesitant about raising adivasi issues in the same manner that a Muslim politician in the BJP would be hesitant about raising issues concerning the Muslims.

'But Soni is fearless. She is not afraid to bring issues to the forefront and take on the system head on to demand accountability from law enforcers. Manish Kunjam of the CPI has also made a great contribution, but Soni's trial by fire, the trajectory she has taken to enter politics, puts her in a different league.'

In the Kukanaar village case, for example, where a few women, protesting the arrests of their husbands, were badly beaten up, JagLAG is helping Sori with the arduous steps to be gone through for basic legal redressal, including filing a complaint, registering an FIR and ensuring action on the FIR.

Until the events of February 2016, the JagLAG team lives in a modest two bedroom apartment in Jagdalpur. Their office is on the floor above their apartment. They spend about three days of the week in court, and the rest of their time preparing for cases. Hearings could be held in Dantewada or Bijapur and involve 8-9 hour bus rides for the round trip, sometimes for an appearance of just 5 minutes. The girls usually like to travel in pairs but that is not always possible. Once when Gera was travelling in a bus, the bus driver was waved to a halt and she was ordered to get off by a police officer who asked her to accompany him for interrogation. When Gera resisted, he backed off and said that he had information that a suspicious woman 'in a bob cut' was on the bus.

There are many uncharted days. Often a phone call will come saying someone has been picked up. In such a situation, Gera says that the most difficult problem is to get information on the identity of the party that had effected the 'arrest'.

'The CRPF is not allowed to detain anyone,' says Khandelwal. 'They are supposed to be accompanied by civil police, but they regularly pick up people. So do a number of other law enforcement agencies. Often the police is in civilian clothing, so we don't even know if it is the Indian state that is involved or some Naxalite faction.'

The next important imponderable relates to the location to which the arrested people have been taken. According to Gera, even though the arrested people have to be presented in court in 24 hours, that often does not happen. When the girls go to police stations to make inquiries they are received civilly enough but they have little success in prying out the information they seek.

In the beginning, the members of JagLAG team were regarded as objects of curiosity. Shortly after arriving in Jagdalpur they had called on IGP Kalluri and told him about the work they were intending to do. Kalluri had received them civilly enough and elaborately described a plan to set up an 'ultra mega steel plant' to create another Bhilai or Raipur in Chattisgarh. (My surmise is that this was the very project that the Tatas' contractor believed had made the government change its priority from the Tatas' dream of creating a new Jamshedpur in Chhattisgarh.) He said that the state had not been able to develop magnificent industries because of the problem of the Naxalites, and that he had been appointed to eliminate rebel influence from the area.

Slowly, as they expanded the scope of their work and their reputation spread, local lawyers started feeling threatened by the competition they represented and grew suspicious of their motives. 'They must be Maoist sympathizers', they speculated. There was also much conjecture about their sources of income, since the women didn't charge their clients fees. IGP Kalluri even addressed a press conference, where he issued a warning to NGOs with 'Maoist sympathies' and took pains to mention that his list included an NGO that provided legal aid. Since there is only one such NGO in the region, it was not hard to guess which one he was targeting.

The authenticity of the degrees earned by the JagLAG

lawyers was openly challenged and they began to be vilified as quack lawyers. On the basis of an anonymous complaint by an '*aam nagrik*' (an ordinary citizen) to the SP (Jagdalpur) and IG (Bastar), the Bastar Police began an inquiry into the issue of the women's legal credentials. A bail application moved by the JagLAG lawyers was rejected on the grounds of their supposed lack of credentials. Their clients were routinely called and told that they would never secure their release if they worked with the women lawyers.

On 5 October 2015, in a move clearly calculated to clip the wings of the JagLAG team, the Bastar Bar Association passed a resolution barring all lawyers not registered with the Bastar Bar Council from practising in Bastar. A day later, the Dantewada Bar Association attempted to do the same.

The legal position on this issue is not clear. While Rule 262 of the Chhattisgarh high court disallows advocates who are not on the rolls of the state's Bar Council from appearing or pleading in court, Section 30 of the Advocates Act allows an advocate registered in any state to practise throughout the territory of India. Moreover, the prerogative of withdrawing the licence to practise arguably rests with the Bar Council of India or the concerned state unit, not the bar association of lawyers.

I bring up the issue with Ashutosh Dwivedi, president of the Chhattisgarh Bar Association. As expected, he claims that the association's decision, passed by two-thirds majority, was strictly in adherence to rules and not intended to target any specific group of individuals.

'I don't know these people,' he tells me, referring to the JagLAG lawyers. 'And I have no interest in knowing them. When I met them once and asked them to submit a document, they behaved impertinently. When a lawyer is not following rules, it is not only the Bar Council that needs to act. The Bar Associaton is liable too. We have received many complaints against them. But we have not acted out of any ill will. If they abide by the rules, I will welcome them.'

JagLAG is challenging the order of the Bastar Bar Association in the high court and the Bar Council. They had already initiated the process of getting registered in the Chhattisgarh Bar Council. However, that process is expected to take several months. Meanwhile, they continued to practise in Dantewada, Bijapur and Sukma, knowing that similar developments could follow in those districts as well. They also tutored their clients to argue their own briefs.

'If they can fight their own cases, what more do we need?' said Gera, laughing.

The JagLAG girls appeared to have made their peace with the existing situation, but events in February 2016 would test their resilience once again.

In a lawless, violent land, the presence of a group of women warriors, each fighting for justice in her own way, is a sign of hope. But it is necessary to understand the logic underlying the violence to assess the possibilities of peace. The life and death of Maoist ideologue Cherukuri Azad raises many questions in this regard.

4

Cherukuri Azad and the Question of Violence

Cherukuri Rajkumar Azad, a top Maoist leader, was killed in an alleged fake encounter, while in the process of negotiating peace talks with the UPA government. It is speculated that his end came about because of a mole in the camp of the government interlocutor Swami Agnivesh.

With his lanky frame, unruly mop of greying hair and ready smile, Azad could have passed off as a college professor. Only a gash running diagonally across his forehead, a reminder, perhaps, of a past encounter, hinted at the life he led as one of the Maoists' most highly ranked leaders.

While he argued forcefully in favour of the use of violence by the Maoists as an essential tool for revolutionary transformation, he was generous enough to write a glowing tribute to K. Balagopal, a civil-rights activist, who had not hesitated to criticize many of the ways adopted by the insurgents, even as he highlighted the repeated excesses committed by the government in their development projects.

Azad defined violence in broad terms to include hunger, humiliation, untouchability and patriarchy, in addition to the usual categories of physical violence. He believed that the ruling classes were inherently violent; that to expect them to surrender power or allow groups attempting to bring about change among the masses to operate without having to face violent reprisals was merely a pipe dream. He cited examples of governments banning and violently suppressing movements that had not resorted to arms, including the Karimnagar and Adilabad movement against the oppression of feudal landlords in the 1970s, the banning in 1981 of the Singareni coal workers' trade union – the Singareni Workers' Federation (SIKASA) – and the killing of unarmed women and children by the police, which would serve as the very genesis of the Naxalbari movement.

According to Azad, 'The violence of the Maoists, which is preceded and provoked by the violence of the oppressors, is not really the main issue; justice is. If Naxalite violence is to be discussed, it should be in the context of violence pervading every aspect of our system. If not seen in this framework, one falls prey to the abstract bourgeois concept that "violence breeds violence", without understanding the structural causes of violence.'

In order to evaluate the impact of Maoist strategies on villagers, one has to understand their military approach. Azad states that the Maoists rely 'on the sea of people in which we swim like fish', harking back to the tactics used by Mao Tse-Tung in the Chinese civil war.[19] In this way, they are able to get the better of numerically superior and better-equipped government forces.[20]

Mao's was not the only approach to guerilla warfare, however. Che Guevara's 'foco' strategy of insurgency, for instance, called for small guerrilla groups (the 'focus' of the revolution) acting without widespread popular backing to carry out daring attacks against highly visible government targets.

The central characteristics of guerilla warfare, as practised by Mao and adopted by the Maoist insurgents, is reliance on small, highly mobile units; avoidance of decisive set-piece battles in favour of prolonged campaigns focussing on hit-and-run attacks, sabotage and other operations designed to increase an opponent's political, military and economic costs; and reliance on local populations for food, shelter and intelligence, as well as 'human camouflage', a mass of people into which the guerillas could disappear to avoid detection.

In the words of Azad, 'All our plans, policies, strategy and tactics will be based entirely on the active involvement of the

---

[19]Rajkumar, Cherukuri, 'Interview to the Hindu, April 14th, 2010', in *Maoists in India: Writings & Interviews*, Hyderabad: Friends of Azad (2010).

[20]Tse-Tung, Mao, *On Guerrilla Warfare*, translated by Griffith II, Samuel B., Urbana: University of Illinois Press, 2000.

vast masses of people in this war of self-defence. The enemy class cannot decimate us without decimating the entire population in the regions we control.'[21]

In order to comprehend the logic of the state's response to Maoist violence, our understanding of the reliance of the Maoists on local populations has to be combined with an appreciation of the ends for which they are carrying out their struggle.

Writes K. Balagopal, 'Maoism is not some social-reform movement that uses guns for greater effect, but a political movement aimed at smashing the existing state and building an alternative state.'[22] He goes on to conclude that 'it would be idle to pretend that any state would, with equanimity, tolerate the proclamation of "liberated areas" within its territory from where its authority is pushed out by force.'

Therefore, the state's inevitable response to the use of guerilla tactics by the Maoist forces will necessarily be to fall back on the means best designed to further its chances of victory against an adversary that 'swims like fish in a sea of people'.

Several academic studies of state action vis-à-vis a guerilla force have argued that mass killings of civilians by the state forces can often be a 'calculated military strategy designed to overcome the difficult problems associated with combating major guerrilla insurgencies'. Here, civilians are defined as non-combatants – those who do not actively participate in hostilities, but may provide food or shelter to the guerillas.

---

[21]'Maoists in India: Writings and Interviews', Azad, Rajkumar; interview on the government's military offensive. (https://revolutionaryfrontlines.wordpress.com/2010/10/19/new-book-maoists-in-india-writings-and-interviews%C2%A0by%C2%A0azad/).

[22]Balagopal, K., 'Physiognomy of Violence', *Economic and Political Weekly* (2006): 2183–2186.

In the Guatemalan civil war of the late 1970s and early '80s, for example, the government faced a Leftist insurgency backed by a large number of active civilian supporters. An estimated 250,000 to 500,000 civilians contributed to the insurgency, many providing food, clothing, shelter and information to the rebels. By 1981, the guerrillas virtually controlled nine of Guatemala's 22 provinces, had established a significant presence in nine others and were carrying out almost daily attacks in Guatemala City. Initially, the Guatemalan regime attempted to suppress the rebellion through a selective campaign, targeting key leaders of the opposition. Over a period of eighteen months, starting from 1982, however, 75,000 people – nearly all civilians – were slaughtered by government-backed forces. In the area of highest guerrilla activity, known as the Ixil triangle, approximately one-third of the local population may have been killed. In contrast, in the Cuban Revolution, where the guerillas were less dependent on mass support, the military regime did not target the local population.

A statistical analysis by Valentino, Huth and Balch-Lindsay (2004),[23] using a data set of 147 wars from 1945 to 2000, reveals that conflicts in which a guerilla group posed a major threat to the government led to a six-fold increase in the risk of a mass killing by state-sponsored forces. Moreover, in insurrections where the rebels enjoyed high levels of support among the civilian population, the possibility of a state-orchestrated mass slaughter taking place rose eight-fold. In democracies, such killings are one a half times less likely.

In brief, inherent in the means adopted by the Maoists is the implication of violent state reprisals that include intentional

---

[23]Valentino, Benjamin, Huth, Paul, and Balch-Lindsay, Dylan, 'Draining the Sea: Mass Killing and Guerrilla Warfare', *International Organization* 58.02 (2004): 375-407.

physical harm to civilians. In India, an additional factor is that the territory controlled by the rebels has strategic and symbolic value because of its mineral wealth and its location in the centre of the country, though the area it covers may constitute a relatively small percentage of the Indian landmass. Hence, the consequences of Left-wing extremism on adivasi welfare have to be assessed – not in a utopian world in which the Maoists are allowed to work unhindered by a government that is willing to cede control of strategic resources in a sudden spirit of large-heartedness, but with respect to the conflict-ridden realities of zones under Maoist control.

This is no justification, of course, for the brutality of the state's chosen counter-insurgency measures. There can be no greater misfortune for a country than when the state begins to turn on its own people. The sane way for the state to counter guerilla forces would be, firstly, to find ways to redress the injustices that had paved the way for the Maoists to inveigle their way into the people's affections; and, secondly, to engage with a group that appears to have won a certain measure of support among the concerned population. But the systemic causes that enable guerilla forces to win over the people – the practices adopted in industrialization and forestry, for example – remain unaddressed by the Indian state, preventing any such reasoned response. Indeed many members of India's ruling classes would deny the presence of any link between our development model and the rise of Maoism, as the following interview will demonstrate.

'Conflicts and armed rebellions reflect the failure of successive governments to provide basic amenities and employment, combined with the capacity of violent movements to misguide the youth,' says Yashwant Sinha, former Union Finance and

Foreign Minister, and long serving MP from Jharkhand, a state affected by Maoist insurgency. We are sitting in the book-lined study of his home office in Noida. Sinha, who first shot to prominence as finance minister in the government of former Prime Minister Chandrashekhar, was at one time spoken of as a future prime minister of the country.

'But to link Maoism only to mining or the commercial exploitation of forests will be a grievous error of judgement,' he continues. 'Maoism is not limited to the excesses of the forest department, or of mining companies. It is many more things.' Among these things, he lists the hope of a better future that Maoists hold out to the youth, the fear they inculcate in them, and the sense of immediate power their cadres feel.

While absolving mining companies from the scourge of Maoism, he also states that the manner in which mining was carried out in the country left much to be desired. 'There is no ideal mine,' he says. 'The Tatas are better than Coal India, but even they leave much to be desired.' He concurs that under the land acquisition act prior to 2013, the state often acted as a 'predator' and acquired land sans consultation and compensation, let alone consent. But he argues that the long list of mining locations and dam sites where Maoism was not present indicated that if I was studying mining as a cause of Maoism I would be 'barking up the wrong tree'.

In India's case, the seething grievances of the adivasis may have simmered on unheeded had the Maoists not been able to take advantage of the access to resources from government and industrial projects, and the availability of abundant forest cover, to convert the embers of adivasi disaffection into a full-blown conflagration. Grievances alone may not suffice to trigger a civil war, a point that would afford some consolation to our policy makers in the context of a country full of deprivation.

But in India's Red Corridor, they certainly played a role as necessary conditions. The relevant grievances cannot be limited merely to the absence of basic services, but principally relate to transgressions on the most fundamental relationships of an adivasi's life – the link to land and community. Mining and forestry are repeat offenders in these acts of trespass.

A failure to join the dots between economic exploitation and the success of the Maoists allows the state to deny any legitimacy to the Maoist problem and to treat the insurgents as a bunch of thugs and exploiters. Likewise, those who support them are simply seen as criminals. Armed with this rationalization, an exploitative state carries out devastating police operations on people stuck between a rock and a hard place, while simultaneously rolling out programmes for 'good governance'.

'Fear plays an important role in recruitment by the Maoists,' observes Sinha, quite correctly. 'One person may be recruited easily, the rest are cowed down by fear.'

But he does not mention the fear evoked by industries and forest officials in the minds of the tribals.

Beyond the means chosen by the Maoists and the response meted out by the state, we have to examine another dynamic that plays a crucial role in allowing the conflict to continue.

The tendency to persist with the heavy-handed approach, despite its counter-productive result of driving increasing numbers of people into the Maoists' ranks, suggests the need to look beyond the development paradigm if one is to discover the seeds from which the violence prevailing in these regions has germinated. To some extent, Maoism and the state's war against it are convenient covers for people at extreme ends of the ideological divide to prosper, albeit in the difficult conditions of an insurgency.

Ignoring the fundamental causes that served as fertile ground for the insurgency to take root, in the first place, the State, along with a variety of entities, uses the presence of Maoists as a pretext for its own failings, at best, and a cover for its own transgressions, at worst. Non-functioning schools, non-existent healthcare services and abysmally poor connectivity, for instance, are conveniently blamed on the Maoists, who may not be responsible for these deficiencies in a number of cases.

Making Maoists the fall guys is not a tactic limited to the government. In inter-corporate warfare as well, the insurgency serves as a major alibi for settling scores between competitors. Acts of sabotage driven by company rivalries are often unfairly ascribed to the insurgents. Finally, in a bid to undermine non-violent resistance to government and corporate transgressions, peaceful activists are labelled Maoists. These are the various ways in which the insurgency is hijacked by the establishment.

Although many officers in government, including a former police chief of special operations in undivided Andhra Pradesh, have shared with me their respect for the ideological commitment of many of the Maoist leaders, the rebels are in no way immune to the strategy of using the revolutionary cause for personal gain.

In 2004, the Communist Party of India (Marxist-Leninist) People's War, or the CPI(ML)PW (also known as the People's War Group or PWG) and the Maoist Communist Centre of India (MCC) merged to form the Communist Party of India-Maoist (CPI-Maoist).[24] The unification brought an end to the internecine conflict that had raged through the 1990s, but also created a more heterogeneous organization, which was ideologically less pure and operationally more unwieldy. Today,

---

[24]http://www.satp.org/satporgtp/countries/india/terroristoutfits/CPI_M.htm

the relationship between the Maoists and the State has acquired elements of 'cooperative plunder', a situation in which two apparently antagonistic forces align for the purpose of siphoning away resources. Vast sums of money are released from the exchequer for Left-wing-extremism-affected districts. Corporate projects also ensure a not inconsiderable infusion of resources into the region. This leads to a nexus between the rebels, pliable government officials, legislators and corporate executives who inevitably come to regard authentic local leadership or genuine members of civil society as a threat.

The case of Noku Koram, narrated in Section 2 Chapter 8 of this book, shows that Maoists are capable of targeting civilians who want to change the system, disturbing the cozy handshake with government administrators and local politicians that allows them to siphon off government funds for their own organization. Such people can be dubbed class enemies when in fact they are merely trying to implement the law as they see it. The death of Noku Koram was not a result of wrong implementation of Maoist doctrine, but an inevitable consequence of the structure under which Maoists earn revenue from government schemes with the complicity of chosen administrators.

The growth of the Maoist movement is accompanied by increasing militarization of untrained civilians who take up arms in self-defence under the tutelage of Maoists. This new cadre of Maoists, which may not have ever heard of Mao or of the Indian state for that matter, presents the risk that the broader group of militia under the Maoists could degenerate into roving packs of armed goons.

Indeed, there is not merely increased militarization of the Maoist zones but also increased criminalization, as all parties seek to maximize their own petty self-interest in the war-like situation.

The onset of the phase of cooperative plunder tends to prolong a conflict situation and extinguishes any hope of systematic economic development of the war zone. The conflict itself becomes the area's main industrial enterprise, crowding out the growth of genuine entrepreneurship and empowerment.

On the issue of cooperative plunder, Yashwant Sinha shares a startling piece of news.

'The blunt truth,' he says, 'is that the recently opened Amrapali coal mine on the Hazaribagh–Ranchi district border is being run entirely by Maoists. They decide who gets the service contracts, who gets employment and so on. This is giving them a huge financial resource. They make lakhs of rupees a day. The scale is unimaginable.'

I search the internet for news of the mine. I find that it is owned by Coal India Limited and was dedicated to the nation by the Union Minister of State for Power, Piyush Goel.

Despite Sinha's assertion, one cannot be too sure which faction or group is actually controlling the mine. In the current political climate, the term 'Maoist' has become a convenient label to slap on anybody one does not like. However, earlier in the interview, Sinha had also alluded to legislative action which led to the MPs having a say in the spending of ₹30 crores per annum that was released for each Maoist-affected district. Would this fund, a mere tip of the iceberg in terms of the resources flowing to quell the insurgency, have been available without the luxury of a civil war?

Ultimately, the relationship that the Maoist shares with the tribal is a doomed love affair between an overweening master and his idealized, fragile beloved, who is overwhelmed at the sudden attention she is receiving, but unable to comprehend the enormity of what she is getting into. Moreover, she is perplexed as her favour is suddenly sought by two implacable foes – her lawful, uncaring consort, the government, and her recent lover, the Maoist.

It was 2010. Operation Green Hunt was under way. Maoist retaliation was equally deadly. The fatalities had touched a peak.

Between 6 and 8 May 2010, Swami Agnivesh and several other activists marched through Raipur and Dantewada, appealing for an end to the endemic violence.[25] On 11 May, P. Chidambaram, then the country's home minister in the UPA government at the Centre, wrote to Swami Agnivesh to clarify the government's position.

'On the specified date (say, June 1), we would expect that the CPI (Maoist) will stop all violent activities,' wrote Chidambaram. 'We would closely observe whether the CPI (Maoist) will maintain the position of "no violence" for 72 hours. It goes without saying that, during the said period of 72 hours, the security forces will not conduct any operations against the CPI (Maoist). It is our hope that talks will begin during [that] period.'

By now, Azad was ready for peace. It is possible that he had begun to sense the magnitude of the suffering innocent civilians were being put through because of the conflict.

In a signed response dated 31 May, Azad wrote, 'Our Party desires peace sincerely in the interests of the lakhs of adivasis who are being cruelly crushed.'

He laid down three conditions that would have to be complied with if the talks were to be held at all: government forces would have to retreat from their position of all-out war; bans imposed on the Party and on mass organizations would

[25]http://www.outlookindia.com/article/the-magicrealistic-slaughter-of-azad/270137, http://archive.tehelka.com/story_main46.asp?filename=Ne170710thirdletter.asp

have to be lifted; 'illegal' detention and torture of comrades had to cease and their immediate release secured. If these demands were met, the very leaders who had been released from jail would represent the Party in the talks. Chidambaram's offer of a 72-hour ceasefire also invited much derision.

In response, the home minister sent a letter to the Maoists via Agnivesh. In it, he explained that the 72-hour ceasefire was only the first step; the ceasefire would continue through the duration of the talks. On 26 June, the letter was despatched to Azad.

Agnivesh waited for the reply which, he hoped, would be positive. Unfortunately, he was to wait in vain. On 1 July, he received news that Azad had been killed in the forests of Andhra Pradesh. The government claimed that its security forces had been attacked while on patrol and had opened fire in self-defence. In the ensuing gun battle, two people were killed. One of them was Azad.

The Maoists claim, however, that Azad was picked up in Nagpur, where he was to meet a party contact at a cinema hall, and killed. The person killed along with him was Hemchandra Pandey, a journalist who was accompanying him and paid the price for knowing too much.[26]

Whatever the truth may be, the fact remains that Azad, a double M.Tech who had seen violence as a necessary weapon in furthering the cause of the oppressed, came to recognize the burden it was placing on the ordinary adivasi and had to die just when he was ready to take a step towards peace.

Swami Agnivesh was racked with guilt over his death and almost broke down at the press conference following the incident. 'It is possible that Azad let his guard down because of my last letter,' he said.

---

[26]http://www.thehindu.com/news/national/unesco-expresses-concern-over-hemchandra-pandeys-death/article518560.ece

In the days leading up to the hoped-for finalization of the peace talks, the Maoists had killed 27 CRPF men. This does not necessarily imply that they were not serious about participating in the talks. Moreover, the government too had killed five insurgents in Lalgarh and continued to arrest and harass civilians. Till the formal announcement of the ceasefire, violence would have been expected to continue. In fact, the higher number of casualties would have intensified the desire for peace.

But the death of Azad, one of the Maoist movement's seniormost leaders and especially one committed to the peace process, was the worst thing that could possibly have happened in the circumstances. It gives rise to questions to which few would have definite answers: did the government cold-bloodedly exploit the offer of peace to assassinate a much-sought-after target? Or was it a case of the left hand not knowing what the right was doing?

In either case, the blow dealt to peace was a devastating one and continues to make its repercussions felt. In the present situation, there is no end in sight to the suffering of lakhs of adivasis, as two enemies, both influential, internally divided on the issue of peace and wilfully mired in the inertia of violence, continue their operations with relentless persistence.

This brings us to the inexorable logic of the state's approach to development, a logic that inexplicably endures in the face of feasible alternative approaches.

5

Reformer, Reform Thyself

Since the early years of the new millennium, there have been frequent cries for 'second-generation reforms'. Investors had high hopes that the new NDA government led by Narendra Modi would kick-start reforms and unleash the potential of the Indian economy.

Of the four factors of production – land, labour, capital and entrepreneurship – the one most easily 'reformed' and made amenable to corporate interests, with, of course, the backing of military power, is land. The creation of a skilled labour force, the optimization of financial intermediation and the unleashing of entrepreneurial forces are, in contrast, more complex and difficult tasks. Even the introduction of greater flexibility in the hiring and firing decisions of companies tends to come up against stiff opposition from the powerful labour unions that constitute a tiny elite perched atop a sea of informal labour.

This criticism of the focus on land acquisition is neither to undermine the need for minerals in an emerging economy like India nor to overlook the importance of offering project-affected citizens more choices than they currently have in their lives of quiet (agricultural) despair. However, the manner in which minerals are being extracted and land acquired has become the cause of intense and widespread conflict, both violent and non-violent, apart from leading to the destruction of ancient cultures and the degradation of the environment. Among the more notorious instances of this are the coal fires that started in the Jharia coalfield due to the failure of the mining contractor to follow due process; they continue to burn a hundred years later.

Even if villagers voluntarily sign on for seemingly sweet deals, deluded by unheard of sums of money, we have to be prepared for the fruits of their disenchantment when they realize that livelihoods are eternal, while cash is quickly squandered. The only way to enable the local population to take advantage of industrialization is by carrying out development activities in the field of education, health and skill-building in advance of and in preparation for the entry of extractive industries. This will allow the people to benefit from industrialization and overcome their deep-seated opposition to mining companies, an opposition that is not merely a product of emotional and irrational attachment to land, but driven by the hard-earned truth that as a general rule, local communities have rarely gained in ways that really matter from the entry of industry into their lives.

In other words, development cannot be an outcome of industrialization, but needs to be a precursor to it. The state must position itself at the vanguard of this development process instead of abdicating its responsibility to corporates. After basic services have been provided to the local population for a certain number of years, industrialization can be allowed to take its course, with the speed of natural-resource extraction being carefully aligned with the absorptive power of local communities.

Two questions arise here: Where will the resources for such development activities come, if not from industrialization? And what will become of the apparently voracious appetite for minerals, in the meantime?

While this book does not aim to be a treatise on the economics of India's development model, the following elements, by no means exhaustive, suggest that there are windows of opportunity available for a path of development that involves a significantly less traumatic and lower rate of displacement of local populations than is currently the case.

To begin with, a higher level of planning to determine India's mineral needs and allocate its mineral resources judiciously would prevent the creation of new mines when existing mines lie unutilized. Such planning would have to be accompanied by the kind of contracts that would allow a new entity to sub-lease part of a mine from an existing leaseholder to commence mining operations.[27] A blog post published by *Down to Earth*, the magazine of environmental research and advocacy group Centre for Science and Environment, states: 'As per 2010 figures from Indian Bureau of Mines, of the 3,480 million tonnes of bauxite resources in India, nearly a third, 1,068 million tonnes, fall under lease-hold areas. The takeaway: at current levels of consumption (12 million tonnes per year), these mines will last for 89 years. If India increases its consumption by three times (36 million tonnes per year), existing bauxite mines will be enough for 30 years. So why do we need to give out more mining leases, say in Niyamgiri hills, at the cost of tribals and their sustainable way of life?'

Such planning when extended to the control of leakages in the supply chain would yield a large quantity of resources for development. For instance, the evacuation infrastructure available at pitheads for coal is insufficient, leading to waste and inefficiency.

Further, efforts to reign in corruption at various levels would lead to huge savings of natural resources. The phenomenon of unaccounted-for trucks leaving mines on a daily basis, for instance, means that resources are being siphoned off by those with the power to do so, rather than being deployed to solve pressing problems of development. The anecdote of a property builder's encounter with the general manager of a national coalfield is instructive. The general manager paid the builder a

[27]http://www.downtoearth.org.in/blog/do-we-really-need-the-bauxite-from-niyamgiri-42005

sum of ₹2 crores in cash within a period of thirty minutes to book a flat in Bhopal. A few months later when the builder had established a social relationship with the general manager, he would explain how he had come into this state of prosperity.

'Fifty trucks of coal leaving the coalfield go unaccounted every day. Each truck contains twelve tonnes of coal,' he had elaborated, before finishing with a flourish, 'it would not be difficult for you to calculate what one lakh eighty thousand tonnes of coal would fetch in the open market.'

It is important for those concerned about 'development' to note that such stories suggest the underlying reason for displacement of the poor in alarming numbers: it helps public-sector executives and sundry politicians and bureaucrats to build their respective nest eggs.

In the context of statistics frequently cited to highlight India's low metal and power consumption per capita, it is important to note the difference between an economy's need and effective demand for natural resources. Our development aspirations certainly require a much higher level of energy or steel consumption per capita than is currently recorded. For instance, India's per capita steel consumption in 2013 stood at 57.8 kg while China's per capita consumption was 515 kg in the same year. However, this does not imply that new power plants or steel mills will inevitably succeed in becoming economically viable. Sustainable growth of our consumption per capita levels requires a matching growth of demand for such resources, either from within the economy or from the rest of the world.

In mining and infrastructure, where project gestation periods are long, the business case often evaporates after the project commences, especially since the rapidity with which the global economy cycles through booms and recessions has increased. For instance, India's iron ore exports rose to a high of 1,015 lakh tonnes in 2009 only to fall to 163 lakh tonnes in 2013. The high variability of effective demand is as much a cause for concern as the lack of a high level of effective demand as it leads to frenetic business activity followed by corporate distress, increasing the distrust of project-affected people and exacerbating social conflict.

As a country whose exports constitute only 1.5 per cent of world exports, it may appear as if India can be optimistic about its ability to steadily expand the export markets for its products, including those based on its mineral resources. However, the prospect of a prolonged recession in the global economy makes such a view unrealistic. In 2014–15 India's exports have declined for twelve months straight since November 2014, with a contraction of 24.4 per cent being registered in November 2015.

In these circumstances India's growth must necessarily be powered by domestic demand. This feature of today's economic landscape is the strongest force militating against an inequitable pattern of development of the kind epitomized by the unjust acquisition of natural resources. And yet old habits die hard, especially when it comes to as visceral an issue as land.

The NDA government spent an inordinate amount of its political capital in the first year of its tenure trying to make it easy for companies to acquire land, when the economy's problem was that far too much land had already been acquired without a robust business case. A problem of lack of demand was misdiagnosed as a problem of too many supply bottlenecks.

The build-up of armed forces in mineral bearing areas of India, including Chhattisgarh, indicates that the model of land acquisition by force continues to be the standard operating procedure. In the past ten years, public-sector banks have worked in tandem with instruments of state power to ensure that money flows to private promoters keen to invest in the exploitation of natural resources. While there is talk of ensuring that banks work with greater transparency and autonomy and the Bank Bureau Board has been created to oversee the operation of public-sector banks, observers will have to wait to see how well this institutional arrangement works in practice.

Both the ruling NDA coalition that claims to cherish the heritage of India, and the UPA that draws inspiration from the vision of Jawaharlal Nehru to make India an industrial economy, place their faith in filling out the missing middle of manufacturing output in India's services-led growth story. The UPA has stressed the need to create 10 million jobs a year, the NDA has orchestrated a highly compelling media blitz on 'Make in India', inviting the world to make India its foundry, much as Taiwan and China had once been. In a world where slowing global growth makes the rise of another country based on the China model of export-led, manufacturing-based growth improbable, the unanimity of approach is a mark, not just of a lack of imagination, but an absence of pragmatism.

A study by ICRIER and the National Bureau of Economic Research[28] shows that our service industries are becoming less skill intensive even as our manufacturing sector is becoming more skill intensive. In this situation, Barry Eichengreen and Poonam Gupta, the authors of the ICRIER study, argue that we need to continue to focus on our comparative advantage in services even as we try to build out a labour intensive manufacturing base.

---

[28]Eichengreen, Barry and Gupta, Poonam, 'The service sector as India's road to economic growth', National Bureau of Economic Research: w16757, 2011. For instance, since the enactment of the Special Economic Zone (SEZ) Act 2005, only 37 per cent of the 60,374 hectares approved for 576 SEZs is being put to use. The CAG audit of SEZs reveals that only 16 per cent of land in the processing area is being used, as against a norm of 50 per cent.

Many alternatives could be considered to grow our services. For instance, let those political parties championing the cause of India's heritage fashion a growth model around the slogan 'Come to India'. Let the world throng to our cultural treasures, our natural wonders, our universities and hospitals. Let unemployed youth become travel guides, cybercafe owners, tour operators, cab drivers. Let our roads, and rail services, airways and hotels serve those who come to sample our hospitality. We will, then, possibly, have a lighter tread on earth and a greater sense of fulfilment than that obtained by following in another's footsteps.

Of course, many 'second generation' reforms are perfectly valid – having a relation with the ease of doing business, rationalizing tax structures and establishing robust regulatory structures in industries with both public and private participation. While appreciating the urgent necessity for India to become 'open for business' and the importance of creating a playing field where new ideas can thrive, one must also exhort the reformist crowd: Reformer, reform thyself!

6

The Prime Minister Comes A-Calling

It was 9 May 2015, a year into his tenure, and Prime Minister Narendra Modi was in Dantewada, stronghold of the Maoist insurgency, addressing a local gathering where he highlighted the need for employment, be it for the poor, the farmer or the adivasi. '*Gareeb bhi chahta hai rozgaar miley*,' he declared, '*kisan chahta hai rozgaar miley. Adivasi chahta hai rozgaar miley*.'

An Indian prime minister was visiting the area for the first time since Rajiv Gandhi's tour in 1985. In his speech, delivered before a ragtag bunch of villagers, schoolchildren and government officials, from whom he was separated by a multi-layered cordon of security, Modi reprised the theme of development that had played a significant part in giving him a historic election victory in May 2014. The BJP had crossed the halfway mark in the Lok Sabha, the first time a party had done so since the Congress under Rajiv Gandhi swept the polls in the wake of his mother Indira's assassination in 1984.

'The priority for India is that our children get employment,' the PM went on. 'No parent would want their child to go far away to a city's slums and shanty towns for jobs. It is the responsibility of the government to usher in a model of development that reaches every corner of the country – be they remote jungles or the huts sheltering the poor.

Alluding to the Maoist insurgency, Modi declared, 'The macabre drama of death will end. A lot of people have been killed by insane men on the path of violence.'

Despite the assertiveness with which the words were articulated, Modi's trip was not going according to plan.

A dome-shaped pandal erected for his public rally in Raipur had collapsed due to heavy winds, injuring 42 people and leading to the cancellation of the event. More worrisome still was the fact that late on the night of 8 May and just hours before the Prime Minister's arrival in Dantewada, the Maoists had struck despite the presence of over 10,000 personnel from the CRPF, the Special Task Force (STF), the state police and the anti-Naxalite wing. The insurgents had abducted the residents of Marenga and some adjoining villages situated within the Tongpal police station's limits and herded them to a nearby forest in protest against the construction of a bridge.

Estimates of the number of people abducted varied wildly. Additional Superintendent of Police, Sukma, Harish Rathore, claimed that anywhere between 400 and 500 villagers had been 'taken away' to the jungles by the rebels opposing the construction of a bridge, while S.R.P. Kalluri, now IGP, Bastar, dismissed the whole episode as a 'fiction' created by the media.

'Around two hundred to two hundred and fifty villagers have been abducted and four to five others (locals) are negotiating their release,' Chief Minister Raman Singh would announce to reporters on 9 May, arbitrating between the conflicting statements from his police officers. Later, the Maoists would kill one villager, who was supposed to have been the supervisor appointed for the construction work to be carried out in building the proposed bridge, and release the others.

In his speech to the people of Dantewada, Modi would stress on the need to wield ploughs rather than guns to bring development to the area, pointing out how Naxalbari, the birthplace of the Naxal movement, had rejected violence.

And putting his money where his mouth was, the Prime Minister signed a slew of MOUs initiating a variety of industrial projects, including a 140-km-long railway line between Rowghat and Jagdalpur, a three-million-tonne ultra mega steel plant, a slurry pipeline and two pellet plants, amounting to a total investment of ₹24,000 crores.

Ultimately, the prime minister's visit to Chhattisgarh prompts us to ask that crucial question: does the new dispensation offer any new hope? Of all the promises Modi made, the one related to employment appeals the most. But whether the new government has the institutional capability or even the honest intention to provide meaningful employment for the displaced so as to spare them the ignominy of working as daily-wage labour on some construction site far removed from their natural milieu is open to debate.

On the way to the Kachche mine during my visit to Chhattisgarh in September 2014, we had passed the Rowghat mines situated nearly 29 km from Narayanpur town in Kanker district. The construction of a railway line from Rowghat to Jagdalpur, announced during Modi's visit, is expected to connect the new mines coming up in Rowghat. A supplementary benefit is that the Rowghat hills overlook Abuj Maad; their development will pose an important strategic threat to the Maoists.

Journalist Kamal Shukla had claimed that the process of obtaining the necessary permissions from the gram sabhas had not exactly been a model of decorum, with villages disappearing from the survey map, villagers being bullied into acquiescence and the more recalcitrant ones being branded as Maoist sympathizers and thrown into jail.

The Rowghat iron-ore deposits, assessed at 731.93 million tonnes, are considered to be the second-largest iron-ore deposits in the state after Bailadila, assessed at 1.34 billion tonnes. The Bhilai Steel Plant obtained approval for mining over 883 hectares of land after nineteen years spent in petitioning the Ministry of Environment and Forests. During that period, the original demand for 3,279 hectares had to be reduced by 2,396 hectares on account of concerns raised by the ministry about the project's impact on the area's rich flora and fauna.

The Chhattisgarh Bachao Andolan (CBA), a non-profit organization working on the region's environmental and human-rights issues, has been a vociferous opponent of the plan to mine in Rowghat. A report prepared by it[29]indicates that the

[29]http://www.kractivist.org/wp-content/uploads/2014/02/Objection_Rowghat_Iron_Ore_Mines_CBA_2014-1.pdf

area leased out for mining is critical for wildlife and constitutes an important wildlife corridor, stretching from south-eastern Maharashtra to north-western Orissa. It is surrounded by tiger reserves, including the Tadoba Andhari Tiger Reserve to the north-west, the Kawal Tiger Reserve to the west, the Indravati Tiger Reserve and the Udanti-Sitanadi Tiger Reserve to the north-east. The stretch also acts as a migratory route for tigers to the Eastern Ghats. According to the CBA's note, the proposed railway line connecting Rowghat to Dalli Rajhara and the metal road leading to the conveyor gallery will completely fragment this important wildlife habitat.

Every project has positive and negative impacts and one is inclined to enquire if the CBA analysis treats environmental and development impacts in a balanced manner. However, their allegations of glaring procedural lapses in the clearance accorded to the Rowghat mine, if proved to be true, would be unequivocally damning.

According to CBA the actual forested land being used by the Bhilai Steel Plant is close to two and a half times the area for which clearances have been obtained. Further, the CBA alleges that the recognition of the rights of tribal and forest dwelling communities in the area, as per the FRA, has not been done. The FRA has set up a process through which the rights of both the individual and the community to occupy, cultivate, use and protect areas are to be given due recognition. No diversion of forest land for non-forest use, such as mining, can be granted under the Forest Conservation Act, 1980, until the process under FRA is complete. A clarification issued by the Ministry of Environment and Forests on 3 August 2009 elaborates on this point and also states that the consent of the gram sabha needs to be sought prior to the forest diversion.

The CBA's note, released to the press, states that in the case of Rowghat, there is nothing in writing from the gram sabhas of the 35 tribal villages surrounding the proposed mining area to establish that they have no claims under the FRA. In fact, the organization alleges that none of the gram sabhas have been consulted to date. What this implies, if true, is that the forest diversion that had taken place in 2009 was carried out without respecting the FRA's due legal requirements.

The CBA alleges that the residents of two villages are to be displaced to make way for a railway station and an explosives factory without a publicly available plan on how the displaced people will be rehabilitated and their issues addressed.

Further, the proposed mine will allegedly encroach on the temple to the Rao deity that is located near the Rao Dongri block of the Rowghat mines. This revered site is visited by communities living in the area who believe that Rao Devi is embodied by the Rowghat hills. This issue remains unaddressed in all the regulatory processes related to forest diversion.

The procedural lapses in the case of the Rowghat mines seem to be a perpetuation of the use of state power to further corporate interests. Many projects are thus born with the birthmark of criminality, involving as they do the violation of people's rights and scant regard for the preservation of the environment. As a result, any CSR activities undertaken in the future run the risk of being perceived as balm to gloss over the original sin involved in the acquisition of land. Such projects can only lead to an intensification of the conflict that is already exacting so heavy a toll on the locals and their environment.

That the public sector is carrying out the mining activity in no way alleviates the transgression. As mentioned earlier in Section 1 Chapter 3 ('Iron-Ore Fines and Tendu Leaves'), the need for the Rowghat mine arose because of the sale of the Ari-Dongri mine to private interests under the specious plea that the reserves were of sub-standard quality.

In any case, complaints by mining activists are equally distributed over transgressions by the public and the private sector. Further, if public-sector companies enter the fray today, their competitors in the private sector are likely to follow suit on the pretext of being given a level playing field. The Rowghat mine contains six blocks, of which only one is currently being leased out. Private-sector companies, including Tata Steel, Nicco Jaiswal and Essar, had unsuccessfully tried to stake a claim on the other blocks around 2005.

Given the significant risk posed by the project, it is not surprising that the Maoists have come out strongly against it. 'The adivasis did not benefit from the mines in Dalli Rajhara and they will not benefit from mines in Rowghat,' they have stated.

The railway line essential for transporting ore from Rowghat to Dalli Rajhara passes through Abuj Maad and will need constant security cover once it is laid. Depending on the strength of Maoist forces, the railway line could well become a source of revenue for them – as the Essar pipeline has become – or a site of pitched battles between the insurgents and government forces, both comprising mostly tribals.

The land acquisition for the three-million-tonne steel plant to be set up by the Steel Authority of India (SAIL) and NMDC, with an investment of ₹18,000 crores, and announced by Prime Minister Modi during his Chhattisgarh visit, has also run into trouble, with the villagers vowing to sacrifice their lives rather than the land given their bitter experience with past projects. In the face of such vehement protest, the government has backpedalled, claiming that Dilimili is a natural choice because of the presence of 600 acres of government land, but other options have not been ruled out.

The script has a monotonous ring to it. Despite the rhetoric, what lies at the core is the same old story now backed by a superb marketing machine.

7

FIGHTING TO THE FINISH

Who decides how a piece of mineral-bearing land is to be used? Who knows where the timber from the forest should go? How should gains be distributed between those who own the land, but do not know how to use its natural wealth, and those who have the knowledge, but not the ownership rights?

The mineral under the ground and the timber above it, unlike the apple in the Garden of Eden, are not forbidden fruit. Neither is the predicament of the adivasi, in the wake of over two centuries of forestry and mining, a fall from grace. But it certainly is a comedown from the carefree days of yore.

Now, with centuries having passed since the tribal lived in his original state of innocence, the only way back to the life he has lost seems to be to move forward. The only option seems to be to claim the right of self-determination, to seek a just share of the spoils, to join the new world, while holding on to the best in his own culture.

But while on this mission, the adivasis must confront the inexorable hunger of an avaricious system, the uncomprehending impatience of modernists who do not seem to realize that their determined embrace is rapidly squeezing the life out of a culture that has survived millennia. The adivasis face a state that becomes increasingly callous about their needs in its quest for 'development'.

In the midst of forest and stream and in this time of peril appears an insurgency, foisted from above, fuelled from below.

When a political movement acquires the shape of an

insurgency, as opposed to a peaceful protest, it inevitably draws a militaristic response. The system becomes 'securitized' and leaves its mark on every organ of the state. There is no institution that the government begins to resemble more than the armed forces. The paradigm of society changes from democratic to militaristic. Elections become, primarily, a stage for the flexing of muscle power. The judiciary becomes a weapon of war.

If the state's focus shifts from development to battling the insurgency in a quest to snuff it out, the original grievance that triggered discontent and anger becomes magnified in response. In its efforts to quash the rebellion, the military is constantly beset by two kinds of errors: allowing citizens abetting the insurgency to go scot-free; and cracking down on the innocent. Since unambiguously classifying locals who live under the fear of the gun is next to impossible, mistakes of both kinds are distressingly frequent.

Further, the ruling class now has additional sources of rent at its disposal from the new resources being pumped in to quell the insurgency. The insurgent too uses his power to gain from these inputs and gathers recruits from the disaffection of the common people.

When the insurgent and the political master begin to drink from the same stream, the problem becomes infinitely more complex, multi-dimensional and destructive of ways of life, cultures and communities.

The rebel's success becomes the cause of his downfall as new cadres fail to imbibe the values that inspired their senior leaders and become susceptible to the idealism-starved mores of the time. The political class too points to the corruption in the ranks of the insurgents to justify its own actions. At this point, the oppression of the people through the collusion of state and non-state actors has reached its final nadir. Jointly exploiting the masses, the government and the insurgent have become comrades-in-arms.

What if the state began to use the pretext of the insurgency to devour its citizens, in a fight to the finish? It would be a fight fuelled by the greed for minerals and spurred by age-old antagonisms, in equal measure. The insurgent would remain just an observer, helplessly and haplessly watching as the tables are turned. He may call for peace, but the call would be denied. It would be decried as a sign of pandering. It would be spurned because the spoils of war are greater than the blessings of concord. For when victory is at hand, when the slate can be wiped clean, only a fool would shake hands. And what of the destruction of the lives of millions of adivasis? That would no longer be collateral damage; it would be the laurel wreath of the victor.

Fast-moving events in Bastar following the Prime Minister's visit in May 2015 indicate that the possibility of events taking a turn for the worse can under no circumstance be dismissed as being merely speculative.

July and September 2015: Two journalists, Somaru Nag and Santosh Yadav, are arrested on the charge of being Maoists. Santosh has, in fact, been under surveillance since May 2013 for managing to reach Jiram Ghati, the site where the Congress cavalcade was ambushed by the Maoists, before the police did. Through their legal counsel, Isha Khandelwal of JagLAG, the journalists deny the charges.

October 2015: Forty women of Peddagelur, Budgicheru and Gundam villages of Bijapur district are reported as having been sexually assaulted, beaten and stripped naked by security forces; three women among them are, allegedly, gang-raped. The police register an FIR based on a complaint by a women's fact-finding group.

The first 22 days of November 2015: According to JagLAG lawyer, Shalini Gera, there are 18 'encounters' between the police and suspected insurgents. She alleges that between 1 Oct 2015 and 1 Feb 2015, the number was fifty-six.[30] A few cases of fake encounters are taken up by Soni Sori and the JagLAG lawyers.

21 December 2015: Journalists from Chhattisgarh, supported by colleagues from all over the country, organize a rally in Jagdalpur to protest against the arrest of Santosh Yadav and Somaru Nag.

22 December 2015: The Samajik Ekta Manch (SEM), a group of citizens later shown to be supported by the state police, organizes a massive rally to protest the brutal killing of a four-month-old infant by Maoists in the Gangaloor area of Bijapur. The district administration and the police support the rally, but adivasi representation at the event is poor. Interestingly, several leaders of the SEM have been involved in the Salwa Judum movement.

11-14 January 2016: Security forces carry out a three-day anti-Maoist military operation in Bijapur's Nendra village, resulting in reports of thirteen cases of gang rape and several cases of other types of sexual violence. Incidents involving physical assault and large-scale looting are also alleged to have taken place. Prompted by the intervention of the JagLAG group, an FIR is eventually registered against the perpetrators.

12 January 2016: Kunna village in Sukma district faces the same fate as Nendra; ten women are reportedly subjected to acts of sexual violence by security forces. Soni Sori is unsuccessful in

---

[30]http://www.caravanmagazine.in/vantage/interview-jaglag-lawyers-evicted-bastar#sthash.Kke89x52.dpuf

her attempt to file an FIR against the forces. As a sign of their diminished strength, the response of the Maoists, apart from a few minor skirmishes with the paramilitary forces and wilful destruction of equipment, is limited to killing villagers whom they supposedly suspect of being police informers. A newspaper report alleges that in their desperation, the insurgents have resorted to enlisting children from Jharkhand in combat roles by using the system of a 'lucky' draw, although villagers are increasingly unwilling to allow their offspring to join the Maoist movement.[31]

21 January 2016: The SEM organizes the wedding of two surrendered Maoists, Laxman and Koshy, who had allegedly been prevented by their comrades from marrying each other. SEM members give away the bride and police officers welcome her into the groom's family. Resplendent in a pink turban, the current SP of Bastar, Rajendra Narayan Dash, whom I had met when he was SP of Kanker, is present at the wedding. He holds the distinction of having been involved with the Salwa Judum in its early years as ASP of Bijapur and is now associated with the SEM, the new vigilante body in Bastar. IGP Kalluri, who is also present at the nuptials, announces that henceforth the weddings of surrendered Maoists will be organized and celebrated in similar fashion.

27 January 2016: ADG of Police (Naxal operation) R.K. Vij is divested of his charge after he announces that the cases of 200 surrendered Maoists, out of a total of 800 recommended for rehabilitation in recent times, have been rejected, following scrutiny by the screening-cum-rehabilitation committee

[31]http://www.deccanchronicle.com/nation/current-affairs/210316/a-lottery-that-no-one-wants-to-win-new-maoist-strategy-to-recruit-children.html

comprising representatives from the police, the CRPF and the home ministry.

Since early 2015, many 'surrendered' Maoists have been inducted into the District Reserve Force (DRF), a group of adivasis hired from the local area to fight the insurgents. For the first time since the days of Salwa Judum, local villagers have reported overhearing Gondi being spoken during attacks by state forces. About the DRF, IGP Kalluri is reported to have said: 'Having a bond with the tribals, they are better mentally conditioned to handle them. They are fighting Maoists efficiently because of their inherent motivation for doing so.'[32]

24 January 2016: According to Nandini Sundar, security forces surround Minpa village in Dantewada district at 6 a.m. and pick up 41 men. Three more men have been picked up on 21 January from Chintagufa market in Dantewada district, where they were attending a cock fight.[33]

Many villagers targeted by the security forces are, at worst, *sangham* members – the unarmed village level workers who carry out, on a part-time basis, developmental activities of the parallel Maoist government, the *janatana sarkar*, as compared to the *dalams* or armed squads, who carry out military operations.

3 February 2016: A team of the Bastar police allegedly kills 40-year-old Hadma Kashyap from Sulenga village in the Bastar district in a fake encounter. The JagLAG lawyers fail in their attempt to file an FIR against the culprits.

---

[32]http://post.jagran.com/District-Reserve-Group-adds-impetus-to-antiNaxal-operations-in-Chhattisgarh-1454663700

[33]http://www.kractivist.org/darkness-at-noon-in-the-liberated-zone-of-bastar/

7 February 2016: SEM organizes a rally against 'Naxalite supporters' (including the JagLAG lawyers) in the marketplace in Jagdalpur, burns their effigies and then proceeds to the house of Malini Subramaniam, a freelance journalist who has been regularly filing despatches on the above proceedings. They surround her house, raise slogans and make insinuations that 'she assembles bombs at home'. Later that night, the house is attacked with stones.

9 February 2016: The JagLAG team helps to lodge an FIR in connection with the stoning incident. However, only a truncated version of the original complaint is registered and all references to the SEM are omitted. On the same day, the SEM specifies its intention to take action against the JagLAG team and to hold a dharna until Subramaniam and the JagLAG team members have been arrested.

11 February 2016: According to JagLAG, the police are guilty of intimidating witnesses in the Malini Subramaniam case.

Later that day, IGP Kalluri, accompanied by SP R.N. Dash, visits Subramaniam's house while the JagLAG lawyers are present and calls for a 'ceasefire'. The SEM calls off its dharna. The situation returns to relative normalcy. Apparently, pressure brought to bear from high-level contacts in Delhi has paid off.

17 February 2016: Things suddenly take a turn for the worse. The landlords of Malini Subramaniam and the JagLAG lawyers are summoned for questioning. The car belonging to the JagLAG lawyers' landlord (who is a driver by profession) is impounded. Malini Subramaniam's 24-year-old maid Prachi is called to the police station for questioning at 10.30 p.m. on suspicion of having engineered the stoning incident.

18 February 2016: The lawyers' landlord's impounded car and Prachi are both released on assurance that the JagLAG team and Malini will leave Jagdalpur. Subramaniam proceeds to leave the city with her two daughters. The police start making inquiries into the identity of the landlord of Bela Bhatia, an independent researcher and activist, who has been doing research on the effects of industrialization on indigenous communities for three decades.

19 February 2016: Police visit the house and office of Bela Bhatia's landlord. On the same day, Soni Sori is informed by the Dantewada district civic authorities that her house in Geedam town in the same district could be demolished as it is built on encroached land. Sori's defence is that no house in the area has been issued a *patta* by the state.

20 February 2016: The police summon Bhatia's landlord for questioning and detain him the whole day for that purpose. The JagLAG team subsequently leaves Jagdalpur. Soni Sori, who has come to bid them good-bye, is heading back home to Geedam on a motorcycle with her associate Rinki, when three young men riding a motorcycle allegedly intercept them at around 10.40 p.m. One of them reportedly catches hold of Sori and forcibly rubs a black liquid over her face. It turns out to be a corrosive agent that causes her epidermis (the superficial layer of her skin) to burn. (A few days after the attack, Sori accused the police and its supporters of complicity in the attack. The police, in turn, accused her relatives of staging the attack to malign the authorities. The relatives, for their part, complained of harassment at the hands of the investigating team. As of April 2016, the chemical is yet to be identified.)

On 20 February itself, Prime Minister Narendra Modi visits Raipur again. While laying the foundation stone of the Pradhan

Mantri Awas Yojana (translate or explain], he announces that five crore houses will be built for the poor in Chhattisgarh by 2022.

On the same day, Sori leaves for Delhi to avail of medical treatment for injuries sustained during the attack on her person.

11 March 2016: Sori returns to Bastar. She is virtually the last person left to alert people about human-rights violations happening there. But her morale appears to be strong. 'It's time for the final battle,' she says, before leaving Delhi to return to Chhattisgarh.

15 April 2016: The SEM is dissolved following a sting operation undertaken by India Today TV showing the Chhattisgarh police directly facilitating the activities of the group. However, the sting also reveals that the group has already put in place contingency measures to deal with such a possibility. Organizations like the Vikas Sangharsh Samiti, the Adivasi Ekta Manch and the Mahila Ekta Manch have been set up in advance to carry on their avowed mission in case action iss initiated against the SEM. These organizations continue to flourish as of 7 May 2016.

On the CGNet Swara yatra in January 2015, I have the opportunity of watching tribals engage in one of their favourite pastimes – the rooster fight.

Hundreds of cheering tribals lean over circular wooden enclosures, shouting and screaming, as a pair of roosters, tied with long ropes to the wrists of their owners, face off against each other. They gaze balefully at each other, step forward and back to sense an opening, like fencers in a sabre–foil contest.

The air grows thick with the cheers of gamblers, the war cries of excited children and the laughter of women. Connoisseurs gaze intently at the combatants and smile, admiring each parry and thrust, each lunge and feint. Suddenly, a rooster makes a break for it and launches itself on the other with a shrill scream that combines fear, rage and exultation in equal measure. Its talons remain suspended in the air, seemingly for a long time, before they land on their intended target, seeking to inflict pain, draw blood and press for victory. The rooster so attacked is grievously wounded, but fights back. The shrieks of the roosters fill the air, lending a knife-like edge to the shrill screams of the blood-thirsty, half-sozzled crowd.

Suddenly, one of the owners pulls back, admitting defeat. He wants his rooster to live to fight another day. He will be back. The other pats his champion and walks around the ring, rooster held aloft, paan-stained mouth bared in a grin, sweat pouring down his shirt front that is unbuttoned down to the ribs.

The crowd settles bets, discusses the contest and disperses to buy the weekly groceries. The fish-seller sharpens his knife in anticipation. It is life as usual at the market.

The tribals are the roosters, Lalsu, the leader of the CGNet swara yatra, tells me as we walk back. The owners of the birds are the different sides in the battle – the Maoists, the government, the corporates. And the crowds are the city dwellers living in remote air-conditioned pads and nests, cheering them on. Then Lalsu turns his gaze on mine and smiles.

'Only the adivasi gets killed,' he says.

Appendix I

A Timeline of Events

1757 Battle of Plassey. The British East India Company under Robert Clive achieves a decisive victory against the Nawab of Bengal and his French allies. Regarded as the start of British rule in India.

1799 Fall of Tipu Sultan, the last bastion of resistance to the British in India.

1800 Commercial exploitation of Indian forests begins. Pressure on customary rights of adivasis gradually intensifies.

1851 Start of Indian railways with a line between Roorkee and Piran Kaliyar. Requirement of wood to make sleepers on railway lines increases.

1857 First War of Independence. Development of railways, now seen as a resource for security as well as commerce, accelerates. Bastar tribals take on British under Dhruvarao, a Dorla tribal leader, and Vir Narayan Singh, a landowner

1859 Koi tribals of southern Bastar refuse to let government contractors undertake the cutting of sal trees.

1864 Indian Forest Department created, state management of forests in India begins.

1865 First Indian Forest Act.

1878 Amendment of Indian Forest Act. Categorization of forests into 'reserved' forest, forests in which no private or customary rights were recognized; 'protected' forest, in which state control is exercised, with some recognition of customary use; and 'village' forest, in which tribals exercise old privileges.

1908 Forest land in Bastar declared as 'reserved'.

1910 Bastar adivasis rise in Bhumkal rebellion, set out from a village called Nelnar, march to Jagdalpur and are able to capture the Bastar Raj for two weeks.

1946 Raja Pravir Bhanj Deo, a 20-year-old man, leases the Bailadila hills, home to the richest reserves of iron ore in the world, to the Nizam of Hyderabad. Then he cancels the lease on being assured of continuation of special privileges in independent India. The incident shows that power over forest resources continues to be an important political tool, even as the British hand over power to Indians.

1947 India achieves independence.

1952 National forest and mining policy instituted. Forest policy includes a new category of forest, the 'national forests', to be utilized for the economic needs of the country. Mining policy emphasizes the urgency of mining for India's development, while putting in place a framework for responsible labour practices.

1957 Congress Party win the elections to the Bastar legislative assembly by a huge margin with the help of Raja Pravir Bhanj Deo.

1958 National Mineral Development Corporation of India set up. Bhanj Deo starts objecting vociferously to the mineral exploitation of the Bastar area.

1960 Bhanj Deo arrested. The state takes a clear stance against a popular leader of the tribals.

1961 Police fire at a group of tribals protesting the arrest, killing 12.

1962 Bhanj Deo forms a breakaway party, the Adivasi Sena Dal, which wins 10 out of 12 seats in Bastar in the assembly elections. A combined princely–tribal front appears to have emerged.

1965 India faces a food crisis. In Bastar, adivasis protest under leadership of Bhanj Deo.

1966 Bhanj Deo killed at the entrance of his own palace. The possibility of strong leadership at the state level is crushed, a phenomenon observed through the fifties and sixties in other states like Kerala and Punjab.

1967 Start of the Naxalite movement in Naxalbari, a small village in West Bengal.

1972 Siddharth Shankar Ray, chief minister of West Bengal cracks down on Naxalites. Thousands go missing or flee the country.

1980 Forty-nine Maoists access the Dandakaranya forest in order to develop a 'rear area', a sanctuary to which Maoists can escape in unusually difficult conditions. They start targeting the excesses of the forest department, including begaar, the coercive use of free tribal labour by the forest department to build roads.

1980s Proselytizer of Hindu religion, Bihari Das, operating in Bastar, claims to be reincarnation of Raja Pravir Bhanj Deo.

1985 Maoists start targeting large tribal landlords. They are targeted by the CRPF. Get training from LTTE cadre on land mines and ambushes.

1991 The ruling Bharatiya Janata Party government, the Congress Party and the Communisr Party of India come together under the banner of the Jan Jagran Abhiyan, led by Congress politician Mahendra Karma. Villagers are forced to take oath, swearing that they will not help the Maoists in any way. Adds to the strength of the Maoists as well as the BJP who emerge as the opposite poles of the conflict between adivasis and the upper classes.

1992–96 Malik Makbuja scam. Mahendra Karma in collusion with a district collector, acquires village land at throwaway prices and sells timber at a huge profit.

1996	Second Jan Jagran Abhiyan launched. Thwarted by Maoists.
2000	New states of Chhattisgarh and Jharkhand formed. A large number of industrial MOUs signed.
2000–2004	Mahendra Karma is Minister of Industries in the Congress government in Chhattisgarh, led by Ajit Jogi.
2005	Raman Singh of the BJP becomes chief minister. MOUs signed with Tata Steel and Essar for two steel plants with a total capacity of 8.7 million tonnes[34] and backward linkages to iron-ore mines.
2006	Citizens' Initiative reports excesses of Salwa Judum, the vigilante movement supported by state.
2008	Essar starts slurry pipeline project linking its iron-ore mines to steel plant in Visakhapatnam.
2009	Operation Green Hunt launched.
2010	CRPF jawans, numbering 76, ambushed and killed near Tadmetla village.
2011	CRPF allegedly attacks Tadmetla and surrounding villages.
2013	Mahendra Karma and V.C. Shukla and 27 others are killed and 30 injured by Maoists in Jiram Ghati ambush.
2014	Tata Steel MOU lapses.

[34]http://www.business-standard.com/article/economy-policy/chhattisgarh-govt-renews-mou-with-tata-steel-112071902013_1.html

Appendix II

A History of Policy on the Scheduled Tribes of Central India[35]

The adivasis' traditional way of life was threatened from the very moment that India's British colonial rulers turned their attention to the country's timber-rich forests. The first official step in this direction was taken with the appointment of a commission in 1800 to enquire into the availability of teak in the Malabar forests.[36] The enactment of the Forest Act in 1865 led to the acquisition of forests by the state. The Forest Act of 1878 introduced the concept of a 'reserved forest' to which local communities would be denied access. The Forest Act of 1927 specifically denied people any rights over forest produce 'simply because they were domiciled there'.[37]

According to the law, at the time a 'forest' was declared as such, a single official, namely, the forest settlement officer, was entrusted with the duty of enquiring into and 'settling' the land and forest rights to which the locals of the area could lay claim. Unsurprisingly, these all-powerful officials either did nothing or recorded only the rights of communities with some clout. Most tribals were now reduced, legally

---

[36]This chapter draws on conversation with Shomana Khanna, a Supreme Court advocate.

[36]Ravindranath, N.H., Chaturvedi, Rajiv Kumar and Murthy, Indu K., 'Forest Conservation, Afforestation and Reforestation in India: Implications for Forest Carbon Stocks', *Current Science* 95.2 (2008): 216 222.

[37]Arora, Dolly, 'From state regulation to people's participation: Case of forest management in India', *Economic and Political Weekly* (1994): 691-698.

speaking, to the level of encroachers on their own land, uncertain if they could access the forests for day-to-day requirements without being penalized.

After the British took swift and decisive action to reserve forests for the purpose of meeting their need for timber, there were close to 200 tribal revolts against colonial rule. Each was ruthlessly quelled. However, laws were introduced to protect the alienation of tribal land. These included the Santhal Parganas Act, 1855, and the Chota Nagpur Tenancy Act, 1908. Tribal communities were also given the power to administer justice in minor disputes.

In recognition of their legacy of exploitation, the Constitution of independent India granted tribals a privileged position. According to the terms of the Fifth Schedule, in Schedule 5 areas, the governor of the state had the right to restrict or modify the operation of laws in the Indian state in the interest of 'good governance'. This covered the prevention of land alienation and moneylending.

The Fifth Schedule has, therefore, been referred to as a constitution within a constitution. There were strict laws on the transfer of tribal lands to non-tribals. In Andhra Pradesh, for example, even sale of land by non-tribals to non-tribals was prohibited. Yet almost 72 per cent of land in the Warangal district is held by non-tribals.

The scheduling of areas in 1950 was rather perfunctory. The first Scheduled Areas and Scheduled Tribes Commission, appointed in 1961, came to the conclusion that 'scheduling is not necessary'. Accordingly, the proposals submitted by various states, notably Kerala, were not considered and scheduling remained incomplete.

The Fifth Schedule, which seemed to be only as efficacious as the totem in a tribal village, was resuscitated with the Tribal Sub Plan of the Fifth Five Year Plan. This plan supplemented the Fifth Schedule in envisaging elimination of bonded labour, liquidation of debts, ownership over minor forest produce and restoration of tribal lands. A policy resolution at the State Ministers' Conference in 1976 conceded community ownership over minor forest produce, a major source of livelihood for tribal people. Allocations in the Five Year Plans increased from half a percentage point to an average of four per cent till the Tenth Plan, at which point, they were reduced, once more, to less than a tenth of a percentage point.

The wildlife conservation movement emerged as a major threat to adivasi well-being in the 1970s. International concern over the fate of the Indian tiger had reached a fever pitch. Subsequently, India passed the Wildlife Protection Act, 1972. There ensued a spate of notifications about national parks and sanctuaries seeking to protect and preserve India's wildlife. Till the 1991 amendment to the act, a sanctuary could be notified without taking people's rights into consideration.

Wildlife reserves, which numbered 131 in 1975, rose to around 572 in 1999, covering about 156,000 sq km, or 4.7 per cent of India's land and 22 per cent of its forest area. A survey carried out in the mid-1980s estimated that approximately 70 per cent of India's wildlife reserves were inhabited by local human communities, whose population was almost 4.5 million; a similar percentage of wildlife reserves were, at least, partly grazed by local livestock; and 57 per cent were subjected to collection of non-timber forest products (NTFP).[38] A powerful lobby of conservationists ensured that the non-use value of species and their habitats in an area overrode considerations of their use values to local people,[39] thus creating a zero-sum game between conservationists and local communities, a game that some believe is harmful to the interests of both.

By the 1980s, it was apparent that the paradigm of forest management was not yielding the desired results and increasing pressure was brought to bear on the state to involve people in the protection and management of forest resources.

In 1990, Dr B.D. Sharma, Commissioner for Scheduled Castes and Scheduled Tribes presented a plan for reconciling the interests of the

[38]Kothari, A., Pande, P.,Singh, S. and Variava, D. (1989) 'Management of Wildlife Sanctuaries and National Parks in India: A Status Report' (New Delhi, Indian Institute of Public Administration)

[39]Rangarajan, M (1996), 'The Politics of Ecology: The Debate on People and Wildlife in India, 1970-1995' (Mumbai, *Economic and Political Weekly*, 31 : 2391-410)

tribal community and forestry development, largely by involving the tribals in the management and utilization of forest resources. Tribals were to be viewed as protectors and sustainable users of forests, rather than as encroachers.

In 1996, the Panchayati Raj Extension to the Scheduled Areas Act (PESA), following the Panchayati Raj Act of 1992, brought scheduled areas under the ambit of the Panchayati Raj, but with significant exceptions that included the right of the gram sabha to be consulted on land acquisition, to make recommendations on the granting of prospecting licences or mining leases for minor minerals (extraction of major minerals is exempt) and to safeguard and preserve the traditions and customs of the people, their cultural identity, their community resources and their customary mode of dispute resolution.

By singling out and empowering the hamlet gram sabha as the relevant entity to be consulted, PESA aimed to increase the power of small sub-communities within a single overarching panchayat to protect their rights.

In 1997, in the Samatha case related to the leasing of tribal lands to private mining companies in scheduled areas, the Supreme Court passed a landmark judgement that established that government lands, tribal lands and forestlands in such areas cannot be leased out to non-tribals or to private companies for mining or industrial operations.

In 2001, the victory of tribal rights activists in the Samatha case was circumscribed by the Supreme Court's judgement in the Bharat Aluminium Company Limited (BALCO) case. It ruled that the Samatha case was not applicable to the dilution of shares of the government to 49 per cent in BALCO, with the remaining part going to a private corporation, since the case pertained to a different state (Madhya Pradesh) and involved the 'leasing' of land.

By the 1990s, the animal-conservation movement was facing the same crisis that had beset state forestry a decade earlier. The soul-searching of animal conservationists would result in a paradigm of 'inviolate' forest sanctuaries, an outcome at variance with the trends emerging in forestry.

Meanwhile, with some judicial help, the Forest Department was about to get much more powerful.

According to the terms laid down by the Forest Conservation Act of 1980, state governments had to seek approval from the Ministry of Environment and Forests (MoEF) for the diversion of forest land. State governments were alleged to have diverted forest land by arguing that they did not legally come under the classification of forests.

In response to a case filed in 1996 by T.N. Godavarman Thirumulpad against the state of Tamil Nadu, the Supreme Court ruled that any area that fit the dictionary definition of a forest, whether falling under the purview of the Forest Department or not as per the legal records, was to be treated as forest for the purposes of diversion. As a result, the forest departments and central Forest Ministry could now extend their control to large areas of forests which had hitherto not been under their jurisdiction, such as revenue forests (that are abundant in MP, Orissa and other areas) and community forests (which are plentiful in the North East).

In 2002, the *amicus curae* Harish Salve filed an application stating that despite the court's intentions, frequent encroachments on forest land were taking place. In response, the court stayed all regularization and conversion of forest villages.

The MoEF followed up the stay by issuing an order to the state governments which directed them to ensure that all encroachers on forest land were evicted. The result was a livelihood crisis for 3.5 to 4 million people threatened by the MoEF order.

The uproar that ensued from the attempted evictions following the Supreme Court judgement resulted in the order being withdrawn. However, by this time, popular movements had sprung up across the country and forest-dependent groups had found a new common cause to unite them. Concerted action, primarily under the national umbrella 'Campaign for Survival and Dignity', as well as through numerous other groups, namely the National Forum of Forest People and Forest Workers (NFFPFW), the Lok Sangharsh Morcha, Gujarat, the Jan Sangharsh Morcha, Madhya Pradesh, and the National Alliance of

People's Movements, Maharashtra, along with human rights and social activists, sought to draw attention to the cause of the tribals and forest dwellers.

In 2004, a new coalition led by the Congress came to power at the Centre on the back of a Common Minimum Programme that emphasized a paradigmatic shift in tribal rights; from a concern with tribals branded as 'encroachers', the issue was now couched in terms of non-recognition of the tribals' customary rights.

In March 2005, the nation was shocked to learn that tigers had disappeared from the Sariska Tiger Reserve in Rajasthan. The trend of the 1990s, promoting people-free conservation by ousting forest dwellers from their natural habitat, appeared to have failed. The animal-conservation movement now tilted towards the side of those who believed that 'the protection of these forests is itself inseparable from the fortunes of people who, in India, inhabit forest areas'. Now the forestry and conservation movements were speaking the same language.

The Forest Rights Act (FRA) drafted by the Ministry of Tribal Affairs and introduced in 2008 granted legal recognition to the rights of traditional forest-dwelling communities and gave such communities and the public a voice in forest and wildlife conservation.

Three kinds of rights were recognized in the FRA: inalienable land titles for up to four acres would be granted for land that had been in cultivation as of 1st January 2005; user rights to grazing grounds, water bodies and the collection of minor forest produce for subsistence or sale; and, the power and responsibility to conserve community forests, which implied the right to veto 'development' projects. For the first time, the right to protect and conserve the forest was extended beyond the states' forest departments and handed to the communities in the form of the gram sabha's consent.

A 2009 notification of the MoEF states that forest rights had to be settled in compliance with the terms laid down by the FRA and the consent of the gram sabhas obtained before environmental clearance could be granted by the MoEF.

Isolated episodes like the cancellation of the licence for bauxite mining in the Niyamgiri hills notwithstanding, the reprieve was not fated to last in the face of increased pressures of 'development'. In November 2012, the PMO of Dr Manmohan Singh under Pulok Chatterjee sent an office memorandum asking the Ministry of Tribal Affairs and the MoEF to revise their circulars in accordance with a decision taken at a meeting in November; they were to remove all requirements for gram sabha consent and certification for 'linear projects', like roads, railway lines and canals. The Minister for Tribal Affairs first agreed with the directive, but later retracted his assent.

In July 2014, according to news reports, the new NDA government pushed for the adoption of the aforementioned PMO recommendation, dispensing with gram sabha consent.

There have also been clear signals that other laws that have a bearing on the tribals' right to self-determination are about to be amended. The Land Acquisition Act of 1894, giving the government the right to acquire land for public purposes, was replaced by the Land Acquisition, Rehabilitation and Resettlement Act (LARR Act), 2013, that explicitly recognized the need for a social-impact assessment to evaluate project impact and required the consent of a certain percentage of the local community, in case the concerned project involved private participation. The power of eminent domain given to the sovereign remains absolute in the case of land acquisition for the public sector.

However, ordinances proposed in 2014 roll back the need for social-impact assessment and the consent of the local population for projects in five categories. These categories are vague and broad enough to allow virtually any private project to go forward without a clear understanding of the costs and benefits – that would have been available through the social-impact assessment or a green signal from the local population – captured by the consent clause. The ordinance was dropped in the face of vigorous opposition in the Rajya Sabha, the Upper House of Parliament, and nationwide protests. Certain laws related to the acquisition of land for specific purposes like coal mining, building highways or railways were exempted from the provisions of LARR Act 2013 for a year. With the Land Ordinance having been dropped, the rehabilitation and resettlement provisions of LARR Act 2013 have been extended to the acts that were initially excluded from their purview. However, these acts are still exempt from the consent and Social Impact Assessment provisions of LARR Act 2013.

The Mines and Minerals (Development and Regulation) Amendment Act, 2015, passed by the Parliament is silent on the issue of obtaining consent from affected communities before mining operations are initiated. Without sufficient safeguards, the increasing pressure for extraction of minerals may end up undermining the PESA structure of governance. The bill prescribes 33 per cent of royalty as the upper limit to contribution by the leaseholder to the District Mineral Foundation, an organization meant to bring about development of affected communities. An earlier version of the bill dated June 2010 included a provision for granting 26 per cent equity ownership to make members of the local community stakeholders in the mining life cycle.

Acknowledgements

This book has been a transformational journey for me in more ways than one. It would not have been possible without a vast support network consisting of research assistants, academic mentors, literary sounding boards, legal advisors and financial sponsors. Above all, it would have been impossible without the moral support of my family and friends.

The journey began with a visit to three NGOs supported by Digital Empowerment Foundation (DEF), through the kind offices of DEF's Director Osama Manzar. In these visits, I zeroed in on the theme of the book, and Shubranshu Chaudhary, who ran one of the NGOs I visited, became a critical resource connecting me to people in remote areas of Chhattisgarh. Having observed the situation at the grassroots level, I wanted a view from the corporate sector. Vijay Mehta, B. Muthuraman, Rajnish Wadehra and J.V. Raghavan enabled me to get access to several current and former executives at Tata Steel.

Srivatsa Krishna, H.N. Sharma and Mohit Mathur provided invaluable assistance and counsel when I became entangled in a legal case in the course of carrying out research for the book. Others who provided leads and links to informants include Shomona Khanna, Pranay Lal, Vaishali Nigam Sinha, Rohit Khanna, Bahar Dutt, Himanshu Thakkar, Aruna Roy, Dr. Sanjay Kumar, Dr. Santanu Gupta, Prianka Singhal, Bill Thies, Aakar Patel, Aruna Chandrasekhar, Vijayan M.J. and Ishita Sharma. Many more have helped but have chosen to remain unnamed.

Gaurav Tiwari rendered valuable technical assistance as I equipped myself with digital tools before setting off on field trips. Archana Vijay and Chirag Jain provided vital research assistance and company during the writing process.

Gautam Kumar read snippets of the book as it came into being and made sure I kept things interesting. Jogendra Singh read the first full draft of the book and shared valuable insights in addition to apprising me on the finer points of environmental laws. Sanjay Ahirwal's green signal on the manuscript was heartening, coming as it did from a veteran journalist as was the appreciation by Nishikanta Verma, a prolific blogger. Dr Kavita Rao provided a valuable critique from the perspective of an economist. Vinay Singh's concerns on the introduction of the book occasioned a significant round of editing.

Every book needs a mentor and this book found its friend, philosopher and guide in Prof. Rajen Gupta, my colleague at the Management Development Institute. I had the privilege of reading the whole draft aloud to Rajen, as it came into being, and gained immensely from the broad sweep of his insights on research methodology. Professor Satish Jain, my teacher from the Jawaharlal Nehru University, similarly, reassured me on the worthiness of my forays into the gray areas that lie on the borders of academic disciplines. In addition, he supplied ayurvedic concoctions to ward off malaria during my field work!

My 'Lemon Tree gang': Amit, Ashesh, Bappa, Madhushree, Sunil, has to be thanked (blamed) for fuelling my explorations with repeated rounds of furious argument broken up by hysterical laughter all in the middle of sumptuous spreads.

Part of the funding for the field trips came from a seed money grant from the Management Development Institute. Prof C.P. Shrimali, the Acting Director, and all my colleagues were extremely supportive even though this is not the usual subject of exploration of a business school professor.

In many places I visited, I encountered the tremendous goodwill that my father-in-law, Lalit Mathur, has earned in his many years in the rural development ministry. He and my mother-in-law, Geeta Mathur, embody the proud multiculturalism that is such a valuable part of our heritage.

My wife, Sonali, has amazed me with her ability to countenance my trips into wild and dangerous territory without batting an eyelid, although stray questions have revealed the anxiety she was keeping at bay. My children, Chaitanya and Soham, one a mad scientist and the other a tree-hugging environmentalist, have inspired me to do something they could both perhaps be proud of.

Heartfelt thanks are due to my editor, Poulomi Chatterjee, whose gentle nudges have surely lifted the level of the book, as also to Mita Ghose.

And last, but not least, my compliments to Grace whose bounty has always been infinitely greater than my deserving.